THE GALLANT OUTLAW

THE
GALLANT
OUTLAW

★

GILBERT MORRIS

BETHANY HOUSE PUBLISHERS
MINNEAPOLIS, MINNESOTA 55438

Copyright © 1994
Gilbert Morris
All Rights Reserved

Cover illustration by Dan Thornberg

Published by Bethany House Publishers
A Ministry of Bethany Fellowship, Inc.
11300 Hampshire Avenue South
Minneapolis, Minnesota 55438

Printed in the United States of America

Library of Congress Cataloging-in-Publication Data

Morris, Gilbert.
   The gallant outlaw / Gilbert Morris
      p.   cm. — (The House of Winslow : 15)
    1. Frontier and pioneer life—Oklahoma—Fiction.
2. Family—Oklahoma—Fiction.
I. Title. II. Series: Morris, Gilbert. House of Winslow : bk. 15
PS3563.08742G27   1994
813'.54—dc20   93-45364
ISBN 1–55661–311–3   CIP

I dedicate this book to Aaron McCarver.
Sometimes a man chooses his friends—but sometimes he *gets* chosen. When someone selects me out of all the people on the planet to be a good friend, I am both grateful and humbled. What an honor that is—to be a friend! Better than silver or gold; better than office or fame!
So, thank you, Aaron, for choosing me. Our friendship is a treasure to me, and I thank God for drawing us together!

GILBERT MORRIS spent ten years as a pastor before becoming Professor of English at Ouachita Baptist University in Arkansas and earning a Ph.D. at the University of Arkansas. During the summers of 1984 and 1985 he did postgraduate work at the University of London and is presently the Chairman of General Education at a Christian college in Louisiana. A prolific writer, he has had over 25 scholarly articles and 200 poems published in various periodicals, and over the past years has had more than 20 novels published. His family includes three grown children, and he and his wife live in Baton Rouge, Louisiana.

CONTENTS

THE HOUSE OF WINSLOW

★ ★ ★ ★

THE HOUSE OF WINSLOW

★ ★ ★ ★

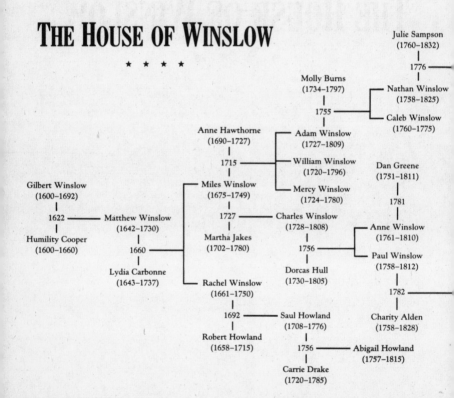

Julie Sampson
(1760–1832)

1776

Molly Burns
(1734–1797)

Nathan Winslow
(1758–1825)

1755

Caleb Winslow
(1760–1775)

Anne Hawthorne
(1690–1727)

Adam Winslow
(1727–1809)

1715

William Winslow
(1720–1796)

Dan Greene
(1751–1811)

Miles Winslow
(1675–1749)

Mercy Winslow
(1724–1780)

1781

Gilbert Winslow
(1600–1692)

1727

Charles Winslow
(1728–1808)

Anne Winslow
(1761–1810)

1622

Matthew Winslow
(1642–1730)

Martha Jakes
(1702–1780)

1756

Paul Winslow
(1758–1812)

Humility Cooper
(1600–1660)

1660

Dorcas Hull
(1730–1805)

1782

Lydia Carbonne
(1643–1737)

Rachel Winslow
(1661–1750)

Charity Alden
(1758–1828)

1692

Saul Howland
(1708–1776)

Robert Howland
(1658–1715)

1756

Abigail Howland
(1757–1815)

Carrie Drake
(1720–1785)

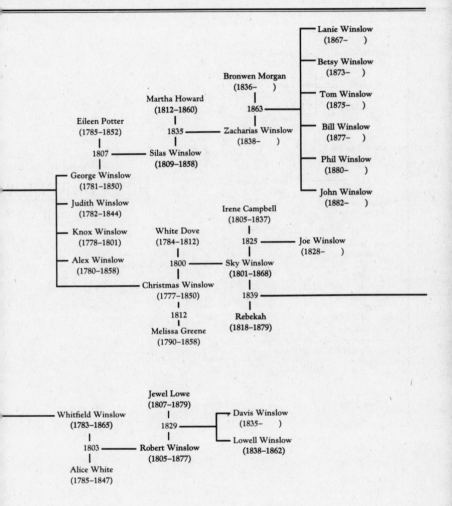

Lanie Winslow
(1867–   )

Betsy Winslow
(1873–   )

Tom Winslow
(1875–   )

Bill Winslow
(1877–   )

Phil Winslow
(1880–   )

John Winslow
(1882–   )

Bronwen Morgan
(1836–   )

1863

Martha Howard
(1812–1860)

Zacharias Winslow
(1838–   )

1835

Eileen Potter
(1785–1852)

Silas Winslow
(1809–1858)

1807

George Winslow
(1781–1850)

Judith Winslow
(1782–1844)

Knox Winslow
(1778–1801)

Alex Winslow
(1780–1858)

Irene Campbell
(1805–1837)

1825

Joe Winslow
(1828–   )

White Dove
(1784–1812)

Sky Winslow
(1801–1868)

1800

Christmas Winslow
(1777–1850)

1839

1812

Rebekah
(1818–1879)

Melissa Greene
(1790–1858)

Jewel Lowe
(1807–1879)

Davis Winslow
(1835–   )

1829

Lowell Winslow
(1838–1862)

Whitfield Winslow
(1783–1865)

Robert Winslow
(1805–1877)

1803

Alice White
(1785–1847)

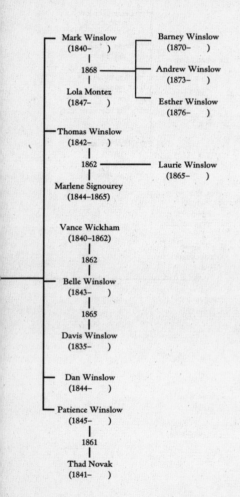

Mark Winslow
(1840–   )

|
1868 ———— Barney Winslow
| (1870–   )
Lola Montez   Andrew Winslow
(1847–   )   (1873–   )
                   Esther Winslow
                   (1876–   )

Thomas Winslow
(1842–   )
|
1862 ———— Laurie Winslow
| (1865–   )
Marlene Signourey
(1844–1865)

Vance Wickham
(1840–1862)
|
1862
|
Belle Winslow
(1843–   )
|
1865
|
Davis Winslow
(1835–   )

Dan Winslow
(1844–   )

Patience Winslow
(1845–   )
|
1861
|
Thad Novak
(1841–   )

THE
HOUSE OF WINSLOW
(continued)

PART ONE

THE RUNAWAY

★ ★ ★ ★

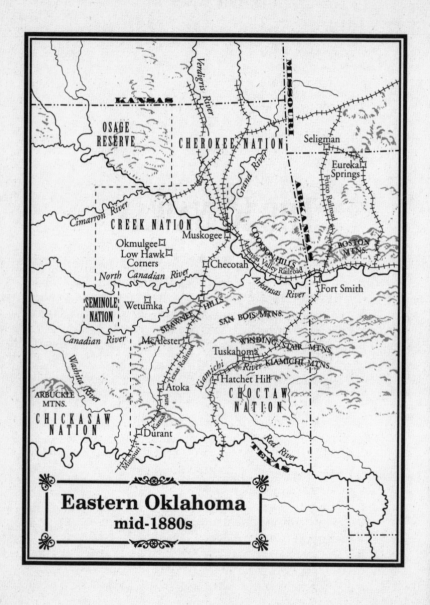

Eastern Oklahoma
mid-1880s

CHAPTER ONE

WHIRLWIND COURTSHIP

★ ★ ★ ★

"I don't really think you ought to take Thor this morning, Miss Winslow. He's too much of a horse for you to handle." Mac Williams, the town's stableman, looked down at the girl and tried to soften his words. "I mean, you're a fine rider but—"

"I'm perfectly able to handle this horse, Mac!" Betsy snapped. "Now give me a hand up."

The stableman shrugged, but he knew better than to argue with the girl. Putting out one hand for her foot, he hoisted her easily into the saddle, then handed her the reins. The big buckskin stirred uneasily, turning a wary eye toward his rider, and seemed to be contemplating some outrage.

"Don't worry about me, Mac, I'll be all right," she said, then spoke to the horse and touched him with her heels. Immediately he started down the riding path at a sedate walk.

Betsy Winslow, in the year of 1890, was, if anything, more sensitive about her horsemanship than her stature. She was a petite young miss with gorgeous deep red hair that one often sees in Irish women, startling blue eyes, and a shapely figure—but the freckles dusting her nose were an abomination to her. She always wore the highest heels she could find to add to her height.

Mac Williams shook his head. "Dang fool girl!" he muttered.

"If she breaks her neck, it'll be me that gets blamed for it! But you never can tell her nothing." He went back to his work, still muttering and worrying. He'd tried his best to warn her. Betsy Winslow might be small, but Mac had decided a long time ago she was one of the most stubborn girls in all creation. He raised his eyes and shook his head as if to confirm his assessment as he watched her moving steadily along.

Betsy held the reins tightly, knowing that if the big horse ever got the bridle between his teeth he could do as he pleased. Her own little mare, Star, had been lame; and it was only after a heated argument that she had convinced Mac to let her ride the big buckskin, Thor. Actually, now that she had won the argument, she was rather nervous about the whole thing. The ground seemed very far away, and the muscles of the big animal rolled and rippled beneath her in a way that was somehow ominous. However, as she made her way down the path, she gained confidence and said, "C'mon, Thor. Let's try a trot."

The big horse responded swiftly, taking off at a rough gait, rougher than that of her own horse. It made her bounce along dangerously as she desperately fought to keep a good seat. Horses could read riders, she knew only too well, and if Thor sensed any hesitation, he would be in control of her, instead of the other way around.

June had begun as a hot month two days earlier, and the noonday sun beating down through the huge elm trees partially shading the riding path made Betsy hot and sticky, though she had gone less than a tenth of a mile. She delighted in the strength of the big horse; riding Star had become too tame for her taste lately. In the three years she'd had the small mare, Betsy had grown increasingly impatient with the horse's unexcitable pace.

I'll tell Daddy to buy me another horse—one with some spirit, she thought as they jogged along. *Maybe he'll buy me this one.* She rode another twenty yards and thought, *No, he won't do it; he'd tell me it's too dangerous. I wish he'd stop treating me like a baby!*

She was being jolted by the horse's rough gait so decided to try a gallop. "Thor, let's go!" she commanded. At once the big buckskin moved into a smooth stride. Betsy was on her guard; she had heard stories from Mac and Mr. Simmons, the owner of the stable, about what a handful a big horse could be when he got an idea in his head. Thor had thrown some men who were considered pretty good riders, Mac had told her when trying to convince her to stay off the animal. Actually, Thor seemed to be an easy horse to ride.

She became so adjusted to Thor's smooth, flowing gait that she forgot to keep a close watch on him. He was crafty as well as big, she had been told, and had learned that with an inexperienced rider he could jerk his head back suddenly and grab the bit in his teeth. Then the rider couldn't control him by yanking the bit back against his jaws.

They were well out of sight of the stable with only one other rider in sight when—without breaking stride—he did this very thing. As soon as he grasped the bit with his powerful teeth, the animal stuck his head out and broke into a dead run. Betsy yanked back on the reins, but she might as well have been whistling "The Star Spangled Banner" for all the impression it made on Thor. He leaned low to the ground, the big trees just flashes of green as he sailed by with his rider. Betsy sawed frantically at the reins, shouting, "Whoa! Whoa!" But, to no avail.

They rounded the turn, narrowly missing another horse and rider moving slowly in front of them. The other horse reared as they swerved, and Betsy caught a brief glimpse of the man struggling to keep from being thrown. Then they were past him, Betsy hanging on for dear life.

When the horse made a sudden bolt to the right, she lost one stirrup. Then, in trying to regain it, she dropped the reins. Now she could only cling to the little English saddle.

The thunder of Thor's mighty hooves pounded in her ears as they plunged along the path. Slyly he drifted over to the edge so the branches began to beat at her. "You beast!" she cried, aware from what Mac had said that the horse knew perfectly well what he was doing. Then he began throwing his weight from side to side. Betsy was no match for this trick, and she began sliding off, panic shooting through her like lightning.

She was falling to the right side, struggling desperately to hang on, but it was no use. Since there was no pommel she couldn't grasp anything. Her heart raced. Suddenly she heard the sound of another horse, coming up hard. Glancing back, she saw the man she had passed. He was leaning low over the saddle, driving his big black at full speed.

The next second the man yelled "Here!" and reached out to her. Betsy had no choice. His arm circled her waist, fastened like a steel hook, and then she was free of Thor. The arm holding her was so strong that it cut her breath off, but at least she was safe!

"Whoa—whoa now, Bobby!" the man commanded loudly. His horse promptly slowed down and began jittering sideways until the man spoke to him again. "Stop that, now!" he yelled, slapping the horse with a sharp jerk of the reins. The horse finally obeyed, his sides heaving from the exercise.

The man lowered Betsy to the ground, and she discovered she was trembling. This was unusual for her. She had been a tomboy while growing up, but the possibility of falling under the slashing hooves of Thor had flooded her vivid imagination with a colorful picture of her own death.

"Are you all right? Come over here, sit down on this log." Betsy felt the man's hand on her arm, but she didn't have the courage to look up. He led her over to a large log lying beneath one of the huge trees, sat her down, then seated himself beside her. "That was a close one," he said, winded.

Betsy gripped her hands together to control the shaking. Taking a deep breath, she glanced up at her rescuer. He was one of the most handsome men she had ever seen. No more than twenty-five or twenty-six, he had bright yellow hair and strangely colored eyes, more hazel than anything else. He was, she noted, a big man, over six feet tall, and very muscular. His clothes were expensive: black shiny boots, a gray riding suit, and a white shirt that was open at the throat, revealing a deep tan.

"I . . . I don't know how to thank you," she said timidly.

"Glad to be of help," he returned cheerfully. He smiled broadly, revealing even white teeth. He ran his hand through his hair and said, "My name's Vic Perrago."

"I'm Betsy Winslow."

"Glad to meet you, Miss Winslow. Most first meetings aren't quite this exciting, are they?" He pulled a tobacco pouch out of his pocket and rolled a cigarette in an accomplished manner such as she had never seen. He lit up with a flourish, and Betsy realized he was giving her time to recover from her frightening experience. He smoked for a moment and then said idly, "Well, I don't think we're going to catch that big buckskin. Suppose we go on back to the stable. You ride and I'll walk."

"Oh no," Betsy protested. "Let's both walk. Or, really, you don't have to go back with me at all. I'm all right now."

"Why, of course I'll go back with you!" Perrago smiled warmly. He rose and helped her to her feet. Holding the reins of his horse in one hand, he kept his left hand lightly under her arm, as if she were something very precious.

Betsy was not accustomed to being treated in this manner— especially by a big, fine-looking man! It happened much more often to her sister, Lanie. As she walked with him, a current of excitement ran through her. When she discovered that he was a rancher, her interest knew no bounds. "How wonderful!" she cried, her eyes sparkling in the summer sun. "I'd rather live in the West than anywhere in the world. Tell me about your ranch!"

By the time they arrived at the stable, Betsy had forgotten all about her near fall. When Mac came running out, she said nonchalantly, "Thor got away from me, I'm afraid. This gentleman saved me from disaster." She saw Mac open his mouth to reprimand her, so she hurried on. "I know, I know! You were right! Thor's too much of a horse for me right now."

Perrago offered gallantly, "Why, Miss Winslow, a few riding lessons at my ranch and you'd be riding fellows like that in no time!"

"Do you really think so?"

"Of course." Perrago handed the reins of his horse to Mac and said to Betsy, "I suppose someone is coming to pick you up?"

"No, I'll hail a carriage."

"Please allow me to see you home."

This was a little bit too fast for Betsy, who knew what her parents would say. "Oh no, I couldn't do that," she said.

She half expected Perrago to argue, but he didn't. Instead, he kept up the conversation, and then saw her into the carriage. Before the coach pulled out, she put her hand out, saying, "I've never been so grateful to anyone in my whole life! Thank you very much."

Perrago shrugged his broad shoulders. "I've always wanted

to be a knight in shining armor and rescue a damsel in distress." His smile flashed as he said, "I'll be seeing you. Goodbye, Miss Winslow."

As Betsy rode toward her home, she decided to tell no one about her adventure. Her father would forbid her to get on a horse like Thor again, and her mother would forbid her to speak to a handsome stranger again.

* * * *

"Betsy! You can't go looking like that!" Lanie Winslow had entered her younger sister's room to find her wearing an ugly brown dress and her hair in careless disarray.

"I'm not going down to the station!" Betsy said petulantly, looking up from the *Harper's Weekly* she was reading. "He's your suitor, not mine." Her face was sullen as she went on. "You're dressed up enough for the whole family, Lanie. You ought to be able to catch him, if clothes will do the trick."

Lanie Winslow stepped forward and jerked the magazine out of her sister's hand. "Nonsense!" she snapped. "In the first place, he's not my suitor! Wesley's a friend of the family, and you're going with me to pick him up and that's all there is to it! Now, let's see . . ." Moving to the huge walnut chifferobe, she flung the door open and began to ruffle through the dresses, a frown on her face. Selecting one, she pulled it out, then turned to say, "This will have to do, I suppose. But next week you are going with me to do some shopping! It's a shame the way you've let your wardrobe deteriorate, Betsy. Not a single dress in style!"

"What difference does it make?" Betsy muttered defiantly. "I look like a stump, whatever I put on!"

"Don't be silly!" Lanie said crisply. "You have a nice figure, and if you'd take care of your hair and your clothes, you'd be very attractive." Lanie, at the age of twenty-three, behaved more like a mother to the girl than a sister. And unlike Betsy, who was merely pretty, Lanie was beautiful by any standard. Tall and stately, her figure was certain to bring admiring looks from men and resentful glares from young women. She had the high cheekbones of her father, but her rich auburn hair and brilliant green eyes came from her Welsh mother, as did the high coloring that required little artifice.

But if her physical appearance was relatively easy to trace, her emotional makeup was more complex. She seemed to have some qualities from each parent. She had the mystic strain of Welsh blood from her mother, and an innate stubbornness from her father, Zach Winslow. At times she would be at the mercy of her emotions, but she was also capable of following through doggedly on any project she set her mind to. She could be carried to the heights of joy, or plunged to the depths of despair—but somehow there was a rock-like quality that overrode this side of her character, giving her a practical side as well.

Both of these facets were evident in Lanie's dealings with her sister. She loved Betsy, and of all the siblings, she was her pet. But Lanie was impatient by what she perceived as her sister's weakness. Lanie was aware that Betsy considered herself the "ugly duckling," a fact that the older girl was honest enough to admit was some cause for complaint. Because of this, she planned to spend more time fussing over Betsy, working on her appearance and her clothes. But Lanie had become exasperated, and did not recognize that what she was doing was trying to force her sister into becoming the same type of person she herself was. This tendency to bully people into "bettering themselves" was a trait that her father Zach had lectured her on from time to time—with no effect whatsoever.

Betsy submitted to Lanie's whirlwind manner, allowing Ellen, one of the maids, to work on her hair and help her dress. She looked in the full-length oval mirror and muttered, "What does it matter what I look like? Nobody ever sees me anyway, not with Lanie there!"

"Why, Miss Betsy! That ain't no way to talk!" Ellen protested. "You look *very* nice! I'm sure Miss Lanie's young man will be very impressed." This was a fabrication on Ellen's part, for she was aware that Betsy would never receive much attention from a man while her sister was present. But Ellen was much fonder of Betsy than Lanie, having been on the receiving end of the older girl's sharp tongue too often. "Now, you just put a smile on your pretty face! Go on now, before Miss Lanie has to come back for you!"

"Oh, all right," Betsy said disgustedly, and went downstairs.

The hall was somber, with brown wallpaper and dark-hued carpet, and on the landing where the stairs made a sharp turn, a tall grandfather clock ticked portentously. The sound of an organ playing drifted on the air as she turned to the left at the foot of the stairs, and entered a large room through a pair of mahogany doors.

In the middle of the room was a large black-walnut table, with a glass dish filled with wax fruit as its centerpiece. Beside the dish was a music box that played six tunes. At one end of the room stood a majestic fireplace, its white marble mantelpiece partly covered by a silk lambrequin of many colors. A yellow cuckoo clock hung over the middle of the mantel, with photographs of the family on each side.

Between the two windows of the room that faced the street, there was an organ with sheets of music and an open hymnbook on it. Betsy's mother sat before the organ playing with exuberance and singing in her rich Welsh voice:

> Come, Thou fount of every blessing,
> Tune my heart to sing Thy grace,
> Streams of mercy, never ceasing,
> Call for songs of loudest praise.
> Teach me some melodious sonnet
> Sung by flaming tongues above;
> Praise the mount—I'm fixed upon it—
> Mount of Thy redeeming love.

Zach Winslow was standing beside his wife. At forty-seven, he looked much younger than his years. At five feet nine, he was thickly built and very strong. As he lifted his right hand to turn the page of the score, Betsy saw again the missing right forefinger. Her father had always enjoyed talking about his Civil War wound: "I lost this forefinger, and got one other wound that nobody can see."

"Well, here you are! And don't you look nice!" Her father walked toward Betsy with his arms out and hugged her warmly.

Betsy could see that he was partial to her, which she felt was a miracle and had often thought ruefully, *I think it's because I'm shorter than he is, and Lanie's taller.*

But for whatever reason, Zach showed his love for Betsy in many ways. Now he stood back and looked her up and down approvingly and said, "You're going to pick up young Stone with

Lanie? Good. Don't want that preacher running off with one of my daughters."

"Oh, he's not going to run off with anyone," his wife broke in. Bronwen Winslow was two years older than her husband. Her hair was a brilliant auburn, and her eyes a sparkling green. A mission volunteer from Wales, she had come to America ostensibly to marry a Welsh missionary she had met in Wales, who had gone to the States a year earlier; but while she was on the boat, she was informed that her fiance had died. So it was Zach Winslow she later married, not the missionary.

She rose and came over to the two, smiling. "Well, it is fine you look now! And a new dress you'll have, is it?" Bronwen still retained traces of her Welsh dialect, so radically implanted in her that she would probably never lose it completely. Her older daughter loved Welsh, and had learned to speak it from her mother.

"I don't know what they want me along for," Betsy complained.

As she was speaking, Lanie entered, dressed lavishly in a beautifully designed blue silk dress, the latest hat, and a jeweled parasol. "I want you along because I'm going to show you off to Wesley," she said, briskly pulling on gloves. "Come along now, sure and 'tis late," Lanie said, her voice reflecting her Welsh heritage.

The two girls left, Lanie continually instructing her younger sister on exactly how to behave. As soon as they were out the door, Zach frowned and turned to his wife. "I wish Lanie wouldn't do that, Bron."

Bronwen raised her eyes, puzzled. "Do what? Oh, you mean bossing her around like that?" A smile played on her lips, but as she thought about it, her smile turned to a frown. "That'll be Lanie's way, Zach," she said. "Saying nothing wrong, she is. I don't think she knows any other way to behave."

Zach wheeled impatiently and went to stand by the window, watching the girls drive off. Looking back at Bronwen he said, "I wish we'd never come to Chicago. We should have stayed out West. Both of us liked it better there."

"I know, dear," Bronwen said sympathetically. "This place is nothing to buy a stamp for." Moving to stand close beside him, she took his hand in hers and stroked it gently. "If *we* have a hard time, it doesn't matter, but I thought it would be better for the boys and the girls to come to the city. Sometimes I think I'd like to just go back to that cabin where we first lived, by Alder Gulch."

"You think of those days?"

Her warm eyes smiled up at him. "All the time." She looked out the window, chewing her bottom lip worriedly. "That would be a better place to raise four boys and two girls than here in Chicago. Are you thinking you'll ever get your business straightened out so we can return?"

Zach Winslow had set his mind to becoming a hermit at one time. He had failed because Bronwen had captured his heart with her comely ways, and he had had to change his mind. Since then, they had become parents of six children, all of which he doted on. He frowned. "If I don't, we'll just buy a wagon and go back, and I'll grub for gold in the Gulch!"

"And I'll raise chickens! And a garden!" Bronwen laughed. Then she sobered. "It is worried I am about Betsy. She feels so inferior!"

"Inferior? Why should the girl feel like that?"

"Oh, go scratch for it!" she snapped impatiently. "You're a man—you don't know women. But Lanie is much more attractive—in the eyes of the world at least," she said hurriedly, to head off his argument. "Anyway, Betsy feels like she's not first-rate."

The two discussed it for a long time. Then Zach sighed heavily. "I wish I could help her—but I don't know how." His face was forlorn as he turned to leave. "I'll go get the boys. I'm taking them to the park, to a baseball game." Stopping at the door he said, "See if you can think of some way to bring Betsy out of it, will you, Bron? You're so good with her—with all the children."

"I'll try," she replied doubtfully. "But with a young girl like that, most of the time you can't tell her anything."

★ ★ ★ ★

Wesley Stone had the appearance of a young Abraham Lincoln. He was tall and lanky, although not weak looking. He had a homely face, deep-set brown eyes, a strong jaw, and a thatch of black hair. He was an eloquent preacher, but when he tried to make conversation with Lanie Winslow, he seemed to lose his flow of words. He had greeted her and Betsy at the station, gotten into the carriage, and driven home. All the way, Lanie talked, telling him what had happened while he'd been gone. Finally she asked, "Was it a good meeting?"

"Yes, the Lord blessed," Stone answered, his eyes lighting up. "The evangelist was the best I've ever heard. And I did some exhorting myself." He smiled at her, saying, "But with you along when we get to St. Louis, I'll have to do better."

"Now, Wes, I'm going to see my cousin Ida in St. Louis—not to hear you preach," Lanie rebuked him. She had agreed to accompany him to a revival meeting in that city, and was looking forward to it. But the most enticing attraction for her was not the revival but a shopping spree she had planned with her cousin.

"Well, I guess I know that," Stone said ruefully. He shrugged. "The train leaves at 9:40 in the morning."

"I'm all packed, Wes."

"I don't see why I can't go with you," Betsy complained, but every effort she'd made to join her sister had been rejected. Betsy had always thought that Wesley Stone was the best man in the world—next to her father.

"You've got to decide if you're going to be a preacher or a lawyer," Lanie said. "I don't think a man can be both."

Wesley was not sure himself which he was meant to be. He was a practicing attorney, the youngest member of the firm that handled Zach Winslow's affairs. Yet he had been saved in a revival meeting in Chicago and since then had spent much time traveling with preachers and evangelists, assisting them with the "exhorting" at various revivals. He'd even been issued a license as an "exhorter," so when Betsy asked him what that meant, he laughed. "Well, I don't know, really. It's someone who tells people to do better than they're doing, I think."

When they reached the Winslow home, Stone was greeted warmly by the girls' parents and the four boys: Tom, fifteen; Bill, thirteen; Phil, ten; and John, eight—like stairsteps, Zach often said. The boys loved Stone, for he spent much time with them, taking them on fishing trips, hikes, picnics, and to ball games.

As the entire family surrounded him, all talking at once, the maid entered with an armful of fresh red roses.

"Oh my!" Lanie exclaimed. "Did you send those to me, Wesley? As a goodbye present? I hope not, they must have cost a fortune!"

Stone shook his head, a regretful expression crossing his face. "No, I wish I had. But a poor lawyer can't afford flowers like that!"

"They're for Miss Betsy," Ellen said smugly, and laid them in the arms of the surprised girl. "There's a card," she announced. "But, I didn't read that."

"Well, now, who could be sending such beautiful flowers to my little girl?" Zach asked speculatively. "You want me to read the card?"

"No," Betsy said hastily. "I'll read it later."

Everyone was curious, but no one except John dared say anything. "C'mon! I wanna know who sent 'em!" he demanded.

Conscious of all eyes on her, Betsy handed the roses back to the maid. "Put them in two vases, please, Ellen. There's enough for my room and your room, too, Mother." When the maid left, Betsy opened the card and immediately her cheeks flushed. "They're from a gentleman I met this morning. His name is Victor Perrago."

"How did you meet him?" Zach asked with suspicion.

There was no escape now, so Betsy told the whole story. As she had foreseen, her father said, "That's all for you, young lady! No more killer horses! You understand me?"

"Yes, Father," Betsy answered meekly.

But Bronwen was much more interested in Mr. Victor Perrago. "Who is this man?" she asked cautiously. They all listened closely as Betsy told what little she knew of him.

"Wasn't that nice," Betsy said as she finished, "to send such lovely flowers? I should be sending flowers to him!"

"He's too bold," Lanie interjected, frowning. "Father, you've got to see that this child stops running around without someone to watch her. Maybe I'd better call off my trip—"

"No," Stone interrupted. "You can't keep her locked up, Lanie. Everything's all set; you *can't* call the trip off now!"

Lanie reluctantly agreed, and Betsy sighed with relief, saying,

"Come on, Lanie, and I'll help you pack."

"I'll be by early in the morning to pick you up," Stone said as he left.

"I'm not sure I like all this," Zach muttered darkly when he and Bronwen were alone. "That girl's too young to be running around by herself."

"She's seventeen," Bron reminded him. "Not much younger than I was when I started *running around* with you."

"That's different!" Zach said. He was very protective of his younger daughter, far more than of Lanie.

Neither one said anything for a while. Seeing their children crossing over that mysterious line between adolescence and young womanhood or young manhood wasn't easy. A loaded silence hung in the air. After a few minutes, Bron said softly, "We'll have to trust God for this, Zach."

He nodded his head. "Yes, I guess we will." He took her hand and they sat for a long time, each lost in thought.

CHAPTER TWO

"DON'T HATE ME!"

★ ★ ★ ★

If Zach Winslow had not broken his leg in a fall from a horse, things might have been better. But he did fall, and he did break his leg—so that when the note came he was helpless.

It was the first day of July. Zach had taken the boys out to the riding stables and had insisted on riding Thor. Almost at once, he discovered that he had lost some of his riding skills over the years. The big horse had caught him unawares as he turned in the saddle to speak to Phil. "Phil! Don't let that—"

Thor instinctively sensed the man's vulnerability. He brought his hooves together and rose into the air in one gigantic buck. Zach made a desperate grab for the saddle horn that wasn't there. Even as he was turning a complete somersault through the air, he was thinking, *If only I'd had a Western saddle—*

His right leg hit the ground, bent under him, and Thor's enormous hoof slammed down right on top of it. Zach heard the bone crack in a sickening snap, and when he rolled over he saw the strange angle at which the leg was bent. The boys stared in horror. He managed to say calmly, "You'll have to go back to the stable and get some help for me, Tom."

Later that day he lay in the hospital, his leg encased in a huge cast from thigh to ankle. "It's just a broken leg, Dr. Miller!" he protested. "I don't need twenty pounds of plaster on it!"

"It's one of the worst fractures I've ever seen—and right in the knee, too," Dr. Miller retorted. "Those tendons are torn to shreds! You'll keep that cast on for a month; then we'll put a lighter one on, and you can start walking with crutches sometime after that." The doctor firmly refused to listen to any more of Zach's protests.

Dr. Miller told Bronwen privately, "For a man like him it's going to be hard, but you've got to keep him off that leg. If you don't, I'm afraid he'll be crippled permanently."

"And sure! I'll see to it that he doesn't do too much, Doctor," Bronwen answered.

Zach was taken home, and everyone hovered over him as if he were a child. He promptly took advantage of it and became petulant, proving to them that he was still childish in some of his ways. For two days he snapped at anyone who came in to wish him well or inquire about how he felt. After a time, though, his good nature took over and he became fairly docile again.

Lanie was notified of the accident and wired that she would come home to help as soon as possible, but Zach had responded, telling her to stay on in St. Louis. Bron did the nursing, going to the office when necessary, and putting up with her husband's grumpy ways. As they were talking one afternoon, Zach asked tentatively, "Where's Betsy today?"

"Where is she every day?" Bron replied, somewhat vexed. "With Vic, of course." She bit her lip and looked at Zach through long lashes that veiled her eyes. "It's worried I am about that situation. She's got a real crush on that man, and I don't know exactly what he has on his mind. She's too young for him, and I can tell you right now that he's a man who knows women."

Her statement startled Zach. He drew his brows together and exploded. "I'll *stop* her from seeing him! I'll run the fellow off!"

Bron laid her hand on his shoulder and smiled. "I know that's what you'd like to do. But in the first place, you have a broken leg, and in the second place, that would be the worst thing you could do." She squeezed his shoulder affectionately. "Betsy's infatuated with him, and the way to drive her into his arms for good is to tell her she can't see him. Or to tell him to stay away." Gently pushing a lock of hair back from her husband's forehead, she went on reassuringly. "He'll get tired of her soon enough. Anyway, I think she said something about his having to go back to his ranch fairly soon."

"I don't like it," Zach growled. "She's just a child!"

Bron wanted to soothe him, considering his helpless condition, and said, "Don't worry, dear. I always know where they're going." This was not true. The two were always going off somewhere; and Betsy was fairly closemouthed about where they had gone. But Bron didn't want to bother Zach with it. "It'll be over in a week or so, Zach. Just having a little romance, she is. Don't worry."

But as the days went on, the romance between Vic Perrago and Betsy did not cool off. Several days after Zach's conversation with Bron, the pair came in on one of their rare visits, and something exploded in Zach. "Perrago," he said ominously, "I need to talk to you—alone. Betsy, step outside." Betsy's eyes flew open and her mouth tightened. She started to speak, but her father interrupted. "Go outside, girl. Didn't you hear me?"

Betsy swung around, set her shoulders stubbornly, and left the room.

Her mother saw the girl's taut posture as she stood outside. "Betsy?" she asked, "what's wrong?"

"It's Dad! He's saying something awful to Vic!"

Bronwen searched her youngest daughter's face and said gently, "It's your father's business to look after you, child."

"I don't *need* any looking after! I'm seventeen years old! I'm a woman! I can take care of myself!"

At that moment Bronwen saw the stubborn resolve in her daughter's eyes. It would be useless to say anything more to Betsy, so she waited to talk to her husband until after Perrago came out.

"What is it, Zach?" she asked anxiously as she entered the room. "Is there trouble?"

"Not to hear that fellow tell it!" Zach struggled to sit up straighter in the bed and struck the cast with his fist. "Blast this thing! If I could get on my feet, I'd throw him out!"

"What's wrong? What did he say?"

"He wouldn't say anything, that's the problem. I tried to talk to him about his intentions, but he's slicker than goose grease,

Bron! He smiled, but that smile never touches his eyes. You ever notice that? He's like a gambler. He's got a professional cheerfulness that I don't like. I told him to clear out and not to come back!"

"Well, devil fly off!" Bron said with exasperation. "You shouldn't have done that, Zach!"

"And why not?" he said, irritated, but then he remembered that she had warned him about this very thing. He dropped his head and twisted his fingers together in a helpless gesture. "Well, maybe not. I just feel so helpless lying here, Bron!"

"Oh, it'll be all right. They'll be upset, maybe, but you can make it up later," she sighed.

Zach slept little that night. The next day when Ellen brought his breakfast, he asked her to send Betsy to him.

"Oh, she's already gone out for a ride, Mr. Winslow," Ellen said brightly. "Her and that Mr. Perrago left about half an hour ago."

All morning Zach fretted and fussed, and finally got Jericho, the yardman, to push him outside in his wheelchair. The sun was hot, but he was sick of the house. Jericho wheeled him around the street to a small park, where he stayed for a couple of hours, then said, "All right, Jericho, might as well go back."

"Yes, suh," Jericho said cheerfully. He pushed the wheelchair briskly down the street, and when they were half a block from the house he said, "Looks like Miz Bronwen's a-comin' to get you. You musta stayed out too long, Mistuh Zach."

Zach looked up to see Bronwen coming down the street, and one look at her face told him something was wrong. He didn't want to mention anything in front of Jericho so he said, "You go on, Jericho. Mrs. Winslow can push me the rest of the way."

"I need to help you up the steps," Jericho reminded him.

"Go on, I said!" Zach snapped, and Jericho took off. When Bronwen reached Zach, he asked, "What's wrong?"

Without a word she handed him a single sheet of paper.

He felt a premonition, such as he had had a few times during the war. Once when, for no reason, he felt compelled to get out of a trench he was lying in. Ten minutes later a shell landed in it, blowing it to bits. As he took the paper, an empty feeling swept over him and almost made him sick. Without reading it, he stared up and whispered, "It's Betsy, isn't it?"

"Yes. This came fifteen minutes ago. She's run off with Perrago," Bronwen said stiffly.

He saw the stricken look on his wife's face and knew that for her to be so affected, it must be bad. His eyes scanned the note:

Dear Mom and Dad,

> Vic and I are in love. I know you would never accept him as a son-in-law, so we are leaving Chicago. I'm going with him to be his wife. I will write you as soon as I can. Don't worry about me—and please don't hate me!

Betsy

The paper trembled in Zach's hand, and then he crushed it, wishing it were Perrago's throat instead. "We've got to do something, Bron!" he said insistently. "I've got to go after them! Right now!"

"You can't do it, Zach," Bronwen replied, looking at his broken leg. "We'll have to hire someone to go."

He looked mutinous for a moment, but then his shoulders sagged as he realized what she said was true. "Yes, I guess you're right. We'll have to get the police onto them—at once!"

"No. They haven't done anything wrong; they haven't broken any laws," Bronwen pointed out. "It'll have to be private detectives."

"All right, we'll get them! The best there is! Send a wire to Lanie. She can find someone for us," Zach said through gritted teeth.

Bronwen reached out, easing the crumpled paper out of his clenched fist, then took his hand. She held it gently, and though her own heart was breaking, she said, "We have to keep on trusting God, Zach. He'll give us our daughter back."

★　★　★　★

The secret could not be kept, of course. Bron immediately sent for Lanie, and she came home on the next train. The family did the best they could, but there were servants and neighbors, so Betsy and Perrago's elopement was soon broadcast in the neighborhood and among their friends.

Zach and Bronwen were naturally the most distraught, but Lanie was not far behind them. She was terribly concerned about Betsy and she blamed herself. "I should have been here to look after her!" she lamented to Wesley Stone. The two were standing outside her father's study, where he was in conference with a private detective. "I never felt right about it! If I'd been here instead of off on a stupid shopping trip—"

"It's not your fault, Lanie. I'm the one to blame—for insisting on taking you with me." Worry creased his brow, for he knew how much this had hurt the family. Besides, he had been close to Betsy, too. Stone was head over heels in love with Lanie, but actually he had spent more time with her younger sister. He had come to the house many times to see Lanie, only to find her gone somewhere, and then had spent the evening playing games or talking with Betsy. When she overcame her shyness, she was a witty and charming girl, more fun than most her age, and with more sense, he had thought. Secretly he thought the Winslows treated her badly, being far too demanding, but he had never said so to any of the family.

"They can't have gone far," he reassured Lanie, knowing even as he spoke that it might not be true. "This detective your father's hired comes highly recommended and he has a good staff. They should find them in a day or two."

"And what then? What if they're not married?" Lanie asked worriedly. This had been in her mind—in all their minds, in fact—from the very beginning. Her mother had revealed that Perrago was not, in her judgment, the marrying kind. "Poor baby, she's ruined, even if they find her!" Lanie moaned. "And how can we make her come home?"

To Wesley's surprise, tears came to Lanie's eyes. He had never seen her cry before, and wanted to put his arm around her. But he sensed that she would resent it.

The study door opened, and a slight man with a closely cut black beard emerged. He looked a great deal like a young General Grant. "Good afternoon," he said courteously, and then left the house.

Lanie hurried into her father's study, followed by Stone. One look at her father's face told her it was not good news, and she asked tremulously, "What did he say, Dad?"

"They traced them as far as St. Louis, then lost them there," Zach answered wearily. "I told the detective to go back and keep looking, put as many men on the case as they had to." Misery cast a pallor over his features, and Lanie ached to comfort him but could think of nothing to offer.

A dark cloud of gloom seemed to hang over them. The three talked about what should be done now that they knew where Vic and Betsy had been. Bronwen came in the room. She listened quietly, then said, "We can't let this destroy us. We've got to be thinking of the boys. Hurting we all are—but they must see that we still have faith."

"Do you really still have faith, Bronwen?" Zach asked her dully.

"I do," she said sturdily, looking at her husband with a direct gaze. "Remember past days, Zach? If you'll think back, God has done marvelous things in our lives, has He not?"

Zach's face lightened just a little, and he nodded. "Yes, He has. All right! I'll just believe, whether I believe or not!"

"And that's true faith," Bron nodded. "The Bible says that when Abraham lost hope, he kept on hoping, and that's just what we'll do!" She turned to Wesley. "Wes, it's glad you're here I am. You're a comfort to me. To all of us."

"I wish I could do more," he said, frustration roughening his gentle voice. "Do you think I should go down to St. Louis and start looking?"

"It'd be like finding a needle in a haystack," Bron stated matter-of-factly. "We'll stay here, and we'll fast, and we'll pray, and God will do something."

★ ★ ★ ★

Four days later God *did* do something. It came in the form of a telegram their detective, Phineas Lowery, brought. After the family had gathered, all except for the three younger boys, who were in bed, Mr. Lowery looked around the little group, opened the telegram, and frowned, saying, "I wish I had a good report, but all I've got is some news."

"Have you found her, Mr. Lowery?" Lanie inquired uneasily.

Lowery turned his sharp black eyes toward her and replied in a carefully measured voice, "We know where she is. My men picked up their trail in St. Louis and traced them to Fort Smith, Arkansas. I hired one of the federal marshals there to find out what they did after they arrived." He hesitated, his mouth drawn in a firm line. "The news isn't good."

"She's not—dead?" Zach asked sharply.

"Oh no—!" Lowery said in a shocked tone. "I didn't mean to imply anything like that. The problem is"—he cleared his throat and continued—"that Vic Perrago is an outlaw."

"An outlaw? What kind of an outlaw?" Bron asked in bewilderment.

"A bad one," Lowery said evenly. "He's got a gang, and they operate out of the Nations, the Indian Territory. They got off the train—we found that much out—and he left the next day with your daughter, both on horseback. The marshal found a man who said he sold them some horses and watched them ride out. So it's definite, I'm afraid."

"What is Indian Territory?" Tom demanded. He was very fond of his sister, and his face had grown apprehensive at the detective's words. "There are Indians there?"

"It's the land set apart for the Indians, son," Lowery explained. "When they were more or less driven out of the South, the government set apart that territory for them. Pretty barren, mostly desert, I suppose." Lowery stroked his beard thoughtfully. "But the thing is, the only law there is tribal law. White man's laws don't apply. So what's happened is that every crook and desperado in the Southwest has taken refuge there. They ride out every once in a while to kill and rob, then they go back in."

Tom's eyes were wide and his voice fearful. "Can't the law do anything?"

"It's under the jurisdiction of Judge Isaac Parker, the federal judge there. He has about two hundred marshals, but the territory is huge and unfriendly. I understand he's lost about fifty of them—killed pursuing their duties there."

Lowery's explanation had cast a pall over the room. Wesley, glancing at Lanie's stricken face, asked, "But, Mr. Lowery, surely we can do something!"

"Of course. We can send a fugitive warrant out after Perrago." He hesitated, looking back and forth at the grim faces of Zach and Bronwen. "Not for taking your girl, of course. There's no evidence that he kidnapped her. She went of her own free will."

They all started talking back and forth about the situation. After about twenty minutes, Lanie's voice rose accusingly over the rest. "Do you mean to say that the marshals won't pick Perrago up?"

"Not for taking your sister, Miss Winslow," Lowery said quietly. "That, unfortunately, was not a crime, though it was very wrong."

Lanie's face was set, her eyes contemplative, Wesley noted. He knew something was going on in her head. He had seen her like this before, as had the rest of the family. When Lanie Winslow decided something, she did it with her whole heart, soul, and mind. Once Lanie was in motion, there was no stopping her.

Lowery remained a little while longer. As he was leaving he offered, "I'll get what information I can, if you like."

"Would you go after Perrago, Lowery?" Zach demanded.

"No. I wouldn't have a chance," he replied. "I'm a city man, and that's the worst territory in the West. I couldn't do you any good. Now, you might find someone in the area who would take on the job, Mr. Winslow. But for me to tackle it would be almost hopeless."

Zach's face fell and he sighed deeply.

"I'm sorry, sir," Lowery said. His voice was respectful but not obsequious, and he bowed politely as he left.

Then the debate erupted again. What could they do? Zach was ready to hobble down to the railroad station to catch the next train to Fort Smith. The others wouldn't hear of it and finally convinced him that that simply wasn't practical. "You can't even walk, much less ride a horse!" Lanie scolded.

"I can ride in a wagon!" Zach said, his eyes flashing. "If I can get within rifle shot of that skunk, I can settle accounts!" Although Zach was basically a gentle man, everyone knew he had been pushed to white-hot anger.

They finally managed to quiet him, and he agreed to go lie down. After he had calmed somewhat, Lanie came to his room. There was a challenging light in her eye that told him she was in one of her determined moods, and he became wary.

"Dad," she said slowly, "I'm going to Fort Smith."

"I thought that's what you had on your mind," he grunted. "What good do you think that will do?"

"If you'll give me the money, I'll find somebody to run Perrago down. Maybe one of the federal marshals, maybe another outlaw—I don't know and I don't care!" She looked at him defiantly for a few moments; then her expression softened and her lips trembled slightly, revealing to her father that she was not as hard as she seemed. "It's my fault—partly at least. If I'd been here, I could have done something. I just have to go, Dad!"

Zach's expression grew somber as he listened to her. For the first time he was seeing something of himself in his oldest daughter. He realized that she had the same steel and stubbornness that he had possessed, and still possessed, although it had moderated slightly with age. He grew thoughtful as he considered the matter, then said, "I think you'd better do it, Lanie. I can't go with this blasted leg. I need to stay with the boys anyway. You can have all the money you need. Just go down there and hire the best men you can find, and stay there until they run him to ground. Bring my girl back." He dropped his head, staring down at his tightly clenched hands and whispered, "Bring her back, Lanie."

CHAPTER THREE

A Sad Awakening

★　★　★　★

As Betsy Winslow stepped up into the train, escorted by Vic Perrago, she had a sudden impulse to whirl around, jump to the ground, and run back to her home. A shudder of fear ran through her as she realized she was leaving everything she had known and loved for a life she knew absolutely nothing about.

At that moment, Vic stepped up beside her, gave her a hug, and smiled down at her, saying, "All right, honey. We're on our way to our ranch." Perrago had seen her hesitation and moved quickly to reassure her. Taking her arm he escorted her down the aisle of the train and found her a seat by a window. He carefully engaged her attention until the train pulled out, talking about his ranch and the life they would have there. He was very skillful at manipulating people and had found it easy to lead Betsy in the direction he chose.

The train gave a sudden lurch, the whistle screeched; then as the big drivers turned the enormous wheels, and the steam engine huffed and puffed its way out of Chicago, Betsy felt small, alone, and vulnerable. She held Vic Perrago's hand tightly; now he was the only security she had left. Looking up at him, she thought of how quickly he had captivated her. Then she thought of her parents. They would be devastated by her decision to run away and marry Vic Perrago. *But they'll be all right*, she tried to assure herself. *We'll come back to visit them soon, and they'll learn to love Vic as I do.*

All day long, the train moved steadily south, and Perrago exercised all of his charm to draw her thoughts from the fact that she was running away with a man she scarcely knew. Night came and Betsy got into her bed made up by the porter. When she was settled, Vic came to her, pulled the curtain back, reached in, and gently stroked her cheek. He whispered, "It won't be long, sweetheart, and we'll be in our own place. It'll be all right then." He kissed her, strongly; and she clung to him like a child until he withdrew and went to his own bunk.

Throughout the next day the train forged southward. Late that afternoon, almost at dusk, they disembarked in order to change trains for another, this one heading west. The station-master told them, "The train won't leave until eight o'clock in the morning. Better put up at a hotel, sir."

Perrago came back with the news, adding, "I don't fancy sitting up in a train station all night. C'mon, Betsy. We'll find a nice little hotel."

"All right, Vic."

He picked up their two suitcases and found a carriage, giving instructions to the driver to take them to a nice hotel. "Yes, sir!" the man said. "The Majestic is a mighty nice place. Nearly all the travelers stays there while they's waiting on trains," he told them with eagerness, his black face gleaming.

When they got to the hotel, Vic helped Betsy down and led her into the lobby. She stood close beside him at the registration desk. "Yes, sir?" the clerk asked.

"Room for two. Just for the night," Perrago said.

Betsy stirred with discomfort as the man's eyes lit on her. She dropped her own eyes to the registration book as Vic signed it "Mr. and Mrs. George Harrison" in a sweeping handwriting. Alarm ran through her, but she said nothing.

When they got up to the room, Vic tipped the bellboy, who then left with a snappy salute. As soon as the door closed, Betsy asked, "Vic, why didn't you use our right names?"

"Just habit, honey," Vic said carelessly. "When you're traveling, you just don't know what you'll run into. So I always just make up names. What does it matter?"

"So then, is Vic your real name?"

"I've told you my name is Vic." Evading her question, he came over and took her in his arms, pressing his lips to hers, holding her and savoring her tender young form. "I'm still Vic and you're still Betsy." He smiled when he raised his head. "That's all that matters."

Betsy struggled and pulled away from him. Her face was troubled and she said in a low voice, "Vic, we can't stay in this room together."

"Why not?"

"Well, we're not married."

Vic Perrago smiled, amusement wrinkling the corners of his mouth. His hazel eyes gleamed and he chuckled. "May as well be, Betsy. We'll get married as soon as we get to the ranch."

"No! This isn't right!" she said. "I can't stay here with you." Betsy was growing fearful, and her lips trembled. She reached down toward her valise, but Vic stopped her.

Taking her arm he pulled her up and said, "Wait a minute, Betsy. Don't be so hasty, now."

"I can't stay here."

Perrago stared at her, his hazel eyes no longer amused. He looked hard and cruel, not at all like the Vic she knew. Then another expression slid over his face, a knowingness she didn't understand.

"Oh, I didn't realize you felt that strongly about it, Betsy. You stay here. I'll go find a preacher to marry us. Will that be all right?"

"Oh yes, Vic," she said, relieved. "That's all I ask."

Betsy reached out to hug and kiss him warmly; then he turned and left the room, saying, "I'll be right back."

She took off her hat and walked nervously around the room. It was difficult to conquer the fear that kept rising in her; she was in a strange town, in a strange room, with a man she didn't know very well. "But I *do* know Vic," she reassured herself, "and I love him. He just didn't understand about sharing the room. Men are so different from women."

For the next hour and a half, she waited nervously. When the doorknob turned she jumped to her feet and stood defensively with her back to the wall. Perrago entered, leading another man, and said, "Honey, this is Reverend Leo Patterson. He's come to marry us."

Patterson, a heavy man with gold rings on three of his fingers, nodded and smiled. "Glad to meet you, miss. Let me congratulate you on your wedding."

"Thank you," Betsy said. She looked questioningly at Vic. "Doesn't there have to be a witness?"

"Not in this state," Perrago reassured her. "All we need is the Reverend, and he's even volunteered to take care of the legal work for us—registering the license and all that."

"Of course I will. Mighty proud to," Patterson agreed heartily. He had a huge stomach and patted it constantly as if it were an old friend. His face was round and red, and his eyes were a muddy brown color.

"Well, Reverend, let's get this over with. Tell us what to do," Vic ordered cheerfully.

Patterson said, "You stand right there, and, young lady, you stand beside him, take his hand there. Have you got a ring?"

Vic snapped his fingers. "No! I forgot a ring!" He looked at Betsy and asked, "Do you want to postpone this until tomorrow?"

"Oh no. You've gone to all the trouble of getting Reverend Patterson. We can get a ring later." Betsy was disappointed at the arrangements. She had always dreamed of a fine wedding in a church, with her mother there and her father giving her away, Reverend Simms leading the ceremony. Once again a feeling of guilt washed over her, but she forced herself to ignore it. "A ring isn't a marriage, is it, Vic?"

"That's right true, honey. I'm glad you see it like that. Tomorrow I'll get you the best ring in this whole town!"

"Well, then, we'll go right on." Patterson had been holding a black book in his hand. "Now, let's get on with it."

Betsy stood, listening to the large man as he mumbled a few phrases. She was too frightened, really, to hear anything but the blood pounding in her temples. The preacher's voice sounded far away; his words didn't sound like those she had heard in other weddings. Vic was holding her hand, and finally Patterson said, "I now pronounce you man and wife." Vic turned her around and gave her a resounding kiss.

Then he reached into his pocket, handed Patterson two bills, and said, "So you'll take care of the license and all that, will you, Reverend Patterson?"

"Oh yes. I have your address, and I'll send them right to you as soon as they go through the court. Takes a few weeks, you understand."

"Well, goodbye and thanks a lot. Here's an extra something to put in the offering plate next Sunday." Perrago handed him another bill, and a wide smile parted Patterson's thick lips.

"Lord bless you, sir!" He turned, put his hand out, and Betsy took it. She cringed at the thick, sweaty, and grimy hand, and was glad when he released hers. "And bless you, little lady! This man will make you a good husband, and you'll make him a good little wife! Well, I'll be going now," he finished, then left, his heavy footsteps echoing down the corridor.

Vic walked over and turned the key in the lock. The clicking of the key struck Betsy like a blow. There was something so final about it. She had gone down a road from which there was no return. Suddenly she remembered climbing a tree when she had been a young girl. She had gone too far up and had slipped. She remembered hanging by a branch, knowing that once she let go there would be no way to stop her fall. Slowly her fingers slipped, and finally she had fallen and sprained her ankle badly. The clicking of the key reminded her of that time; and she realized that in these last moments she had turned loose of everything she prized in her life. She had been an unhappy girl in many ways, envious of her sister, Lanie, discontented with her appearance. But now that she was here, there was no more entrance for her at her parents' home, and a sense of loneliness cloaked her. When Vic came close to her, she threw herself into his arms and said, "Oh, Vic! I'm afraid!" She buried her face in his chest, holding on tightly, as if she were a little girl.

Perrago looked down at her and smiled. He swept her up in his arms, moved over to the bed, and laid her on it. "Don't worry, Betsy," he grinned. "You're going to love being married to me!"

★　★　★　★

Ordinarily Betsy would have enjoyed the last stage of the train ride. They were going, she discovered, to Fort Smith, Arkansas. She had never heard of the town, but Vic told her he had a little business to do there before they could go on to the ranch.

She was sitting beside him in the narrow coach, gazing at the gold band on her left hand. It was a simple ring, but Vic had told her he would get her something nicer when he had more cash. A gusty wind boiled against the car's sides. Out in the bleak landscape a band of antelope rushed up from a copse, then scudded away into the darkness. A window behind Betsy squalled open, and the man sitting there pumped seven quick shots from a rifle—fruitlessly—and slammed the window down again.

The shots startled Betsy and she jumped as the rifle went off. Perrago put his arm around her, laughing at her expression. "Don't worry, sweetheart. I know things like that don't happen much in Chicago, but you'll get used to it."

"I hope so, Vic," Betsy said quietly. Her brief married life had been a disillusionment. Perhaps she had read too many romance novels. But the one thing she had come to expect from a husband was tenderness, gentleness. She would have no other complaint had she received this; but as fine as Vic's manners were, he was demanding, in a physical sense, not asking what her preferences were, making Betsy feel used and unfulfilled.

Betsy was not totally uninstructed. Her mother had given her the basic details of what it was to be a wife. But somehow what her mother had told her seemed very different from what had happened between her and Vic. After Vic was asleep, she buried her face in her pillow, choking back the sobs. That morning she put it behind her—at least outwardly. *It'll be different when we get home,* she comforted herself. *He'll be more gentle then.*

Fingers of cold crept through the car as the train steamed along at forty miles an hour. They had been traveling most of the day, and it seemed very long to Betsy. As the train made its way around a sharp curve, the steel wheels of the car chattered. "Won't be long now," Vic said with satisfaction, staring out of the window. Down the tracks, the lights of the Fort Smith station were coming into view, making a yellow glow in the gathering gloom of the late afternoon. "Are you anxious to see Indian Territory?" He grinned at Betsy.

"What is that, anyway?" she asked curiously. She wanted him to talk, and held his hand as he explained.

"Well, the Osage went into the Territory first; there were some other tribes as well, but mostly Osage in the beginning. Then more tribes started coming in from the Southeast. Later they were removed by the government, who wanted them out of the Deep South. These were called the Five Civilized Tribes." Vic seemed to enjoy explaining this to her, stroking her hand as he spoke. "They were herded into the territory west of where the Poteau and the Arkansas Rivers flow together—and that's Fort Smith. There's five of them: the Choctaw, Chickasaw, Seminole, Creek, and Cherokee."

"And Indians are the only ones who live there?"

An undiscernible smiled etched itself on Perrago's lips. Shifting back in his seat, he crossed his arms and glanced out the window. "We're almost there, station's just ahead." Then he answered her question. "It's supposed to be just for the Indians, but there are quite a few white men out there now. Some of them are on government business."

He didn't explain further. The conductor stuck his head into the car and called out, "Fort Smith! Fort Smith! Everybody out!"

Betsy and Vic joined the crowd piling off the train—most of the passengers men. It was completely dark as they started down the street. "This is Garrison Street," Vic informed her. "We'll stay here tonight before we leave for the ranch."

"All right, Vic," Betsy agreed meekly.

Betsy felt easier that night. Vic was charming; he took her all around the city by lantern light, finally showing her the famous gallows. "Lots of men been hanged there," Vic said, looking up at the platform. He rubbed his neck. "Must be pretty unpleasant. Hangman's name is George Maledon." The sight of the gallows seemed to fascinate him as he stared upward. "You know, they put the 'hangman's knot' in the rope. Has thirteen loops around it. When they put the noose around you, the knot goes right behind your left ear. That way, when you fall, it breaks your neck. You don't strangle to death." He shivered a little. "Once, I saw a man hanged—a little fellow, no more than a hundred pounds—when the drop didn't break his neck. He hung there for thirty minutes, it seemed like, his hands tied, kicking and squirming while he strangled to death."

"Don't tell me things like that!" Betsy said in a frightened voice. "Let's go, Vic, I don't like this place!"

Perrago laughed. "Me neither, honey! C'mon, let's go get something to eat!" He led her to a hotel called "Betty's Place," which was somewhat of a disappointment to Betsy. There were a lot of women there—loud and wearing a lot of paint on their faces. Several of them drifted by and started to speak to Perrago, but he waved them off, saying, "Don't bother me, girls, I'm on my honeymoon!" He put his arm around Betsy, and the hard-looking women laughed raucously, then went about their business.

After they ate, a tall, painted, gaunt-looking woman came over to them. "Do you want a room for the night, Vic?"

"Sure, Betty! This is my wife, Betsy. Betsy, this is Betty, an old friend of mine."

"I'm glad to know you, Betty."

The woman looked at Betsy with a strange expression, and a caustic smile turned the corners of her painted lips upward. "I wish you many happy years of marriage," she said formally to Betsy. Then she glanced at Perrago. "I'll send you up a bottle for a wedding present, Vic."

Perrago seemed to find this amusing and laughed. "That's fine, Betty, we'll drink a toast to you. Come along, Betsy, we've got a long trip tomorrow." He led Betsy upstairs to a small room. It was sparsely furnished, with only a bed and one small table. A long time after they went to bed, they could hear the tinny piano and its raucous tunes downstairs and the voices of men and women going up and down the corridors.

Once in the middle of the night there was a gunshot, then the sound of running feet. Betsy jolted upright and Perrago mumbled, half awake, "Huh, what is it?" Then he rolled over, saying, "Oh, don't pay any attention to that, honey. Always stuff like that at Betty's place." His head dropped on the pillow and he was fast asleep again.

The next morning Betsy was exhausted from lack of sleep, and her nerves were drawn as tight as a wire. Nothing seemed to be going as she had imagined it. She had pictured herself going to a fine ranch, being introduced as the wife of Victor Perrago—the crew lined up to take their hats off, mumbling her name worshipfully. Then she saw herself moving into a big house with high ceilings, fine western furniture, a horse of her own.

But that morning she sat alone, looking around the unlovely room. Vic had risen early, saying, "I'll get us geared up and we'll be leaving." She stared with distaste at the leprous-looking floor, the faded wallpaper, the shabby, beaten-up bedside table. *It'll be better when we get to the ranch,* she told herself for the umpteenth time.

An hour or two later Vic finally came back and handed her a package. "I picked you up something to wear. You can't wear a dress where we're going, on horseback." He insisted on watching her put it on, and she flushed, still embarrassed by the intimacies of marriage. He laughed at her discomfort. "You'll get over that soon enough, honey. I want to see that outfit on you."

Betsy slipped into it as quickly as she could. It was a fawn-colored riding outfit with a divided skirt, a pale blue cotton shirt, and a jacket of the same material as the skirt. The jacket had silver dollars for buttons. There was a flat-crowned hat and a pair of riding boots to complete her outfit. When she had finished, he laughed and said, "Now you look like a real western girl!"

"Oh, Vic, thank you! It's lovely! I'm so glad to be off that train, and I can hardly wait to be riding again!"

"You'll get plenty of riding," Vic said dryly. "Let's go. I want to get an early start."

He had bought two horses, a big roan stallion for himself and a brown mare for her. "Oh, she's beautiful!" Betsy said breathlessly. "What's her name?"

"Anything you want to call her."

"I think I'll call her Dolly," she decided, ecstatic over the small trim mare.

Vic had also bought two pack mules, which were heavily loaded. "What's all that for, Vic?" Betsy asked interestedly.

"Just taking some supplies to some friends of mine," he said. "You ready?"

"Yes!"

The two rode out, the pack animals trailing behind on a tether tied to Vic's saddle horn. They rode all morning along the banks of the Arkansas River. It was hot, but Betsy was so glad to be off the train and out of hotel rooms that the ride was a delight to her.

They camped that night on the bank of the river, rolling into their blankets just after dark. They rose at daybreak the next morning and rode all day again, crossing another river.

When she asked its name, Vic said, "This is the Verdigris. I don't know what that means." It ran alongside a set of railroad tracks for a while, and he told her that was the Arkansas Valley Railroad. He turned and smiled at her. "I've made a lot of money on that railroad."

"You have railroad stock?" Betsy asked in surprise.

"Oh, I have sort of an interest in it," he said idly, gazing off into the distance. "Once in a while I rake off a little of the profit." He laughed as if he had made a joke, then said, "I'm not really a railroad man, though."

They crossed the railroad tracks, and at noon entered into a set of low foothills that began to rise steeply as they headed farther north. The sun beat down on them and once Vic asked, "This too hot for you? I know it's pretty rough on a northern girl."

"No, it's fine, Vic," Betsy said quickly. Her tender skin had blistered, and she congratulated herself on having bought some lotion to coat the backs of her hands and her neck. Still, her fair complexion was pink and rosy. "How much farther is it?"

"Oh, we'll be there by dark," he said.

They rode steadily all afternoon, the low hills breaking up into sharper ones. Finally a bunch of "razorback hills," as Vic called them, broke the horizon in front of them. Up ahead there were long draws like fingers going back into the hills. He nodded toward them, saying, "Sometimes cattle get up into those. Have to be rousted out by the Indians who keep them. Sometimes they never get found."

"What kind of Indians?"

"Cherokees here," he said shortly. "Don't like to get cross-ways with them if I can help it."

His words made Betsy nervous, and she said no more but rode close to him. The little mare was a delight to her; although Betsy was not accustomed to such long rides, the mare was an easy mount so she fared well.

It was late in the afternoon when Vic suddenly drew up and said, "We'll meet my friends right over that rise, I think. At least, that's where they told me they'd be."

They passed through a group of scrub trees. Beyond the trees was a small, dilapidated farmhouse, the eaves drooping like rumpled covers from the corners of an unmade bed. Along with a few outbuildings, it sat in the midst of cleared ground. The sun was setting as they drew close. Betsy saw that it was a rough place, with a clutter of trash scattered about the yard. A few chickens were still pecking about at the debris. She heard a rooster crow, and a dog came out, barking menacingly.

"Hold it!" A voice ordered. A man stepped from behind one of the outbuildings with a rifle, which he leveled at the two. Betsy grew frightened.

"That you, Mateo?" Vic called out.

The man peered toward them and lowered his rifle. "Vic," he called out.

"It's us!"

Perrago turned to Betsy and said, "This is Mateo Río. Mateo, this is my wife, Betsy."

The man came forward. He was, Betsy saw, Spanish or Mexican. He was tall, with an olive-colored face, a thin mustache over an equally thin mouth, and the blackest hair she had ever seen. His eyes were like black coals as he frowned at Vic. "You didn't say nothin' about this, Vic."

"Didn't know it, Mateo," Vic said cheerfully. "When a man falls in love, not anything to be done about it. Everybody else here?"

"No. Honey, Jack, and Grat ain't here."

"Well, we're hungry; we're going to go in and get something to eat. Take care of the horses and mules, will you, Mateo?"

The Mexican took the reins of the animals, closely inspecting the pack animals. "You bring the stuff?" he asked.

"Sure," Vic nodded. "Come on, honey, let's go inside." He led Betsy to the house, which was an ugly shack that had never known paint. Many of the boards were warping off, and the boards that were still intact were held in place by nails that looked as if they could pop loose at any moment. The shack had been fried and baked by the sun, washed by the rains, and frozen by the snow, and its dilapidated look reflected the effects of years of harsh weather. Vic opened the door and stepped inside, saying, "Hey! Anybody here?"

Betsy followed and saw three people sitting at a table. A lamp gave off a yellow light, making their features look almost Oriental. One of them, she saw, was a woman.

"Got a surprise for you," Vic said. A big grin was on his face, and Betsy could see he was enjoying the moment. "I got married while I was gone. This is my wife, Betsy. I want you all to be nice to her. Betsy, this is Angela Montoya, Bob Pratt, and Buckley Ogg."

Betsy waited for them to speak, but no one did for a moment. Then the man identified as Buckley Ogg said with disgust, "That was a dumb thing to do, Vic. Bringing a woman out here." Ogg was at least fifty, with a balding head. He had deep-set black eyes and a beautifully modulated voice that matched neither his appearance nor his demeanor. He was tremendously fat, and his belly spilled over his belt.

"You're just jealous, Ogg," Pratt said. He was a young man of no more than twenty. Even sitting at the table, Betsy could see he was extremely well built and muscular, with black hair in tight curls, a wedge-shaped face, and eyes that angled into slits. He looked at Betsy with a leer. "I wish you woulda brought me a wife, Vic."

He frightened her a little, and she shifted her gaze to Angela Montoya. Angela was obviously Mexican, and Betsy would have thought she was married to Mateo Río, except for her name. She had jet-black hair, black eyes, and an olive complexion. Her lips were full and generous, yet there was a streak of cruelty in them. She studied Betsy so brashly that Betsy grew embarrassed and reached up to grasp Vic's arm. Finally the woman spoke. She cursed fluently and ended by saying in an ominous tone, "Ogg is right! You were a fool to bring that girl here! If you have to have a woman, why don't you go into town?"

Vic did not appear to be disturbed by all this. He put his arm around Betsy and squeezed her, saying blithely, "Don't worry, honey. They'll love you when they get to know you. Now," he went on, rubbing his hands together, "Bob, fix us something to eat. Then we're going to go to bed. Married folks go to bed earlier, you know."

Pratt laughed loudly and slapped the table. "You're a sight, Vic! A real caution!"

Vic sat Betsy down in a chair, and she listened while they talked. Much of it she didn't understand. The woman sitting across from her stared at her almost continuously, even when she spoke to the men, and it made Betsy very uneasy. Pratt fried bacon and eggs and put plates in front of Betsy and Vic. Vic ate voraciously, but it was so greasy Betsy couldn't stomach it.

"Angela, you show Betsy to the honeymoon suite," Vic ordered. He grinned at Angela arrogantly and said, "You two can get acquainted. I'm sure you'll be good friends."

Vic got up and walked out of the shack, followed by the other men. Angela did not move from her seat, her black eyes still fixed on Betsy. There was a chilled silence in the room.

Finally Betsy said in a small voice, "I—I hope I won't be too much trouble." She was afraid of the woman, who was quite a bit older than she—twenty-seven or twenty-eight—and wished that Vic had not left her alone with Angela Montoya.

"Where did Vic find you?" Angel demanded in a tense voice.

"In Chicago. But we were married on the way out here."

The dark-haired woman's eyes flickered, but her face was unreadable. "No, I don't think so. Did he bring a man in that he introduced as a preacher?"

An icy hand closed around Betsy's heart and her breath became ragged. "Why, yes, there was a Reverend Patterson—"

"He show you any credentials?"

"No—no—not actually—"

"You see the marriage license? Did you sign it?" Angela went on relentlessly.

Betsy licked her lips, which were suddenly very dry. "N-no, he's supposed to mail it—to us—"

Angela Montoya rose to her feet. "You little fool," she spat. "You're not married! Vic's done this before!" She turned on one heel, cursing again, then said, "Come on, I'll show you the bedroom. But don't think you're his wife, because you're not! Vic will never marry any woman, because he doesn't like women!" She turned back to Betsy, her hands on her hips. "Didn't you know that? Couldn't you tell it?"

"No, no, that's not true! You're lying to me!" Betsy cried,

coming to her feet. She wanted to protest more, but suddenly the words were choked and she couldn't say anything else. Pictures rose unbidden in her mind: Vic signing a false name in the hotel, the man that had been introduced as a preacher, the incoherent marriage vows. Vic had lied to her—it had all been a lie—and now she was trapped. She stared mutely at the Spanish woman and knew she would get no sympathy from her. Angela Montoya's eyes were black as night, and cruel as death. As Betsy stood there, she knew she was irrevocably and totally lost.

CHAPTER FOUR

TRIP TO FORT SMITH

★ ★ ★ ★

Once Lanie had decided what to do, she threw herself into organizing all the details with a furious energy. By the next day she had made arrangements to have all her father's business taken care of by a young clerk in his employ, who was rather apprehensive at the responsibility. She had also written letters, explaining that she would not be able to attend various functions she was committed to.

It was late that afternoon when she looked up from dispatching final bits of paperwork to see Wesley Stone enter the study. "Oh yes, Wesley," she greeted hurriedly. "I'm glad you came. I have a few errands I want you to run while I'm gone."

"I won't be able to do that, Lanie," he replied gravely.

Surprised, Lanie searched his face. He had never declined any request before. Now she noted a look of determination on his craggy features. "I won't be able to," he went on, "because I am going with you."

Lanie stared at him and said in a puzzled voice, "I don't know what you're talking about, Wesley. You mean you're going to the train with me?"

"No, I mean I'm going to the Indian Territory with you." He walked across the room and looked into her startled eyes. "I decided it wouldn't be safe for you to go alone, so I'm going along."

"Why, you can't do *that*! What about your practice?"

"I told Mr. Ratliffe I had to have some time off." The corners of his wide mouth lifted slightly. "He didn't like it much. I may not have a job when I get back."

Lanie put her pen down and rose to her feet. Wesley was a deliberate and methodical man. Normally everything he did was by the book—but now he was breaking out of the character she had thought was as set as if it were carved in stone. "It's sweet of you, Wesley," she said warmly, "but you can't throw your career away. I'd better go alone."

"It's all settled," he said as if he hadn't heard a word. "My bags are all packed; so what time does the train leave?" He was casually leaning against the mantel, apparently relaxed.

"You're really worried about me, aren't you?" Lanie probed.

He gave her a curious look. "Yes. You don't have any business going off by yourself in that kind of world. But that's not the real reason I'm going." She looked at him questioningly. He shrugged. "I'm worried about Betsy. I wouldn't count myself half a man if I didn't do everything I could to get her back. Now, when do we leave?"

"The train leaves at 8:15 in the morning—" Lanie began, but was interrupted by Phil and John, who were arguing about who got the honor of pushing Zach's wheelchair.

"Whoa, there!" Zach yelled. "You want to break my other leg?" Reaching down, he grabbed the wheels and yanked them hard. "You two wild Indians run along, now! You can break the rest of my bones after I talk to your sister."

They left, still arguing noisily. Zach grinned as he released the brakes and rolled toward his daughter. "Hello, Wes," he said as he passed him and turned to Lanie. "Lanie—"

"Mr. Winslow," Wesley interrupted, "I've decided to go on this trip with Lanie."

Zach wheeled his chair around and stared at him. He had become an astute student of human nature through his years on the frontier and in business. He had always liked this young man, but somehow Stone seemed to lack drive. Wesley wasn't the kind of go-getter that Zach had envisioned for Lanie. He had never thought Wesley had much of a chance with Lanie, anyway. Now he raised his eyebrows and asked, "What's all this?"

He listened carefully, his head cocked to one side, as Wesley explained why he felt he had to make the trip. When he finished, Zach slapped the arm of his wheelchair and said with enthusiasm, "By heaven, that sounds good to me, Wes! What did your boss say?"

"Said I might not have a job when I get back," Wesley answered with a crooked smile.

Zach laughed. "Don't worry about that, boy. You take care of this girl here, and find Betsy, and we'll see that you got plenty of lawyerin' to do!" He rolled over to his desk, opened the drawer, and took out a worn gun belt. He lifted the .44 from the holster, hefted it, then shoved it back. Handing the weapon to Wesley, he said, "You'll probably need this."

Wesley disliked guns. He was a man of peace and opposed violence in any form. He looked down at the gun, started to hand it back, then decided it would hurt the old man's feelings. *I'll take it, but I'll never use it*, he thought.

Zach said, "Now, let's talk about this trip. How much is it going to cost?"

They discussed finances for a time and made arrangements for cash to take with them for expenses and emergencies. As the final preparations were made and the last details taken care of, Wesley was his usual methodical self. Lanie seemed a bit nonplused, but Zach was grateful that his daughter would have a man along. He had not missed the expression on Stone's face when he'd taken the gun. *He'll have to change when he gets in the Nations*, Zach thought.

At 8:15 the next morning, Lanie and Wesley pulled out on the train headed for Fort Smith, Arkansas. The family had said their goodbyes at home, so no one had come to see them off. As the train chuffed loudly, its locomotive driving wheels pulling the big engine along, sending it out of the station in an increasing speed, Lanie looked out the window and said in a low voice, "I hope we find her, Wesley. It's killing my folks."

"It's hard on all of us, Lanie. We'll do the best we can." He knew that Lanie was not a deep-rooted Christian. Her religion had always seemed to be a fashionable thing, like her dresses—

always the latest style, perfectly designed for public view. The trauma that had torn apart the lives of the Winslow family could not be fixed by the expensive, tasteful stained-glass windows of First Church, or the trained choir, or a theologically sound message from the fancy walnut pulpit.

Wesley cast a sideways glance at Lanie's profile. *As tragic as this trip is, if Lanie learns a little bit about what real life is like, where faith is tested, that may be good for her.*

★ ★ ★ ★

The trip from Chicago to Fort Smith brought Lanie into close contact with the harsh realities of life. Accustomed to the comfort of short train rides on palatial coaches in Chicago, she was not prepared—any more than Wesley—for the crudeness of the narrow-gauge passenger train that wound around mountains until it reached the city of Fort Smith.

As they stepped off the coach into the bright sunlight, Lanie looked up at her companion and groaned. "We look like coal miners, Wesley! I tried to get clean in that washroom, but all I did was smear the dust and soot!"

"Yes, it's been pretty rough," Stone agreed. He rubbed his aching back. "I won't mind sleeping in a bed tonight. Sitting upright in a hard seat for two nights running is little better than some of the medieval tortures I've read about that they used at the Inquisition!" There had been no sleeping coaches available on the last leg of the journey. Two nights in the dingy, tobacco-smelling smoking car had drained both of them of their vitality.

"I expect we better find a hotel first; then we'll see what we can do," Lanie said. She looked around expectantly and spotted a man in a carriage, evidently waiting for passengers. "Come on," she urged, "let's see if that man will take us to the hotel."

It proved to be simple enough. The driver collected their baggage, loaded them in the back of the buggy, and climbed back up onto the driver's seat. A garrulous man, he informed them that his name was Shaughnessy O'Quinn and that he had been born in Ireland. Waving his whip expansively, he asked, "This your first trip to Fort Smith?" Seeing their affirmative nods, he continued. "Well, it's a right nice town we have here. We've a paved street—down Garrison Avenue here—and we have street-lights, and two newspapers."

As he proceeded along Garrison Avenue—the main street that led from the rail yards—he added, "Ten years ago, you wouldn't have seen none of that. No paved streets, no sidewalks, no decent hotels. What we did have was thirty saloons, which did a thrivin' business what with the steamboats and the railroad men. Lots of cowboys coming by from the Texas drives. Was about the wildest place you'd be wantin' to see."

"It still looks pretty wild to me," Wesley remarked to Lanie quietly. "Look at how many of these men are carrying guns."

Lanie's eyes followed his nod and saw that at least half of the roughly dressed men sauntering along the avenue were armed.

"Here we are, folks!" O'Quinn announced proudly. "The Main Hotel! Real fine place!" He jumped out and began carrying luggage in. After paying the fare, Stone helped Lanie to the ground, and they walked into the lobby of the hotel. With surprise and delight they saw that it was actually clean and new.

"We'll have two rooms, if you have them," Stone said to the clerk, a thin, mousy-looking man with an imposing set of front teeth and a head of flaming red hair parted precisely in the middle.

"Sign right here," he directed. He watched as they signed, then gave them two keys. "102 and 104," he said, winking, "right next to each other."

Stone flushed at the innuendo, grabbed the keys, and turned to lead the way to the stairs. "That fellow has a wicked imagination," he muttered resentfully. Lanie made no comment.

They found their rooms and distributed the luggage. "Why don't you get washed up," Wesley suggested, "then lie down for a nap. And I'll do the same." He put one hand to his back and stretched painfully. "I feel as if I've been beaten with a hoe handle."

"I don't know," Lanie replied wearily. "I'd really like to get started right away, but it's tired to the bone I am. Maybe you're right."

It was almost three in the afternoon, and Wesley insisted, "Let's get some rest, and tonight we'll go out and get something to eat. Then tomorrow we'll get a fresh start at it." He fiddled with the large watch he had pulled out of his vest pocket and said with concern, "It's a different world here, Lanie. Both of us are aliens. I've got a gun, but don't want to use it. Wouldn't know how."

Lanie's lips tightened, and the determined look he was so familiar with leaped onto her face. "We'll find her, and we'll get her home again, too, Wesley."

They went to their rooms, washed, then lay down for a nap. When Lanie awoke, it was pitch dark outside, and she fumbled for the tiny watch she wore pinned to her blouse. It was eight o'clock. Exclaiming with dismay, she got up and started dressing. A knock sounded on her door. Stone stood there with a sheepish look on his face. "I guess I was more tired than I thought," he said.

"So was I." They smiled, both realizing how much the trip had already taken out of them.

They found that the hotel had a dining hall. Soon their orders were taken and while they were waiting for the meal, they discussed what they should do next. In reality, neither of them had much of a plan. After some vague and fruitless discussion, Lanie said resignedly, "I guess we'll just have to wait and see what the judge says. You know, Mr. Lowery said Judge Parker has nearly two hundred marshals. Surely one of them ought to be able to help us."

They finished their meal and decided to go for a walk. In spite of the vaunted streetlights, there were menacing dark places along the street; and the crowds roaming the city were so rambunctious that Stone cut the walk short and escorted Lanie back to her room.

"Tomorrow," he said confidently, "we'll find out what to do." They were standing in front of her door, and Wesley wanted to kiss her but couldn't gather his courage. This statuesque, self-assured girl intimidated Wesley Stone. He had come from a poor background, and, to him, she was a rich girl, sought by many of the wealthy young men of Chicago. He knew he was facing a long, hard fight to get to the top of his profession; therefore he had never spoken of marriage to her. Now he said tentatively, "I wish we had some of your people here—that you're always talking about."

"Oh," Lanie said with a slight smile, "you mean like Thomas Winslow, the gunfighter? Yes, I expect he'd be much more useful than either of us." She saw his face change and quickly put her hand on his arm. "Oh, Wesley, I don't mean to make light of you. But after all, you said yourself that we don't know this world." She withdrew her hand and straightened up to her full height. "But I will before I'm through! Good-night, Wes."

Lanie closed the door behind her and prepared for bed, determined that the next day they would make a start toward finding Betsy. Lanie had no idea what Betsy would do if they did find her. They couldn't force her to return, Lanie knew. "But when we find her," she said resolutely into the darkness, "we'll figure out how to get her home."

The next morning Lanie rose early, washed thoroughly, and dressed in one of the two extra dresses she had brought, a simple pearl-gray taffeta. She knew that it was much too fancy for this part of the world. It was, however, by far the simplest dress she had, so she finished dressing and went to meet Stone. After a hurried breakfast, she said, "I want to try to see the judge before court opens."

This proved to be difficult. When they arrived at the courthouse, which was only a block from the Frisco Depot, they found it already stirring with activity. The streets swarmed with men, mostly white, with a plentiful sprinkling of Indians and black faces. The courthouse was not set square with the compass. Instead, it favored the Arkansas River, which meandered a few blocks away. The building itself ran from northeast to southeast. Half of the main floor, they discovered, was used for the courtroom. The other half was given to the minor court officers. The entire lower floor, a basement really, was used as the jail.

Wesley and Lanie entered the building, looked down the corridor to the left, and saw several offices. "We'd better go that way," Wesley said, pointing. "I expect that's where the judge's office would be."

They did find Judge Isaac Parker's office, but their entrance was barred by one of the clerks. "The judge can't be disturbed before court," he told them sternly. But he had never faced a woman with the tenacity of Lanie Winslow, and somehow he found himself going inside with a promise to *see* if the judge would talk with them. He was back in a moment and said with some confusion, "Uh—yes, ma'am, you can go on in now."

The man behind the desk was an imposing figure—over six feet tall and weighing about two hundred pounds. "I'm Judge Parker," he said, indicating two chairs. "Won't you sit down? I have just a few minutes, though."

He was in his mid-thirties; and Lanie was surprised to find him an unusually handsome man with brown hair, blue eyes, and a neat, well-trimmed beard. He was genial and pleasant, and he listened politely as Lanie explained their mission. But when she finished he shook his head and said briefly, "I'm afraid there's nothing I can do to help you."

"But surely, since Perrago is wanted—"

Judge Parker held up his hand, cutting off Lanie's words. "I wish there were something I could do," he said with obvious sincerity, a compassionate look in his eyes, "but even though I have two hundred marshals, they are covering an area about the size of New Jersey. The outlaws have banded together, striking fear into the people who live in the territory, including the Indians. Most people know only too well that if they give assistance to one of my marshals, they're likely to be burned out, or shot, or both, in retribution."

"But, Judge," Stone said when he paused, "that doesn't leave us any recourse! Only a federal marshal has authority to do this for us, isn't that true? I mean, we can't even hire a private detective to go in and look for this man and Miss Winslow's sister."

"That's true," Parker nodded. "It has to be that way. Actually, the Nations were set apart for the Indians, and tribal law governs there. But now, my court has been established because the area has become a haven for white renegades. The Indians really have no authority over a man like Perrago."

Lanie tried to find a basis for reasoning with him, but she finally had to concede that there was nothing the judge could do. She stood up—and both Wesley and Judge Parker hastened to stand as she did. "I understand your position, Judge Parker—but my sister is out there somewhere. And somehow, I'm going to get her back!"

"Well might you labor to that end, Miss Winslow," Parker said, and inclined his head as a gesture of respect. "I am truly sorry that I am unable to help you. However, I will do this much—I will alert my marshals to be on the lookout for Perrago and his band. But they're a slippery bunch—vicious, unprincipled, and sly. Very hard to run down, they are. Even my best men haven't been able to find them."

"Thank you, Judge, I appreciate that very much," Lanie said graciously; then she and Wesley left.

When they were back in the hall, she gritted her teeth. "Well, there's no help there. We'll have to do something else."

Wesley Stone had no inkling of a suggestion. As they walked down the corridor he said, "Look, Lanie—court's about to start. Let's sit in on a little of it. Maybe we'll get some kind of a feeling for this place, and for Judge Parker too. Who knows, we might find a way to get him to help us yet."

They entered the courtroom and found the room filled—some people were even sitting on the windowsills. Lanie and Wes got their seats by the grace of a short, undersized man, about sixty, wearing a marshal's badge. When he saw Lanie he stood up at once and said in a courtly manner, "Here, ma'am, you set down here." He looked at a sloppily dressed man sitting in the next chair. "Fred," he said tersely, "go stand over against the wall." The man gave him a sullen look but immediately got up and slouched away.

"You're one of Judge Parker's marshals?" Lanie inquired of the man.

"Yes, ma'am. Name's Lorenzo Dawkins. Been with the judge from the very beginning." He looked down and saw that an Indian was sitting in the next chair over and said, "Spotted Horse, go over there and stand with Fred. I need your chair." The Indian grunted and left. Dawkins stepped past Wesley and Lanie, taking the chair the Indian had vacated.

"I'm very grateful to you, Marshal Dawkins," Lanie said with a glowing smile. She turned on the charm, and though Wesley appeared to be idly looking around the courtroom, he was listening. He knew exactly what Lanie was doing—he'd seen it often enough before. *She's decided that this old man can tell us something we need to know,* he thought. Reluctant admiration crept over him as he watched Lanie deftly use her charms to play on the marshal's kindness.

The old man was obviously flattered by the attention of the beautiful young woman, and he talked freely until the bailiff came in and said loudly, "Hear ye, Hear ye! The Honorable District and Circuit Courts of the Western District of the Indian Territory is now in session! Judge Isaac Parker presiding!"

Judge Parker came in and sat in a high-backed, ornately carved walnut chair, then said, "First trial will now begin."

The trial was rather simple. A boy was brought in on a whiskey charge. He pleaded guilty to buying whiskey at two dollars a gallon and selling it at ten. Judge Parker listened to the evidence, took into consideration the boy's age, and gave him a light sentence and a severe lecture. When he finished he said, "I hope this will be a lesson to you, and that from now on you'll try to be a good and honest citizen."

The boy choked up, then said loudly, "As good and honest as you, Judge!"

Laughter ran around the court, and Lorenzo Dawkins leaned toward Lanie and whispered, "The judge liked that. You don't see him smile often."

There were several cases that went by quickly. Stone said once under his breath, just loudly enough for Lanie to hear, "He's more like a king up there than a judge. That's what I've heard about him."

Lorenzo Dawkins overheard and fixed a sharp gaze on Wesley. "We've got so many cases here, he's got to run 'em through quick, Mr. Stone. Ain't no time for foolin' around."

A man was brought in for horse stealing, and Judge Parker asked, "Are you represented by an attorney?"

"No, sir," the small, dingy-looking man said.

"Don't you want someone to plead your cause?" the judge asked.

"Can't I plead my own?" he said indignantly.

"Yes," Parker said shortly and waited for the man to state his plea.

The man paused for a few minutes, then said, "Well, in that case, I'll plead guilty."

The most interesting case was one involving a woman. She was brought in by a lady bailiff and was identified as Connie

Wright. The charge was horse stealing, and her husband was a co-defendant.

The trial proceeded with dispatch, and Lorenzo Dawkins gave a little background to Lanie and Wesley as the preliminaries were taking place. "That Connie, she's a caution," he said, shaking his head. "She's been in and out of this courtroom seems like half a dozen times. But the judge, he's always lenient to women. He believes they should be punished, but in a woman's case—well, I don't reckon he'd ever hang one."

"That's her husband, there with her?" Lanie asked.

"Well, that there's one of 'em, I guess. Connie changes husbands pretty often. That one there's the first half-breed she ever had, though," Dawkins commented with the conscientious manner of a tour guide. "I think Connie adopted him, on a notion, don't you see? Then wound up marrying him one day because it occurred to her."

"She'd do that?" Lanie exclaimed. She was studying the woman closely. Connie Wright had a shapely figure, but her face was not pretty at all. Her mouth was pulled downward in a constant frown, and her small eyes flared with anger when the prosecuting attorney belittled her husband.

Dawkins listened to the trial and nudged Lanie with his arm. He seemed to be in the habit of touching people while speaking to them. "Yep. Well, looks like Connie and Sam's goin' away for a while—going where the dogs won't bite 'em," he commented sagely. "I've seen the judge a lot, and I can almost tell what he's gonna do. You watch, now."

Parker had the two defendants brought before him. "I sentence both of you to a year in the federal penitentiary. You're both guilty of crimes worse than horse stealing, but that's all that's been proven against you." He gave Connie a severe look and said, "Connie Wright, if you keep on the way you're going, you may be the first woman I've ever hanged."

Connie looked up, smiled, and said boldly, "Then I'd be hung by one of the best-lookin' judges I ever seed!"

CHAPTER FIVE

A BROKEN PLAN

★ ★ ★ ★

After two days of sitting in the sweltering hotel room, the monotony broken only by the activities in the courtroom, Lanie finally made up her mind that she was going to do *something*. Putting on her hat, she marched to Wesley's room and knocked forcibly on the door.

When he opened it, she blurted out, "Come on, Wesley! We've got to do something! We can't spend the rest of our lives in this awful place!"

His eyes widened and he grabbed his hat, then hurried along behind Lanie as she stalked down the hall. She kept up her fast pace, and he finally caught up with her as she reached the street. "What are you going to do?" he demanded.

Lanie answered brusquely, "I'm going to find someone who'll go over into the Nations and pick up the trail of Perrago's gang."

"Find someone?" Stone looked at her in bewilderment. "What do you mean, 'find someone,' Lanie? You don't know any bounty hunters around here! And the marshals won't go; Judge Parker made that clear to both of us."

"There must be someone," Lanie said stubbornly. "I think I'll go find that nice old man we talked to in court the first day. What was his name—"

"Lorenzo Dawkins," Wesley said automatically.

"Yes. I've been listening, Wesley, and they say that in his day he was quite a marshal."

"You're not thinking he'll go with you?"

"No. But he knows just about everyone in the Territory, and he can tell us who to hire."

When they arrived in front of the courthouse, they found a large crowd gathered.

"What's going on?" Stone asked a man standing nearby.

"Prison wagons coming in. The marshals are bringing in the men they caught out in the Territory," he answered.

As the wagons approached, the scene looked a lot like a circus. Some of the bawdy girls from the houses of prostitution joined the parade, with a number of the men following after them. When they reached the jail, the prisoners inside pressed their faces against the bars, whooping and yelling like madmen. Lanie stared at them in bewilderment, not understanding why men in jail would be glad to see others join them.

The marshals unloaded the prisoners from the wagons, poking them sharply with their Winchesters. The men were all chained together like fish on a string. They were mostly white men, with a few Indians and half-breeds and Negroes.

"They look like a rough bunch, don't they, Lanie," Wesley murmured. "Murderers, robbers, train wreckers, and no telling what else. Tough-looking crew. If that's what we're facing to get Perrago—I just don't know."

Lanie didn't reply, but set her mouth in an even tighter line. Her eyes scanned the crowd until she found the man she was looking for standing near one of the wagons, talking with a marshal who was dusty from head to foot after the long ride. "Come on, Wes. There he is," she said and started weaving her way through the crowd. When they reached the two men, she said without preamble, "Marshal Dawkins, may I speak with you, please?"

Dawkins turned and at once snatched off his hat. "Why, shore you can, Missie. See you later, Box." He took Lanie's arm and guided her through the crowd, shoving his way roughly when one of the onlookers didn't move fast enough to please him. Inevitably, when those in the crowd recognized the marshal, they stepped back quickly, according him a respect that made Wesley wonder as he trailed in their wake. *Must be a pretty tough old codger,* he thought, *the way they back off from him like that. He sure doesn't look like it.* He followed the pair as they cleared the street and stepped up on the sidewalk to talk.

Lanie had decided to waste no more time. She said succinctly, "I want to hire someone to go into the Territory to find Vic Perrago."

Dawkins cocked one eyebrow and asked, "Perrago? What do you want to find that one for? Most folks would just about rather do anything than go findin' him!"

"He ran off with my sister," Lanie said. She explained the situation briefly. Dawkins listening intently.

When she finished, Dawkins blew out a long breath. "Missie, you just don't know what you're asking. You ever hear tell of a bandit name of Ned Christie?"

"No, I don't think so."

"Well, he was a tough one. Ran marshals all over the Territory for a long spell. We got word where he was at, and we went out to get him, just him—Ned Christie. You know how many marshals rode? Seventeen—and it took every one of 'em to get Christie. And Perrago, he's almost as big a rattlesnake as Christie, and he's got a bunch with him. Ain't no one man gonna take him, even s'posin' he could find him." He repeated adamantly, "Ain't no one man gonna take him."

Stubborn in her resolve, Lanie Winslow lifted her chin and said, "If I could talk to Perrago, I'm sure I could reason with him. Marshall Dawkins, please give me the name of a man that will just *find* Perrago's crew."

Dawkins scratched his head, then clapped his hat back on. He looked up and down the street. Finally he said resignedly, "I don't know. Earl Waters might do it. But he's gone way over on the other side of the Territory and won't be back 'til tarnation knows when." A half smile flickered over his face and his gaze met Lanie's. "Lobo Smith could do it. But he's in jail, of course." He continued to name men, all of whom were either unavailable, unsuitable, or unreachable. He finished cheerfully, "Well, I guess you better leave this up to the marshals, Missie. We'll run Perrago to the ground sooner or later."

"I can't wait, Marshal," Lanie said stubbornly, "but thank you for your trouble." She turned and walked away, not even looking at Wesley.

Feeling utterly frustrated and inept, Wesley sighed and hurried after her.

"What are you going to do now?" he demanded.

"I told you, Wesley, I'm going to find a man to take us to Perrago," Lanie answered emphatically.

"Lanie!" Stone reached out and stopped her, pulling her around to meet his eyes. "You can't do it! You're not thinking of going out into the Nations yourself?"

"Yes, I am!" Lanie said fiercely. "But you don't have to come along if you don't want to, Wesley!"

This was all it took to fill Wesley Stone with do-or-die determination. If he had been alone, he would never even have thought of the wild scheme now running through his head— going into a place like the Indian Territory, which fairly bristled with outlaws, desperadoes, killers, and wild Indians. His back stiffened at her tone, and he retorted, "If you're going, I'm going, and that's all there is to it! Now, let's hire these men!"

The grim expression on Lanie's face wavered, then dissolved. Putting her hand on Wesley's arm she said gently, "You are a jewel sometimes, Wesley. It's glad I am that you came along!" Then in a brisk, businesslike tone she said, "So let's find the man."

★　★　★　★

Dobie Jacks and Conn Bailey made a strange-looking sight. Dobie was six foot two, knock-kneed, and lanky. Conn Bailey was five foot six, roly-poly, and bow-legged. Someone once remarked, "When Dobie and Conn stand together, they spell 'ox.'" The pair had been drinking at the Cattleman's Bar most of the day, and were now solemnly contemplating spending the rest of the day doing exactly the same.

The bouncer, a man aptly named Bulge Raymond, came over and said, "You hear about the girl trying to hire someone to take her into the Territory?"

Dobie glanced down at Bulge and asked owlishly, "What girl, Bulge?" He listened carefully as Raymond explained that a young woman and man were trying to find someone to guide them.

Raymond grinned. "And you'll never guess who she's wantin' this guide to find."

"Who's that, Bulge?" Conn Bailey asked. He had a round face and a pair of muddy brown eyes.

"Vic Perrago."

The two men stared at Raymond; then Conn Bailey laughed harshly. "She'll be sorry enough if she finds *that* one!"

"I guess so," the bouncer shrugged, muscles rippling along his shoulders. "Just thought you two might like a job."

"I don't want no job tanglin' with Perrago," Dobie said flatly.

"Wait a minute," Bailey jumped in, his brow wrinkling. He was the thinking one of the pair. "Mebbe there's something in this after all. Thanks, Bulge." The bouncer nodded and left. Bailey looked up at Jacks. "I've had about enough of this town for a while. Whaddya say we become jen-yoo-wine, cert-ee-fied guides?" he said slyly.

Jacks shook his head. "Not me. I ain't so stuck on staying in Fort Smith any longer, but I'd like to cut out for California. I ain't huntin' for Vic Perrago, that's for sure."

"I think that just shows your good sense, Dobie," Conn Bailey nodded. "But I think I just figgered out a way to get the money and the supplies to pull outta here." He winked broadly at his partner. "Let's go find that there couple. Try to look as much like a tough guide as you can, will you?"

They had no trouble finding out that the lady's name was Winslow and the man's was Stone. And finding them was no trouble either; they just went to the "main hotel" and asked for them at the desk, and the clerk politely supplied the room numbers. They walked upstairs and knocked on one of the doors. When it opened they both pulled their hats off and Conn said, "Miss Winslow?"

"Yes. What is it?"

"My name's Conn Bailey and this here's Dobie Jacks. We heard tell you're lookin' for a couple of guides to go out and find Vic Perrago."

Lanie's eyes brightened and she said eagerly, "Yes, come in." She stepped back, and as the two men entered she motioned to a tall man standing by the window. "This is Mr. Stone." She made the proper introductions and then asked Bailey, "Do you think you can find Perrago?"

Conn was slow to answer. He turned his hat around in his hand two or three times and shifted back and forth. "Hard to say for sure. But if anybody can find him, it's Dobie here. He can track better than a Indian. Best tracker I ever seen in my life. Once we cut their sign, it won't be no trouble, ma'am."

Dobie heard his cue and put in, "Naw, it won't be no trouble, Miss Winslow. Not *findin'* him, that is." His eyes momentarily fixed on Bailey, then back to Lanie. "'Course, there's only the two of us, and Perrago's got eight or ten pretty tough hands. In a fight I don't think we'd have a chance."

"There won't be any fighting," Lanie said quickly. "All we want to do is talk to him. How much would you expect to be paid?"

Conn said deprecatingly, "Oh, Miss Winslow, we heard about the bad luck you had with your sister. We don't want to over-charge a lady, especially one in your situation. Would twenty-five dollars apiece be too much?"

Lanie was surprised at the small figure and said, "Oh no, that would be fine."

"Of course, you'd have to buy a couple of good horses and outfits for both of us. We're a little shy at the minute. And also for yourself, of course. Saddles, guns, grub, supplies." Bailey named off quite a few things and when he finished he said, "Be pretty expensive, I reckon. But when we get back you can sell the horses and get your money back."

"When could we leave?" Lanie demanded.

Conn held his palms up. "Why, Miss Winslow, we're ready any time you say." He looked out the window and said specu-latively, "Probably it'd be best to pick out some good outfits today and leave early in the morning."

"Would you help me pick out the horses? Neither Mr. Stone nor I are really experts."

"Be glad to do it, ma'am. You wanna go now? I think I could get you a good deal down at the blacksmith's. He's got some good stock there that he's picked up pretty cheap," Conn replied helpfully.

"Yes!" Lanie said excitedly. "Let's go. Right now." She

jammed her hat on her head and the four left the hotel, Lanie talking animatedly and Bailey smiling and nodding.

They spent the rest of the day getting supplies. It was exciting to Lanie. She didn't know much about horses, but Bailey and Jacks apparently did. She was well-satisfied with the small horse they picked for her, a pretty mare almost coal-black with an easy gait, which Lanie knew she'd need. She drew even more pleasure from going into the General Store and outfitting herself in a divided skirt, a white cotton blouse with a vest to go over it, and topping it off with a flat-crowned black hat with a cord that held it tightly in place.

Wesley bought himself two pairs of jeans, some blue chambray shirts, a pair of riding boots that hurt his feet as soon as he put them on, and a wide-brimmed hat. By the time they finished it was nearly dark. Bailey said, "If you'll be here in the morning, before sunup, it'd be good to get an early start."

"We'll be here," Lanie said firmly and bid the two men goodnight. Lanie and Wesley returned to the hotel, stopping first at the front desk to make arrangements to keep their extra luggage and money in safe keeping while they were gone. Then they went to their rooms, talking, making plans, and admiring their clothes. Wesley was not as enthusiastic as Lanie, however. He was now realizing the enormity of what they were proposing to do. He had a lawyer's mind and was able to analyze things better than Lanie, who acted and reacted mostly according to her emotions.

They went to the dining hall for supper, and when Wesley didn't say much throughout the meal, Lanie asked, "What's the matter, Wesley?" Her eyes were bright with excitement, and she looked very pretty in the light of the lamps that lined the walls. "I think we're going to be all right!"

Stone hesitated. He had learned long ago that Lanie was impatient with anyone who interfered with what she had her mind made up to do. But he felt compelled to say, "Lanie, I think we ought to take some more men. Maybe one of the ex-marshals might go with us. After all, we don't know these two. Maybe we ought to ask around."

"Oh, there's not time. Besides, they've been more than helpful," Lanie replied impatiently. She flushed and then said imploringly, "I just *have* to go, Wesley! It just kills me to think of Betsy being out there with that awful man. And there's no telling how he's treating her." She put her hand across the table and squeezed his. "Please, Wesley. This one time, don't argue and analyze! For once in your life I'd like to see you do something out of pure impulse, just because you think it's the thing to do!"

Stone flushed; he was aware that she thought he was too rigid, never spontaneous. He had no dash, no romantic flair that would catch a woman's eye. The steadiness and evenness of temper that a woman would come to value long after romantic fevers had passed, Lanie Winslow had never been able to see. Now, feeling like a weakling, he caved in. "All right, Lanie," he sighed, "have it your way. We'll try it, and God help us once we leave this town, because I've got a bad feeling about the Nations."

★ ★ ★ ★

The first day out of Fort Smith, the small party followed the south bank of the Arkansas River as far as the Canadian River. They camped that night at the fork in the two rivers so they could get an early start the next morning. Bailey and Jacks set up the camp, which consisted merely of building a fire and throwing blankets down around it. Then they cooked some steaks they had brought along.

Lanie and Stone were too tired to do anything but sit down. Both of them had chafed thighs, almost blistered, and Lanie wondered how she could possibly stand days of this. She'd have to find some way to apply ointment—if she could find ointment.

She fell asleep as soon as she put her head down. More than once that night she woke to the cry of a lonesome wolf somewhere out in the hills.

They rose before daylight and Lanie splashed her face with water from the stream nearby, ate some cold beef left over from supper, and climbed into the saddle, stiff and aching in every joint.

They waded their horses across and followed the smaller stream, camping that night just past the Missouri-Kansas-Texas Railroad.

The next day they crossed some of the most barren country Lanie had ever seen. They passed through no settlements, although several times Indians rode in the distance and there were occasional small villages outlined on the horizon.

At dark they made camp again, and once more Stone and Lanie were so tired they could hardly talk. They pulled their blankets close around them, discouraged, aching all over, and slept like logs. The next morning when Lanie awoke, she moved very carefully to avoid pain from the stiffness in her joints. Sitting up, she looked over to where their two guides had slept and saw that their blankets were gone. She whirled around to where the horses had been picketed. Gone!

Fear shot through her like lightning. "Wesley!" she cried. "Wesley, wake up!"

Stone sat up abruptly. He rubbed his eyes and finally focused on Lanie. "What is it?"

"They're gone! Look!"

Stone looked over to where the horses were supposed to be picketed and exclaimed, "Where are they?" He scrambled out of his blankets and hobbled over to where the horses had been, but even the rope that had held them was gone. He turned around, wildly searching for some sign of the men. His heart sank. All they had left were the two blankets he and Lanie had slept in.

Lanie got to her feet and looked across the open distance in every direction. It seemed more lonely than any country she'd ever seen. "Maybe they just went hunting!"

"I don't think so." Stone was no tracker, but in the dusty earth the marks of the horses' hooves were evident. He followed them as they led out of camp, and looked to the west. He walked back and said quietly, "They've left us, Lanie."

"They can't have!"

Stone looked at her with pity. He walked over to his blanket, picked up the gun and holster he had hidden beneath it and strapped them on. "Pick up your blanket, Lanie. We've got to walk out of here."

Lanie stared at him and licked her lips. She, who had never doubted her own abilities for a moment, suddenly felt small and defenseless and alone. The land stretched out in all directions, wild and unbroken. Any human form they might see could be more dangerous than a wild animal. She had only half listened to the stories of the wild, restless, and deadly men that prowled this area. But now that she was in the middle of it, stifling fear filled her, leaving a bitter taste in her mouth.

"Come on," Stone said. He picked up his blanket, then hers and tossed it to her. "We won't get lost. We'll just go back and find the river, and it'll lead right into Fort Smith."

"But—what if we—run into . . ." Lanie did not finish her sentence and knew there was no point in it anyway. So she just said nervously, "All right, Wes. Let's go as quick as we can."

They began the long trek back. Stone was counting in his head and after a while said, "We rode for three days. So that means it'll probably take us six days to walk back—if our feet hold out."

Lanie looked down at the riding boots she had been so proud of and knew they were not the proper footwear for walking across such broken country. Already they were pinching her feet.

An hour later they had to admit what deep trouble they were in.

★   ★   ★   ★

Lanie's throat was parched, and she was aching in every joint. She leaned back against the tree that offered the only shade from the burning sun and pulled off her boots, wincing as she did so. When she had pulled off one sock, she stared soberly at the huge blister that had formed on the heel of her foot. Then she pulled the other sock off and found a matching blister on her other foot. Carefully she lowered her feet into the tiny stream that seemed to rise out of the earth and trickle down between some huge rocks.

Wesley's face was set. He took off his boots and sighed softly. His blisters were even worse than Lanie's. "Next time," he said evenly, "I'll wear sensible shoes. Or carry some, at least." He looked up, squinting at the merciless sun. "But there won't be a next time. If I ever get out of this desert, I'll never want to come back!"

They had walked all day and knew that they had not come far. There was little danger of their getting lost as long as they followed the river. Wesley thought they had reached the little stream just before they became totally exhausted. All day they had endured the blistering sun until their eyeballs seemed to crackle. The air entering their lungs was almost like fire. Now the sun was going down, giving a little relief. Stone sat by the stream, so tired he could hardly lift his head. He muttered, "We'll make it, Lanie. The good Lord will help us."

Lanie did not answer. She had never in her life been so tired— or so afraid. But there was still bitter anger inside her. "I'll find those two swindlers!" she said viciously. "You wait! I'll have the law on them, no matter how much it costs!" Her fair skin was burned by the sun, and her lips were cracked. Still she had enough energy to rail at the two who had robbed them.

"I wouldn't worry about them if I were you," Wesley said mildly. "I wish we had something to eat. Maybe we'll find berries or something tomorrow. But I doubt it."

They sat wearily, sometimes in silence, sometimes talking, letting the water soak their feet. They washed their faces again and drank until they were satisfied. The sun was fast setting, leaving a rosy glow in the west. "It'll be cold tonight," Wesley said. "We don't have any matches to build a fire. Why don't we—"

He broke off abruptly. A movement to his left had caught his eye. He jerked his head around, and his breath stopped. There, not twenty feet away, stood an Indian. Wesley swallowed hard and tried to speak, but nothing came out. Lanie, he saw, had turned to look at the Indian as well; her face seemed frozen.

"You lose horses?"

Both of them relaxed a little and Stone managed to squeak out, "You speak English?"

"I speak English good." The Indian came forward. He was short and dark. His raven-black hair was tied behind his head with a leather strip. He wore doeskin breeches and moccasins, with a white man's shirt, the shirttail hanging out. He had a .44 in a holster and carried a rifle in his left hand, loosely and pointed at the ground. He was a villainous-looking man—at least to Wesley and Lanie at the moment. His eyes were obsidian and half hidden in the deep crevices of his eye sockets. He stopped a few feet away, studying them, and waiting silently.

"We—we were robbed," Lanie said. "Two men took our horses and all we had. Can you help us get back to Fort Smith?"

Stone was hoping that, at best, the Indian wouldn't kill them for their clothing and blankets. Stone had his hand close to his gun and was tempted to reach for it. But he knew he couldn't possibly beat the speed of the Indian who watched them, his face impassive.

"I see tracks. Four horses, two men. That way," the Indian said, pointing.

"That's them!" Lanie cried. "Is there any way to catch them?"

The Indian regarded her gravely, then shook his head deliberately, first to the left, then to the right. Again his unwavering gaze fixed on them; he stood immobile, almost like a statue.

Lanie didn't quite know how to speak to him, but she went ahead. "My name is Lanie Winslow, and this is Wesley Stone. If you'll take us back to Fort Smith, we'll be glad to pay you."

A slight smile touched the stern lips of the Indian. "Men took your money," he remarked.

"But I have more, in town," Lanie said with desperation. "What's your name?"

"Woman Killer."

Lanie blinked and gulped convulsively. Stone's hand brushed the butt of the .44. But the Indian smiled. "I good Indian. Good Christian Indian. Brought up in mission school."

A long-held breath escaped Stone's lips and he said, "Thank God, Woman Killer! I've been worried about how to get this lady back to Fort Smith. Can you help us?"

"I help." The smile had disappeared as suddenly as it had come, and he turned and walked away without another word, vanishing behind the jutting rocks.

"Where'd he go?" Stone asked. Then came the faint sound of hoofbeats. The Indian came out, riding one horse and leading another.

"You ride. Woman Killer walk."

The Indian guided them, walking silently, seemingly tireless, in front of the horses. They rode into Fort Smith at dusk. Lanie had to endure the stares of the townspeople, which was more humiliating than anything she had ever experienced. But in her heart she said, *I'll go back if it kills me!*

CHAPTER SIX

NEEDED—ONE KILLER

★ ★ ★ ★

Lanie Winslow was not accustomed to failure. Her life had been one long series of successes, and the catastrophe with Jacks and Bailey left her crushed and despairing of ever finding Betsy. She kept to her room, refusing to see Wesley Stone. But on the second morning she came out, wearing a brown dress that set her figure off nicely, and her hair was done up stylishly. This told him that she was ready to go into action again.

"Wes," she said decisively, "we can't allow ourselves to dwell on what we've done wrong so far." As always, her head held high and her eyes glinting with determination indicated she had fully made up her mind. "The thing to do is profit from what we've learned."

"Well," Wesley said cautiously, "I think we've established that finding Perrago is not going to be easy." He looked out the window and nodded. "Look at that crowd out there."

"What is it? What's going on?"

"A hanging," he replied starkly. "It looks like everyone in this part of the world has come for it. Come along, let's take a stroll."

They walked outside to the overflowing streets. Garrison Avenue was crowded almost to capacity, with a sense of holiday atmosphere filling the air. They passed an ice wagon where a man was chipping ice from a three-hundred-pound block and passing chunks of it out to the young people. Grabbing the huge pieces, they ran along the sidewalks, sucking the ice, letting the cold water run down their arms.

"Just like back home," Wesley murmured. "When I was a kid, the biggest treat I had was to get a piece of ice in the middle of summertime. That was even better than ice cream, I always thought."

They walked along with the crowd. Abruptly Lanie said, "I want to see the hanging."

"Whatever for?" Wesley exclaimed. "It's not something a woman ought to see—or anybody else, for that matter! They ought to be held in private where people can't watch."

"That ain't the way the judge figgers it," a voice said non-committally. Startled, Stone looked around and saw that Lorenzo Dawkins had joined them. He wore his big white hat pulled down almost over his eyes, his droopy mustache dripping with sweat. "The judge," he continued in a lecturing voice, "figgers that the more of these outlaws the people in the Territory sees get hung, it'll cut down on crime."

"Do you think it's working, Marshal?" Lanie asked.

Dawkins shook his head sadly. "Not that I can tell. It's just that no matter how many you hang, there's always gonna be a bunch more that are willin' to take a chance on it. You goin' down to see the execution, Missie?" He looked at Lanie with faint disapproval.

Lanie lifted her chin and nodded. "Yes," she said firmly. "I want to see it. I never thought I'd want to watch a thing like that, but I want to know just exactly what kind of world this is—here in the West."

"Well," Lorenzo Dawkins said pensively, his dark eyes studying her, "I s'pose this here hangin' is a part of the real West, Missie, if that's what you want to see. C'mon, it's gonna be crowded. I'll find you a good seat."

They followed close behind him as he made his way through the crowd. They passed the federal courthouse, rounding to the north end, and there they saw the platform where the hangings took place. To Lanie, the scaffold looked like a band shell. It stood at the southwestern end of what had been the old army fort compound, the size of a city block or more, surrounded by six-foot stone walls. The scaffold had thirteen steps—Lanie counted them as they came to stand about ten feet from the platform. The floor of the scaffold extended twenty paces under a slanted roof and back wall.

"That trap runs the entire length of the platform," Dawkins informed them. "They say eight people can be hanged at one time. Biggest crowd they ever had, back in June, on a single drop, was six." A serious expression came over his face. "The local citizens called it 'The Government's Suspender.' "

Lanie felt nervous standing in this place and almost turned to leave. She had always prided herself on being able to look at reality, though; and if she was going to face the reality that lay outside this city in Indian Territory, she reluctantly decided that this might be the right place to begin. *I'll watch it,* she told herself sternly, *even if it makes me sick. I want to see the worst there is here before I go on.*

A man appeared at the foot of the gallows and climbed the steps. "That's George Maledon," Dawkins said, nudging her with his elbow. She was accustomed to his nudge by now; she realized that the marshal was not even aware he did it.

"Who's he?" she asked.

"The hangman."

Both Stone and Lanie gazed intently at the man. He was small, with a huge beard and deep-set eyes. His forehead projected so far that his eyes looked as if they were in a cave. "He brought his ropes from St. Louis," Dawkins said informatively. "He oils them every morning before a hanging. Comes out and tries 'em on a sack of sand to be sure they're all workin' right."

"He doesn't look like a hangman," Wesley observed. "Why does he wear those big guns?"

"He's an official of the court. He's shot more'n one man trying to escape. Funny sort of fellow, Maledon is," Dawkins philosophized. "Strange job, I guess, bein' a hangman. Lots of folks won't have anything to do with him. Superstitious folks claim they see ghosts around those gallows," he went on with relish. "I've heard 'em tell about how the spirits gather there. Nothin' to it, of course." He looked back up at the small man who was busy on the platform. "I asked Maledon one time if he had any qualms of conscience about the hangings. He just said, 'Nope. I simply do my duty. I never hanged a man who came back to have the job done over.' "

"I wonder what he's thinking about, that man who's going to hang," Wesley Stone murmured softly.

"Couldn't tell you," Dawkins said. "He ate a big breakfast, I know that. He was smokin' a cigar thirty minutes ago." He smoothed his mustache, another gesture that had grown familiar to Lanie. "He's a hard one. Name's John Childers. Been a member of one of the worst bands of brigands and plunderers in Indian Territory. Killed an old man for his horse, dumped the body in the river, then just rode off." His voice softened with regret. "I tried to talk to Childers last night. Told him he was going to face God and it weren't too late to repent, to trust in the Lord. He just laughed at me."

"How awful!" Lanie exclaimed.

Dawkins was silent for a moment, a faraway look in his eyes. Then he looked at Lanie and his voice grew brisk and business-like again. "Awful enough. They get mighty hard out here on the frontier, Miss Winslow. Sometimes I think they're more beast than animal. But that ain't the way the Bible says it. They're all of 'em men the Lord Jesus died for."

Stone studied him with renewed interest. "You're a Christian, I take it, Marshal."

"Well, my pa, he was a Methodist preacher, and I guess some of it stuck on me. Hard to be a Christian and a marshal out here at the same time, but I do the best I can."

Just then, three deputy marshals armed with Winchesters appeared and took positions around the gallows. Toward the river a freight train passed, the engine whistle giving out shrill warnings to those coming from Choctaw territory. There were crows in the elms and sycamores along the Arkansas River, and their raucous calling came strongly on the wind.

"Them crows are always here on hanging days," Dawkins said. "Now, that's somethin' a little spooky. Don't know how they know about things like this. Just the crowd, I reckon."

Lanie looked up at the crows circling overhead. In spite of the somber situation, Lanie noticed little things: the yeasty odor of fresh bread that the wagons from the nearby bakeries had unloaded on their morning runs; the barking of a dog; a mill whistle sounding out a call to work. Then a bank clock along the avenue struck. Ten o'clock.

With the last stroke of the clock, George Maledon began to attach a heavy rope to the bar at the top of the gallows. A man came up on the platform—evidently his assistant. Every eye was glued to the actions of the man with the rope.

Shortly, two deputy marshals armed with rifles behind a man came out of the courthouse and started through the human corridor, which the deputies kept open despite the press of the crowd. The man was middle-aged, muscular, with a shock of black hair and a pair of dark eyes. Twice in the short walk to the gallows, he brushed his hair back from his face, lifting both hands in the manacles to do so. A minister followed behind him, carrying a Bible. Once the prisoner turned and said something, seemingly unkind, to the preacher, who fell back a few steps.

When the man passed in front of Wesley and Lanie, horror gripped her as she looked into his face. He was hard-looking beyond belief, cynicism marring his face, his jaw painfully set. He climbed the thirteen steps, and one of the marshals faced him and read the death warrant. Childers puffed a cigar with an air of indifference.

"Are there any last words you wish to say, Childers?" the marshal asked, folding the paper and putting it into his pocket.

Childers tossed his cigar away and began to talk. He documented his entire trial, claiming that he had not done the murder he was accused of, and that they were hanging an innocent man. Then he looked out at the crowd, which was eagerly drinking in all of his words. "Someone else done that murder," he said stoutly. "It was one of my pals, maybe, but not me."

The marshal who had read the death sentence said, "If you'll give me their names, Childers, I pledge not to hang you now. What's your answer."

It grew so quiet that Lanie could hear the drone of insects in the nearby trees shading the crowd. Dust and tobacco smoke hung motionless in the air. The heat was stifling.

The condemned man's gaze jerked away from the marshal and flickered over the crowd. His eyes focused and paused momentarily here and there. Stone whispered, "He knows some of them. His buddies are in the crowd."

Lanie half expected Childers to point them out, but suddenly he waved farewell with a general sweep of his hand, then turned to the marshal. He spoke out in a firm, loud voice that everyone could hear. "Didn't you say you were going to hang me?"

"Yes," the marshal replied.

"Well, why in blazes don't you?" Childers rasped.

The marshal's head jerked back, and he nodded at Maledon, who stepped forward and put the rope over Childers' neck, adjusting the hangman's knot below the convict's left ear. Then Maledon pulled a black hood over the man's face.

A solemnness enveloped the courtyard; every eye was fixed on the doomed man.

Maledon walked to the lever that released the trap and gave it a hard jerk. John Childers' neck tilted to one side as he shot down to the end of the rope.

And at that moment, as the door fell from under his feet, a tremendous clap of thunder shook the earth, completely drowning the noise of the cumbersome trap. A bolt of lightning shot from the black cloud overhead, striking the frame of the gallows and shooting a thousand tiny sparks into the air.

"John Childers' soul has gone to hell—I done heerd the chains a-clankin'!" screamed an elderly black woman as she hysterically waved her arms and fell to the ground in the center of the throng. For several minutes the rain poured down, soaking the frightened and confused people.

"Let's get out of here," Stone said and grabbed Lanie's arm. By the time they had escaped the courtyard and reached the hotel, the dark cloud seemed to have vanished and the thunder had stopped.

"That was frightful . . . frightful!" Lanie said in a shaky voice. Her face was ashen and her lips trembled. "I don't know why I wanted to see a thing like that! I must have been crazy!"

"We both were," Wesley said briefly, then added, "You ready to give up on the idea of going after Perrago yourself, Lanie?"

Her eyes shot up to meet his. Her face was still pale, but she drew her lips into a firm, tight line and retorted, "Give up? No! I'll not give up! You stay here if you want to, Wesley, but I'm going to find my sister." She whirled and stomped into the hotel, letting the door slam behind her.

Wesley stood on the sidewalk, considering whether he should knock her in the head, or perhaps throw her into a train and kidnap her. Maybe take her back to Chicago and have her father deal with her. Of course, he knew he would do nothing like that, and his anger slowly dissolved.

I'll have to go with her, he sighed. *But we'll need better help than we had last time.*

★ ★ ★ ★

Wesley awoke with a start, hearing a loud pounding on the door. He rolled off the bed, confused, disoriented, and so befuddled that he reached for the gun he had left on the table beside his bed. Then the insistent voice penetrated his consciousness; it was Lanie.

"Wes! Open the door! Let me in!"

He quickly crossed the room and stuck his head out the door. "What is it, Lanie?" he demanded.

"It's a telegram! It just came!"

She handed it to him and he scanned the words:

LANIE,

HAVE WORD FROM BETSY STOP BELIEVE SHE IS A PRISONER STOP AM CONVINCED SHE WANTS TO COME HOME BUT CAN'T STOP MAKE THE CHARGE KIDNAPPING STOP URGENT THAT YOU FIND HER SOON STOP

ZACHARY WINSLOW

"She's been kidnapped!" Lanie exclaimed.

Stone's lawyer mind, already dissecting the new information, was cautious. "It doesn't say that, Lanie. I mean, Betsy hasn't said that—not to any of us."

"What do I have to do to make you see it, Wes?" Lanie said wildly. "My sister is in trouble—my little sister! She's been kidnapped, and we've *got* to find her!" Her face was twisted with anger, but there was a vulnerability Stone had never seen before.

"All right, Lanie. Let's go see Lorenzo Dawkins again," Wesley said calmly. "That old man's got a lot of sense. He can tell us what to do now."

Wesley closed the door and dressed. Although he was very quick, he could hear Lanie pacing impatiently outside his door.

"Hurry up, Wesley!" she said furiously.

Grabbing his hat, he rushed out, Lanie already running ahead.

They found Dawkins at the courthouse and asked him to step outside with them. Lanie showed him the telegram, then waited with bated breath.

After reading it, he looked up at her with sympathy but spoke with finality. "There's already a warrant out on Perrago. I don't think addin' kidnapping is going to bring him in any quicker, Miss Winslow."

"But we've got to *do* something! Please, Marshal Dawkins, can't you help us?"

Dawkins ran his hand through his shaggy white hair with obvious frustration. He finally said reluctantly, "Well, one thing's sure, you can't wait for us marshals to go pick him up. Right now we got two hundred marshals out there. But you know how many we've done lost? Shot, or stabbed, or clubbed and left to die in some ditch? Over fifty!" He clapped his hat back on his head. "Why, the things that go on here makes some of them towns like Dodge City and Hayes look like a girls' school promenade! We have over 74,000 square miles to cover! That's bigger than New England!"

"I know, Marshal," Lanie said meekly, "but she's my only sister. And she's so young! Isn't there *something* you can do? My father will gladly pay whatever it costs!"

Dawkins rammed his hands into his pockets and dropped his head, evidently trying to come to some decision. After a few moments he looked back up at Lanie and said thoughtfully, "Well, it don't hurt to have some money. You wouldn't believe how much it costs to go on these here escapades." Lanie and Wesley glanced at each other painfully, reminding Dawkins of their mishap with Jacks and Bailey. He shrugged and said, "Oh, yeah, I guess you do know about that. Well, you'll have to outfit all over again."

"That doesn't matter." Lanie waved her hand in dismissal. "Just tell us, how can we do this?"

"All right," Dawkins said, drawing the last word out slowly.

"I guess you gotta have a man like Lobo."

"Yes, you mentioned him before," Wesley said. "Who is he?"

"Lobo Smith's a cross between an outlaw and a marshal, I guess you might say," Dawkins answered cryptically. "Now he ain't got no badge. But he could have one. Judge Parker, he's tried to make a marshal outta Lobo many a time, but Lobo, he just won't do it. He's just a—just a—" Dawkins seemed to be carefully choosing his words, "a triflin' sort of fellow, I reckon. But he knows his way around the inside of that Indian Territory, even better than the Indians do. Raised by a Indian, so they say."

"Is he tough enough to take on a bunch like Perrago's?" Stone urged.

Lorenzo Dawkins' weathered face creased into a grin. "That fellow Smith would fight a steam sawmill! I reckon," he said with relish. "Lobo Smith is tough enough to raise perdition—and put a chunk under it!" Then he grew sober. "But it ain't no good anyways. You can't get Smith right now."

"You mean it would cost too much?" Lanie probed.

"I mean he's in jail. Charged with selling whiskey."

"That's not much of a charge," Lanie said as if the man had been jailed for swatting flies. "Surely we can get him out."

"You might do that," Dawkins said with spirit, "but what would you do with him when you got him out? That fellow's stubborn as a blue-nosed mule! Never knowed Lobo to do nothing he didn't want to do, and something tells me he ain't gonna want to do what you want, Missie!"

"Can you arrange it so I can talk to him?" Lanie pleaded.

Dawkins shrugged. "I reckon I can do that. Come on, and I'll set up an appointment for you right now." He turned and started toward the jail, Lanie keeping pace with him, and Wesley trailing behind as usual.

When they got inside, Dawkins said, "Now, I'm going to put you in this here office, and bring Smith up to you, Miss Winslow. You ain't a-going downstairs with that bunch of yahoos!"

He disappeared and Lanie turned to Wesley. "We've got to get this man, Wes." She looked at him imploringly and stepped a little closer to him. "I want to talk to him alone."

"Why?" Wesley was suspicious. "It'd be better if both us did, wouldn't it?"

She laid her hand on his arm. "Just let me have my way this time, Wes," she pleaded. "There're some things I might want to say to him that would be private."

"All right." His feelings were hurt, but he promised to leave the room once he had met the convict.

Lanie began to pace back and forth. She had never seen a man she couldn't bend to her will, and she was mentally practicing how she was going to persuade him to do exactly what she wanted.

CHAPTER SEVEN

"I WON'T WORK
FOR A WOMAN!"

★ ★ ★ ★

"This here's Lobo Smith," Marshal Dawkins said. "Lobo, like you to meet Miss Lanie Winslow, and this here's Wesley Stone."

Wesley hesitated, not knowing what response to make. Then he put out his hand, and the prisoner, after giving him an amused look, took it. "Glad to know you, Smith," Stone said. For some reason Stone didn't like the looks of the man and said shortly, "I'll wait outside while you two talk." He left, followed by Marshal Dawkins.

"Thank you for coming to see me, Mr. Smith," Lanie said.

"I wasn't all that busy."

The dry humor in the man's reply made Lanie revise her plan. She had been expecting a rough-looking man, much larger than this one, a man who looked more like those she had seen being taken from the prison wagon. Lobo Smith, she saw, had a neat appearance, for the most part. She guessed he was about twenty-six or twenty-seven, and not tall, no more than five foot ten. He probably weighed around one hundred and sixty pounds; and there was a roundness to his arms revealed by the tight tan shirt that he wore. He had a muscular chest and carried an aura of strength about him. His hair was curly and brown, and a fresh cut would have suited him well. But the most striking aspect of the man was the black patch he wore over his left eye. It gave him the look of a bandit or a pirate, she thought. The right eye was an unusual shade of blue—indigo, really. He was tanned very deeply—a dark golden color; and his teeth were perfect and startlingly white against his skin.

He was not much older than she. However, Lanie had Dawkins' word that this man could do what she wanted done, so she set out to achieve her end.

"Mr. Smith—"

"Lobo's about all I go by."

"Oh. Well—Lobo—then, uh—that means 'wolf,' doesn't it?"

"Yes."

His brief answers gave her no opening, but taking a deep breath, Lanie plunged right into her story. "Mr.—I mean, Lobo—my sister left home a short time ago," she began.

She finished the story by saying, "So what we need is to go into Indian Territory, find this man Perrago, and get my sister back."

Lobo Smith was lounging back in a chair opposite Lanie, watching her with his one indigo eye. His voice was soft, very quiet. He shrugged his trim shoulders. "That's what they got marshals for, Miss Winslow."

"But they won't go," she said impatiently. She wanted to push him, to force him to help her, but she knew that would achieve nothing. Putting on her most charming smile and making her voice as winsome as she possibly could, she said, "My father would be willing to pay almost any amount to get my sister back. Marshal Dawkins has told us that you are the one man who might be able do it."

"Lorenzo's got a vivid imagination." Lobo Smith stretched in a sudden motion that reminded Lanie of her big longhair cat at home when he extended his claws. "I'm no marshal. Wouldn't do any good for me to go looking for Vic."

"Vic—Perrago? Do you know him?"

"Bumped into him a few times. He wanted me to join up with him . . ." Lobo's voice trailed off.

"What kind of a man is he?" Lanie asked, intrigued. "I never met him. I was in St. Louis when Betsy got involved with him."

"Oh, Vic's a dandy," Lobo grinned. "Dresses fancy and talks like a gilt-edged lawyer when he wants to. But underneath, I think he's the wolf, not me."

Wanting to steer the conversation back to this stranger she was thinking of hiring, Lanie asked, "Why do they call you Lobo?"

"Indian name. I was raised by Comanches. That's the name they gave me," he said matter-of-factly.

"Was it awful?" she asked. "Being with the Indians?"

"I liked it better than anything I ever had since," he answered. He saw her surprise and smiled. "Thought a lot about going back, but the Indians are gone now. They're all trapped in places like the Nation over there, squatting on five acres and raising goats. Wasn't that way in the old days."

She leaned across the table to move a little closer to him, and deliberately held his gaze. "I know it's a lot to ask, and it's dangerous work." Her voice was low and intense. "But doesn't it mean anything to you that there's a girl out there, helpless, being mistreated, maybe in awful danger?"

"Nope. Doesn't mean anything to me," he said nonchalantly.

Lanie was shocked at his indifference, then outraged. She sat up stiffly. "What kind of a man are you?"

"Lots of opinions on that," he said, refusing the argument. "Guess maybe I won't win any popularity contests. Except maybe among some of the Indians." He got to his feet, looking at her with boredom, and said as an apparent afterthought, "Besides, I won't work for a woman." Without another word he turned and walked out of the room.

Dawkins was standing just outside the office door and Lobo said, "Visit's over, Lorenzo. Take me back to the honeymoon suite." Then he walked down the hall, Dawkins following.

Wesley came back into the office. He'd gotten over feeling left out; he was not a man to hold a grudge. "Well, will he do it?" he asked expectantly.

"No. He says he won't work for a woman," Lanie answered.

Surprised, Stone grinned. "Well, not much of a compliment to you, is it, Lanie? When a fellow would rather stay in jail than work for you. Some men like that, I suppose. What do we do now?"

Lanie rose abruptly from the chair and began to pace the floor without responding. She had the ability to set her mind on a single target and block out everything else. Stone had seen her with this concentrated, purposeful manner before, so he remained quiet, allowing her to think.

Back and forth she continued to pace, hugging herself with her arms, her head down. Her lips moved slightly, as if she was making some sort of speech to herself. After a while she turned to Wesley and said quickly, "We've got to see Judge Parker again. Come on."

She's got the bit in her teeth, Wesley warned himself. *Now she'll be like a turtle that won't let go 'til it thunders*. He followed her doggedly anyway, and watched her charm her way past Judge Parker's clerk once again. Soon they were in the judge's office.

"Well? What is it, Miss Winslow?" he asked genially. "I heard about your misfortune. I wish you had counseled with me, or one of my men, before you hired those two." He shook his head sadly. "I'm afraid there's more of that kind than the good around here."

"Oh, Judge, you're so right," Lanie said remorsefully. She sat down in a chair, and Wesley awkwardly stood behind her. "I should have talked to you first! But that's why I've come to you now. I don't want to make another mistake."

Parker listened to her with great sympathy, not suspecting for a moment that he was being beguiled by this beautiful young woman. His sympathy was real; he could only imagine what it would be like to have a beloved sister held captive in the Nations by a man like Perrago. "I wish I could think of some way to help you," he said, "but the best I could do is promise to assign a marshal to the case as soon as one is free. And this I will do."

"I've been talking to Marshal Dawkins. He's been with you a long time, hasn't he?" Lanie asked sweetly.

"Yes, from the beginning. He's one of the best marshals on the force," the judge said stoutly.

"He mentioned that a man called Lobo Smith might be able to catch up with Perrago."

A smile touched Judge Parker's lips. "That'd be like putting the fox to watching the chicken house, wouldn't it? I mean, Smith's an outlaw himself. I believe he's in my jail right now."

"But the charge is only selling whiskey, isn't it?" Lanie asked innocently.

"That's all we could find evidence for," Parker said tersely. His lips drew in a taut line and he added, "He's done more than that. Smith is right on the verge of being very bad." Leaning back in his chair he said thoughtfully, "I've seen this before, over and over again. There are a lot of men who go bad out here, and the worst is when a good man goes bad. And Smith, right now, is headed toward being one of those. He has all kinds of potential. Why, I've tried a dozen times at least to hire him as one of my marshals! But he just laughs at me and says it's too much work," he added in disgust.

"But he can't be all bad if you want to hire him as one of your marshals, Judge," Wesley Stone put in.

Parker sighed deeply. "I have to say that not all of our marshals have turned out so well. Grat Dalton was one of them—turned out to be a bank robber. And there have been others." He stood up and walked to the window, looking down on the gallows.

Lanie and Stone wondered what he was thinking as he studied the people milling around. Was he thinking of the hanging that had taken place? Someone had told Wesley that on the days of the hangings, Judge Parker stood right at that window and watched, reading his Bible, and sometimes wept.

He turned then and said, "All I can say is that I don't think even Lobo Smith himself has any idea whether he'll turn out to be a saint or sinner. Could be either one. But right now I'd lay odds on his being a sinner."

This was an interesting concept to Lanie. "I've never heard it put quite like that. But I do have an idea. If he could help me get my sister back, my father could do a lot for him. He's in business, and he can always use talented young men."

"I doubt if Lobo Smith would ever go to Chicago, Miss Winslow," Judge Parker answered. "He's born for this world out here."

"Well, perhaps my father could set him up with a ranch or something," Lanie insisted. "But he won't help me, Judge. He says he won't work for a woman."

Judge Parker's lips parted in an ironic smile. "That's only an excuse. Lobo Smith just doesn't want to work—for anybody."

"Well, I want you to help me with him, Judge," Lanie said firmly. She sat up straight and began to talk earnestly, convincingly making her case. There had to be a way to force Smith to do what she wanted.

"Force him?" Judge Parker repeated incredulously. "I don't think so. He's as stubborn as any man I ever saw," he told Lanie heatedly. "Right now, Lobo Smith could be out, free, if he'd just agree to help me with this territory. But he won't do it! He'd rather stay down in that hole than be a federal marshal."

"I'd think he would hate it down there," Lanie said. "Any man would. So, Judge, will you try one thing for me, please?"

"What's that?"

"Offer to suspend his sentence if he'll help me find my sister. And," she said purposefully, "tell him that you will keep him in jail for a year, waiting for a trial, if he won't."

Parker was not a man of vast humor, but this idea definitely tickled him. His eyes, usually so stern, twinkled as he looked at Stone. "Does she often do things like this?"

Stone shrugged. "More often than I'd like to admit, Judge."

Parker said simply, "I'll do it."

Lanie beamed up at him, and he smiled back mischievously. "Maddox!" he called out, his eyes still on Lanie. The clerk— Lanie's victim twice-told—appeared at the door. "Bring Lobo Smith to my office," the Judge ordered, and the clerk disappeared again.

"Do you really think this will work, Judge?" Stone asked meaningfully. "I'm a little doubtful about Smith's . . . talents, if you will. He doesn't look like all that much to me. He's undersized, doesn't look tough like some of the outlaws I've seen around here."

"I don't know if it'll work or not," Parker admitted. "If he gets his head set wrong, he'll stay in jail the rest of his life. But maybe I can put it in a way that'll help him make the right decision," the Judge said with heavy irony. "As for being tough, he is . . . deceptive. He's smooth. But if you ever see him mix up with a bunch of desperadoes, watch them. They never take their eyes off him. One of them told me he's like a keg of dynamite, and they treat him that way. Like he might go off at any minute, and everyone might get hurt."

They talked about Smith until a knock sounded on the door. "Bring him on in, Maddox," Parker said. The door opened and Lobo Smith strolled in.

If he was surprised, he did not show it. He walked to the judge's desk and said pleasantly, "Good afternoon, Judge. You're looking well."

A smile touched Parker's lips again. He was having an amusing afternoon, a relief from the stress of being a judge in this desolate place, perhaps. "Lobo, I understand Miss Winslow here has made you a rather attractive offer, which you refused."

"That's right, Judge."

"I think you ought to reconsider," Judge Parker said slowly. "In the first place, this lady needs help. I know you fellows take a lot of pride in showing how tough you are, and there's a young woman out there who needs someone to give her a chance to get away. That's number one." The judge went on. "Secondly, I think you ought to have had enough of that jail down below."

"Well, I don't know about number one, but number two's right enough, Judge Parker," Lobo agreed. "How much longer are you going to keep me there before we get to the trial?"

"That depends on you, Lobo."

"Me? Then I say let's have it today."

Without a smile, Parker picked up a worn book on his desk and ruffled through it, running his forefinger down the pages, obviously looking for an opening in his court schedule. Then he looked back up. "Seems we're booked up here for quite a while, Mr. Smith. I think you might be in my jail a long time before we can get you a trial. Then, of course, there's a good chance that you'll be convicted and given the maximum sentence—in a case like this it's a year, you know."

Lobo Smith was watching the judge carefully. Once again Lanie thought how much like a bandit he looked with that black patch over his eye. She saw him study her with his good eye, and it made her feel as if he were reading her mind and knew exactly what she was up to. Then he turned back to the judge. "It looks as if you're holding the winning hand, Judge." His voice was soft as a summer breeze. "I feel that I'm going to be doing whatever Miss Winslow wants me to do."

"That's very wise, Lobo," Judge Parker said approvingly. "Now, here's what I'll do. I will suspend this charge against you, and if you bring the young lady back, we will of course forget all about it. And one more thing," he said in a businesslike voice, "if you catch up with Perrago you'll need some authority. I will make my offer one more time. I insist that you become a federal marshal, at least while you're on this foray into the Nations." He pulled a star out of his desk drawer and said, "You've turned this down before, but now I don't see that you have a choice."

"Like I say, Judge, you're calling the shots."

Parker came around to stand in front of Lobo Smith, dwarfing the smaller man. Then the judge said gravely, "Do you, Lobo Smith, swear and affirm that you will, to the best of your ability, perform the duties of a Special United States Deputy Marshal for the government, and for this court, taking no fees other than those due you, so help you God?"

"I do," Smith said quietly. Once again his gaze went to Lanie and he remarked casually, "I guess you're my new boss."

"I'm so glad you're going to be taking over, Lobo," Lanie said. "When can we leave?"

"Soon as I can get some help."

"How many men do you think you'll need?" Parker asked.

Lobo thought for a moment, chewing on his lip. "It'll either take a big bunch, or just a few. I'd say offhand we can move better with just a few. I'd like to take Woman Killer with me."

"Woman Killer? Why, he's the one who brought us in from the desert," Lanie burst out.

"Best tracker in the Nations. And a dead shot, too," Lobo said laconically. "And I want to take Lorenzo with me, if you can spare him, Judge Parker."

"Lorenzo? He's too old to go on a hunt like this!"

"He won't be too old if he lives to be ninety," Smith said, smiling.

Lanie spoke up doubtfully. "Well, I like Marshal Dawkins, but this does seem to be a job for a younger man."

Lobo Smith seemed somehow set off from them, as if he were a different specie. In his presence one could sense a sort of wildness that they did not have nor understand, but they could feel it. He said evenly, "Sometimes you need a fox. And that's what

Lorenzo is. He's smart. I'll do the shootin', and he can do the thinkin'."

There was silence in the room for a moment. But Lanie felt a shiver go down her spine.

Judge Parker finally conceded. "If Dawkins wants to go, I'll release him from his other duties." He leaned back in his chair and said, "I'll make out your release papers and see that you get your things back." He pulled a form out of a drawer and filled it out quickly, then walked to the door. "Maddox," he said, "take care of this for me."

He turned back to the three and shook hands with Lanie. "My wife and I will pray for your success, my dear. I know how hard it must be for you."

Lanie was charmed by the tall judge. She put her other hand lightly on top of his and said quietly, "Thank you, Judge, for all you've done. My family and I will never forget it."

Parker looked a little anxious. "I'm not certain I'm doing the right thing. I want to urge you to let Dawkins and Smith handle this matter. You'll only slow them down if you try to go with them."

Lanie did not answer. She just thanked him warmly again. As they left, Smith stopped in the outer office and picked up his gun, which he immediately strapped on, then retrieved a small sack full of personal belongings.

When they got outside, Lanie watched Smith's face carefully. His eye lit up and he took a deep breath. "Good to be in the open air," he said gratefully. He looked at her and asked, "When do you want to leave, Miss Winslow?"

"As soon as possible. I know you'll have to get us outfitted." She fished in her purse and took out a roll of bills. She counted a few and held them out to Smith. "If this is not enough, come and see me about some more."

He looked at the bills and shrugged. "That ought to be plenty." He stuffed them into his shirt pocket, turned, and walked away.

"I wish we had more men going with us," Wesley said anxiously. "I don't see what good it'll do if we do catch up with Perrago. The marshal can shoot, as can Woman Killer and Smith, no doubt, but what could we do?"

"I don't know, Wesley," she said with a trace of weariness. "All I know is I have to do all I can to get Betsy back." She bit her lip. "I still think it was my fault. I should have paid more attention to her."

"You can't always know how to act," Wesley replied softly. At times she was like this, soft and gentle, with a vulnerability that charmed him. At other times she was immovable in her desire to get her own way. She was two women in one; and he was in love with one, but feared that he would never be able to fully love the second. "Let's go," he said. "I have a feeling we'll be leaving pretty soon. We need to get our things together. Those other men are probably used to rough living, but I'm taking some extra blankets this time. And some comfortable shoes," he added ruefully.

"Well, at least," Lanie said with a hint of a smile, "these three won't run off and leave us." She hesitated, then asked, "Do you feel safe? I mean, do you trust them?"

"I trust Dawkins," Stone answered firmly, "and we both know Woman Killer is all right. But Smith . . . I don't know. He's a different breed. I'd guess he doesn't know a lot about stability, or have much of it. He's like a wolf, I think. Kind of looks like one, doesn't he?"

"Well, I think he's nice looking," Lanie declared.

"So are wolves. Especially when they're in motion. But I don't think loyalty is their best quality."

"You think Smith is untrustworthy?"

"I think we don't know anything about him," Wesley replied. "Even the judge doesn't. I know I'm going to watch him every minute, even though I don't know what I could do if he got out of line. Hit him over the head with a stick, I guess, while he's asleep."

"Oh, stop talking like that, Wes," Lanie said with amusement. She was excited about going into action; adventure always seemed to animate her. She was not good at waiting around idly. Once things started to happen, she was ready to move. Now she said impatiently, "Come on, let's go. And we certainly will get some comfortable walking shoes this time!"

"I don't expect we'll be walking much, not with that bunch," Wesley said. "Maybe getting a soft pillow for the saddle would be a good idea."

CHAPTER EIGHT

WOLVES DON'T HAVE RULES

★ ★ ★ ★

The skies were still gray when Lanie and Stone came out of the hotel and met with the three men, who were already mounted. Lanie looked at them and whispered to Wesley, "They've got enough guns to take on a regiment, haven't they?"

Both of the white men were wearing gun belts. Lobo Smith had a .44 with a cedar handle, while Lorenzo sported a pair of white-handled pistols. Lanie noticed that Lobo's gun belt was not fancy—only a plain, narrow belt with no cartridge loops. She wondered where he carried his bullets. She saw also that he had a dirk knife, and that he as well as Dawkins had saddle rifles and two more revolvers in saddle scabbards at their thighs. They were huge pistols, big enough to knock down a bear.

The Indian, Woman Killer, had the biggest rifle Lanie had ever seen. "That's a Sharp rifle," Marshal Dawkins said, seeing her staring at it. "It'd kill a buffalo nearly a mile away."

"Let's hope we don't get jumped by buffaloes," Lobo remarked dryly. "Are you ready to go?"

Lanie wanted to ask why they couldn't start at a reasonable hour but knew that was no way to begin the trip. "Of course," she said shortly. She marched to the horse Woman Killer was holding and mounted awkwardly. She wished now that she had spent the number of hours riding that Betsy had; she was aware that she looked out of place. There was some satisfaction in noting that Wesley had done little better.

When the two of them were settled in their saddles, Smith turned without a word and led them down the silent streets—Smith and Dawkins first, Wesley and Lanie following. Woman Killer, leading a pack mule, brought up the rear.

None of them talked as they left town. Lanie was upset with Lobo Smith, who had disappeared the whole previous day. She had expected to have a talk with him and lay out their strategy, but at breakfast Dawkins had simply said, "Lobo's scoutin' around, looking for some kind of trail."

"When will he be back?" Lanie had demanded.

Dawkins looked amused. "When he gets here, I reckon, Missie."

As they rode along, Lanie mulled over the events of the day before. It had been after supper when Lobo appeared. Lanie and Wesley were sitting on the front porch of the hotel, watching the sun go down, when suddenly he seemed to materialize from nowhere. Lanie was startled and still unhappy over what she considered his irresponsibility. "Well, we've been waiting for you!" she snapped.

Lobo smiled lazily. He was wearing jeans and a deerskin shirt, like a mountain man's, with fringes. He also wore something she had not seen before on a cowboy—a pair of Indian moccasins. All riders, it seemed, wore high-heeled boots with big rowels. *That's why we didn't hear him,* she thought.

He wore a black low-crowned hat held by a leather thong. "Picked up something," he told her, shoving his hat back, his voice soft on the evening air.

"What is it?" Lanie demanded.

"Got word that Perrago might be in Eureka Springs. We'll have a look there before we head out into the Territory."

"Where's Eureka Springs?" Wesley asked.

"Few miles north of here. We could take the railroad, but then we wouldn't have any horses. So be ready before sunup." He gave Lanie a cursory nod, then disappeared into the gathering darkness of the street.

★ ★ ★ ★

Unknown to Lanie, Lobo had left to see Dawkins at the

boardinghouse where he stayed. "Got a sniff of our man," Lobo had said, leaning back. "Ran into Pete Summons. He said that Perrago was at Eureka Springs not long ago."

"He's probably not there now," Dawkins observed.

A half smile touched Lobo's lips and he agreed. "You're probably right. But it'll be a good little ride, enough to break those two in. They're not ready for the Territory yet, Lorenzo."

"Got to say you're right about that," Dawkins said. "I don't know what that girl thinks she can do. She ain't gonna talk Perrago out of a thing he don't want to do."

The two men discussed the situation for a while, then Lobo excused himself. He went to his room, dropped into bed, and slept soundly.

★　★　★　★

Leaving Fort Smith, the party crossed the Arkansas River on a ferry, then followed the foothills of the Cookson Mountains for most of the day. These were really just hills, rising slightly to the west, like the backs of turtles. The ride was pleasant enough, though Lanie became tired by afternoon. She would rather have died than show it, though, and finally when they made camp that night, she forced herself to stay up, just to show the men that she was not going to be a handicap on this trip.

Just after noon as they crested a small hill, a buck had burst out of a thicket. Lanie was behind Lobo, watching him, and saw what happened. For most of the ride Lobo had been lounging in the saddle, seemingly half asleep. But the moment the buck showed, Lobo whipped out his pistol and got off one shot. The buck leaped into the air, then fell to the ground kicking.

"Not a bad shot, Lobo," Dawkins had observed.

Lobo grinned. "Yeah. Deer don't shoot back at you. They don't make a fellow so nervous."

He skinned and butchered the deer quickly and efficiently. Lobo had elected himself cook. They thoroughly enjoyed the steaks broiled over the campfire. Lorenzo pulled out some cans of peaches and passed them around. They fished the sweet fruit out with their fingers, then drank the juice from the cans. Afterward they sat around the fire, listening to the muted sounds of the night.

Lanie wondered when they would talk about Perrago and

their plans to catch him. But Lobo sat motionless, silently staring into the fire as if he saw something in it that the others couldn't.

Wesley began to talk with Dawkins about religion in general, and the conversation wandered to specifics about the frontier. "What about the Indians?" Wesley asked. "The missionaries have been coming here for quite a while, haven't they? Are there many Christian Indians?"

"Ask Woman Killer there," Dawkins answered, indicating the Indian with his head. He groomed his mustache and went on. "All I know is, them missionaries ain't done much good. The Indians get shifted around so much by the government that the missionaries can hardly find 'em, much less catch up with 'em. Ain't that right, Woman Killer?"

Woman Killer's eyes were expressionless and obsidian, glinting as they reflected the flames of the small fire. "Missionaries good," he said assertively. "I go to missionary school, find Jesus God."

That was the extent of the Indian's testimony. But Wesley wanted to know more about Lorenzo's faith. "What's your theology, Lorenzo?" he inquired seriously.

Lorenzo Dawkins pulled out a pipe, filled it, lit it with deliberation, and got it glowing heartily before he finally answered. "Well, I ain't got none, I reckon. I've led a pretty rough life. Rode with Quantrill back during the war. That's enough to send a man to perdition, if you get my meanin'. Some of the things I did I don't like to think about." He stared blankly into the fire for a few moments, then roused himself and took a long draw on the pipe. "But," he said, sending a small cloud of purple smoke upward, "the good Lord's forgiven me for all that." He considered the question again and finished succinctly, "And theology. Well, all I know is I was in a mess, and God sent Jesus to straighten it up."

Lanie was listening to Stone and the others, but she watched Smith. He took no part in any of it, giving the impression that he didn't even hear it, but at Dawkins' last sentence Smith looked across at the marshal. He didn't exactly smile at him, but his expression was one of warmth and approval. Lanie saw that he had a great respect for the older man, and wondered about Lobo's own beliefs.

Stone and Lorenzo Dawkins talked for a long time, mostly about the efforts to Christianize the Indians. Woman Killer did not join in the conversation, but his stony black eyes rested on each speaker in turn, unblinking and intent.

After a while, Lobo stretched indolently, reminding Lanie of her cat, and said in his particular way, "Better get some sleep. Long ride into Eureka Springs tomorrow." He rose and walked outside the camp, disappearing into the darkness.

"Where's he going?" Stone asked in surprise.

Lorenzo watched him go and answered, "I don't know if that man ever sleeps. He's just like a cat at night." Lanie smiled at Lorenzo's words. Dawkins continued. "You know how cats are. They take little naps all day long, but at night they're out, ready to find any trouble roamin' around. That's the way he is—Lobo."

"Any danger of Indians attacking us here?" Lanie asked nervously.

"Missie, there's always that danger. Never can tell what an Indian will do. Ain't that right, Woman Killer?"

Woman Killer nodded solemnly. "Yes. Especially Kiowa. Bad. No good Kiowas."

Lanie had to smile at the Indian. "You're a racist, are you, Woman Killer?"

She felt his steady, expressionless gaze on her as she spoke. Suddenly she was too tired to continue the discussion and didn't want to offend the stone-faced Indian, so she quickly excused herself. She found her blankets and eased her aching bones into their welcoming comforts; almost at once she was asleep.

The next afternoon they arrived at Eureka Springs and found it packed with tourists. This was like no town Lanie had ever seen before. The hardwood foliage in the town was like a jungle, and up through the leaves of the trees she could see the slopes on which the town was built. There were fine Victorian houses and hotels. The streets were so narrow and winding that two wagons could barely pass. And all along the sidewalks were stone benches that pedestrians could rest on before climbing up to Hotel Row. Here they could sit and admire the spectacle of houses built almost on top of one another up the shoulders of all the surrounding hills.

"I'll drift around," Lobo said. "See what I can find out. Lorenzo, why don't you go down to the courthouse and check out any of the marshals. Maybe they know something about Perrago."

"What'll *we* do?" Lanie asked.

"Guess you might as well get yourself a room, Miss Winslow," he replied easily. "Not much you can do along this line. You and Mr. Stone there get some rest. I'll come for you when it's time to leave."

Actually, Lanie was relieved. The two days' ride had drained her, and her legs and thighs were so sore she could hardly walk. "We'll be ready when you are," she said defiantly, locking her eyes into the gaze of Lobo Smith.

She and Wesley found two rooms in one of the hotels, and it was a real pleasure to take a regular bath. Lanie soaked in the hot water for almost an hour. Getting out reluctantly, she dried off and put on the one nightgown she had brought for the trip, then crawled into bed. The clean, crisp sheets were wonderful, and she relaxed with a sigh, glad for the big window that allowed a cool, fragrant breeze to come into the room and made the summer heat bearable.

She lay in the bed, thinking about Betsy and the family at home. Lanie was not a girl who had doubts about herself; she had little reason to. She had been successful at just about everything she had set out to do. But she knew that this was something altogether different—the success of this venture wasn't entirely in Lanie's hands. She drifted off gently, but no sooner had she settled into a deep sleep than there was a loud knock on her door.

"Who is it? What—What is it?" she cried, sitting bolt upright in the bed, eyes staring. The room had grown dark, lit only by the bright moon shining through the open window.

"It's me. Lobo."

"Just a minute!" Lanie jumped out of bed and realized she hadn't brought a robe. She walked to the door, unlocked it, and pulled it open just a crack, hiding behind it.

Outside the door, Lobo Smith stood leaning against the wall with his hands shoved deep in his pockets, excitement gleaming in his good eye. "Get ready, we're pulling out," he said cheerfully.

"Pulling out! What do you mean, pulling out? I just got to bed!" Lanie wailed.

Lobo grinned at her. For the first time, it was a full grin, and it made him look much younger, almost boyish. The dim light of the corridor threw his face into blue-gray shadows. "Well, might be best," he said with a hint of mischief in his voice. "You and Mr. Stone stay here while Dawkins, Woman Killer, and me go run this fellow down."

Lanie lifted her face haughtily. *He's always trying to make me look weak and helpless!* she thought. "I'll be right down," she said stiffly, slamming the door. Hurriedly she threw on her clothes, grabbed her things, and ran down the steps in a flash. Her eyes were still gritty with sleep, and she knew it would be all she could do to hang on to the saddle for the night ride. But Lanie was on a rampage and there was nothing that could stop her, especially an outlaw seemingly set on exposing any weakness.

Downstairs, she found the four men waiting outside with the horses. "Where are we going?" she demanded.

Lobo answered in a straightforward tone, "Been a train robbery. From what I hear, might have been Perrago."

"Where was this?" Stone asked grumpily. He had been roused by Woman Killer from a sound sleep and was bad-natured for once. "I don't see that it's going to do us any good to go rambling around these mountains in the middle of the night."

"Be quiet, Wesley," Lanie commanded. She looked over at Lorenzo Dawkins and asked, "Where did the robbery take place?" She deliberately ignored Lobo, which for some reason amused Woman Killer, who was observing the scene from his large bony gray horse.

"Somewheres close to Muskogee," Dawkins informed her. "The Arkansas Valley runs through there. 'Course, it mighta not been Perrago, but from what we was able to pick up, it's a good bet."

"How far is it?" Lanie asked intently.

"Oh, 'bout two whoops and a holler," Dawkins chuckled, but then saw that his humor was not appreciated, and went on, "Well, we gotta ride over to the Boston Mountains. We can either ride through the middle of them or swing up north and go around them. Or south, all the way back to the railroad." He squinted into the darkness for a moment. "I expect we'd better get there quick as we can."

Lanie swung into the saddle and felt her muscles protesting, but she kept all signs of pain off her face. "Well, let's go then! What are we waiting for?" She looked up at Lobo rebelliously. "You won't have to slow down for me!"

Lobo nodded. "That's good to know, Miss Winslow." He mounted, turned his horse, and left town at a hard gallop.

"You shouldn't have told him that," Wesley chided her as the two spurred their horses to catch up. "I would have asked him to take it easy. I'm about to fall out of the saddle. Don't those three ever rest?"

"Hush, Wes," Lanie retorted. "Hurting a little you are, that's all." In her tired state the Welsh strain of her mother's speech flowed unbidden. Then she added, "Oh, devil throw smoke! I could shoot that man sometimes!"

"Who?" Wesley asked in confusion.

"Lobo Smith. Him!" She did not amplify her remark for some time, but finally she said, "He thinks I'm worthless. But I'm going to show him how wrong he is!"

Later that night they stopped for a break and a drink of water at a cool mountain stream. Lanie found herself almost unable to get off the horse. She staggered when her feet hit the ground, her legs numb. As she was about to crumble, she felt a steely hand catch her arm. Turning around she saw that it was Smith, who remarked smugly, "Long ride for someone not used to being on horseback."

Yanking her arm away petulantly, she said, "Don't worry about me. I'm all right." He did not answer, but she could see that her remark amused him, and it drove her to again challenge him. "I don't see why we have to ride all night. We could at least be a little—a little . . ." She could not think of a word and finally finished lamely, "civilized about all this! After all, there are rules!"

Lobo stood silently for what seemed to Lanie a very long time. He was a lean, strong silhouette in the darkness. He seemed to be listening to something far off in the deep woods of the mountains that rose up darkly in front of them. All Lanie could hear was the gurgling of the small stream and somewhere far off the dim cry of a night bird. After a while, he looked directly at her and said softly, "Wolves don't have rules, Miss Winslow." There was a softness in his voice that conflicted with the roughness of his statement, and Lanie realized again that she knew nothing about this man. Fear ran through her as she thought of the danger that lay ahead—but she could not stop now.

"All right," she said evenly, her eyes fixed on his. "We'll do what we have to do."

PART TWO

THE CHASE

★ ★ ★ ★

CHAPTER NINE

"I'M NOT ANYBODY'S WOMAN!"

★　★　★　★

The train robbery had alerted not only the marshals in Arkansas and Missouri, but also the Indian officials inside the Territory. It was obvious that the robbers had escaped deep into the Nations, and Dawkins had said, "Best we go down and see what Johnny Bear Claw knows about this here matter. He knows every frog that hops inside his territory."

Dawkins' statement had precipitated a hard ride, and by the time they arrived in the Indian settlement, Lanie and Wesley were pretty well reduced to clinging to the saddle horn.

The settlement had less than a dozen buildings, the principal one being the store of Johnny Bear Claw, a Cree who operated a general merchandising business. As they dismounted their horses, Dawkins explained to Lanie, "Johnny Bear Claw is pretty much the buffer between the federal marshals and the Indian government. He used to be an officer himself, but he decided clerkin' would be easier, so he set up in this store. C'mon in. I'm sure we'd all welcome something good to eat."

Lanie nodded and followed the marshal, her knees weak after the long ride. She was glad to see a table.

"Sit down there, Missie," Dawkins said. We'll see what we can get from this jaybird in the way of groceries." He turned to a tall thin Indian who had stepped from behind the counter and came toward them.

"Hello, Marshal Dawkins," he said. "Do you all want something to eat?"

"Yeah, whatever you got, Johnny. I'm so hungry my stomach thinks my throat's been cut."

"All right. Take a few minutes, though."

As they waited for the food, Lanie looked around the store curiously. It was a long building, with what seemed to be living quarters at one end; the rest was taken over by a long counter with a coffee grinder and a hand-crank cash register perched on top. There were shelves and boxes and barrels, all in a clutter, scattered liberally about; a coal potbellied stove; leather and metal gear suspended from pegs all along each wall; and two tables with chairs and benches for those who wanted to eat. Along the rear wall were two large windows. A number of Indian men were standing in a cluster talking in their native tongue. They reminded Lanie of a tintype picture she had seen one time, a picture of Indians solemnly gathered, wearing white men's clothes, and looking dolefully at the viewer.

Soon Woman Killer and Lobo Smith came in and sat down. "You talked to Johnny Bear Claw yet, Lorenzo?" Lobo asked.

"Not yet." The marshal glanced over at the men lining the wall and said, "We'll get him alone after we eat."

After a short wait a young Indian woman brought the food in, which consisted of chili, crackers, and tin cups full of apple cider. "Not much grub," Johnny Bear Claw said apologetically. "If you want to wait longer, I'll cook you up some steaks and potatoes."

"This'll do fine," Dawkins said. He nodded toward a chair and when Johnny Bear Claw sat down Dawkins went on almost in a whisper, "We're looking for Vic Perrago."

The Indian listened, unmoving. He showed no sign of understanding or recognition, giving Lanie the sinking feeling that he knew nothing about Perrago's whereabouts that would help them.

Then, almost without moving his lips, the tall Indian said, "Be careful, Marshal." He glanced meaningfully at the men around the wall and spoke almost inaudibly, "He did the train, though."

"That the true goods?" Dawkins demanded. "How do you know?"

"One of the witnesses saw Perrago, or someone who could have passed for his twin brother."

"Judge Parker will never get to hang him with that kind of identification," Lobo murmured. He was spooning chili fast, shoveling it down hungrily. He took a deep draft of the apple cider and added, "Vic's too smart to get caught like that. But I don't have any doubt he did the train."

The talk ran around the table for a while. The Indians sat at the other table and were soon playing cards, the sound of their voices growing louder; they ignored Johnny Bear Claw and his visitors. Lanie listened as Dawkins and Bear Claw did most of the talking. She was not surprised that Lobo said little. After he finished eating, he shoved back in the chair, leaned against the wall, and pulled his hat down over his face.

He could at least pretend to be interested, Lanie thought angrily. *You'd think this was none of his concern at all! I never saw a man so irresponsible!*

After a while Lobo pushed his hat back and rose to his feet. He had an animal-like grace about him, lazy and slow-moving at times, but always with a hint of the energy that lay beneath the surface and could explode at any moment. "Guess I'll take a little stroll," he said idly, and walked out the door without looking back.

Lanie glanced at Wesley, who shrugged and said, "It doesn't look like we're going to get anywhere here, does it?" He was worn thin with fatigue. City life had not prepared him for the long hours in the saddle, the poor food, and the primitive sleeping conditions. His craggy face had sharper lines than usual, and his eyes seemed to have sunk farther back in his head. He was discouraged and despondent, though he said nothing. Lanie could see the weariness that weighed him down and understood, for she too was trembling with fatigue.

Twenty minutes later Lobo stepped back inside, and Lanie noticed immediately that something had lit up his single indigo eye. It seemed to sparkle as he walked over to the group to stand beside Lorenzo. "Old friend of ours here, Lorenzo," he said in a low voice.

Dawkins looked up with surprise. "Old friend? Who's that?"

"Tyrone Biggs."

The name meant something to Marshal Dawkins, who leaned back in his chair and began to groom his mustache, his eyes beginning to glow a little. "He been around here long, Bear Claw?"

"Coupla days," the Indian shrugged. "He's become a peddler. Got a wagon full of junk and he goes around trying to get rid of it. At least, that's his story."

Both Dawkins and Lobo grinned, a glint of humor in their eyes. "A little something under that pile of junk?" Lobo asked.

Johnny Bear Claw's chiseled face changed for the first time; a faint glimmer of humor hovered in the hawk-like eyes. "Never caught him at it. But the word's out that if you find Biggs alone, he'd sell you a bottle of whiskey."

"Why, that's against the law!" Dawkins said with indignation, the grin widening on his face. "I'd best have a talk with our old friend!" He turned to Lanie and said cautiously, "Now, Missie, this may be a wild goose chase. This here Tyrone Biggs, he's been just about everything up to and includin' an informer for most of Parker's marshals. Bank robber, too. More important than that, he did a spell in Perrago's gang, and I'm guessin' if anybody knows what Vic's up to, it'd be Tyrone Biggs. Why don't you sit here and rest up while Marshal Lobo Smith and me go invite him to share all his information with us?"

"All right, Marshal," Lanie agreed wearily.

The two men walked out, Dawkins' boots clonking loudly on the wooden floor, Lobo's moccasins sounding not a whisper. As soon as they were on the street Lobo said, "Tyrone's not going to be glad to see you, Marshal. Fact is, he wasn't all that glad to see me."

Dawkins bristled, "I don't give a dead rat what that ol' bandit's glad about! I'll have it out of him where Perrago is, or I'll throw his rear in Parker's jail!"

Lobo led the way to a cantina, where they found Biggs inside sitting at a table talking to the proprietor. Biggs was a sharp-featured man of forty. He had bright brown eyes, a long, pointed nose, and was bald except for a fringe around the crown of his head. As soon as Biggs saw the two men, he grew alarmed but covered it quickly with a hearty greeting. "Well, hello, Marshal Dawkins! Lobo didn't tell me you was here! I was kinda surprised to see that star pinned on Lobo's chest."

Dawkins walked over to the table and said to the proprietor, "Go wait at the bar, Willie." The stubby Indian rose at once and without a word went to the other end of the room and began busily polishing glasses. Dawkins' eyes narrowed and he said, "I ain't wasting no time on you, Tyrone." Lorenzo Dawkins had been dealing with outlaws for many years now and had learned that gentleness played little part in negotiating with them. He leaned over the small round table, his face close to Biggs' and went on in a low, serious voice, "We want to know where Vic Perrago is."

Biggs shrugged and held his hands up. "I don't know, Marshal," he said earnestly. "I ain't seen Perrago now, in, oh, must be nigh on a year, I guess. Lobo knows all of Vic's hideouts as well as I do—"

"Shut up!" Dawkins snapped. "We didn't come here to listen to that fodder! What we did come here for is to find out where Perrago is now. You know he has a dozen hideouts in the Territory. We just need to know where he's headed so we don't end up on a wild goose chase—Lobo can take us. We just need the inside information from you. Now, are you gonna cooperate with two federal marshals, or would you rather see the inside of Parker's jail for the load of *goods* in your wagon?"

Biggs' mouth opened and shut like a beached fish. "Now wait a minute, Marshal! You can't do this to a man! I don't—"

"I told you to shut your mouth," Dawkins said. "If I wasn't such a gentle cuss, I wouldn't even be givin' you a chance like this. But I'll tell you what I'll do. You help us find Perrago, and I'll see that you don't go to Judge Parker's jail. At least, not for a while."

The conversation was short and sweet. In less than three minutes, Biggs, who knew all about the conditions in the basement of Judge Isaac Parker's jail, told them that he knew Perrago and his gang were at one of two hideouts near the Boston Mountains, and that they had been seen at different times roaming the hills with a woman.

The three men left the cantina, and Dawkins walked back to

Johnny Bear Claw's store, while Lobo walked with Biggs, still discussing what Vic might be up to.

Dawkins thanked Bear Claw and led Stone and Lanie outside. "All right, Biggs told us where Perrago probably is. Lobo's gonna take us there. He don't know 'zactly where he's at, but he knows all his hideouts. So we're gonna load up with supplies and take off soon as we can." He turned to Lanie and said sternly, "Now, Missie, lemme tell you one more time. I think it'd be better if you stayed here. It's awful rough out there."

Lanie smiled and put her hand on the marshal's arm. "That's sweet of you, Marshal," she said. She was taller than he, and looked down into his eyes. "I realize that's good advice, but it's proud I am." She laughed slightly and said, "My father always said I had a little bit of Old Scratch in me. A temper and stubborn as the devil himself. But they have my sister, you see," she went on grimly, "and I'll have them for it, or know the reason why."

Admiration beamed in the old man's eye, and he smiled beneath his bushy mustache. "There is somethin' about you, Missie," he said, shaking his head, "danged if there ain't!" He glanced at Wesley Stone. "Well, hope you enjoyed your meal. Last one you'll have sittin' down at a table for a while."

Thirty minutes later, the party left with heavily laden pack animals, ready for the long hunt.

* * * *

Whether or not Lobo decided to stop because he could see that Lanie and Stone were exhausted, or whether it was just a whim, Lanie was never able to figure out. Whatever the reason, he led them through a draw to a creek that murmured sibilantly as it wound its way among the rocks. There were a few trees there, which provided some shade. Lanie practically fell off her horse, heartily grateful for the halt.

Woman Killer staked the horses out while Lobo made a fire. Soon they were sitting around the small, comforting blaze, eating peaches and nibbling chunks of tender beef that they had bought from Bear Claw's store. "I like my grub, surely do," Dawkins said, loquacious and ready to talk. "I shoulda been a chef in some fancy restaurant. I coulda handled that, always was a good cook."

It was still daylight. Lobo stood up and brushed himself off, his indigo eye on Lanie. "Been meaning to give you a little training. You and Mr. Stone," he said in his soft voice. "Come with me."

"What for?" Stone asked.

"Going to teach you how to shoot those guns you've been carrying," Lobo answered blandly.

Wesley shook his head stubbornly. "I don't want any shooting lessons. All I wear this thing for is self-defense."

The eyebrow above the patch went up sarcastically. "Interesting theory, Mr. Stone. Don't think it's going to work too well out here in the Nations, though. What about you, Miss Winslow?"

Lanie got to her feet and said defiantly, "All right. Where do we go?"

"Over by that big rock is good enough." He picked up the empty peach cans, and Lanie and Lobo walked toward the rock.

When they got about a hundred yards away from the camp, Lobo said quietly, "Right here, Miss Winslow." He put three cans on top of a large rock and moved back about thirty feet. Nodding at them, he told Lanie, "See what you can do."

Lanie pulled out the .38 that Lobo had gotten for her, held it in both hands, shut her eyes, and pulled the trigger. The gun went off, making a loud explosion in the wilderness. She opened her eyes and saw that the three cans were still in place.

"Go on," he said.

She shut her eyes and pulled the trigger twice more, and opening them, found the three cans still mocking her.

"Look," he said gently, "you're not going to be in a gun fight, I don't think. Someone might come for you, though—you never know in this country. You shouldn't have to shoot anyone far away; in fact, the best thing would be if you can shove that gun in someone's stomach and pull the trigger. That'd stop 'em."

Lanie winced and said doubtfully, "I don't think I could do that."

He eyed her curiously. "Not even if it was to either fire the rifle or become a Kiowa squaw?" He came over and stood behind her and said firmly, "Now, look, let me help you." He checked the load in the gun. "You've got three more shots. It's all right to use both hands, Miss Winslow, but don't shut your eyes.

Here." He put his hand on her wrist and pulled her arm out to its full length, then took her other hand, cupping it on the other side of the firearm, and said, "Now use your other hand to steady your stance. Good. Hold steady, take a deep breath, and don't shut your eyes. Now, pull the trigger."

She did as he directed and was surprised to see one of the cans disappear. It wasn't the one she had aimed at, but she didn't mention that to Lobo. "How was that?" she asked triumphantly.

"Not bad," he encouraged her. "Now try another one."

She had gained confidence and fired the other two bullets quickly. Neither of them hit the can, but one of them left a long scar on the rock. "Woulda been a dead man if it had been a man," Lobo told her. He loaded her gun several times, and Lanie fired determinedly at the cans. He would go get them when she hit one, which wasn't often, and reset them for her.

After several rounds she asked, "Isn't that enough?"

He nodded and said carefully, "Always keep your gun loaded. And don't pull it unless you mean to use it, Miss Winslow."

They had walked back perhaps another thirty feet when she stopped and looked back at the cans. "Can you hit those cans from here?"

She hadn't even finished the sentence when suddenly Lobo's gun was blazing in his hand. The shots were so close together it sounded like one continuous roar. Lanie's eyes batted as the cans almost simultaneously went flying into space. When she turned back to him, his gun was back in the holster and he was standing, smiling at her, a smirk in his eye. "I never saw anyone that could do that," she said with undisguised admiration.

"Well, like I always say, Miss Winslow, cans don't shoot back," Lobo shrugged, then glanced at her. "You know, I've wanted to ask you something."

"Ask me something? What?" Lanie thought he meant to ask her something about her family, or about life in Chicago.

"Are you Stone's woman?" The question came with unusual abruptness from Lobo's lips.

Lanie's eyes narrowed, flashing abruptly with temper. "I'm not *anybody's* woman." She bit the words off. Her cheeks grew red and her back stiffened. "And I resent your asking that."

"You do?" Lobo seemed genuinely surprised. He kicked the shells out of his revolver, pulled three shells out of his shirt pocket, and deftly reloaded the empty chambers. Replacing the gun securely in his holster, he looked back up at her, obviously puzzled. "I don't understand that."

"You don't understand why a woman doesn't want to be classified as somebody's woman?"

"No." He was searching her face, evidently very sincere. "If someone came up to me and asked, 'Are you Lanie Winslow's man?' why, I'd just say yes—If I was, that is."

The artlessness of his reply irritated Lanie even more and she retorted, "Well, you are not 'my man,' and I don't want to *have* a man, anyway! Any more than I want a man to *have* me!" Her heated replies seemed to be all out of proportion to his calm inquiries. She took a deep breath and tried again. "When you say, 'Am I Stone's woman?' you're asking, 'Do I belong to him?' I don't think people should *belong* to—people," she finished, frustrated.

"You don't?" There was a genuine look of interest on Lobo's face. "Well, I always thought that was the way it was."

"The way what was?" Lanie asked in spite of herself.

"The way love was," he answered. There was a dryness in his tone, and the quickly setting sun carved the hollows in his cheeks. The single eye was steadily fixed on her. "'Course, I don't know much about love."

Lanie could not understand what he was talking about. "You think people ought to belong to each other? Why, that's slavery!"

"No, not the way I look at it." He seemed to be searching for words, speaking slowly and carefully. "I've known cases where the man and the woman somehow seemed to belong to each other. Wasn't slavery to them."

"I don't think you're qualified to talk about love," Lanie said impatiently. "Have you ever been married?"

"No."

"Have you ever been engaged?"

"No." Then he added, "Have you?"

Lanie glared at him. "I've never been married or engaged."

"Guess you're no expert either, then. Are you, Miss Winslow?" He did not smile, but she knew instantly that he was amusing himself at her expense. She wheeled and walked back toward the camp, Lobo following without another word.

The others looked at them as they came in, and it was obvious that Lanie was upset. She stalked over to her blanket and sat down, staring into the fire without speaking. Dawkins began talking about outlaws, and the conversation went on for some time.

Finally, Lobo said, "We better get some rest so we can head out to Perrago's hideout. He's probably using that shack he has in the Cherokee Nation. It'll be a good two-day ride, as I figger it." He cocked his head to one side and continued pointedly. "I can find the shack. Perrago may or may not be there. But I can tell you one thing, Marshal."

"What's that, Lobo?"

"You ain't gonna walk in unexpected on Vic and that bunch. They're ready for whatever comes."

No one answered. Wesley Stone had been listening, trying to stay awake, and now he looked at Lobo. "There's no way to sneak up on them?"

"A man don't make it in the business Perrago's in unless he learns how to keep folks from sneakin' up on him. Nope. I expect when we go to fetch Perrago that he'll be there to furnish the reception," Lobo said as if he were instructing a child.

CHAPTER TEN

No Escape

★ ★ ★ ★

Every day was the same. Betsy got up wearily, dressed, ate what she could—although it was hard to choke anything down—and then spent the monotonous days either wandering around the shack, always under strict surveillance, or else sitting on the front porch, staring out over the emptiness of the hills that surrounded the house.

She had learned within the first few days that she was trapped with an outlaw crew. They made no attempt to hide their exploits from her. It made her blood run cold when they talked about killing the way other men talked about planting crops.

Almost two weeks had gone by, and Betsy had lost weight. Dark circles emphasized her dull eyes, and she made no attempt to make herself attractive. She wanted to lose her prettiness, for whenever Vic came close to her she felt unclean. She could not avoid him at night. He merely laughed at her attempts to get away from him, at least for the first week. Then he grew tired of it. Night was coming on, and she sat out on the front porch listening to the men inside cursing and yelling. The eternal poker game was going on, and she dreaded for it to be over.

Betsy knew that she couldn't just walk away, for usually at least two of the men were watching her. Sometimes they were invisible, but she knew they were there. Tonight Honey Ward, a burly man of thirty-five, was out there somewhere in the falling darkness, perhaps to the hills to the west, watching all the passes that way, while Grat Duvall, a small rider whose eyes almost looked crossed because they were set close together, was probably watching from the east. Jack Masterson, a dark, muscular man with sharp black eyes, frightened her the most—he stared at her constantly.

The house had been chosen because no one could sneak up on it. There were only the low hills, void of anything except shrub timber that was shriveled by the heat. The only water was a small creek that flowed behind the house, some greenery edging its banks.

Betsy sat on the porch stoically, her thoughts dull and sad. She had been sitting there for hours, and finally she got up and walked to the creek, scooped some fresh water up in the bucket she carried, and drank deeply. The water was the only good thing here; the cooking was greasy, the food usually half done. But the water in the creek was fed by a spring somewhere, and it was deliciously cool. She sat down stiffly and bathed her face with it. She was well aware that she would never be allowed to get more than a hundred yards away from the shack, and that right now sharp eyes were watching her. Taking off her shoes, she bathed her feet, then took her handkerchief out of her pocket and bathed her face and neck, enjoying the cool water against her hot skin. It was always hot here, and her face was beginning to pick up a golden tan, although the freckles still showed.

Freckles, she thought dismally. *To think I was once worried about freckles and not being tall.* Her mind wandered back to the old days, and she dropped her head and ground the heels of her hands into her eyes to shut off the tears. She had cried herself out long ago, and she knew too well that tears would not bring her any sympathy.

For a long time she sat motionless, her head down, trying not to think of home. But the thoughts came to her, like faint music comes to one who listens. She thought of her mother, hearing her voice again, the Welsh strain so rich in it. She thought of her father and how he had always made a pet of her, thinking that no one knew it, while everyone was totally aware of it. What she would give to see him again, to have him put his arm around her and hold her close! A sob escaped, and she thought, *That will never be again. I can never face him, never!*

At last the yells and curses died down, and she knew that most of the gang would be going to sleep soon. They usually drank heavily on idle days like this and fell into a drunken stupor early in the evening. Slowly she picked up the bucket and carried it back to the house. When she got to the porch, she set it down on a small rickety table by her chair and went inside.

Buckley Ogg sat like a huge idol, staring down at the cards on the table. He was playing solitaire. The rest of the crew seemed to be asleep, except Vic and Angela. They both looked up as she came in. "Well," Vic said, "you're too late to join the party, sweetheart." When she didn't answer he grew angry. His hazel eyes sharpened and he said, "Did you hear what I said?"

"Yes."

"Then answer me. Blazes! You're no good; you're like a dead woman!"

Betsy stared at him blankly. She knew fear, but she was too exhausted emotionally to do anything about it. When she didn't say anything, Vic got up and came toward her menacingly. He grabbed her hair, pulled her head back cruelly, and kissed her. She could smell the alcohol and tobacco, and he held her so tightly she could not move.

Holding on to her hair, he shook her. "Can't you smile? What kind of a woman are you, anyhow?" He was aware of Ogg and Angela watching them, and without warning he let go of her hair and slapped her sharply across the cheek.

Betsy was driven sideways by the blow, and she saw bright flashes for a few seconds. But she didn't utter a sound, nor did she raise a hand to rub her bruised cheek.

Angela spoke up in a mocking voice, "You're a tough hombre, aren't you, Vic? With women, anyway."

Perrago whirled catlike and stepped over to Angela, his eyes flashing angrily. She stared at him, her own face smooth and unmoved. Her lips curved with amusement. "Go on," she taunted. "Why don't you slap me?"

Perrago stared at her; he wanted to slap her, but he didn't. He growled, "Better watch yourself, Angela."

Angela Montoya smiled brilliantly. Her teeth were beautiful against her dark skin. There was a feline look about her, more tiger than house cat. "You know better, don't you, Vic? You know I'd have a knife in you if you laid a hand on me," she said, her voice as smooth as velvet.

Perrago cursed and whirled around. He had been drinking heavily and had lost a great deal of money in the poker game. He looked again at Betsy, his eyes narrowing.

Again Angela mocked him. "Go on, Vic. Hit her again; show us what a big man you are."

Perrago turned back to her, furious. "You're just the one to do it, too, aren't you, Angela? Stick a knife in a man while he's asleep!"

"You know I would," Angela said calmly. "Now, go sleep it off. We've got work to do tomorrow."

Vic gave Betsy a venomous look and spat, "Sleep on the floor. See how you like that." He entered the bedroom and slammed the door.

Ogg looked up from where he sat, eyed the door, and murmured in his deep voice, "Vic's letting himself get out of hand." His gaze went to Betsy and he added, "He never should have brought you here."

Betsy wanted to beg, *Let me go home*, but she knew it would be useless. She didn't know what to do, for he had never shut her out of the bedroom before, but she was glad for it anyway, and looked around for a place to lie down.

"I have an extra blanket," Angela said in an offhand manner. She went down the hall to her bedroom and came back with a blanket and a pillow. "Curl up over there. He's too drunk to do any more tonight, and nobody else will bother you. If anyone does, just let out a yell."

"Thank you," Betsy said quietly.

That night Betsy slept well, curled up on the hard floor with just the blanket. She was bone-weary and emotionally drained, and she simply passed out. She was so exhausted that she didn't even wake up the next morning when the majority of the band rode out. When she did get up she found only Angela Montoya and Grat Duvall left behind.

"The boys went out on a little job," Angela informed Betsy,

a mocking light in her dark eyes. Looking Betsy up and down, she ordered, "Sit down and have something to eat. You're going to turn into a skeleton."

"I don't want—"

"Sit down, I said!" Angela commanded. She pushed Betsy into a chair and began cooking an omelet. When it was finished she slammed it down in front of Betsy, along with a tall glass of milk, and said shortly, "Eat."

Surprisingly, Betsy found herself ravenous. She had not eaten, except for a few bites here and there, for several days. Now she devoured the omelet, washing it down with the warm milk. "That was so good," she sighed, sitting back in her chair. "Thank you, Angela."

"I'm not much of a cook. But I'm better than anyone around here." She was studying Betsy with a scrutinizing gaze and finally asked, "Where did Vic find you, Betsy? Why did you leave with him?"

Betsy just shook her head and said wearily, "I don't know. I thought I was in love with him. I thought he loved me."

"He never loved anyone but himself."

"I know that now. But I didn't then. I'd never had a boyfriend before, not really. My sister, Lanie, she's the one all the men liked." Betsy talked for a long time, unaware that she was revealing a great deal. Angela began playing solitaire, barely glancing at Betsy. For Betsy, speaking openly to Angela was a relief. She was afraid of all the men—most of all Vic Perrago. Though Angela Montoya was a cruel woman, different from anyone in Betsy's experience, at least she was a woman and wouldn't hurt her. Or so Betsy thought.

The next three days went by quickly. There was a peace in the desert that descended upon Betsy. She was allowed to ride her horse, as long as either Angela or Duvall went with her, and she savored this new freedom. She kept her eyes open at all times, seeking an opportunity to escape, but none came.

Three days later the men arrived back, late in the afternoon. They were covered with desert dust, exhausted, and ravenous. Duvall scrambled around, frying meat, throwing together a quick meal for them. They ate hungrily and then began to drink. Ogg was the one, Betsy had discovered, that planned the jobs.

He looked like anything but an outlaw, but she had become aware that there was a shrewd brain ticking away inside his bald head.

Mateo Río never got drunk like the rest of them. There was always a coldness in his eyes as he watched Betsy, and it frightened her, much more so than Bob Pratt. Río leered at her with open lust. She could never allow herself to be alone with him.

Honey Ward, big, burly, and simple, said nothing unless spoken to, for the most part. He loved to play cards but was terrible at it, so he always seemed to be broke, having lost his share of the money from their various jobs.

Late that night, after the rest of them had gone to bed, the moment Betsy dreaded came. She was left alone with Vic. He was studying her with a strange light in his eyes; they looked yellow and feral. He asked casually, "What have you been doing with yourself?"

Ignoring his question, she looked at him directly and said, "Vic, let me go."

He grinned, "You'll go home pretty soon."

Her heart leaped; then she saw the mockery in his eyes and she dropped her head. She wept bitterly, knowing that she was entirely at his mercy. "Please," she begged, raising her eyes to his. "I'm no good to you out here!" She lifted her eyes, anger flaring in them. "You must know I despise you!"

Perrago laughed out loud. Perversely, her words seemed to please him. "Well, I'm glad you have a little fight in you! You've been like a worn-out dishrag! Oh, you'll be going back, all right." His lips curled with disdain. "Your folks just have to get a little bit more lonesome for you. Then they'll be ready to pay a nice sum to get their little girl back."

Betsy's shoulders sagged. "I can *never* go home. Not after what—not after what you've done to me." She stumbled over the words, shame rising in her throat thickly. She could not face his eyes, and her head dropped again.

Again Perrago laughed coarsely. "Sure you can! Lots of girls have fellows!" He stalked over to her and grabbed her shoulders roughly. "Just keep your mouth shut, and your father will never know about our little romance when you get home."

She looked up at him hopelessly. "He would know. He couldn't help but know."

Perrago cocked his head to one side. He had known many women, but there was something about this small young girl that baffled him. "You're taking all this too seriously," he said. "A man's a man, a woman's a woman. We don't have too long down here. Have some fun, Betsy!" His grip on her shoulders tightened and he shook her lightly. "You didn't have any fun back in Chicago. Remember how you told me that! How your sister got all the men, and all you got to do was go to church?"

Betsy burst out, "Oh, how I wish I was back there now! I wish all this had never happened!"

Perrago grew impatient. "Never mind all that. I'm tired of hearing you complain. C'mon, let's go to bed."

Betsy drew back and stiffened. "No. I know you're gonna whip me, so you might as well start in. But I'm going to scream and fight until you kill me! So go on and start!"

Perrago's eyes flared with anger. Then somehow, the humor of it hit him. He grinned. "Well, a little more of that kind of spirit and you'll be a fit woman for me after all!" He shrugged, then turned. "Suit yourself. I'm tired of fooling with you," he said and went down the hall.

Betsy sighed with relief. She had fully expected him to grab her and haul her into the bedroom by brute force, and she had prepared herself to fight him until she was unconscious. Feeling somehow liberated, she started to tremble. At first, when the realization of the intolerable situation she was in began to come home to her, she had prayed; then she had grown bitter. But now she said simply, "Oh, God, thank you, thank you!" She blew out the light, then curled up in Angela's blanket and pillow on the floor, where she had been sleeping since the night before Vic had left. Somehow, while Vic was gone, she couldn't willingly force herself to sleep in the bed in which Vic had defiled her.

As she lay there on the bare floor, hugging the blanket tightly, she began to pray, feeling hopeless and faithless. Yet she prayed.

★　★　★　★

The next day when Angela and Vic were alone, he told her his scheme. "I'll hang on to the girl for a while. Let her old man sizzle a little bit. He'll be glad to pay plenty to get her back."

Angela's lips twisted—a red slash across her olive face. "That trick will get you killed," she said. She was smoking a little black cigar as she often did, and now she took a puff and blew the smoke at him. "You can get away with stealing money. But this sort of thing men don't forget. She's told me a little bit about this father of hers. He was quite a man in his day, I understand. And he'll be coming after you, Vic. And he probably won't come alone."

Perrago laughed disdainfully. "Let him come," he said carelessly. "Nobody knows the Nations better than I do. There's a thousand places we can hide out." He moved over toward her. "What are you so mad about, Angela?" He reached out and ran his hand down her glossy black hair. "Maybe you and I can get together after we get rid of her. How would you like that?"

"Take your hand off me, Vic. If you ever touch me again, I'll kill you. I swear it," she said smoothly.

He jerked his hand back as if it had been burned, and Angela Montoya watched him indifferently, taking a drag from the little cigar. Without another word, he turned and walked out of the room.

CHAPTER ELEVEN

"SOME THINGS ARE LOST FOREVER"

★ ★ ★ ★

The afternoon was half gone and the heat had reached its unbearable intensity as the four riders moved eastward. There was no relief from the sweltering sun. In all the days they had followed the trail, this one held the most punishment to Lanie.

She labored for breath and her nerves grew raw. *Must be a hundred and twenty out here,* she thought. The edges of her saddle were too hot for comfort, and the metal pieces of the bridle shimmered in the bright sunlight, making her eyes hurt from the intensity of it.

Finally, at five o'clock, the countryside rose from its flatness into rolling dunes of sand and clay gulches. Here and there a pine tree stood as an advance, announcing the rolling hills far away to the north. The hills before them were black and bulky and high, with the yellow streak of a road or trail running in crisscrosses up them, then vanishing into the distance. The riders crossed a shallow creek, pausing long enough to let the horses have a short drink, then started the roundabout climb into the benchlands.

"How much farther?" Lanie asked wearily. Her lips were so dry she had to lick them before she could form the brief sentence.

The heat devils danced before her eyes across the broken land, distorting the view of the horizon with its steamy haze.

"Just another hour. Maybe two," Lobo murmured. He looked back at her, his eyebrow cocked. "You ready to pull up and make camp?"

"No!" Lanie said shortly. She said no more and spurred her horse forward in a gesture of defiance.

After the last two weeks of crossing and recrossing the land that made up the Nations, Lanie had grown rather proud of her tenacity. Lorenzo had complimented her on it more than once, saying things like, "Not many gals could make it like you've done, Miss Lanie."

Even now Lorenzo leaned across and said quietly to Lobo, "Pushin' it a little bit, ain't we? Maybe that gal ain't wore out, but I'm here to tell you I am."

Lobo glanced at the older man, and it was evident that fatigue and weariness had indeed taken a toll on Dawkins. His eyes were droopy and his shoulders were slumped. "Well, I guess another hour won't help much," Lobo shrugged. "There's a ravine up ahead, Lorenzo. Little creek there. We can make camp."

Lobo touched his horse's flanks and the party moved ahead. The shadows ran before them longer and longer as the sun dipped, and Lanie turned to catch the last great bursts of flame as the sun dropped below the rim of the mountains, like the explosion of a distant world. After that, the land was changed: blue and still, the smell of pine trees in the hills. Coolness wafted across her face, soothing the sting of the day's heat from her.

Just at dusk Lobo led them around a bend and down into a small canyon where he pulled up. "This'll do as good as any," he announced. "Let's make camp here."

Wearily they piled off their horses. Wesley found that his knees were weak and he stared at them as if they had betrayed him. Then, as if to show them that he would not be dominated by a pair of spindly limbs, he announced loudly, "I'll get the firewood."

As he staggered off into the gloom, Lorenzo looked after him fondly. "That boy's got spunk," he observed. "Not many city folk would stick it out like he does."

They had begun a ritual in the last few days. Wesley gathered firewood; Dawkins did the cooking. Usually Lobo and Woman Killer took a ride, just to be sure there were no bands of Indians or renegades in the vicinity. Now they pulled away, their horses moving slowly, and made a wide circuit around the camp. When they got back, the smell of frying meat was in the air and they dismounted, tying their horses to the small saplings that lined the bank of the creek.

"Come and get it! What there is of it, anyhow," Dawkins called. He was squatting in front of the fire, holding the handle of a large black skillet. He stared down into it, made a face, then turned his sharp-featured face to Lobo and said morosely, "Last of that antelope you shot, Lobo. If we don't get something to eat, we're gonna have to turn back."

Dawkins dumped the small portions of meat into the tin plates and added two or three pieces of baked potatoes to each. "This is the last of the potatoes, too," he said. "Cupboard's done gone bare. Even the coffee's done run out."

Lobo didn't answer. Moving over to the small fire, he squatted on his heels and took a tobacco pouch from his pocket. As he rolled a cigarette, he let his gaze circle the small group. All of them, he noted—except Woman Killer—were worn down by the chase. He was somewhat surprised by Lorenzo's obvious fatigue, for he knew the old man could be a tough one. But then, at sixty, Dawkins had been following a hard trade for a long time, and it had taken its toll. Even now he saw the old man sitting with legs crossed, hands in his lap, and barely able to chew the tough meat. *Lorenzo can't make it too much farther,* Lobo thought soberly.

Lobo took his plate and began to chomp on the tough meat. After he swallowed he said thoughtfully, "We'll go to the store tomorrow."

Woman Killer looked at him and nodded. "Otumka? We go there? That good. I got friends there."

"What's Otumka?" Lanie asked. The meat was so tough she could hardly chew it; but she couldn't remember ever being so hungry, so it tasted good. She had always been a finicky eater, but that had changed now. Chewing on the tough gristle, she extracted from it every bit of savor and strength that it offered. Lanie had learned what it was to live on the edge of starvation. The food that she consumed was only enough to provide energy for the day, and it seemed that she was always hungry. *When I get back home, I'll never take a meal for granted again,* she vowed.

"Otumka? It's just a little trading post about ten miles from here." Lobo studied Lanie, his hat pulled down low over his brow so that the gleam of his eye could not be seen. The girl was a puzzle for him. He had never been around a city woman before, and somehow this one had been different from all his expectations. He admired the sheen of her cheeks, noting that they were more sunken than when the chase had begun. He had never thought she could take this kind of punishment; in fact, he had deliberately kept the pace up, hoping that she would cave in so he could send her back to Fort Smith, along with Wesley Stone.

Wesley devoured the small morsel of meat and the potato, then looked sorrowfully at his empty plate. "I'd like to have a steak big enough to choke a horse," he murmured.

Woman Killer grinned suddenly. Ordinarily he was a sober man, smooth-faced and expressionless, but now the smile that appeared broke the solemnity of his features. "Maybe we kill spare horse. Pony's good eating," he said, rubbing his stomach.

Lanie laughed. "You know, if we don't get something pretty soon, I'll vote in favor of that, Woman Killer."

Silence then fell upon the small group, broken by the crackling of the dry wood that sent red and yellow flames leaping high. The creek made a bubbling sound, soothing, as it flowed across the rocks. Lorenzo put his plate down and said, "I'm goin' to sleep." Without further ado he stood up, walked slowly to his horse, and pulled a blanket from his gear. Spreading it on the ground, he tossed his hat beside it, sat down, took his boots off, then pulled the blanket about him.

The marshal's collapse was as sudden as if he had been struck in the head, and Woman Killer said in a muted whisper, "Lobo, Dawkins no make it on long trip."

Lobo could offer no remedy. "We'll see how it goes," he murmured.

"Well," Wesley said, "I'm worn out myself." He pulled his blankets from his horse, rolled up in them, and was soon snoring loudly.

Lanie was tired, but she sat in front of the fire, her legs crossed. "There's just something about a fire, outside, in the open . . ." she said softly. "It's not quite the same as a fire in the fireplace, is it?"

No one answered. Woman Killer stared at her, his eyes solemn. "You like it here?" he asked.

Lanie shot him a surprised glance. "Like it?" she repeated. The question puzzled her. She had not liked it at all. The weather and the heat and the poor food had all combined to drag her down, and at times she wondered if she could stand it. And yet as she considered the question, the answer did not come easily. Her whole life had been the city; only a few rides on stable horses had been the closest she had been to open country. But here—there was something about the desert and the far-off mountains, the openness, even the very wildness, that drew her. "I don't know, Woman Killer," she sighed, staring into the fire. "It's hard on a city woman like me. And yet, if I'd been raised out here, I know I'd love it." Lanie looked up at the Indian and suddenly asked the question that had been on her mind since she had met him. "Why do they call you Woman Killer?"

The grave face of the Indian broke into a grin. "They gave me that name because the squaws like me so good," he answered.

Lanie's face grew skeptical. The Indian did not seem like one who would be given to practical jokes. But as he sat there, short and muscular, holding the rifle across his knees, she became aware of the glint of humor—almost mischief—in his dark eyes. "Oh, really?" she answered blandly. "We call those 'lady-killers' in our world."

The Indian got to his feet suddenly, then disappeared as silently as a ghost, without another word. Lanie stared after him, disconcerted by his abrupt departure. Looking across at Lobo she asked, "Do you think I hurt his feelings?"

"Not likely."

"Well, I guess I—I didn't—I guess I was a little afraid of that name," she said lamely.

"Indians like names like that," Lobo shrugged. "Have you heard of the one called 'Young Man Afraid of His Horses'?"

"No! Is there really an Indian with a name like that?"

"Sure is." Lobo idly poked the fire with a stick, his hat shading his single eye. "But if he was afraid of his horses, he sure wasn't afraid of anything else. Great war chief."

Silence fell again, only the hissing and the crackling of the fire breaking the hush as Lobo poked at the burning timbers from time to time. After a while he looked up and said, "You know, this probably is not going to get any better, Miss Winslow."

"Oh, for heaven's sake," she said irritably, "you can call me Lanie." Then she leaned back, removed her hat, and ran her hand through her hair. It felt dirty, stiff, and gritty. Lanie was usually fastidious about her hair, but lately she had let it go, as she had all other items of personal care. "You're hoping I'll give up, aren't you? That Wes and I will go back and let you handle this alone? That's what you're thinking, isn't it?"

Lobo was taken by surprise. *This young woman is not only beautiful*, he thought, *but has a quick and active mind*. He nodded now in agreement. "Be best," he said succinctly. "We've had good luck so far, but if we ever meet up with Perrago it might not be so easy."

"I didn't come out here to fight the man. I think there are ways to get my sister back without that."

"Not if Vic wants her. He always hangs on to what he wants. Stubborn hombre."

Lanie looked across at the motionless form of Lobo and said, "You're a stubborn fellow yourself, Lobo."

"Have to be in this country, I guess."

"Have you lived here always?" Lanie inquired curiously. She knew almost nothing about him, he rarely spoke of his past. "Do you come from the West?"

At first she thought he would not answer, but at length he nodded. "Born in Texas," he said. There was a hesitation then, and Lanie did not move or speak, hoping that he would go on. She let the silence run on and finally he added, "I didn't have a very good life. My mother—she gave me away when I was three years old."

"Gave you away!" Lanie was astonished and horrified. "What do you mean, she gave you away? Women don't do that with their children!"

"Mine did." His voice was even and calm, and yet there was a desperation, or hopelessness, in his voice that Lanie had not heard before. "I don't fault her for it," he went on quietly. "She must have had a hard time. My old man was killed by a wild bull, and there were two other children, a brother and a sister of mine. I don't know the real story about it. I only remember her a little bit. Remember she always wore a blue dress." He lifted his head; his face was tense. A bitterness lined his mouth as he continued. "I can remember the shack we lived in, the well out back, and we kept chickens. It was my job to feed the chickens, I remember that much. Then something happened, I never knew what. But one day she came in and told me, 'I gotta leave you kids with the neighbors.' She'd been crying, and we all were scared. I said, 'Don't go. I'll help you, Ma.'"

Far away a coyote lifted its plaintive voice, sending the mournful sound over the desert air. When it died down, Lobo suddenly broke the stick he'd been poking the fire with, threw it into the blaze, and pulled his hat down over his eyes again. "She never came back. So the neighbors kept us for a while, but I ran away when I was fourteen."

"What did you do then?" Lanie whispered.

"Cowboy'd some. Went to Oklahoma, that country right over there, the Territory. The Indians took me in and I stayed with them for five years."

"You—you never heard from your family again?"

"I went back one time," he said, his voice distant, "where I was born. Tried to pick up my mother's trail, but nobody even remembered her. It was like the earth just swallowed her up. My brother and sister had been given away and were gone. Don't know where they are now."

"I'm sorry."

Lobo glanced up sharply and saw tears in her eyes. He shook his head, his lips tight. "Shouldn't have bothered you with all that. Don't know why I did. Never told anybody else."

Lanie said, "I'm glad you did." She desperately wanted to say more but couldn't think of anything. Lanie had never had the kind of trouble he'd had, and she knew from that moment on that she would not be as quick to fault the man. He had been forged in a hard school, and what had come out now was pure steel—hard and vengeful.

"I think I'll go to bed," she said. "I'm tired." She went to her horse, unstrapped her blankets, made a place for herself a few feet away from the men, and lay down on the hard ground. The exhaustion that was her companion now washed across her. She felt her muscles relax, and she looked up at the sky. The stars were swarming like a million fireflies overhead. For a long time Lanie thought of Betsy. She had spent a lot of time lately thinking of how she had failed to be a good sister, and the thoughts pricked her spirit with pain. *I'll make it up to her*, Lanie promised herself. *I'll find her and get her away—and take her home—and I'll be good to her* . . . Her thoughts trailed off.

Across the fire, Lobo Smith sat, his hat pulled low over his forehead, studying the flickering fire. Long hours passed as he watched it die down to a solid red glow. He held his hand out to it, felt the heat, and thought about the days to come. He rose and out of habit made a quick survey around the camp but saw nothing ominous. Returning to the small circle, he found the others still sleeping peacefully, and he too pulled his blankets out and joined them.

★   ★   ★   ★

Otumka was not really a town, Lanie saw, but merely a small collection of rude huts and shacks, made primarily of warping cottonwood planks. The most impressive building—if it could be called that—was the General Store, where they pulled up wearily.

Slipping from her horse to the ground, Lanie joined the others as they trooped inside. One look around convinced her that although they would not have silks and satins, they would have food and a few items she longed for. The proprietor, named Slim John, was a lean man with a cadaverous face—a Cherokee, Lanie was informed. Silently he began to pull out the items Lobo named off: coffee, bacon, flour, cans of peaches. Lanie noted that Slim John was watching them carefully. She expected Lobo or Marshal Dawkins to ask the Indian something about Perrago; but they did not mention his name. That puzzled her, but she said nothing.

After the supplies were all ready, Lanie wandered around the tiny store, looking at the scant selection of clothes. She managed to find some men's socks in a small enough size to fit her, or almost fit her, and also a pair of moccasins, which she held up with delight. "Look!" she breathed to Wesley. "Look how soft these are!"

Wesley watched as she slipped them onto her feet. "Do they fit?" he asked. Receiving her nod, he said wistfully, "I wish they had some big enough for me! But I've got feet like logs. These boots—I'll never get used to them."

They looked over the supply of footware and indeed could find nothing that would fit Wesley. But he did buy three pairs of the heavy wool socks. "Maybe they'll cushion some," he told Lanie resignedly. "Save me from some blisters."

Meanwhile, Lobo and Lorenzo Dawkins had retired to a corner table after instructing the proprietor to fix them something to eat. As the Indian disappeared into the back room, they began drinking long drafts of the tepid water. "Come on and sit down, Miss Lanie," Dawkins called to her. Lanie sat down at the table and Dawkins grinned. "Take a load off your feet. I reckon we'll stay here tonight—might even find a bed somewheres."

"That would be wonderful," Lanie said, but after looking around, her expression grew doubtful. "But it doesn't look like they have much along that line."

"I don't guess they do," Lobo shrugged. "But at least we can rest up a day while we try to get some kind of word on Perrago." His eye searched the store. "Where did Woman Killer get off to?"

"He has some friends here, I think." Dawkins took another sip of the water and made a face. "Water sure tastes bad here. I'm gonna see if Slim John's got any of that beer he sells when no marshals are around. See if I can convince him that he won't get arrested if he sells me some."

After Dawkins had disappeared into the back room, Lanie poured herself some water from the container and took a sip. She wrinkled her nose and said, "Dawkins's right. Water's bad." She looked at Lobo, aware in a new way of the man across from her. "I thought about what you said last night, Lobo. How you were raised." Her lips softened and she folded her hands in front of her, lacing them together. She noted the broken fingernails and the beginning of calluses from the reins, then raised her eyes to his. "It's been a hard life for you, hasn't it?"

Lobo gave her a searching look. That one eye of his seemed to penetrate her thoughts, its indigo color making it shine even brighter. Lanie had discovered that out of that one eye, he had amazing vision—no depth perception, of course—but with that one eye, he could see as far as she could with a pair of binoculars.

Lobo seemed embarrassed about the reference to what he had told her of his life. Lanie knew that he was not a man to speak freely of himself. Then he smiled at her, which made him look much younger. "I guess I'm getting to be a blabbermouth," he said. "Shouldn't have told you all that." He studied the glass of water in front of him, then met her eyes. "I envy men like Dawkins," he murmured. "And your friend Mr. Stone."

"Envy them? Why?"

"Because they believe in God." He hesitated, then added almost tonelessly, "I'd like to believe in God. But how can I when He lets such bad things happen?"

Lanie was softened by his confession. At first, she had seen only the hardness of the man, the sudden violence that had lurked below the seemingly careless demeanor—and had judged him for it. But this made things different. She thought back to what he must have been like when he was a boy—alone, forsaken, cast off; and she sensed that he had never had any security—nor anyone to love him. Without meaning to she leaned forward and put her hand on his. He looked up, startled. "You've lost someone," she said softly, "and so have I, Lobo. You've lost your mother, and I've lost my sister."

He was tremendously aware of the touch of her soft hand on his and did not move for a moment. He had known women before, but never one like this one; a rough life had put him in contact with rough people. He was aware that there was a quality in her that had been missing from the other women he had known. Shoving the thoughts of her as a woman out of his mind, he drew his hand back, trying to make their touch seem accidental, and answered, "But I can never get my mother back."

Lanie was aware of his discomfort, that he had deliberately withdrawn his hand from her touch, so she changed the subject. "You think we'll find my sister?"

He shook his head. "You never know about things like that." He put his thoughts in order and finally said, "I feel as if I'm searching for something. I can't turn around and go back. I know what's behind me, but I don't know what's ahead. I don't know what it is I'm trying to find."

"You'll find that something," she said.

He listened intently to Lanie's words and understood them, as well as the unspoken words—the words of kindness written on her face. Gradually he relaxed, and reached up to touch his ear in an absentminded gesture. "Not everything is right or wrong. Lots of things are half right and half wrong," he observed. "I've quit judging people. We're all in the same wagon, passing through the same scenery, bound for the same place. But every man has a different set of eyes, and that's the beginning of right and wrong." He looked at her suddenly and said, "I hate to think of it hurting you—your sister being lost."

She sat up straight in the chair, startled at the change in him, and what the change did to her. He had become important to her; what he thought of her mattered to her. At first she had seen him as an adversary, but now he was becoming a true friend. He was saying things that might have come straight from her own private thoughts. Quickly, to cover her own feelings, she said, "We've both lost something. But we can't give up, can we?"

He looked at her with a directness in his gaze. His thoughts were fully on her, warm and embracing. "Nothing comes the way you think it should. And the world is deaf and dumb to some of us. Finally you figure you're just making pictures in water." He hesitated, then added, "That's why I like to be around fellas like Wes Stone and Marshal Dawkins, and even Woman Killer. They've got something I don't have. They believe in something, anyhow."

Very quietly Lanie answered, "You'll find something, Lobo. I know you will."

He looked at her, warmed by her words and charmed by the gentleness that he had not known existed in her until the night before. Shrugging, he said only, "We'll go on. You're praying you'll find your sister, and I hope there's something in it—this prayer business. I'd like to think so anyway."

She would have answered, but at that moment Lorenzo came back with two mugs of beer, set them down, and grunted, "I weaseled these out of Slim John. Promised to throw him in jail if he *didn't* give 'em to me. Now," he ordered Lobo, "let's talk about how we're going to find this man Perrago. I'm gettin' tired of chasin' him around all over the country."

CHAPTER TWELVE

A CHANGE OF MOOD

★ ★ ★ ★

To the surprise of Lanie and Wesley, Lobo did not lead them out on the chase the next day. "Why do you suppose he's giving us a rest?" Stone wondered. "It's not because he has any tender feelings for us, I don't think."

They were sitting in the shade of a small cottonwood tree, seeking relief from the blistering heat of the sun. They had gotten up late, eaten a leisurely breakfast of eggs and bacon, and had been prepared to ride out. But they had discovered that Woman Killer and Lobo had ridden out before dawn. Now, Lanie stared out into the distance where heat devils danced across the desert floor. The land was so flat it was hard to tell where the land met the sky. Absently Lanie commented to Stone, "I don't know . . . They're like hunting dogs. Always on a scent. Have you noticed, Wes, that even when we're riding, their eyes are never still? They're always looking at trees, or a rock, or *something*."

"I suppose that's a result of always being alert for trouble."

"I wish they'd come back!" she snapped with exasperation. "I feel useless, just waiting around here." She bit her lip as she looked toward the barn where they had bedded down the previous night. "Did you see how bad Lorenzo looked? He could hardly eat anything this morning, and then he told me he had to lie down for a while."

Stone sighed deeply. "He doesn't need to be doing this kind of thing—he's too old for it. Besides that, he's sickly. I wish he'd go on back to Fort Smith. But I don't guess he will—he's stubborn, just like Smith."

The two sat talking companionably for a while, mostly about unimportant things. There was a lull in the conversation, and Lanie glanced at Stone and smiled sadly. "I think you ought to go home too, Wes. This isn't really your affair, and you've done more than you needed to already." She considered the idea of telling him that she would never marry him; and the intrusive thought surprised her, for she had considered it seriously at one time. Wesley was not flashy or handsome or rich, yet she had always liked him enormously, and thought that someday her feelings might become deeper. But these last few days together had convinced her that he would never be more than a good friend. She wanted to tell him this as gently as she could, and muttered, "I know you're doing this for me, but—Wes—we—we could never be more than friends."

To her surprise, Stone grinned cheerfully at her. "I know that," he answered. "And maybe I've known it for a long time." He sat cross-legged, holding his bony knees, looking more than ever like a craggy, youthful Abraham Lincoln. The planes of his face were angled and sharp. From the struggles and hardships of the last days, his eyes seemed sunken. Wesley Stone was an honest man with others, and even more so with himself. Actually he had known for some time that his chances with Lanie were slim. With determined lightness he continued. "I guess that's one good thing that's come out of this trip."

Lanie was overcome by surprise; she hadn't anticipated this reaction. "Wh—what do you mean by that?" she asked.

"I mean, I've found out just like you that we're not for each other. Not," he added hastily, "that you ever had any serious idea of marrying me, but you knew how I felt about you. Or thought I felt about you." A puzzled look came over his face. "And it took a thing like this to show me that you and I can be good friends, but never anything more."

Lanie leaned over and patted his hand warmly. "It's true, isn't it? But after all, good friends are worth so much! I don't have all that many of them."

"We never have many good friends," Stone mused thoughtfully. "Lots of acquaintances, but not many really good friends. I wish that—" He broke off suddenly and lifted his head, squinting his eyes, gazing across the desert. "Look! I think that's Smith and Woman Killer coming in!"

They watched the two trails of dust to the north, and eventually Lanie recognized the pair. "Yes, it is! Let's go see what they've been doing." They rose to their feet, but it was twenty minutes before the men rode in, so deceptive was distance in the clear air of the desert country.

Lobo Smith and Woman Killer were layered with dust, and their mouths were parched, so Lanie got them a pitcher of cool water from the spring house and waited until they had drunk their fill before she asked impatiently, "What did you find out?"

"Not a thing," Lobo said in disgust. His lips were cracked with dryness, and he took another deep drink from the long-handled tin cup he held. "Nothing in this world better than water when you're thirsty," he grunted, and handed the cup back to Lanie. "Wild goose chase. We'll have to try something else."

Woman Killer said, "I go to my people. Might know of Perrago." His smooth copper skin did not appear to have been affected by the blistering sun; he seemed to not even notice the stifling heat. Turning, he gathered the tired horses and walked toward the stable, the animals barely able to lift one hoof in front of the other.

"Those horses are almost used up," Stone remarked. "Think I'll go help Woman Killer give them a good rubdown and some feed."

He hurried off, leaving Lobo and Lanie alone. "The heat is terrible," Lanie said. "Let's go inside. I'll get Slim John to fix you something to eat."

"In a minute. I just want to stand on my own two feet for a while." Lobo stretched his legs, did two or three deep-knee bends, then swung his arms around, loosening the muscles in his shoulders. Looking out across the desert, his single eye almost shut against the brilliant sunlight, he said in a low voice, "He's out there somewhere. But this is a big place, Lanie." His thoughts obviously troubled him. "I'm going to take a little walk, get my legs loosened up. Then I'll be back to get something to eat." He turned and glanced back at her. "Come on. I'll show you what I found the other day."

"All right." Lanie, anxious to break the monotony of the morning, found herself relishing the invitation. She walked beside him through the scrub sagebrush, broken here and there by a spindly cottonwood struggling to make it in the drought-stricken land. Studying one small, malformed specimen, she broke the silence. "You know, it's amazing how worthless this land is, isn't it? Yet men fight over it."

"Men will fight over almost anything, I guess," Lobo replied. Silently he led her down a beaten path, and then they passed cottonwoods somewhat taller and stronger than those around the settlement. "Look," Lobo said, pointing.

Across a small field, Lanie saw an area with about ten or twelve graves. "A cemetery? Here?"

"Burial place for those who didn't make it." They walked over and Lobo stooped and stared at a board that rose up out of the dusty ground. He read the crudely carved letters slowly. "Fella's name was Jedediah Ransom. Died twelve years ago." The name seemed to hold some fascination for him and he said in a low tone, as if to himself, "His mother was proud of him when he was a baby. He grew up having all kinds of hopes and dreams, just like the rest of us. He probably had a woman who cared for him, loved him, hoped he'd always be there for her. Maybe a son or a daughter . . ." Silently, he reached out and traced the rough lettering with his forefinger. "Here he lies," he murmured, "and I wonder what it all means to Jedediah Ransom now."

Lanie could sense a curious streak of mysticism in this hard-looking man. She didn't know what to say, although she herself had had such thoughts. Gazing around the little cemetery now, the same thoughts and questions rose within her. "Why, I've thought about things like that," she said to Lobo, her eyes traveling over the roughhewn markers dotting the hidden field. "They had their lives, just like we have ours. They left footprints on the earth, their hands worked hard to make a living. And now . . ." She looked down at a grave next to the one where Lobo still knelt. "Somewhere, someone still remembers the touch of these people. But I guess we'll never know about that."

She stood motionless, thinking of these things. Then, in a

gesture of rebellion, she began to draw her moccasin along the fading edge of the grave to sharpen its outline, and thus postpone its inevitable oblivion. Lobo stood and backed off a step, watching her wordlessly. When she had made the complete rectangle, Lanie looked up at him; he was staring at her, studying her. Laughing in embarrassment, she shrugged and said in a light tone, "I guess there's something in all of us that makes us want to live longer than we do, isn't there, Lobo?"

"Some people feel like that."

"No. All people do. Some just don't talk about it."

"You may be right," he admitted. "Some of the toughest men I've ever known were superstitious and afraid of what waits for them on the other side of death. They took life easy enough, but when it came their turn, they went out into the darkness like little kids—afraid."

The two stood close together, looking down at the grave of Jedediah Ransom. Something else was on his mind, Lanie felt, so she waited quietly. Finally he said, "I've been wanting to talk to you about Betsy."

Instantly she turned to him, hearing the somber tone of his voice. A note of fear sounded in her voice. "What? What is it? What do you want to tell me?"

Lobo had sensed the dread in Lanie, fearing that her sister was dead, that she was beyond help; and he saw that fear in her now. "I don't think you're going to be happy, Lanie," he answered her reluctantly. "Even if we find her." There was the faintest hint of tension in his body and voice; he didn't know how to say what he knew he must. Lobo felt awkward; her gaze unnerved him and he shifted nervously. "I think we'll find her, all right. But you come from a family that's uh—well off. And your parents, you tell me, are religious people. Well . . ." He searched futilely for words.

"What is it?" she prompted him. "What do you want to tell me, Lobo? Just say it!"

"All right. I know Perrago. He's used your sister, like he uses all women. That's what he does. He never loved a woman in his life. To him, they're something to be used and then thrown aside. And he'll throw her aside, too, as soon as he gets tired of her."

For a long time thoughts like this had threaded darkly

through Lanie's mind. But she shook her head and said defiantly, "I don't care. I don't care what's happened, or what she's done. Betsy's my sister! And my parents feel the same way. No matter what she's gone through, we still love her."

"You may love her," Lobo said, his eye narrowing, "but what about the way she feels? Do you think she can just walk away from this?" His voice grew full of warning. "When these things happen they leave scars!"

"You're wrong!" Lanie thrust her hand in front of him, her voice growing loud. "See that scar?" He saw a tiny white scar tracing between the thumb and forefinger of her left hand. "I almost cut that finger off, and it bled, and it hurt, and I cried. Even after it was bandaged it hurt for weeks, and was sensitive for months, even years! But look at it now. Touch it." Tentatively he held his hand out and she took it, putting his fingers against the scar. "See? It doesn't even hurt. I know it's there—I know something happened that day—but the pain is not there anymore. Just the memory. And that's what it will be when we get Betsy back. We'll take her home, and take care of her, and love her, and she'll be all right."

Lobo's gaze was full of wonder. "You always think the best, don't you, Lanie? Well, I'm glad you do, and I hope you always do." He seemed to be affected by the conversation and abruptly turned from her, saying, "Let's go talk to Lorenzo. We've got to do something besides wander around this desert."

Late that afternoon, after having disappeared, Woman Killer came around the corner of the General Store with a gleam in his eyes. He immediately walked to Lobo, who was sitting on the front step, staring out across the desert. "I find them."

Lobo looked up and exclaimed, "Perrago?"

"Uh. My cousin. He comes from the north, Cherokee Nation. He married Cherokee girl. Says he saw Perrago three days ago, close to Grand River."

"Let's go tell the others," Lobo said.

Quickly they called a council of war. They all gathered together and heard what Woman Killer had to say. When he finished, Lobo exclaimed, "Why, I know where that is! I'd forgotten about it! Perrago don't use it much. But sometimes he goes out and robs a train, then ducks back there. Handy place to hide—

and hard to get at. They can see for miles in every direction. If too big a bunch comes after 'em, they can split up and fade into the hills, then come back together somewhere else."

"What do you think, Lobo?" Lanie asked eagerly. "Think we might go after them?"

"Yeah. We'll travel tonight, be much cooler that way."

Dawkins' eyes were bright, and he looked much better than he had when they had first arrived at Otumka. "C'mon, let's get goin'. And let's be sure we take enough grub this time! We'll load those mules of ours good. I ain't intendin' to go hungry while I'm chasin' around after that bunch!"

They pulled out shortly before dark, just as the air began to cool, and traveled most of that night. They made camp just before dawn, the horses beginning to tire. They rested there all the morning, then started out again after eating at noon, and traveled hard for the next three days, making quick camps and taking short rests.

Lobo was pleased to see that Lanie and Stone stood the hardship of the journey better than before. "I believe they're gonna make it," he remarked to Lorenzo Dawkins as the two trailed them. "They're doing better than I thought they would."

"Guess so," Lorenzo nodded. He took off his hat; a slight breeze lifted his fine white hair. He was tired again and looked more frail than ever, but he was a tough man and rode without complaint. "I wish they weren't here," he said, his voice troubled. "Ain't no place for a woman like that. Or him either, for that matter. They could both get killed. You thought of that?"

"Yeah, I've thought of it. But I don't know what to do about it. That woman's got more determination than a hungry mule!"

The marshal laughed. "You sure got a way with words! Comparin' a young lady like that to a mule!"

Lobo turned slightly in the saddle to search Dawkins' face. "What do you think of her? Lanie, I mean?"

"Good-looking woman. Stubborn, though," Lorenzo replied.

"Always liked a woman with grit in her," Lobo remarked, laughing.

They rode hard all that day, and the next day Lobo sent Woman Killer ahead to scout. The Indian left at three o'clock while the others made camp.

Darkness fell as they were finishing their evening meal, and Lobo lifted his head. "Somebody coming," he said in a low voice, rising to his feet. Picking up his Winchester, he moved over to a large rock, listening carefully. The others didn't hear a sound, but after a moment he lowered the rifle and said, "Woman Killer."

The Indian rode in, excitement lighting his smooth face. "Found 'em!"

"You saw him? Perrago?" Lobo asked.

"No. Perrago not there. But the black-haired woman is there—and Mateo."

"It's them, then," Lobo said tonelessly.

Lanie was watching Lobo as he spoke and noticed that his face changed at the mention of the woman. "A woman?" Lanie asked curiously.

"Yes," Woman Killer nodded. "Name is Angela."

"Angela Montoya," Lobo added. "It's them, for sure."

"Only two men and two women," Woman Killer told them.

"You saw another woman? Did you—could you see her?" Lanie asked anxiously.

"Yes. Small woman with red hair."

"It's Betsy!" Lanie cried. "We've found them!"

Dawkins was excited. "Found 'em at the right time, too! If there's only two men there, the rest of 'em must be out on some kind of a raid. What do you think, Lobo?"

"Sounds good," Lobo agreed. "We'll take 'em in the morning. Or maybe tonight would be better, catch 'em off guard," he added thoughtfully.

"I'd say morning," Dawkins argued. "You get to shootin' in the dark, no tellin' who could get hurt. Tomorrow we can get there, surround that cabin at daylight. Soon as the men come out, I'll take one and you take the other. With only two, we can kill them first thing and they won't be causin' us no trouble."

His words sent an icy chill through Lanie. Wesley Stone's jaw dropped. "K-kill them? Without warning?" he stuttered.

Dawkins stared at him in surprise. "Why, you didn't think we'd get that little lady back without shootin', did you?"

"Well, uh, no, I guess I didn't," Stone stumbled, "but we need to give some warning, don't we? Give them a fair chance?"

"You're thinking like a man that works in an office," Dawkins said grimly, and spat on the ground. "Don't you understand? We let 'em know we're there, one of 'em grabs her, puts a pistol to her head and threatens to kill her if we don't leave. And they'd do it, too, any one of 'em. They don't think any more of takin' a human life than you'd think of takin' a drink of water!" He took a deep breath and spoke in a gentler tone, "I know it sounds rough to you two. But out here it's different. These men—you just have to treat 'em like wild animals. If you want your sister back, Miss Lanie, that'll be the best way."

Lanie was troubled, and she exchanged distraught glances with Wesley Stone. The two of them knew they were out of their element, but Lanie could not quite bring herself to face what Dawkins and Lobo were planning. "Maybe we can think of another way," she said quickly. "Let's wait until the morning."

That ended the conversation. The group gathered around the fire as Woman Killer ate his late meal. Lobo took guard duty; Woman Killer would take the next watch, followed by Lorenzo Dawkins. The old man seemed to be strengthened and invigorated by the thought of action.

But that night, as everyone else lay asleep, Lanie stared blindly into the darkness, troubled in spirit. Finally she got up and looked around at the still forms lying on the ground. The fire cast a feeble glow in the immense darkness of the open country. Moving off about thirty yards from the fire, she stood gazing at the moon and the stars. It was a brightly lit night and she could see the shadows of the hills over to her right. For a long time she stood motionless, thinking about what was to come.

To her left, Lanie heard the sound of a twig snapping, and she whirled quickly. At the same time Lobo's voice came softly, "Lanie?" He had been walking around the camp, as was his custom, and she released a sigh of relief. He came closer, the silvery moonlight washing over his face. He had put aside his hat, and his hair looked crisp and curly as he moved closer to her. "You all right?" he asked.

Lanie answered, "I'm worried about tomorrow."

"I knew you would be. But Dawkins is right. The important thing is to get Betsy out of there. And if you give those men one chance, they'll kill her, Lanie."

There was a heavy stillness in the air as Lanie stared into his face, wanting comfort. In the bright moonlight he looked younger; Lanie noticed distractedly how his neck joined into his smoothly muscled shoulders. He was strong, and she found that strength comforting, and yet it was that strength that would kill, she knew.

"I—I just can't think straight," she whispered. "It goes against everything I've ever thought of."

"I know." He stood silently, his face impassive. Lanie was very beautiful as she stood close to him, and the vulnerability of her spirit was reflected in the troubled lines of her face. Her eyes seemed enormous and they glistened in the ghostly light of the moon. She was trembling, he saw, and he muttered, "I wish you didn't have to go through this."

She stepped closer to him. She felt lonely and alienated out in this vast, wild desert. It was a place of death and mercilessness; she had known it from the first, and now she felt it pressing down on her. Lanie had never been faced with a decision such as this, and she knew instinctively that she could choose what to do. If she said to go ahead, they would kill the two men. But she could stop them with a word. The pressure of it had been building up inside her, and her knees felt strangely weak. The thought of bloodshed at her own hand made her feel almost sick. "I—I just don't know—what to do," she whispered tremulously. Unconsciously she reached out and touched his arm, as if to gather strength from him.

Lobo was starkly aware of her closeness and of the aura of femininity that seemed to emanate from her. Lanie was a woman—shapely, beautiful, full of vigor—and her nearness made him desire her in a way he'd never wanted a woman before. He looked down at her lips, full and inviting, then raised his eyes to meet hers. He could see the weariness etched on her face, in her eyes.

Lanie caught the expression of concern and it moved her. He was so strong and protecting—and suddenly desire swept over her.

He put his hands at her hips and pulled her upright against him and kissed her full on the lips. His mouth bore down hard and heavy on hers, and he could feel her wishes joining his. Her response touched the deepest chord of his heart, and at that moment he thought he had never known such exhilaration.

As for Lanie, she knew that a barrier had fallen, a barrier that could never be entirely restored. She suddenly realized with shock that she and Lobo were on the edge of the mystery that every other man and woman faced—neither of them knowing what good or tragedy would come of it.

And then, she drew back and said breathlessly, "I don't know why I let you do that." Her voice was distraught; she was unnerved at her own strong reactions. Instantly she drew a tight rein around her emotions and she said resolutely, "That must never happen again."

"It probably will," Lobo said calmly. But he knew that the moment had passed and that Lanie was flustered. Finally, he said, "You've got to decide, Lanie. What will we do?"

The time of decision had come. Taking a deep breath, Lanie fought to stop the thoughts that flew aimlessly inside her head. She would never be able to make a clear, unfettered decision, knowing that whatever she decided, she would have regrets about later. But uppermost in her mind was *Betsy*.

"All right," she said. "Do what you have to do. I want my sister back."

CHAPTER THIRTEEN

THE BEST-LAID PLANS

★ ★ ★ ★

Dawn had not yet come, but a thin, milky line of light had begun to appear in the east. The face of Lorenzo Dawkins was hidden under the shadow of the brim of his hat so that Lanie could only see his lips as he spoke. "I know you two don't wanna shoot nobody, but we've gotta do whatever we can to make this work. Even if you can't hit nothin', you can let off a few rounds and make 'em think we're an army."

As the small group bunched around the marshal, they could feel the warm breeze of the coming morning. And yet, despite the warmth, both Lanie Winslow and Wesley Stone were chilled. Neither of them had slept that night, and one time Wesley had said to her, "Lanie, I don't think you ought to do this. You'll think about it the rest of your life." She had shaken him off, but now, with the action upon her, she began to wonder if he had not been right.

As if discerning her thoughts, Dawkins gave her a penetrating look. "Missie, you sure you wanna go on with this? We can back off right now. Or, we can take you back, and me and Lobo can try to get at it another way."

But Lanie knew that the "other way" would still involve shooting and killing. She was convinced from what she had heard of Vic Perrago that he would never give up Betsy without a fight. So she answered briefly, "No. I want Betsy back now."

"All right then," Dawkins said, and his voice grew hard as granite. "We're gonna surround the house. Missie, you and Mr. Stone, take these here guns. If anything happens, fire off as fast as you can in the air. We're gonna make 'em think they're outnumbered."

"I don't want to have anything to do with it," Wesley Stone said stubbornly. In the light breaking upon the landscape, he looked older and very scared. "I just don't think I could kill another person."

"You won't be doing any killing," Lobo shrugged. "Just pull that trigger. We won't have any trouble with just two of 'em down there."

"That's right," Dawkins agreed. "If anything happens and you see we're in trouble, just shoot up in the air, like I tell you. Now, they'll be comin' out pretty soon. So, Lobo, let's mosey on down and take up a position behind them rocks. Soon as the two men come out, we'll pop 'em and this'll all be over. You think we need to worry about Montoya?"

"Angela's an old friend. I think we can leave her alone. What if the men come out one at a time?" Lobo asked, eyes roving over the layout.

Dawkins shook his head. "No good. Only chance we've got is to get both of 'em away from the girl. Best thing is gonna be to get 'em both at once. They'll have to come out together sooner or later."

"Well, everybody keep still and quiet then 'til that happens," Lobo ordered.

The plan seemed simple enough, and they headed out toward the cabin. When they arrived, the two noncombatants were positioned carefully by Lobo and Dawkins. Then Woman Killer, Lobo, and Lorenzo moved down closer to the cabin.

At first light a lantern came on, clearly shining through the single window in the front of the house. Half an hour later, a young man, with black curly hair stepped outside. He walked to the well, let the bucket rattle down, drew it up full of water, then went back inside. The individual members of the group waited impatiently, but nothing happened for the next hour. Finally a Mexican man came out, sat down on the porch, and began rolling a cigarette. Lanie could see him plainly from her position behind a bunch of scrub oak. He had to be Mateo Río, a bloodthirsty killer, from what Marshal Dawkins had told her.

Time crawled on. Río did nothing but smoke and stare out across the desert. Suddenly, Lanie's heart leaped; the door of the cabin opened and Betsy came out. Even at that distance Lanie could recognize her, and she almost cried out to her. Betsy walked around the house to a small shed, entered it, came out shortly holding something, then reentered the house.

Time seemed to stop. For fully an hour longer, Mateo Río sat on the front porch smoking and staring out across the desert. Finally he rose, stretched his legs, then went to the well and got a drink of water. Lanie watched the door, hoping that the other man would come out, and yet dreading it at the same time. But he did not come out; instead, a woman came through it—the woman that was called Angela Montoya. Curious, Lanie stared at her; she had seen the strange expression in Lobo Smith's eye as he spoke of this woman. She was, Lanie saw, very attractive, with black hair and a shapely figure. She went to the barn and came out ten minutes later, mounted on a beautiful black mare. Calling out something to Mateo, she spurred the horse and rode off to the west. *I'm glad she's out of the way, at least*, Lanie thought. *Surely the other man will come out soon!*

All morning long they waited, the hours dragging by eternally, it seemed. As fortune would have it, the two men never appeared at the same time. The younger man with the black curly hair mostly stayed in the house. At noon Río went inside and the younger man then came out, mounted a horse, and rode off in the direction that the woman had taken earlier. As soon as he disappeared, Lobo left his position and crawled over to where Dawkins was hidden behind a huge outcropping of rock that broke the floor of the desert.

"What do you think, Lorenzo?" Lobo hissed. "Only one in there now."

"If he comes out, we nail him. That's all there is to it," Lorenzo answered in a hoarse whisper. "We try to rush him, sneak up on him, it might tip our hand. And he'd have the girl."

"Where do you suppose those two went?" Lobo asked, shading his eyes to look off to the west.

"I don't know, but I hope they stay gone. That bird's got to come out sooner or later."

The pressure was mounting; the lack of action was crawling on Smith's nerves. "I never could stand waiting," he grunted to Dawkins. "Once I'm in a fight, it's different. But the waiting—that's what gets me."

"Always that way, I reckon," Dawkins replied calmly. "I remember once, before that charge at Gettysburg—that last one—I was nervous as a June bride." Memories washed over the old man as he reflected on those days of loss. "All of us knew we was in trouble, and that most of us wouldn't make it up that there hill. But once it started—it was all different."

"Yeah, I felt that way myself a time or two," Lobo said absently. He was trying to think of a plan, but discarded each as quickly as he formed them. The cabin sat up on a steep shelf that rose at least twenty feet above the barren desert floor. It would be impossible to sneak up on it; there was no cover whatsoever. Lobo stared at the door, willing the man to come out. "You know that fella? The one with the black hair?" he asked the marshal.

"Sure. Bob Pratt. He done a year in the pen for cattle rustling. Didn't know he'd hooked up with Perrago," Lorenzo answered. "Pretty hard one, though, 'specially for one so young."

"That's the only kind Perrago wants."

"Reckon that's true."

Dawkins and Lobo stared at the small cabin, studying it with intense concentration. After a few moments Lorenzo Dawkins shifted uneasily and said, "Somethin' don't feel right to me. I got a Injun arrowhead stuck in my back they never could dig out, right next to my backbone. Always hurts just 'fore it rains, or 'fore trouble comes."

"Hurtin' a bit now, Lorenzo?" Lobo grinned.

"Little bit." The older man yanked on the brim of his hat and smiled faintly. Then he sobered and said, "I don't like this, Lobo. I wish we coulda come in, taken 'em nice and simple, and gotten it over with."

Lobo's mouth tightened. "Maybe when Pratt and Angela ride back in, Río'll come out. Then we can get 'em with one blast."

Dawkins sighed with exasperation. "I hope so. Longer this runs on, worse it gets."

Back where he was hidden, behind some small cottonwoods

in an old creek bed, Wesley waited uneasily. He looked down at his torn and worn clothing, the scuffed boots, thought of the blisters on his feet, his sunburned hands, and wondered, *What in the world am I doing here? I wouldn't be any good in a fight.* But he knew that something in him demanded that he stay, so he put leaving out of his mind.

Wesley had thought a great deal about Betsy Winslow during the last few days; he had even had dreams about her. He wasn't prone to dreams, so this had struck him as very unusual. And he had thought much of the times he had spent with Betsy—when he had been put off by Lanie. He remembered Betsy's humor and her quick wit, which always seemed to bubble out in his company. The thought surprised him; he had been so focused on Lanie that he had overlooked her vivacious sister who lavished him with attention. The thought of harm coming to Betsy ran a sharp stab of pain through him. *What would I do if she doesn't come out of this okay?* he thought anxiously. *So much harm has already been done. . . .* He knew Betsy was a sensitive girl, and if she had been abused by Perrago, Stone was sure that it would devastate her. He fingered the Winchester that Lobo had handed him, wondering if he really could use it on a man if he had to.

The afternoon wore on sluggishly. At about three o'clock a thin column of dust rose to Lobo's left. Cautiously he called out to Dawkins, who was still in his hiding place about forty feet away. "Looks like they're coming back," he said almost inaudibly. "Montoya and Pratt."

"Likely Río'll come out and meet 'em," Dawkins warned. "If he does, I'll take the Mexican. You take Pratt."

"All right."

But Río did not emerge from the house, nor did Betsy. The two horses galloped up to the front of the cabin, and the riders dismounted and hitched their horses there. No movement or call came from the house, and Angela Montoya and Bob Pratt went inside.

Lobo blew out a frustrated sigh, then sat back on the ground, resting his rifle on a rock. After a while he called softly to Dawkins, "We need some water. I'll go fetch the canteens. Won't take long."

"No, I'll go," Dawkins countered. "We need to talk to everybody. If this thing don't come off before dark, we'll have to give it a try again in the mornin'." Lorenzo edged back out of view of the cabin and straightened up stiffly, then made the rounds. Finally he had drawn the whole bunch together and told them, "Well, I don't think it's gonna do any good for you all to be staked out. Me and Lobo can watch the house good as anyone. Give me that big canteen, Woman Killer, and the rest of you pull back and rest. I don't think anything's gonna happen before mornin'." He took the canteen, and despite protests from Lanie that they might be able to help, he insisted the three pull back. "No, Missie, go on. Me and Lobo can handle it. Woman Killer, you keep a watch over these two," Lorenzo said stubbornly. "We may stay out all night and give it another go in the mornin'."

Dawkins went back to Lobo and the two filled up on the tepid water, which tasted delicious to both of them. "What do you think?" Lobo asked with obvious impatience. "We can't hang around here all night! That bunch could come in any time!"

"You're right," Dawkins nodded. "So here's what we'll do. Soon as it gets good and dark, I'll sneak down front, and you go around to the back. You peep in the window, and if you can see the two men, break the glass and let 'em have it. I'll rush the front door when I hear your shot. Risky," he shrugged, "but so's hangin' around like this."

Lobo didn't like it. "No. I don't think it'll work, Lorenzo," he argued. "I don't know about Pratt, but Río's quick as a cat. First sound he hears, he'll be pulling his iron and blastin' away. That girl could get killed easy."

Dawkins was silent for a while. Finally he said, "Well, let's try to get closer, anyway. Maybe them two will come out on the porch to get some cool air. They gotta come out together sooner or later."

They waited until darkness fell and the lantern glowed through the cabin window. As they crept closer, they could smell meat cooking. "Look, Lorenzo," Lobo said, "you stay here. I'm gonna go around and try to catch a look at the layout of that cabin. But if it looks bad, we'll pull back and wait for morning, right? I don't think we ought to bust in, too much danger to Betsy."

"You may be right, son," Dawkins agreed reluctantly. "All

right. I'll wait here while you go take a look. If you get a good shot, take it. If not, come on back."

Lobo nodded and slipped away into the darkness. He took a roundabout way, staying well clear of the cabin, knowing that even in the fading light the sharp-eyed Río might be able to spot him. Finally he found a vantage point behind the cabin where he could see one small window with a yellow light beaming out into the night. He moved carefully across the ground until he reached the side of the house, then silently flattened himself against it. He could hear muted voices inside. Holding his breath, he removed his hat and slowly crept so that his head was below the window.

Looking inside, he caught a glimpse of the girl he had been seeking. She was standing before an ancient iron cookstove, frying meat. Across the room, at the table, Mateo Río and Bob Pratt sat playing cards. He did not see the woman and assumed that she was down the hallway, in one of the bedrooms. Deliberately he drew his gun and held it in his left hand.

Lobo had no false modesty; he was a swift, sure shot and he knew it. But in order to get the shots off, he would have to break the glass in the window, and he well knew that every second mattered if he were to be successful. He knew also that if he missed, one of the two men might easily shoot the girl. Tense and silent, he stood in the darkness, weighing the risks.

Finally Lobo decided that it was not his risk to take. He slowly sheathed the gun and stepped back from the window. All of a sudden, the sound of gunfire screamed through the night, somewhere in the front of the house. Instinctively he leaped to one side, clearing the window, and dashed around the corner of the house. When he reached the front he saw the winking spots of fire that revealed several men shooting. It was almost pitch dark, but he could see that they were firing at the spot where he had left Lorenzo Dawkins.

They're back! The thought hammered Lobo's brain.

The two men inside the cabin burst out the door. Lifting his gun, Lobo pulled off one shot and missed. Mateo Río shouted, "Over to the side, Bob! They're over there! Take 'em!"

Lobo ran forward, holding his gun ready, and Río and Pratt opened fire on him. He heard the lead whistling through the air all around him and tossing up dust almost at his feet. He laid a heavy fire on the two men, but knew that he was missing them; he was shooting blindly at the flashes of their revolvers. Their fire returned even heavier. He loosed one final shot, then ducked and ran across the desert toward where he had left his friend.

As he neared their hiding place he yelled, "It's me! Lobo! Don't shoot!"

Instantly Woman Killer, who had joined them after seeing Perrago's gang ride in, was at his side. "No good, no good! We leave now!"

"Good idea," Lobo gasped. "C'mon, Lorenzo, let's move!"

Lobo couldn't see the marshal, but the older man's hoarse voice sounded out, "I'm coming!" Then Lobo realized Dawkins was busy returning the fire of the group across the ravine. The sound of gunfire continued to split the night air.

"This is hot work," Lobo grunted. "We've gotta lead that bunch outta here, away from everyone. C'mon, Lorenzo! We'll fade over to those rocks over there. They won't charge us there."

"Right! I'm—" Suddenly Lorenzo's voice broke off and Lobo's heart sank.

"I think they got Lorenzo!" he muttered to Woman Killer. "You wait here." He dodged through the darkness, feeling his way through the brush; a low cloud cover obscured the moon and stars. He found Lorenzo Dawkins lying in a heap, and gently rolled him over. "Are you hit bad?" Lobo asked, trying desperately to see where the old man was bleeding.

"Don't—know. Somewhere—low down," the old man gasped.

Lobo knew he couldn't help him there, crouched down in the darkness and surrounded by flying lead. He picked up the old man and slung him over his shoulder, grunting, "This is gonna hurt, Lorenzo, but I've gotta get you outta here." Dawkins didn't answer.

Despite the heavy weight he carried, Lobo moved swiftly back toward Woman Killer. "Don't shoot," he warned when he got close. "They'll know where we are if they see the muzzle flashes. C'mon, let's get back to the others."

The two men moved cautiously, their moccasined feet silent, but shortly Lobo began to gasp from the effort of carrying Dawkins. Woman Killer took the slight form without a word and Lobo drifted slightly behind. He could hear their pursuers getting closer. *Got to slow them down,* he thought.

He stopped and waited until he could see the vague outlines of the men; then he let off a round into them. Instantly he heard a shout of pain and someone yelled, "This way! C'mon, we got 'em, Vic!"

Perrago's voice ordered, "Spread out! Now! Surround them!"

Lobo grimly lifted the rifle and began to lay down a heavy fire, but knowing that he was being quickly cut off, he retreated. He caught up with Woman Killer and said, "I'm worried about the others! They're liable to blunder right into the middle of Perrago's bunch! We've got to cut 'em off!"

The men made their way through the blackness, stumbling, falling, scrambling to their feet and running, until the sound of yelling and crashing was behind them. Then they heard a shaky voice call out, "Who's there?" It was Wesley.

Lobo said, "It's us, Stone! Don't shoot!" He and Woman Killer came staggering into the camp, where Lanie and Wesley were waiting.

"Oh no! What happened?" Lanie cried. Woman Killer laid the still form of Marshal Dawkins down and knelt by the small man.

"Perrago," Lobo spat out. "Came back and surprised us. Dawkins got hit. C'mon, we've gotta get out of here, get Lorenzo to Fort Smith, to a doctor." He looked back, motioning for silence, then turned back to the group. "You and me'll have to stay here and hold 'em off, Woman Killer. Stone, you and Lanie take the marshal. Lanie—go. Now."

Lobo and Woman Killer instantly picked up Dawkins, who was still unconscious but groaning faintly, and laid him on the back of his horse, securing him with a rope from the saddlebag. "I'm staying," Lanie said, but was seized roughly by Lobo and shoved forward.

"You get going with them," Lobo growled, "and we'll take care of this end."

Perrago and his men were closing in fast. Lobo loaded his rifle and Woman Killer did the same. "We'll hold 'em off for a while," Lobo told him, "and give Stone and Lanie time to get a clean start. Then we'll make a break for it."

"Too many," Woman Killer said impassively.

"I know," Lobo said, "but all we have to do is hold 'em for a little while."

Five minutes later the fight began in earnest. Perrago was a good general; he had sent his men around in a semicircle so that Woman Killer and Lobo were caught in a crossfire and were slowly forced backward. As they retreated, Lobo's mind raced desperately, trying to think of a way to throw them off. He heard a sound directly behind him and almost shot it, but then a voice whispered.

"It's me—Stone. We couldn't leave just yet." The tall form of Wesley Stone materialized, Winchester cradled awkwardly in his arms. "I'm not much of a shot," he said ruefully, "but I'll do the best I can."

Smith thought with fleeting amusement that Stone sounded as if he was apologizing for some breach of courtesy at a tea party, and a feeling of warmth swept over him for the young man. Lobo knew that Wesley Stone had never been in a situation like this before and that it took more courage for him to come than for a native westerner.

He told Stone, "Don't shoot until you see a rifle flash; then just shoot in the general direction. You'll hit something."

That was the way it went. They backed up until the sounds of pursuit seemed to fade; but even as they did, Lobo heard Stone grunt and he jerked around to see Stone's tall gangly figure slowly slump to the ground. Lobo cursed under his breath and called hoarsely, "Are you hit, Stone?"

"Uh—think so—but it's not bad."

Lobo moved cautiously but quickly to him, scanned the landscape carefully, then knelt down. "Where? Where is it?"

"Here, in the arm."

Lobo could see nothing in the murky darkness, and he hoped it hadn't hit the bone in Stone's arm. "Get back," Lobo urged him quietly. "Just leave the rifle. Go back to Lanie and you both just take off. Me and Woman Killer can track you in the morning. Get as far as you can, as fast as you can. Got that?"

"Yes," Stone gasped and scrambled to his feet. Lobo rose with him, his hand running lightly over Stone's limp right arm.

"Here," he said, yanking the bandanna from around his neck, "I'm gonna tie this around your arm, up here. This'll keep it from bleedin' so bad." In the blackness, lit only by spasmodic fire from scattered guns, Lobo bound up Stone's arm. "Doesn't seem to be too bad," he assured him, squinting closely at the arm, "just a flesh wound. Now, get on back as quick as you can."

"All right, Lobo."

Stone disappeared and, with grim determination, Lobo said to Woman Killer, "We've gotta cover for 'em, Woman Killer. Let's move in."

Woman Killer nodded; Lobo couldn't see him but he felt the Indian's assent, and the two men stopped retreating and stood still, listening. Then they started forward like dark ghosts, flitting soundlessly from rock to rock, until finally both of them faced a shadow in the darkness. A man appeared in front of Lobo; a huge form hulking before him, and he recognized Honey Ward, a giant of a man. Ward fired in Lobo's direction, and instantly Lobo drove a shot toward the looming form. It struck dead center. Ward screamed a wild cry that was cut off abruptly, threw his hands toward the sky, and was driven backward to the ground.

At the same time, Lobo heard someone else call out, "I'm hit! I'm hit, Vic!" Woman Killer had found a victim.

Lobo began to methodically lay a volley in the direction of the men as they approached him—more cautiously now—and finally was rewarded for his coolness when he heard a panicked voice call out, "We've gotta get out of this! Too many of them! They got Honey!"

"Pull back, then!" Vic's harsh voice called, strain and disappointment obvious in the curt order.

It was the moment Lobo had been waiting for, and he made his way back, knowing that Woman Killer would hear Perrago's retreat. As soon as Woman Killer appeared beside him, Lobo muttered, "Let's get on back to the others. They're not coming any farther tonight." The two men ran lightly across the broken, dusty ground and found Lanie and Wesley with the wounded marshal securely tied on the back of his horse, Lanie leading the way.

"Let's go, as fast and far as we can," Lobo ordered calmly.

"They'll be after us as soon as it's light enough to track us. But we can be clear by then. Woman Killer, now that we've found 'em, I hate to lose these rascals. There's no way Vic'll stay here now that he's been found out—I need you to track 'em until they settle on a new hideout. Then you can meet us in Fort Smith."

"Yes. I go. Back soon." The Indian nudged his horse's flanks and forged ahead into the night, ready to follow Perrago and his gang.

CHAPTER FOURTEEN

DEATH IN THE DESERT

★ ★ ★ ★

"We've got to get back to Fort Smith," Lanie said desperately.

She had drawn Lobo aside from where Marshal Lorenzo Dawkins was lying flat on the blanket they had thrown down beside the small fire. The sun was now high in the sky, and the horses had been pretty winded by the inexorable pace all last night and half the day.

They had reached a small creek and decided it would be best to rest the wounded men and the horses before going on. All of them were dead tired. Lanie's face was drawn and pale as she glanced back at Dawkins and Wesley. "How far is it?" she asked Lobo worriedly. "How long is it going to take?"

Lobo shook his head. "Best part of two days," he answered, "at least, riding slow enough to keep from shaking 'em to death. We need to make a travois so Lorenzo can at least lay down instead of bouncing along on the back of that horse." He looked around the barren landscape and the one indigo eye narrowed. "But you're right, we sure can't stay out here."

"Do you think Lorenzo will be all right?" Lanie's eyes were large, pleading.

An apprehensive look crossed Lobo's face, and he chewed his lip nervously, not meeting her gaze. "I don't know, Lanie. He wasn't too strong to begin with, and that bullet's hit something around his lower back. Last time he woke up, he said he didn't feel any pain." Lobo sighed softly, "Bad sign. . . ."

They stood talking quietly, trying not to let the others over-hear their anxious words. Lobo finally made a decision. "All right. We'll rest here until it cools off. We've got plenty of food, but no grain for the horses. I'll take 'em out, find some graze, and then rub 'em down and let 'em rest tonight. We can make it in two days, I think."

Lanie was worried. "Wesley's arm looks bad, too, Lobo. I've heard of gangrene coming from things like that."

"Yeah, I've seen it happen," Lobo admitted, "but we got it cleaned out pretty good. If we keep puttin' fresh bandages on it and keep him quiet, I think he'll be all right. I'd rather he saw a doctor, though," he went on almost to himself. His eye searched the rising hills they had struggled over the night before, and thought of what they had left behind. He looked back at Lanie and said shortly, "Sorry we didn't get your sister. I made a bad play."

Lanie sighed deeply and shook her head. "No, Lobo, it wasn't your fault." She lifted her eyes to his questioningly, "By the way, what *is* your name? It can't be 'Lobo.' Makes you sound like the big bad wolf."

Despite the strain and weariness that had engulfed him, Smith grinned suddenly. "I'll tell that only to one person, Lanie."

"One person? Who?"

"When I stand in front of a preacher and say 'I, Something Smith, take thee to be my lawful wedded wife . . .' That's the one time I'll let my name slip," he teased.

Lanie's full lips curved upward, soft and gentle. She was so tired and scared of what lay ahead, but suddenly her heart light-ened and new strength seemed to surge through her. "Let's go back to the others," she said softly. "And please quit beating yourself up. You did the best you could, Lobo. No one could have known that Perrago would return at the wrong time."

"All right. It's hard not to think about it, though."

During most of the day, Lobo busied himself making the tra-vois. He cut two saplings down, tied them together at one end and secured a blanket between the two poles, creating a trian-gular stretcher for Lorenzo to rest on as they traveled.

They stayed beside the cool trickle of water all that day and night. Early, before dawn, they loaded up and continued on again as fast as they could. The stop had given the wounded men some respite. At about eleven o'clock that morning Lobo, who was pulling Lorenzo on the travois, suddenly reined in his horse. "Stop!" he cried out to the other riders. "Stop the horses!"

As they obeyed, Lanie asked, "What's wrong?"

"I don't know," Lobo said. "I just felt I needed to check on him." He pulled the stretcher down, looking worriedly at Lorenzo's gray face. "Something's gone wrong. I'm not even sure he's breathing."

Holding his breath, he put his hand over the frail chest of the old man. Lorenzo did not move. Lobo leaned over with his head on Dawkins' still chest and listened for a moment, then straightened up. "Heart's beating like crazy," he said quietly, "real fast, then not at all. I don't know what that means."

Stone, who was hunched over on his horse, whispered, "I think he's dying, Lobo. That's the way the heart does sometimes when it's giving out." Then he slowly dismounted.

"Let's get him into the shade," Lobo said. "At least bathe his face with some cool water." The only shade they could find was under two sickly looking pine trees. They quickly detached the travois from the horse and carried it to the cooler spot, trying not to jog Lorenzo too much.

Lanie took a canteen, wet one of her handkerchiefs, and began bathing his face. "He looks—awful," she whispered in anguish.

Lobo spoke up, his voice filled with frustration, "I always feel so blasted helpless in a situation like this! If we only had a doctor!"

Lanie turned to him, her face strained. "I'm not sure a doctor would help now." She dampened the handkerchief and tenderly touched the ashen face of the still form.

Lobo stalked around in circles, pounding his hands together as if looking for some way to ease the old man's torture. His voice reflected his feelings of futility, "Well—I guess—we'll stay here until he comes to. Or maybe I'll ride on ahead, see if I can bring out a doctor."

"No, don't leave us!" Lanie cried. She was more afraid of the country and their current predicament than she had let on; but now her face revealed the fear that lurked within her, and Lobo knew that leaving would be out of the question.

"All right, Lanie," he reassured her; "we'll just camp here and see how he does."

★ ★ ★ ★

As the afternoon passed, the burning, raw heat changed into a cooling breeze. A small fire crackled cheerily and blew aromatic drafts around the group as the mesquite brush burned. No one had any appetite, though Lobo had fixed a meal. They sat, silent and forlorn, staring disconsolately at the merry flames.

Wesley drew close to Lorenzo. Stone's movements were clumsy and slow, pain etching his face as he looked down at the still form. He had not once moved. Mutely he stared at the man's blank face, then inched back to his place without a word.

His own wound was painful. The bullet had torn through the flesh of the upper arm, leaving a ragged exit hole. But it had not broken the bone; so if infection didn't set in, Wesley knew he would be all right. But the wound had sapped his energy greatly. After the long chase, he did not think he could take any more. Hopelessly he thought, *I've just come to the end—I can't go on anymore!*

Lobo's sharp gaze rested on Wesley. Lobo had seen men like Stone before; a final, numbing exhaustion would set in, and they would seem to distance themselves from the concept of life and death. It just didn't matter anymore to them. And they would die.

Lanie seemed to be in shock; her face was deathly pale, her eyes enormous and unfocused.

Lobo's shoulders sagged. Quietly he said, "I dunno what to do. We can't go on, and we can't stay here."

Silence lay heavy and thick, like a stifling cloak, on the group. No one moved or said anything for a long time. Minutes stretched on endlessly. Lobo got up and fed the fire, then turned and walked away into the gathering darkness, holding his rifle loosely in his hand. The desert night slowly surrounded them, but no one went to sleep.

About ten o'clock Lobo returned and Lanie and made a pot of coffee. It was black and bitter, but the hot liquid was refreshing and seemed to break the twilight trances over them. "Better eat something," she said listlessly and fished a baked potato out of the glowing coals, cracked it open, and began to pick the steaming white pulp out, not even bothering to salt it. She was not hungry, but she had learned that she had to eat to keep going. Lobo ate too, but Wesley couldn't gather the energy to down anything.

Hours passed. Finally Wesley leaned back and fell asleep. Overhead the skies were clear. Lobo pushed his hat above his forehead, leaned back on the saddle he had thrown on the ground, and looked up. As always, he wondered about the stars: who made them, how they all stayed in place, what they were made of. He was lost in his reverie.

Suddenly a faint sound came from Lorenzo Dawkins. Like a cat Lobo sprang to his feet; almost as quickly Lanie was there. The wounded man lay close to the fire under a light blanket. Stone woke up and crawled over to them.

"Can you hear me, Lorenzo?" Lobo asked, kneeling beside him.

At first there was no answer. Then Lanie saw the old eyes slowly open and recognition dawn in his face. She cried out, "Lorenzo, Lorenzo! Can you hear me? Are you in pain?"

Dawkins gazed up at her and licked his lips as he whispered in a weak croak, "Water . . ."

Lanie ran to the supplies and returned with a canteen. Lobo held the frail figure upright. "Can't move my arms," Lorenzo muttered. "Can't move nothin'."

"Here—" Lanie knelt at the old man's side and held the canteen to his lips.

Lorenzo managed to drink awkwardly, most of the water running down his chin. Finally his head dropped back and he sighed. "That was good." He stared at Lobo, then at Stone and Lanie. "Well, I guess I've torn it this time, huh?"

"You'll be all right," Lobo said stoutly. "We'll get you to a doctor, and he'll fix you up."

His bluff made no impact on Lorenzo Dawkins. He shook his head and said in a voice of wonder, "Can't move nothin' 'cept my head! Ain't that somethin'? Feel like my whole body's gone to sleep." His eyes began to droop, and they were afraid he was drifting into unconsciousness again, but then his eyes widened. He looked at Lanie and whispered, "Sorry about your sister, Missie."

"Don't worry about it." Lanie reached up and gently brushed a lock of his white hair back from his forehead, then lightly wiped his forehead with the handkerchief she had dampened. "We'll find her, Marshal, and you'll be all right," she said in a soothing voice.

"Nope. Not this time," Dawkins whispered mildly.

Lobo exchanged a quick glance with Lanie and said gruffly, "Oh, sure you will, Dawkins. You've taken bullets before. We're gonna get you—"

"Nope," Dawkins said again, a certainty in his voice. "This is it for old Lorenzo, son." There was a peacefulness on his face and in his eyes that surprised them all. He began to talk, and he spoke slowly, forming the words with great care and effort. "This time," he said, "I'm on the receivin' end." Lanie's eyes welled up with scalding tears, and, inexplicably, the dying man was filled with compassion for her. "Don't you cry now, Missie," he chided her gently, breathing heavily. "Don't you cry for ol'—ol' Lorenzo Dawkins."

"I—I c-can't help it," Lanie said, biting her lip. "It's all my fault! I never should have dragged all of us out here in the first place!"

"I was here 'cause I wanted to be here, Missie." His voice was growing weaker. "I been out on lots of hunts that I wasn't proud of, but this time I was proud. Wish we coulda done it." There was silence, and for one moment Lanie thought he was gone. She held her breath and leaned closer to him, tears streaming, her eyes fixed on his face.

Slowly Lorenzo began to speak again. "I ain't been the man I shoulda been. Hard to be a Christian in this line of work. I tried to be fair and honest—but I've had to handle some rough characters, and that takes rough ways. Don't it, Lobo?"

"That's right, Lorenzo. But everybody who knows you knows you're a good man," Lobo said gently. He felt helpless kneeling by him. Lobo loved the old man. He had known him and respected him for a long time, but now he saw the life slipping away, like sand sifting through an hourglass. Lobo knew that

Lorenzo Dawkins was almost gone.

They waited. The moon crept slowly across the sky. The stars twinkled and burned quietly against the velvet black curtain of night. The desert silence reigned, broken from time to time only by the cry of a night bird or the howl of a coyote—all sounds of nature, all sounds of the familiar world each person was living in. Yet now each one felt strange and alien to the cries. As the old man's life flickered weakly and seemed to be fading away, all of them were struck dumb by the awesomeness of the moment. Finally Lorenzo Dawkins roused and whispered, "One thing— one thing . . ." He faltered, but then his voice returned, stronger than before. "One thing—I done. Long time ago. I took Jesus as my Savior. I ain't been faithful to Him always. But I always loved Him, and I always studied His Word. And now, I guess, when I go to meet my God, all I'll be able to say—is—Jesus paid for me—for all my sins."

His voice trailed off, but his eyes opened wide and brightened, and suddenly he smiled, a fine strong smile. Then he looked straight at Lobo, the mysterious smile warming his face, and said, "Son, I'm going. . . ." Lorenzo seemed to slump; then faintly they heard, "Praise . . . Praise . . ." The fading blue eyes closed.

"He's gone," Lobo said, almost angrily. "One of the best men I ever knew. Shot by a no-account dog!"

Lanie heard his bitter words, but she was too filled with grief to focus on their meaning. In the few days she had known Lorenzo Dawkins, she had learned that he was a good man. He had been unfailingly kind to her and truly caring. Now he was gone. One moment he had been with them, living, breathing, sharing the stage where they all acted out their parts. Now in one brief moment of time, he had stepped from that stage and had gone to a new place, to another world, another land. Lanie wanted to cry out, but she could not. Great scalding tears ran down her face, and a knot formed in her throat. Carefully, tenderly she laid Lorenzo's head down, crossed his frail arms over his chest, stood to her feet, and walked away to stand in the darkness alone. There no one could see the river of grief flowing down her desolate face.

A while later she heard light footsteps and knew Lobo was

coming up behind her. "We'll leave as soon as you're ready, Lanie," he said quietly. "We still need to get Wes to a doctor, you know. And we need to get Lorenzo—in this country, it needs to be quick . . ." His voice trailed off awkwardly. Turning her around with a desperate gesture, he saw the tears making silver tracks down her smooth cheeks. "I—I know how hard it is, Lanie. You loved the old man, didn't you?"

"Yes," she whispered in a stricken voice, "I did."

Lobo sighed softly in the darkness. "Me too. Known lots of men, but never one more faithful than Lorenzo Dawkins. He was the kind of man I'd like to have been—but the cards just didn't turn up that way."

Lanie looked up at him, wiping the tears from her cheeks. "It's not too late, Lobo. Maybe all this happened so you can see— what it's like. It's made me see. I called myself a Christian, you know. But I couldn't go out to meet God like Lorenzo did! I'd be scared to death."

He searched Lanie's upturned face, his expression puzzled and questioning. Lobo was disturbed by her confession, but he could think of no word of comfort or strength that would ease Lanie's grief and fear. He muttered, "I can tell you one thing. I'm coming back, and I'll get Perrago. I'm gonna put a bullet right between his eyes, and I'll get your sister!"

Lobo's voice was hard and adamant and cruel, and Lanie protested, "No, don't talk like that."

"Why? It's what you want, isn't it?"

"I want Betsy. But if you turn out to be a man who does nothing but kill, it's—it's all for nothing, isn't it?"

Lobo's features were shadowy and dim, but an intangible aura of hatred seemed to surround him, and his voice chilled Lanie. "I don't know any other way to get the job done."

Lanie stood there, unable to think clearly, unable to argue with him; she didn't have any other answers. And yet she saw that if this man went on this way, letting the bitterness build up in him, he would become just like the outlaws that rode with Perrago. But words refused to come to her, and soon weariness overtook her. "Come on, Lobo," she said, her shoulders drooping, "let's don't talk about it now. We'll go back to Fort Smith and then we'll see what can be done once Woman Killer arrives with news."

She turned and slowly walked back to the fire, her steps dragging, and blindly looked into the glowing red coals for a while. Lobo was reattaching the travois, holding Lorenzo's body, to Lobo's horse again. Lanie straightened up and walked over to him as he finished. "Can we move on now?" she asked. "Even if we ride slowly, I'd like to start."

"Sure, we can." Lobo nodded at Wesley. "We're gonna head out now. Get you to a doctor. How're you doin'?"

"Fine. I'm all right."

They mounted their horses, and at a word from Lobo they were on their way. The three made their way through the darkness of the wasteland—all lost in their own thoughts. The farther they went, the blacker the pall seemed to become as it hung upon Lanie Winslow's heart. She still grieved for her sister, but now she knew that the price that had been paid was terribly high—and it wasn't fully paid yet.

PART THREE

THE TRAP

★ ★ ★ ★

CHAPTER FIFTEEN

"HE'S MY KIND OF MAN!"

★ ★ ★ ★

"Well, devil throw smoke!" Bronwen Winslow exploded, putting both hands on her hips, thrusting her chin out, and staring at her husband as if he had just announced he had decided to flap his wings and fly to the moon. She grew angry very rarely, but when she did, the strong Welsh temper flared like a torch, and her green eyes sparkled in a most ominous manner.

"Now, Bron—" Zach Winslow said in a placating fashion, "this is just something I've got to do! I've moped around here like a whipped dog long enough! I can't sit around on my rear end in this wheelchair, doing nothing, while my girls are out there in trouble!"

"Go and scratch, Zach Winslow!" Bron snapped impatiently. She folded her arms across her chest and stared at her husband, and when she spoke again, her voice carried a cold chill. "So you'll be leaving me and your family alone! Is that it? And *you* in a wheelchair—"

Zach rolled over and put his arms around her. She sat stiffly, refusing to yield herself to his embrace. "You know I've got to do it, don't you, Bron?" he murmured against her fragrant hair.

For one moment Bronwen held out. Then she grabbed the front of his shirt with both of her hands and looked at him, tears shining in her eyes. "It's stubborn you are, Zach Winslow!"

"You knew that when you married me, Bron," he said gently. He drew her closer and kissed her, then held her tightly. The two clung to each other, her hands clasping his neck. In truth, Bronwen Winslow had seen this coming. Ever since Lanie and Wesley Stone had left, her husband had been like a caged lion— restless and fidgety. It had almost driven her insane, knowing that sooner or later he would have to do something. Bron knew him so well. Drawing back, she looked into his eyes and smiled. "Well, go get him, then—and bring the bones hot from his body!"

Zach laughed suddenly at her bloodthirsty words. "You haven't changed a bit, woman! Not since the first time I saw you!" he declared. "I thought you were the stubbornest woman in creation, and nothing's happened to make me change my mind!"

"Ah, well," Bron shrugged, "no matter if I get lonesome and sad. You'll do what you have to do." Then she smiled again and dashed the tears from her eyes. "I knew you would be doing it sooner or later, Zach. When will you leave?"

Guilt crossed his face and he said casually, "Oh, I've got tickets for the nine o'clock train in the morning."

"It's an old liar you are!" Bron grumbled, and playfully struck his broad chest with her fist. "Didn't say a word about it, did you now? Telling me you're going to the office!"

"I'm always afraid of *you* more than anything else," Zach grinned. Then his voice dropped with emotion as he went on. "Afraid of hurting you, or displeasing you, Bron." He took her hand, held it for a brief moment, bent and kissed it. "I have to do it. You know that, don't you?"

"Do I know you?" she whispered. "I only wish I could go with you."

"Someone has to stay here and take care of the boys, my dear."

"You can't go alone. Someone needs to go with you. How about Tom? He'll be having a fit here if he can't, Zach," she said thoughtfully. "Maybe you ought to take him."

Slowly, the idea formed and took hold in Zach's mind. He was a methodical thinker, always stopping to consider his options carefully—except when the action started; then he seemed to explode. "You may be right. He's fifteen now. You could take care of the other boys by yourself, then?"

"Am I a rat with green teeth?" she retorted heatedly.

"No!" Zach replied in a knee-jerk reflex.

"Well then!" Bron said with supreme satisfaction. Zach was still trying to work out the incongruity of her statement as she went on smugly. "And haven't I been taking care of *you*? And aren't you more trouble than the rest of them put together!" Bron hated being separated from Zach and spoke out of the unwelcome twinge of fear she felt. Never before had they been apart for very long, but this time might be much longer than she'd like. She took a deep breath and said, "I'll help you pack." Then she turned to go.

He caught her, pulled her back, and kissed her again. She threw her arms around him and hugged him fiercely. "Oh, Zach," she breathed, "it's hurting I am—but only a little. I'll be all right. You go find Betsy and bring her home."

"All right," he said sturdily. "I'll do it."

At that moment, he looked like the young man he had been when she had first seen him. A young soldier just out of the army—hard and tough; determined to make no friends and to know no woman. Abruptly she said, "Remember? You were set to be a hermit. And I disrupted your life, along with all the needy people from the mission."

He smiled and ran his hand over her hair. "That you did," he said ruefully, "and it's the best thing that ever happened to me!" They were quiet for a moment, remembering. Then he said huskily, "I'll miss you, Bronwen." She clung even tighter to him, enjoying his nearness and the familiar sense of closeness they shared.

After a few moments Zach spoke again, and his voice took on a distant quality. "You know, Bron, I think we made a mistake when we left the West to come to Chicago. The boys need elbow room, and the city's sure got none of that. I wish we'd never left Montana."

"Do you now?" Bron replied with some wonder. "I think of those days too." Visions of the past rose in both their minds, and they thought of the mountains of Montana, so far away but so clear in their memories. "We'll go there," Bronwen whispered, "and see it again. As soon as we get our girl back."

"Yes, we'll go there," Zach echoed her in a strong voice. "We'll do it, or I'll die trying."

★ ★ ★ ★

Lobo and his caravan moved along slowly, the horses' heads low. They were weary, and the people no less so. It had been a hot day. They had driven hard these last few days, knowing they had to get Lorenzo Dawkins buried as quickly as possible. Lanie was glad to see the outlines of Fort Smith shimmering just ahead so didn't protest when Lobo muttered, "Let's step it up and get this over with."

They entered the town, attracting attention from the people on the streets. Lobo rode in front with the canvas-wrapped body of the slain lawman on his travois in the back. Lanie rode close beside Wesley, who by now was reeling in the saddle from weakness.

When they pulled up in front of the jail, a man with a star on his chest emerged promptly. "What happened?" he asked curtly.

"We got ambushed, Jeff," Lobo answered wearily. "They got Lorenzo."

The tall marshal's eyes flew to the still form on the travois; then he turned and said to the two deputies who had followed him out, "Take him down to Robertson's place. He'll take care of him."

One of the deputies climbed up on Lobo's horse and rode slowly down the street.

As the deputies followed, Marshal Jeff Samuels spoke to Lobo. The marshal was deeply affected and the pain in his voice was obvious as he said, "I hate to see it. Lorenzo was a good man."

"He was that," Lobo nodded.

"Who done it?"

Lobo stared at him, shook his head slightly, and answered in his dead-weary voice. "Can't be sure. Most likely Perrago."

An ominous light glowed in the tall marshal's eyes, and his lips drew into a thin white line. "We'll nail his casket shut." Turning on his high boot heel he added, "I'll go tell Judge Parker. He'll be sorry to hear it. Dawkins has been with him a long time." He disappeared into the jail.

Lobo turned and walked to Lanie and Wesley, who had somehow managed to dismount. Now Stone was clinging to his horse's reins, holding himself up, his face ashen. "Come along with me, Stone," Lobo ordered. "We'll have a doctor look at you and—"

"Lanie!"

Lanie whirled at the familiar voice. Her eyes grew wide as she looked toward the boardwalk where a young boy was pushing a man along in a wheelchair. She blinked in shocked disbelief, then cried, "Dad!—Tom!" and ran across the dusty street.

Lobo watched in surprise and finally he asked, "That her dad, Stone?"

"Sure is. And her oldest brother."

Oblivious to the stares and remarks of those around her, Lanie rushed to her father and fell into his arms. It was awkward, leaning over the wheelchair, but Lanie didn't care. Familiar sensations flooded her. As a little girl she had done the same thing— run to him whenever she had hurt herself. Now she held tightly to him and tears of joy and relief came unbidden to her.

After a few moments she stood up in front of him, blinked back the tears, and held both his hands. "What in the world—"

"I came over to straighten this mess out," Zach announced firmly. "That right, Tom?"

Tom Winslow, a sturdy carbon copy of his father, grinned at Lanie. "Yep, we sure did, sis. I've pushed Dad around in circles in this town so long, I swear I've done worn down two, three inches shorter!"

"Well, don't just stand there now, boy," Zach growled. "Let's get outta this blasted heat!" He glanced over to the small knot of men who were waiting, staring at them, and called out, "Come on, Wes! I need to talk to you!"

Stone started toward them, his head low and his steps faltering. Lanie told her father anxiously, "He's been wounded, Dad. We've got to get him to a doctor right away."

"Wounded? What happened?"

"Let's get Wes taken care of. Then we can go somewhere and talk."

"I've got a room in the hotel you were staying in before," Zach nodded. "Two of them, really. One's waiting for you."

"All right, Dad, but first I want you to meet someone." She motioned to Lobo. When he walked over to the Winslows, Lanie said, "Dad, this is Lobo Smith. He's the man we hired to get Betsy back."

Zach stuck out his hand to meet the hard grip of Lobo Smith. Zach studied the man carefully, and for a moment he didn't speak. Zach Winslow sized the man up, methodically weighing the close-knit shoulders, the quick movements, the steady look in the single indigo eye. Finally he said, "No luck this time, I reckon."

"Not this time," Lobo shrugged. "Goes that way sometimes—"

"Let's get Wes to the doctor," Lanie broke in. "Then I'll feel better."

It was nearly two hours later when Smith and Lanie stepped into her father's hotel room. Zach sat by the window in his wheelchair, and Tom was perched on the bed. As soon as they appeared Zach greeted them briefly and asked, "Well? How's Wes?"

"Not as bad as I thought," Lanie said with relief. She walked forward and stood close to her father, drawn to him more than she had ever thought she would be. "The doctor dressed the wound, put bandages on it. He said he most of all needed to lie down and get lots of rest."

"He did look tired," Zach observed. "Now. You two sit down and tell me the whole thing. Don't leave anything out."

Lanie glanced at Tom, considering if she should tell him to leave the room. But he looked back at her with mutiny in his eyes and a stubborn set to his jaw, and Lanie realized that it would be useless to tell her brother to leave. So she smiled gladly and said, "Oh, it's good to see you, Tom! Is everyone all right at home?"

"Everybody's fine," Zach interrupted impatiently. "Now, tell me about Betsy and this man Perrago."

Lanie began to speak, and for the next ten minutes she sketched their aborted attempt to free Betsy. When she was through she sighed deeply. "I've made a mess out of it, I know, Dad, but—"

"You did fine!" Zach snapped. He slapped his hand down on the wheelchair irritably. "Blast this leg! I won't be able to ride a horse for another month!" His eyes went to Lobo Smith and he asked gruffly, "Well? What about you, Smith?" But before Lobo could answer, a rakish grin suddenly lit up Zach Winslow's face. "Way I hear it, you're a rangy wolf with long teeth and whiskers of metal shavin's! Scare little children in the night, do you? And make the girls scream and run for cover. So what's your side of it, Smith?"

Lobo's grin was as roguish as Zach Winslow's. "Isn't any."

"Just as well you think so, then," Zach nodded. Zach had an ability to make decisions about people—and when he did, he seldom changed his mind and almost never made a mistake. He had made up his mind about Lobo Smith. "I know you feel bad about your friend Marshal Dawkins," he said soberly. "I'm sorry about him, too. He was a good man."

"He was straight. Never let a man down and never broke his word," Lobo replied. Zach Winslow nodded his understanding. Lobo cleared his throat. "Well, I don't guess you'll be needin' me anymore."

"Oh no, you're not getting off that easy, Smith," Zach said calmly. "We're going back to get that girl of mine, and you're the one who's going to have to do it. I can't go with this bum leg. So sit down and let's make medicine." Lobo awkwardly took a chair, seemingly uncomfortable with the older man's mandate. Lanie sat on the bed beside Tom. For some time they discussed possibilities.

Finally Zach Winslow said, "Well, there's nothing to be done tonight. I know you two are dead tired. Tell you what. Let's go get something to eat, and I'll get a few more rooms here."

"No need in spendin' your money on me, Mr. Winslow," Lobo protested.

"Got more money than I have good sense, I think sometimes. And so does my wife," Zach replied cheerfully. "I want you to be fresh. I want something done, you're the man that's gonna be doing it, and I want you rested up and ready. C'mon, Tom. Get me out of this place, and push me on along to that restaurant. See if they've got anything fit to eat."

After their supper, Zach had Tom take him to the desk where he procured a room for Lobo and Wesley. He wheeled around and ordered Lobo and Lanie, "You two go get some rest. And when you get up in the morning, we're going to get together and decide what to do. I'm going to ask the good Lord for an answer, and if either one of you knows how to pray you might do the same. Good-night." He wheeled back around and said, "Let's go, Tom."

When Zach was gone, Lobo remarked, "He's quite a fella, your dad. Is he always like this?"

"He's the kindest man I've ever known," Lanie said. She bit her lip and looked after him. "It's taken something out of him, this thing has. I know Mother's suffering, too."

"Best thing to do would be to get twenty marshals and throw a chain around that bunch," Lobo growled. "Pull Perrago up in a chokehold."

"But what would happen to Betsy?" Lanie asked quietly. "Couldn't she get hurt?"

"She can get hurt any way we go about it," he said. "But you're right, Lanie. First sight of something like that, and Perrago's going to threaten to kill her." He noted her weariness. "You're wore out, Lanie. Go to bed."

"Yes," she readily agreed. "I'll see you in the morning, Lobo. Good-night."

Lobo nodded and turned to go, but she caught his sleeve. "I know it didn't work out as we wanted it to," she said softly, "but you did get us out of there. And now—do you think we have another chance, Lobo?"

He studied her face, the lines of fatigue deep at the corners of her mouth, her eyes darkly shadowed. Her vitality seemed to have drained away. Still, he felt admiration for Lanie; she had borne days of hardship and heartbreak in a way few city girls ever could have. "Always a chance," he told her, then added, "Your dad said something about praying. He's a praying man?"

"Yes, he is, and my mother! She's more for prayer than anybody I know of!" Lanie was watching Lobo steadily. "Do you ever pray, Lobo?"

"Nope. Wouldn't be right."

"Not right? What do you mean?"

"Fella like me," he shrugged. "Never think of God, never do anything for God; then out of the blue I start beggin'. Seems pretty small to me."

Lanie chose her words carefully before she spoke. "I think all of us have to reach some point where the only thing we can do is ask God. Until we get there, we're pretty likely to stay stubborn and go our own way. At least that's what I've found." She smiled at him as she rose. "Now I'd better get some rest. Good-night, Lobo."

Lobo watched as she disappeared down the hall. *What a woman!* After a few minutes, he sighed, got up, and walked to his room, pondering her words all the way. He took off his boots, shirt, and trousers and scrubbed the dust from his face and arms in the washbasin in the corner, then dropped onto the bed and was asleep instantly.

★   ★   ★   ★

"What do you think about this fellow, Lobo Smith?" Zach asked.

He and Lanie were alone. She had come to her father's room early the next morning; Tom had gone on an errand. "Think about him? Why—I don't know."

"You must have had some thoughts about him, girl! You trusted him enough to go off gallivantin' around the desert with him!" Zach said, frustrated at her silence. "C'mon, speak up!"

Lanie found herself awkwardly trying to define her feelings to her father. "I—I don't really—know. He's—a strange man," she stammered. She dropped her eyes to the floor, confused by her own muddled feelings as her father studied her.

Zach Winslow knew his eldest daughter. Lanie had never acted like this about a man before, and her difficulty in speaking of Lobo Smith made him want to ask more, but he decided not to press her. *I'll just keep my eyes open and find out for myself*, he thought silently. Aloud he said, "Well, I've discovered one thing. Smith's tough as a bootheel. And as far as I know he's not vicious. On the borderline," he added thoughtfully, "but so far even Judge Parker thinks enough of him to put in a good word."

"He's had a hard life," Lanie said. "I think if he'd had more chances he'd have made something out of himself. He's very quick. Not educated, but he—he—knows things, learned things by himself. What you used to call 'country smart,' Dad."

"He's quick-witted, all right. And looks kind of like a wolf, huh? That one eye of his so sharp, looking right through you. Funniest shade of blue I ever saw. How'd he lose that other eye?"

"I don't know," she answered, wondering to herself. "He never told me."

"Nothing simple, I bet," Zach observed. "All right, let's go to that dining room. I'm going to tackle another one of those tough steaks."

They went down the hall into the spacious lobby, Lanie pushing the wheelchair. There was a saloon on one side and a dining hall on the other. Lanie and her father found a table, and ten minutes later Lobo came in, accompanied by Tom. The two had evidently met somewhere.

Something about Tom's attitude alerted both Zach and Lanie. The way the boy was acting toward Lobo. It was the same way he acted whenever he was around men he admired—furtive sideways glance and inordinate attention to what Lobo said; indeed, the boy was hanging breathlessly on every word. Tom had even begun to walk like Lobo Smith. *Next thing*, Lanie thought, *he'll be wanting to strap on a gun, just like Lobo*. Her amusement faded as she thought of the dangerous path her brother could follow.

They had breakfast, eating enormous amounts of food and speaking little during the meal. When they had shoved back from the table Lobo said abruptly, "I've thought of something that might work." He looked directly at Zach Winslow; an air of fatalism seemed to be reflected in the gleam of his single eye and the set of his shoulders. "But it might not work, either."

"Let's hear it," Zach demanded.

Lobo leaned forward and said slowly, "If you send a big herd of marshals in after Betsy, she's got maybe a fifty-fifty chance. First thing Vic Perrago will do if he sees a star flash is use her as a hostage."

Zach nodded in agreement. "Yep. That's the way I figure it too. I talked about it to some of the marshals, and they said it'd be real dangerous for my girl."

"Go on, Lobo," Lanie urged him. "What's your idea?"

Lobo ran his hand through his crisp brown hair. He was obviously reluctant to speak; but then he sighed, seemingly resolved to tell his plan. "I've been thinking. If somebody was there—you know, on the inside, right there with Perrago—well, he could make a chance to get your daughter away, Mr. Winslow."

"You thinking about yourself?" Zach's voice was quick and sharp.

"Can't think of anybody else," Lobo replied offhandedly. "I know Vic a little bit. And all he really knows about me is that I've had my share of run-ins with the marshals. Matter of fact, he made me an offer a coupla times to join up with him, and I did ride with him for a while. Seemed kinda anxious to have me."

Zach leaned back in his wheelchair and studied the smooth countenance of the young man lounging across the table. "Be a bit dangerous," he idly remarked. "If they found out what you're there for, I guess they'd kill you before your next blink. You think he knows you were in the shootout when Dawkins got shot?"

Lobo straightened up, crossed his arms, then grinned impudently. "No, it was pretty dark—I was hid good in the brush. I'd just have to keep 'em from finding out my real intentions is all."

Lanie ignored his lightness. "But, Lobo," she asked plaintively, her voice troubled, "how could you do it? I mean, even if you were there, they'd be watching you. They'd be suspicious, wouldn't they?"

"They're suspicious of everybody, that bunch is," Lobo shrugged. "But, like I say, if I was right there I could make a chance for Betsy. They'd ride out sometime, leave just a man or two with her, like before. I might just be one of the men they'd leave! Then I'd just take Betsy, and ride out with her. Once Woman Killer comes in with word of their whereabouts, I can ride out. You can bet they didn't stay in that shack after we found them out."

Silence fell around the table. Every face—except Lobo's—was troubled. After a while Zach sighed with exasperation and said, "I've thought of everything in the world, Lobo. And not one idea would work. Maybe, just maybe this would." His eyes grew sharp as they met Lobo's. "But this is dangerous, real dangerous. I'd pay you well for it, though."

Lobo didn't answer.

"How could the rest of us help?" Lanie questioned him. "You can't go out there alone."

"Better that way." Lobo looked at Lanie, then at her father

and drawled, "So if you agree to it, I'll pull out. Soon as Woman Killer comes. Probably a couple more days. Besides, I need to get my horse shod anyway."

"But we've got to make a better plan than this," Lanie protested. "You propose to just disappear into the desert. You can't get in touch with us, we won't know what's happening—" The vehement flow of words stopped and her eyes narrowed.

Zach Winslow studied his daughter's determined expression and demanded, "What's going on in that head of yours, girl? I know that look, and I want you to give it up right now!"

"I just had an idea. But—I have to think about it a little bit." She got up and left the table without another word. The men watched her as she walked outside and paced along the sidewalk.

"Well, there she goes," Zach said with resignation. "We've seen her look like that before, haven't we, Tom?"

"Yep, sure have!" Tom grinned at Lobo and told him with admiration in his voice, "Whenever Lanie gets to looking like that, she's hatchin' something, you can be sure of it! Usually some devilment!"

Lobo said warily, "I don't know what she'd be able to think up in this kind of situation."

Suddenly Tom piped up, "Lobo, can I go with you? Please! I could come back and bring messages."

Lobo grinned at the eager boy. "Yeah, you'd like that, wouldn't you! And so would I! But I guess right now, your job is to take care of your dad. Maybe next time, Tom." He saw the eagerness melt away, so he reached out and slapped the boy's shoulder lightly.

Zach appreciated the way Lobo took time with Tom and treated him with simple respect, like he'd treat another man.

Lobo got up and said, "I'm going to go check about getting my horse shod, Mr. Winslow." He put on his hat, nodded briefly to Zach and Tom, and left the dining hall.

Tom's eyes followed Lobo all the way out. "I sure do like him, Dad. And I betcha he's a dead shot with that gun."

Zachary Winslow's eyes were on Lobo, too. "Well, Tom," he said quietly, "I'll tell you one thing. He's my kind of man!"

CHAPTER SIXTEEN

A PARTY OF TWO

★ ★ ★ ★

When the sun dipped westward, touching the ragged rim of the hills, its livid red ball seemed to break like the yolk of an egg, spilling out against the spires and peaks and rough-cut summits of the mountains far to Lobo's left. He looked quickly as light flashed in a thousand sharp splinters against the sky, creating a fan-shaped aurora against the upper blue. And then the spectacular burst faded, and the deep purple of twilight began to trickle down against the canyon slopes. Lobo Smith studied the far ridge line closely. He had watched the mountains all day; now they grew vague before his eyes. Hot silence covered the summit as he stared, but, as the twilight began to envelope him, the stillness seemed even greater. Suddenly the staccato beat of a woodpecker clattered, rocketing startling waves of noise out into the distance.

Then, as if he had received a clearly spoken warning, a sense of danger overtook Lobo. He drew his horse in sharply and took shelter behind a large outcropping of rocks. He dismounted, led his horse back into a thicket, tied the animal, and crept back. Inching his way on his belly, he worked to the top of the outcropping of rocks. He lay flat; his outline would be invisible to any onlookers, appearing only as a darker part of the stone. There was still enough light to see, and now he heard what he thought he had heard more than once on that day: the sound of hoofbeats coming from the same direction he had traveled.

Lobo lay as motionless as the rock beneath him. Every nerve was tingling; a familiar sensation, one that he always felt at the approach of danger. More than once since he had left Fort Smith, Lobo could sense that someone was following him. But never— until now—had he caught sight of a horse or heard the sound of pursuit.

The hoofbeats of a single horse sounded along the trail that wound directly beneath the rock. With extreme caution, Lobo moved into a crouch, his legs gathered beneath him, his moccasins gripping the rough surface. He could have used his gun, but he was wary of the sound of gunshots carrying to other ears. Lobo had felt ever since the fiery clash with Perrago that danger was close. Who was sticking so close to his trail?

A horse appeared with a single rider. Lobo tensed his muscles, his rifle ready to fire at the slightest movement. The animal had slowed to a trot. Lobo's nostrils flared as he tried to judge distance and timing with his one eye. The rider would pass within five feet of him; he could easily ambush the stranger without having to arouse any unwanted attention, he judged. He waited. When the shadowy figure appeared directly in front of him, he released himself in a powerful spring, the muscles of his legs thrusting forcefully, his arms outstretched.

Tearing the rider from the saddle, the two of them flew to the ground. The horse reared and neighed shrilly; from underneath Lobo came a muffled grunt. Lobo pinned the rider down and ran his hands down the sides of the coat, looking for a weapon.

"No gun?" he muttered, then stood up and pulled the man upright by his collar. "Who are you?" he demanded roughly. "Why are you following me?"

Even as he spoke he caught the faint wisp of delicate scent. He whirled the rider around and knocked the low-brimmed hat back, then stared in shock. "Lanie!" he gasped.

Lanie was gasping desperately for a breath. "You didn't— have to—" she began.

Hot anger coursed through Lobo, and then a chill of fear at what might have happened. "You crazy fool woman!" he shouted. "I almost shot you!" Clutching the lapels of the jacket she wore, he shook her hard and bellowed, "What are you *doing* out here? Don't you know you could get killed? Assuming I didn't shoot you first." He shook her again. "There are Indians and outlaws and who knows what else in this country!"

Lanie was finally able to draw a deep breath, but her knees still shook. The blinding shock of being knocked out of the saddle had sent a lightning bolt of fear through her, and even now she could not speak except in convulsive short bursts. "I was—following you!"

In disgust Lobo muttered, "Fool woman, coulda gotten killed!" He stalked around in a circle, Lanie turning nervously to watch him. "Are you hurt?" he asked roughly.

"N-no. Just had the breath knocked out of me." She knew he was furious, so she immediately began to plead with him. "I had to come, Lobo! I *had* to! You're going into danger, and I didn't like—I mean, it won't—" She stopped, trying to calm herself. "I just didn't think it would work."

"Does your dad know you're here?" Lobo asked, his tone still menacing.

"No, I left him a letter telling him what we're going to do." Lanie's voice was studiously even, but the whites of her eyes showed as she warily watched him. He was still stalking around her.

"What *we're* going to do!" He jerked to a stop and looked at her squarely. "*We're* not gonna do anything! *You're* going back to Fort Smith! Right now!"

"Wait a minute! Please, Lobo!" she begged. "Just let me tell you my idea, just give me one minute. Please?" She saw his face soften, and she drew in a deep breath to calm her nerves.

"Oh, for the love of—" He blew an exasperated breath and said, "Well, let me go catch your horse. He's halfway to the next Territory by now." He turned and scrambled back up the steep rock outcropping, went back to his horse, and swung into the saddle. It was an easy job to catch her mount, for the little bay had not gone far before she stopped. Lobo found her dawdling along, nibbling at some scrub bushes, reins dragging. On the next rise he could see the form of a rider. Even in the darkness, he recognized Woman Killer's familiar mount.

Lobo grabbed the reins and went back to Lanie, her mare following him. "Well, let's get riding," he grunted. "Woman Killer's up ahead there."

"All right," she said meekly. She swung up into the saddle, proud that she was getting better at it, and the two moved along, Lobo's eyes relentlessly searching the gloom ahead.

"I hope he doesn't shoot us," he grumbled. "Now, what's this all about?"

Eagerly Lanie said, "I thought of a way that would be better. You were just going in blind, without any plan at all. I don't think it would have worked, Lobo. You would have been found out. They would watch you every second. You know they're suspicious."

The chafing of the leather broke the silence of the night. Ghostlike, the moon began to glow over to their left. *Bright moonlight tonight*, Lobo thought. *Killer's Moon, to the Indians.*

"All right, what's your great plan, Lanie?" he said sarcastically, still angry at this impossible woman.

She knew Lobo was mocking her, but she began to explain anyway. "All right. I thought about this a lot—and here it is." She took a long, deep breath. "You take me into the outlaw's camp. You tell Perrago that I'm the daughter of one of the managers who works for the Western Express Company over at Durango. I was in St. Louis when Vic and Betsy were in Chicago, so he won't know who I am—we've never met. Anyway, they ship gold coins every so often by train."

"How do you know that?"

"Some of the men were talking at the hotel," she shrugged. "That's what made me think of it."

Again there was a short silence. Lanie waited. Finally Lobo said, "All right, what comes next?"

"You tell them," she explained, "that you've kidnapped me, and you're going to make my father give you the number of the train, and when it's due to leave with a big shipment of gold on it. A million and a half dollars, or something like that."

"Well, that oughta be enough to get Vic's attention," he admitted. "So how does it work?"

"We'll locate someplace out here, in the desert, and plant a sealed bottle there. Your story will be that my father is going to send us a message about the train."

"Yeah, I follow," he said grudgingly. "Then?"

"So." Lanie held her hand palm upward, gesturing. "You tell him that you've got this big shipment of gold located, but you don't have a gang to hold the train up. Vic's got the gang, so the two of you go together. You see?"

Lobo had an active imagination. He rode along without speaking, the clopping of the horses' hooves on the dusty ground the only sound. The dust rose in the air, and Lobo could smell the spicy aroma of sagebrush, and the thousand other indefinable scents of the desert that he had grown to love. His mind toyed with what Lanie had told him, turning it over, prodding and poking at it. At length he said reluctantly, "Well, it might work. It has possibilities anyway." His head snapped up sharply and he said, "There's Woman Killer up ahead. Guess I better ask him not to shoot us." Pulling the horses up he cried out, "Woman Killer! Come in here."

Out of the darkness the Indian appeared. *How does he sneak up like that?* Lanie thought with irritation. *Even his horse doesn't make noise!* A rifle was slung across his saddle, and he greeted Lobo almost cheerfully. "As soon as I found out about her lame idea, I took out to follow you. I can take her back to Fort Smith in the morning." He nodded toward Lanie. The moonlight was strong now and his white teeth gleamed in his bronzed face.

"It's a good thing you knew where I was headed," Lobo said drily. "Me and Miss Winslow's been talkin' about this great plan of hers—to get Betsy back. Actually, it sounds promising. I don't think you'll need to be takin' her back just yet. Now, let's find a place and make camp. We can't ride all night."

Within an hour the three were sitting around a small campfire, eating a brace of rabbits and a stock of biscuits that Woman Killer had proudly produced. They ate hungrily and washed everything down with cool creek water from a small spring. When they finished, Woman Killer stood, picked up his rifle, and disappeared as usual, without saying a word.

"That's what an Indian likes," Lobo observed, watching him go. "To prowl around, 'specially in the night. Woman Killer's a Christian, but he still likes the hunt. Still got that battle thirst that so many Indians have."

"You ever wish you could go back to them?" Lanie asked quietly.

"Nothing to go back to," Lobo murmured. "It's all gone now. It was good while it lasted. But everything changes, and most things disappear."

"Not everything," Lanie said quickly. "Some things last."

"Like what?"

"Some say," she said hesitantly, "that love never changes. That it's eternal."

Across the fire he searched her face, curious. "That's an odd thing to say. Everywhere I look I see love breaking up and going off in different directions."

"I know that happens," Lanie shrugged, "but sometimes it doesn't. There's my father and mother—why, they're just like one person. I can't even imagine one without the other! They love each other now more than they ever did."

Lobo didn't answer. He dropped his head and, as was his custom, picked up a stick and began poking at the fire. Red and yellow sparks shot up, grew cold, and died out—and Lobo watched, reflecting on Lanie's words. "That's nice," he finally grunted. "I admire your dad."

Lanie sat quietly for a while. There was a hardness about Lobo, but underneath she thought she sensed a tenderness. She hesitated to call it that, for there was nothing feminine about him. It was the same quality, she suddenly realized, that she admired so much in her father, who was also a tough man. Lanie sought for words to express this to Lobo, but looking across at him, she knew she could not form the words so that he would understand her. Finally she asked, "What about my great plan?"

"Been thinking about it." He tossed the stick into the fire, leaned over and picked up the coffeepot and poured some of the tar-black liquid into a tin cup. After replacing the coffeepot, he drank a swallow, and continued, measuring his words. "I think it'll work. But I hate to see you go into it, Lanie. You just don't know what rough characters those men are. They don't *think* about killing—they just kill you, like swattin' a fly."

Lobo's concern for her safety warmed her, and she said, "You're taking the same chance I am, and Betsy's not even your sister."

"Different with a man," he shrugged. He was restless and fidgeted with the cup, now empty, his eye roving continually around them. "Your dad and your mother, they'll blame me if anything goes wrong."

"No they won't, Lobo. They know what I'm like." She smiled suddenly, looking very young. Her cheeks were the smoothest he had ever seen, and her eyes were alight and glimmering in the shadowed night. Leaning forward she said earnestly, "I told them in the letter that you didn't take me, that I had to waylay you. And that it wasn't your fault, whatever happened. It was what I had to do."

"Still, I feel responsible," Lobo argued. "Better not do it."

"Oh, I'm going to do it," Lanie said stoutly. "They've stolen my sister, and somehow, some way, I'll have them for it."

Lobo searched her face and smiled briefly. "I always liked stubbornness. Even in a horse. Somehow I got the idea that it means a strong character." A faint tinge of mischief touched his voice as he went on, "Maybe not. Maybe it's just orneriness, wanting your own way. I think you've got some of that in you, Lanie Winslow."

"I didn't ask your opinion of me!" she said defiantly. "Now—tell me what we're gonna do."

"All right. We can plan some, but most of it—well, we'll just have to see how the cards fall, and be sharp." His tone was light, but now he leaned forward and his face grew grave. "One thing that bothers me, Lanie . . . Here we go, galloping in. Suppose Betsy looks up, sees you, and calls out to you before we can stop her?" He snapped his fingers and it rang out like a shot. "Game's over," he finished soberly.

"I know. I'll try to do something—give her a sign." Lanie lifted her chin and met Lobo's gaze undaunted. "But Betsy's very sharp. I think she'll realize something's up as soon as we parade in there. Of course, she's got to know Dad's sent someone after her."

"It's taking a big chance," Lobo said tensely.

"It'll be all right. Betsy's quick," Lanie said with a dismissive gesture. "So now what?"

They huddled close to the small fire and talked for a long time, Lobo outlining his plan. Then silence settled on them like a cloak. It was a night full of stars. The little fire snapped and crackled merrily between them, lending cheer to the moment. After a while, Lobo stood up and stretched restlessly, looking around.

"Where are you going?" she asked.

"Nowhere. Just can't rest easy, next to a fire," he answered carelessly. "Not good strategy, usually. Draws everybody from a hundred miles, seems like. Could be all kinds of Cherokees, Choctaws, Osages lurkin' around. They'd shoot us for the horses and think they were rich." He paused for a moment, then said, "Come on, let's pull the blankets back. 'Course, I guess with Woman Killer out there it doesn't really matter, but . . ."

Lanie obediently rose and they moved the blankets back a ways, then sat down again and wordlessly watched the fire dwindle. As the flames flickered lower Lanie shivered.

"Are you cold?" Lobo asked.

"No. To be truthful, I guess I'm—I'm a bit afraid."

He turned toward her, drawn by her closeness. She was a woman, full and rich in a femininity that some women never know. There was nothing bold or crude about Lanie; on the contrary, gentleness and softness were in and around her, permeating her being.

Lanie could feel his eye on her and was aware of his scrutiny. After some hesitancy, she voiced the difficult question. "Why haven't you ever married, Lobo?"

He turned her words over in his mind, then finally said, "Guess I haven't found anyone I'd like to get hitched to—for life, that is. Oh, I've known a few women, but nothing—permanent. I haven't lived that kind of a life, you might say. What about you?"

Lanie shrugged slightly. "I never found a man I trusted enough to put myself in his hands."

"That's a funny way to put it," he mused. She had a way of speaking that made him want to get inside her brain, to discern her thoughts. The way she said things, expressed herself, revealed a quick mind, capable of dredging up old things and making them new. After he mused on that for a few moments he asked, "Do you think you'll wind up an old maid?"

She laughed, a gentle and kind sound that rippled right into

Lobo's heart. "If that ever happens, look for me on the floor! No! I'll never be an old maid!" She sobered and gazed back to the dying coals. "A woman's made for a man, and a man's made for a woman."

The boldness of her words caught him by surprise. Her lips were parted slightly and, to him, looked most inviting.

His face betrayed a struggle, and she asked pertly, "I can see something's in that mind of yours! What is it?"

Lobo wanted to ask Lanie if she would ever consider such a man as himself. But even as the words took form in his mind, he forced them back into oblivion. Lanie came from a prominent family, was used to privilege and having the best of all things. He had known nothing but difficulty, hardship, and a life of danger.

"Nothing," he answered quietly. Then he looked at her and murmured, "I haven't forgotten. That kiss."

She stared at him and said almost absently, "I haven't made a habit of doing things like that." Overhead a bird broke the silence of the desert air with a thin, keening cry. Lanie looked up. "What was that?"

"A hawk, I guess. Late for them, though." Lobo's voice, too, seemed distant and unconnected to the words he spoke as he studied her with a piercing gaze. Finally he drew a deep breath and said, "Not safe for you to be out here."

"You mean outlaws?"

"No. I mean me."

"You'd never harm me, Lobo."

"Don't be too sure of that. You don't know me."

Lobo's voice was low, intense, but Lanie shook her head in an imperious gesture. "I know you. You can be hard—even deadly. But you, Lobo, are never mean or cruel. I know men that much, at least."

He cocked his head, his forceful gaze never wavering. "How do you know? Where did you learn about men?" Then without waiting for her answer he reached over, put his arms around her, drew her in, and kissed her. As their lips touched, something struck Lobo like the peal of a bell, so clear and complete—the sudden understanding that sometimes passes from man to woman. He had heard of this, disbelieved it, and certainly never imagined it happening to him. He held her for a moment.

Lanie did not struggle, but returned his kiss. Then gently she put her hands against him and pushed him away. "That was a warning, I take it," she said evenly.

"No," Lobo said wearily. "You are right. You're safe with me." Her nearness made him uncomfortable and he sat up straight. "Tomorrow we'll start, and I think we'll find Perrago pretty soon. When we do," he warned, "I'll have to treat you rough. You understand that? They won't believe us otherwise."

"Be as rough as you have to," she said firmly. "I'll understand."

They lapsed into silence for a few more minutes, then Lanie said, "Good-night, Lobo. Got to get some sleep," and began tucking her blanket around her. After she was settled, he picked up his blanket, moved to the other side of the fire, and sat down, staring into the flickering flames, drinking coffee until it was cold. Then he poured the rest of the brew over the fire and rolled up in his blanket. Once he heard the high piercing cry of a night bird, but Lobo knew that it was Woman Killer saying that no enemies were near to do harm.

CHAPTER SEVENTEEN

RIGHT THROUGH THE FRONT DOOR

★ ★ ★ ★

The band of outlaws that Vic Perrago had put together was not noted for their congeniality. He had picked them carefully for their fighting abilities, sometimes making it difficult to switch off their tempers. Ever since they had lost Honey Ward in the fire fight outside the cabin, the members of the gang had been sullen and irritable. Perhaps some of this was because the last raid had been nearly a total failure, netting just over a thousand dollars which, divided so many ways, left very little for any of them.

The day after the gunfight they had fled to a hideout between the Cookson Hills and the Boston Mountains. Even if their attackers hadn't been marshals, Vic knew enough to get out once they'd been discovered. Anyone could inform the marshals of their whereabouts, especially if someone had gotten hurt in the showdown.

The atmosphere in the cabin had grown thick with antagonism. Grat Duvall and Jack Masterson had fallen into an argument about a horse; the mild disagreement had escalated into a vicious, cursing, shouting match, and would have exploded into an all-out gunfight. But Perrago had stepped in and told them disgustedly to shut up and get away from each other.

All of them were tough men, but Perrago held authority by the unmatched swiftness of his gun and the hair-trigger edge of his temper. Duvall and Masterson grudgingly gave up the fight, both still sulking and edgy.

Late one afternoon Buckley Ogg was playing solitaire on the scarred oak table. Vic was pacing the floor. The others were out of the cabin, for once. Ogg looked up and said, "Ain't no sweetness in this outfit, Vic. It's fallin' to pieces."

Perrago halted and turned his cold hazel eyes on Ogg. He wanted to lash out at him, but Vic knew the man was right. Shrugging, he conceded. "You're right, Ogg. But it'll be all right when we get a new job. What have you got for us?"

Buckley Ogg, for all of his almost three hundred pounds and simple demeanor, had a brain as keen as a scalpel, and wielded the power it gave him as skillfully as a surgeon. He could sit in the cabin, or walk around outside, staring up into the skies, apparently a fat, harmless old man. Yet beneath the seemingly aimless, worthless exterior, that cunning brain of his would be reaching out—all over Indian Territory, or into Fort Smith, or Missouri, or Arkansas—for Buckley Ogg knew this corner of the world better than anyone. He would think of banks, payrolls, trains, possibilities of banditry and robbery, and all the permutations. An astute general he was; and that was why he had lasted much longer than others who had operated out of the Territory.

True enough, it was Vic Perrago who made it work and held the band together by the sheer animal force of his will. But it was Buckley Ogg who envisioned and planned the jobs.

Now he laboriously laid a black four down on a red five and stared down at the coupling. His face was round and smooth and unlined, almost youthful in its appearance, even though he was over fifty. Ogg never mentioned the past, including how old he was. In a fight he wasn't much, but his keen brain made him priceless.

Perrago was waiting impatiently. "Well? What about it, Buck? Have you got anything in mind for us?" He paced again, up and down, and still Buckley Ogg didn't speak. "You're right about the boys," Vic went on. "They're mean and jumpy. If we don't do something pretty soon, they're sure gonna start shooting each other."

Ogg looked up from the dog-eared cards. "What about that young woman of yours?" he asked mildly. The deep-set black eyes studied Vic Perrago like a thick curtain, hiding what went on in his brain. "I thought you were gonna get a ransom for her."

"I'll take care of that!" Vic snapped. "That wouldn't solve our problem. We need to get the boys involved in something useful. We need *action*."

Ogg sighed, his huge chest and stomach billowing. "I'm working on it, Vic. Not as easy as it used to be, you know. Those marshals are plumb touchy now. But I'm thinking on it."

At that moment the door opened and Betsy walked in, carrying a load of wood. Briefly she glanced at the pair, strode over to the fireplace, and dumped the wood in the tinderbox. Straightening up, she walked to the single kitchen cabinet that held most of the cooking supplies and began pulling out the ingredients for biscuits she had decided to make for the evening meal.

Perrago watched her thoughtfully. Her back was to him, and he moved across the room silently. Without warning, he put his arms around her and pulled her back. She did not fight, but remained motionless in his arms, holding a box of baking powder in one hand. Cruelly Perrago squeezed until he heard her gasp as the breath was forced out of her, but still she said nothing. Angrily he whirled her around and grabbed her forearms, his fingers digging into her flesh. Perrago had done everything he could to shame Betsy, to humiliate her, to break her spirit; but still she looked at him as fearlessly as ever.

In one sense Vic admired her stamina, but he was a man well accustomed to women obeying his bidding. This small girl defied him constantly, and it continually grated on him. He could do as he pleased with her bodily, but never could he get inside that strong spirit. Now he said savagely, "What's the matter with you? You don't know how to appreciate a man!"

Betsy's gaze was steady, her blue eyes veiled, and she remained silent. With a curse he shoved her away so that she fell against the cabinet and spilled the baking powder in a long streak of white, tracing her fall. From across the room Ogg watched and listened. *She's got the best of that boy,* he thought shrewdly. *A woman never outsmarted Vic before. It's made him downright mean. If we don't watch out, he'll do something crazy and we all might get shot up. Got to get that girl out of here.*

Betsy picked up a towel, stooped and cleaned up the baking powder. Composed, she turned and took a large bowl, dumped some flour into it, and started adding ingredients for biscuits. Betsy had given up on escape; she knew they all watched every move she made. She was also aware that if it weren't for Vic Perrago, she would have been attacked long ago. These men were cruel, remorseless, and would never have shown her a moment's mercy. But knowledge of this dependency on Perrago inspired no gratitude in Betsy's heart. She had come to despise Vic Perrago more than she ever thought she could another human being.

The door creaked open again and Jack Masterson entered. In the gunfight with Lobo a bullet had creased his side and bounced off a rib, inflicting a painful wound. They had bound him up to stop the bleeding, and he had begun to heal almost at once. A very tall man with haggard, wolflike features, Masterson's slanted eyes glittered malevolently; together with his V-shaped face and cavernous cheeks, he indeed looked like a lean wolf. Jack Masterson spoke in a soft voice and smiled from time to time, but the smile never reached his eyes. He grabbed a chair, leaning it back against the wall, sat down and intoned, "After the fight, I went out and looked around. Those tracks. That wasn't no Indians that hit us."

"I know that," Perrago said shortly. He had looked over the grounds himself. "The horses were all shod. No such thing as an Indian war party shoeing their horses."

"We got one of them," Masterson nodded with satisfaction. "Left blood all over the place. Hope we killed the dirty dog." His soft voice clashed with his hateful words.

Perrago looked at him straight-faced, then turned to Ogg. "Who do you think it was, Buck? What were they doing way out there? You think they were looking for us?"

With great deliberation Ogg laid down a red queen on a black king, then systematically filed through the cards by threes. His movements were sluggish as his mind raced. "It's hard to say. Marshals wouldn't have run off like that—unless someone was hurt bad. I don't know, Vic. Maybe just some hardcases who ran blind into something a little harder than they thought and got drove off."

Perrago was unconvinced. He had a suspicious mind and he nurtured it; suspicion had kept him alive so far. It seemed that Vic had a sixth sense for danger.

Ogg continued playing cards, never glancing up. He concentrated laboriously on the simple game, which was typical of the man. Whatever he did, he did with the whole power and force of his intellect.

Perrago went outside. Betsy became uncomfortably aware of the slate-colored eyes of Jack Masterson as he leaned back in the chair, watching her intently. Ignoring him, she continued to work on the meal. Somehow, Betsy had learned to operate inside herself by building a barrier as protection against the abuse around her. Once she had visited a science laboratory where a glass bell jar had captured her imagination. It was a round, curving, symmetrical piece of glass that served as a cap for an animal used in an experiment. That memory had helped Betsy during a time when her spirit was almost broken. She had cried out to God hopelessly, ready to do away with herself, when a vision of the bell jar had risen in her mind. *Just get under that kind of protection. Don't think of anything outside of it. Picture yourself covered with a bell jar. They can beat you and abuse you, threaten you and humiliate you, but inside there, underneath the glass, you'll be safe.*

Once Betsy had learned to think this way, the protection had become a tangible thing to her, and she had realized that it was a matter of the spirit, not the mind alone. Never before had she faced such trouble, and never had she been a girl to pray. Like her sister, she had been dutiful in her religious obligations. But after that vision, it seemed that she could just call out and God's globe of protection would descend on her, invisible to everyone. And as it settled over her, no matter what went on outside, there was an inner peace that kept her safe. Betsy had learned to be humbly grateful for it, realizing that it came from God.

She went about her work preparing the meal. When it was ready the men all trooped in and sat down. Bob Pratt was the only one who had ever shown any sign of decency toward her. He helped her set the table and bring the food in. Grat Duvall watched him and smirked maliciously. "You'd make a mighty fine waiter, Bob. If you don't get rich bein' an outlaw, you kin always git a job waitin' tables in a fancy restaurant."

Pratt's face flushed with anger and he turned with a heated retort on his lips. But Duvall grinned up at him with mocking innocence and Pratt shrugged it off.

Bob Pratt was the youngest of the band and had been with Perrago the shortest time. Some redeeming qualities were still there, down deep, although there was no doubt he was a rough young man and had led a violent life. Once, as he was helping Betsy clean up a mountain of dirty dishes, he had told her about himself. Pratt had come from a good family. His father and mother were godly and kind people; but they had died together from some sickness, leaving their only son alone. Rough people had taken him in, and the young orphan had followed in their ways.

"I sure do miss Ma and Pa," he had said almost plaintively. "They was good folks."

"I can see that, Bob," Betsy said gently. She smiled at him. "You're too good for this kind of life. I wish you'd get out of it."

Pratt stared at her, flushed, then muttered, "Too late for me. I ain't got no education nor nothin'."

Betsy said little more to him, but she thought of him often. If she ever made her escape, it would require help. And Bob Pratt, she realized, was the only one who had any semblance of human kindness left in him. He might, just might, help her if she needed it.

Honey Ward—who had been killed—had seemed simple enough, but the others could not be trusted. Ogg would never help her, under any circumstance. Masterson frightened her, as did Mateo Río, the tall, immaculate Mexican. Grat Duvall was a snake, she knew, for all his smiling. He was a man of fifty, homely, with a sly sharpness that would let nothing get by.

After the meal, the men shoved back from the table and smoked cigarettes. When their bellies were full, there was usually a short respite from the tensions of close-quartered living. Masterson finally said, "When are we gonna get out on a job? I'm broke, Vic. We can't stay around this place forever!" Duvall and Pratt jumped in the conversation, more than ready to break the monotony.

A loud argument was in full swing when suddenly Vic glanced out the window. Betsy saw his face change, and he jumped to his feet. As he stalked to the door, his hand fell to his gun, freeing it from its leather sheath with incredible speed. "Somebody comin'," he growled. Immediately all of them leaped to their feet. Every man was always at the ready, expecting the law to ride over the hills, or another band of outlaws, or renegade Indians. Betsy backed up against the wall, her heart thudding, hopeful that this might be someone sent to find her.

"Who is it?" Ogg asked. "I can't see so good anymore."

Vic Perrago could see very well. His eyes were almost as good as an Indian's. "Two of them," he answered. "Not marshals, I don't think. They wouldn't come ridin' up to the front door like this. C'mon—get out there and get ready. There may be more of 'em," he warned.

They all filed outside and spread out, Pratt stopping to pick up a rifle on the way. "If they move, or if they give any signals, put 'em down, Bob," Perrago ordered harshly, then turned to face the approaching riders.

When the horsemen had gotten two hundred yards out, Vic squinted his eyes and said in astonishment, "I know one of 'em, anyhow. That's Lobo Smith."

"Lobo!" Pratt lowered his rifle. "Haven't seen him in a long time. Who's that with him?"

Perrago squinted, trying to see Lobo's companion. "Got a woman with him." Suspicion darkened his deceptively handsome face and he muttered, "Never heard of Lobo takin' up with any woman." They waited, guns ready.

When the riders were fifty feet away, they stopped. "Hello, Vic!" Lobo called out. "Got our welcomin' party all ready, I see!"

The two riders pulled up. They sat calmly on their horses as Perrago stared up at them, masking his suspicion with a smile. "Hello, Lobo. What are you doing out here, in the middle of nowhere? And who's your lady friend there?"

Lobo slipped off his horse and stretched indolently, like a cat, and arched his back stiffly. "Came lookin' for you, Vic." He turned around and indicated the still figure of the woman. "Like for you to meet Miss Irene Johnson."

Perrago and all the other members of the band zeroed in on the woman. It was a hard moment for Lanie. She had never seen Perrago, but as his intense gaze turned full force on her, she was afraid he would see the anger in her. It had become a flame, burning inside her, in the weeks since he had deceived her sister. She glanced at him briefly, then looked back down at her hands, which she kept folded on the saddle.

"You don't come visitin' very often," Perrago said as he turned back to Lobo. The note of suspicion marked his voice. "But come on in and bring your lady with you. We were just eatin'."

"Sounds good to me," Lobo said with a languid grin. "My stomach's been rumblin' some time." He grabbed the reins of Lanie's horse and barked, "Get off that horse, lady." When Lanie did not move his face grew stern. Moving around his own horse he reached up, grabbed her arm, and dragged her from the saddle. "Didn't you hear me? I said, get off that horse!"

Lobo kept his hold on her arm and half dragged her across the yard, talking to Vic all the while. "She's a little bit . . . shy, Vic. But she'll be all right after I've had a chance to tame her down. You know how it is with a spooky filly. Just have to use the spurs on 'em until they learn who's boss."

Vic was staring at the girl, and when Lanie raised her eyes there was one terror-filled moment when she thought he recognized her. For the very first time the thought came to her that Vic may have seen a picture of her at their house. She wouldn't have been surprised to see the man pull his gun and blast them into the dust.

But then Vic smiled—a cruel smile, to be sure—and said, "I didn't know you were a ladies' man, Lobo. Come on in, both of you." He led the way into the cabin, adding, "Maybe I can give you some lessons. I've got a woman of my own now."

Inside, Betsy had come to the window, which was open to admit fresh air. Her heart had almost stopped when she saw Lanie. For several moments her mind reeled and somersaulted as she tried to impose some mental order. Then she heard Lobo's introduction—not Lanie's name—and quickly she grasped what was going on. *She's here to get me,* she thought exultantly, *and that man with her, he's in on it!* Resolutely she calmed herself and thought with heightened perception, *I'll have to be careful! Real careful!*

When the men trooped back into the room, accompanied by Lanie, Betsy was standing calmly and expressionlessly, as usual. "This is my lady friend, Betsy Winslow," Vic said. "Betsy, show a little hospitality. We have company for lunch."

Without so much as a glance at her sister, Betsy began putting clean plates on the table. Her heart was racing, but she was determined to show no emotion whatsoever, and her hands remained steady, her face composed.

Lanie felt overwhelming relief when Betsy did not respond to her. *Thank God*, she thought fervently. *If she had given us away, all of us would be dead.*

She and Lobo had meticulously planned how to get into the outlaws' hideout. Lobo had said, "You know, we can plan all we want to, Lanie. But after we get there, there'll be other players, and we sure can't plan *them*! So we'll just have to play it close to the vest." His words were cautious, but he smiled at her with encouragement. "We don't know what we'll find, you see. The chance to get Betsy away may not come for a while—probably won't. They'll be watching us like hawks. Vic is sharp, crafty as any wolf you ever saw. He'll have to be convinced before we have any chance at all."

Now, as Betsy set the table, Lobo took Lanie's arm and ordered her roughly, "Sit down and eat. I'm tired of your snippy ways. Eat!" He looked across the room at Vic Perrago and shrugged. "She's been nothin' but a nuisance ever since I left with her."

Perrago's eyes narrowed, and he furtively glanced at Buckley Ogg. The fat man's muddy eyes held the same suspicions as Perrago's. "You two on a honeymoon?" Perrago asked caustically.

"Might say that," Lobo replied and began shoveling food into his mouth. He grinned at Lanie roguishly, then looked back at Vic. "She's not used to the idea yet, but she'll be fine when she is."

At Lobo's sharp command, Lanie began to eat. She wanted desperately to look at Betsy, but knew that she simply must not, and kept her eyes riveted on her plate. When they were through, Perrago said mockingly, "Well, this isn't exactly a hotel for honeymooners, Lobo. Was you thinkin' to stay the night?"

Lobo leaned back, rolled a cigarette slowly, struck a match on his thumbnail and lit it. He watched the smoke rise in the air; his hand was so steady that the thin blue wisp rose as straight as a ruler to the ceiling, and Lobo nodded with sleepy satisfaction. "Thought we might, Vic." Idly looking down at the back of one hand, he went on in an offhanded tone. "Got a little business deal you might be interested in."

The hairs on the back of Perrago's neck stood on end and his voice sharpened perceptibly. "Business deal? What business deal?"

Lobo let his eyes run around the room, then said easily, "Aw, let it rest for a while. You and me'll have a private talk later."

Perrago did not argue the point, even though Buckley Ogg's bland face momentarily tightened. Vic ignored him and matched Lobo's nonchalant tone. "Yeah. I'm always interested in business." He nodded sharply toward Bob Pratt. "Pratt, you and Jack are gonna have to move out of your bedroom—for our honeymooners here."

Pratt grinned and Masterson scowled. "C'mon, Jack!" Bob said, "let's go make some room for these two lovebirds!" They went through a door in the hall and shortly came out dragging their various possessions. Bob volunteered, "We'll sleep out in the shack tonight."

They disappeared and Vic said, "Betsy! Take our guests down to their room and make 'em comfortable!" He stared hard at Lanie as he spoke, noting the girl's cheeks growing pale. Something about this woman interested him, and he kept his gaze fixed on her so steadily that Lanie became nervous, although she did not show it, keeping her eyes down and saying nothing.

Betsy moved next to Lanie and said, "This way, and if you like, I'll help you get settled down."

Lanie got up and followed her down the hall. As they passed through the door into Lanie and Lobo's room, Betsy said loudly, "The room's a mess, but you and I should be able to get it cleaned up pretty quick." She stepped inside, followed by Lanie, and they closed the door. At once they fell into each other's arms, saying nothing but clinging desperately to each other.

"Oh, Lanie—" Betsy whispered softly. "I'm so glad you came!" She looked fearfully at the door and murmured, "We've only got a minute. Be careful! I know you came to take me away, but they'll kill us in a minute if they get suspicious!"

Lanie looked at Betsy and whispered, "Oh, I'm so glad to see you, Betsy! I've been so worried!"

Betsy dropped her eyes and turned away. She walked to the window and stared out. Her back was stiff and there was a set to her head that told her sister that she was ashamed. Betsy said, "I—I'm not the same as I was when I left. I'm so—I'm so—" She broke down crying, dropped her head, and her shoulders began to shake.

Lanie rushed to her, not allowing her footsteps to make a sound. "Don't do that, don't cry! It'll be all right, Betsy!"

"I'll never be the same again!"

"God can take care of it," Lanie assured her. "We'll get you home, and you'll be all right, Betsy. It'll be like it was before."

"No," Betsy sobbed, "it'll never be like it was before." She turned to Lanie and her fine eyes glistened with tears. She pulled a handkerchief out, wiped her face, and whispered fiercely, "Be careful. I'd die if anything happened to you!" She paused, catching her breath, and continued. "And who's that man with you?"

"Lobo Smith."

"Is he an outlaw? Vic knew him. And that's the only kind of man Vic knows."

"N-no, he's a good man, Betsy. He's been a little wild, I guess, but now he's risking his life to get us out of here." Betsy, searching her sister's face, nodded, and Lanie went on, "Dad's in Fort Smith, waiting. With Tom. And Wes is there, too. Don't worry! It's going to be all right!" Then they started moving around the cluttered room, making loud cleaning noises.

In the other room, Perrago was listening to Lobo as he talked. "Haven't seen you lately, Vic. But I heard about that train job you did over on the Arkansas Valley. Musta cleaned up on that."

Vic glanced over at Mateo Río and Buckley Ogg. Río had ridden him hard after the robbery because of the scanty take. Now Río said, "No, Lobo, we didn't get rich on that one. They musta heard we were coming."

His words stung Perrago. "I can't guarantee what a train's carrying," he snarled. He was sensitive over the failure and glared at Mateo. But Río was a tough man and stared right back at him, his black eyes expressionless.

Lobo lounged in his chair, amusing himself by blowing smoke toward the ceiling and watching it curl upward. He looked slack and lazy, but his mind was racing madly. *Got to play this right*, he said sternly to himself. *Make one mistake and we're all dead.* He blew out a long smoke feather. *Perrago—he's the key to the whole thing!*

CHAPTER EIGHTEEN

THE WAY OF A WOMAN

★ ★ ★ ★

Angela Montoya pulled her horse up and stared out across the shadows that were closing over the land. The brilliant afternoon sunlight had faded, and now shadows rested on the eaves of the house, and the dusty road took on soft silver shadings. Evening's peace magnified the distant sound of the coyote's mournful howl, and for a moment she sat on her horse wishing she did not have to go down. All day she had ridden aimlessly through the wasteland, glad for the solitude of the open, rolling land.

With a sigh she touched her horse and murmured, "Come along, Lady." At the command, the mare immediately stepped out briskly toward the house. Angela was tired from her day-long ride, but physical weariness was what she had sought—maybe she would sleep tonight. As she rode in she saw two strange horses loose in the corral and wondered if they had visitors, or if one of the men had mysteriously "procured" the horses.

Riding straight to the stable, she dismounted and stripped the saddle off. She gave the mare a quick rubdown, grained her, and then turned her out into the corral. "Good girl," Angela murmured affectionately, slapping the animal's muscular flank.

The mare pranced around the corral after answering with a lively whinny.

"You're the best friend I have in the world, Lady," Angela said. Her full and rounded lips drew tight as the forlorn words hauntingly echoed and died. *Not a very good world where the best friend a woman has is a horse!* she thought wearily. Abruptly she turned toward the house, refusing to let her mind entertain something that could never be.

Stepping up on the porch, her sensitive ears picked up the clatter of dishes and the muted tones of men talking, and she knew she had come back at suppertime. She stepped inside the door, took one look in the room, and then halted. Angela Montoya was not a woman subject to frailties or weaknesses—but the sight of the man sitting on one side of the table with the black patch over his left eye unnerved her.

"Hullo, Angela," Lobo said. "You're looking well."

Lanie recognized the woman as the one who had been with the gang since Woman Killer's first sighting of the cabin. But she was totally unprepared for the cool beauty of Angela Montoya. She had the black hair, black eyes, and olive complexion of the Spanish race—all strong and fine features. Her figure was striking and lush. Angela Montoya was a woman men would be drawn to. But what caused Lanie to stare at her was the single fleeting expression that crossed the woman's face as she stared at Lobo—that, and something odd about Lobo Smith's tone as he spoke to her.

There's something between them, Lanie thought instantly. Her eyes flashed to Lobo; but no emotion showed on his face, just the same lazy expression as usual. He nodded, adding, "You're looking better than ever."

"What are *you* doing here?" Angela asked harshly. She walked closer, took off her hat, and tossed it onto a chair, then came to stand by the table. Her eyes scrutinized Lanie, making her feel as if she were being stripped raw.

Angela's back was to Vic Perrago, her eyes still riveted on Lobo. "What are these two doing here, Vic?" she demanded.

"Dropped in to talk a little business," he said casually. "On their honeymoon trip, I understand." A grin crossed his lips, and he looked devilishly handsome as he sat there, his hazel eyes bright. Vic wore fancy clothes, despite the crudeness of his surroundings. Something in him evidently demanded the finery he wore.

Then Perrago's expression changed as he addressed Angela Montoya again. "You're not being very friendly toward our guests, Angela. You and Lobo go back a long time, don't you?"

There was a barb in the question, and Angela turned to cast a poisonous stare on Vic. Then she walked over to the coffeepot, poured herself a cup, and came back to sit at the table. "What sort of business?" she asked, her sultry gaze again locked with Lobo's eye.

Lobo shifted, then leaned forward and rested his hands on the table, loosely clasped. "Guess I'd better talk it over with Vic first," he said idly.

"You will talk it over with all of us!" Angela snapped. "If it's business, the rest of us will be in on it." Antagonism edged her voice and sharpened her face, and Lobo felt the heat of it. He *had* known this woman for a long time. Angela had dangerous mood shifts; sometimes she was as sweet and tender as a summer breeze, and other times her temper slashed out as fast as lightning and as sharp as a wolf's fang.

Lobo shrugged. "All right with me. How 'bout you, Vic? You don't have any secrets from anybody?"

"Just say what you got on your mind," Vic said, irritated. Somehow the presence of Angela Montoya had made him apprehensive, and he shot out a challenge to Lobo. "Last I heard, Parker was trying to get you to be one of his marshals! For all I know, you might be wearing a badge under that vest."

Lobo reached up and pulled his vest away from his shirt, grinning at Vic. "No badge," he said cheerfully. "But if Parker wants me to work for him, that shows you what a good cover I have, doesn't it?" He glanced around the circle, gauging the faces of the gang. His own grew serious. "I've got a job coming on, Vic. But I'm not sure your bunch is able to handle it. Down a few men, aren't you? Where's Honey?"

"Dead," Perrago said shortly. "We're able to handle any job you come up with, Lobo. What is it? Spit it out!"

"All right," Lobo nodded. "Here it is. Miss Irene here has a very important father. Mr. Ralph Johnson. Now, Mr. Johnson works for the express company over in Durango."

Every member of the gang grew alert. They were aware that the Western Express handled large amounts of gold and silver. There were no mines where the offices were located, which always seemed strange, but they received shipments of gold and silver coins from the Treasury in Washington and transported it over the central parts of the country.

Buckley Ogg's muddy eyes began to glow as he pulled his massive bulk up straighter. "Western Express? Not planning on holding *that* place up, I hope. They've got enough guards to furnish an army!"

Lobo grinned at Ogg. "No, Buck, nothing like that. What I've got in mind is helping the 'transport' end of things."

Every man in the room—as well as every other outlaw—had thought of that. Vic said impatiently, "You know every train robber in the country's tried that, Smith. But they're clever. They ship out empty boxes this day, boxes loaded with rocks that day, and any day they might or might not ship out the real stuff. Anything to throw us off. Nobody ever knows what, or when."

Lobo leaned back in his chair and ran his fingers through the dark hair falling over his forehead. He looked over at Lanie and said softly, "That's right, Vic. *We* don't ever know—but Irene's father knows, don't he, sweetheart?" He let the silent tension build up in the room and then added indolently, "Your dad's in charge of the shipping, isn't he, Irene? He always knows."

An electrifying current shot around the room. Bob Pratt spoke up with excitement, "Why, if we knew which train to hit— we'd all be rich!"

"Shut up, Bob!" Perrago snapped. He leaned forward, his yellow hair gleaming in the lamplight, and stared at Lobo. He was silent for a moment, then turned his eyes on Lanie. "That right, Miss Johnson? Your father works for Western Express?"

Lanie swallowed, blinked, and nodded. "But he'll never tell you. Men have tried to get at him before. You wouldn't believe how much money he's been offered just to tell those things!"

Lobo grinned broadly, his eye gleaming in the lamplight. "But then, they didn't have his only daughter, held in Indian Territory, away from the law. Did they, honey?" he said menacingly.

"He'll see you hanged!" Lanie muttered, glaring at Lobo. "You won't get away with this!"

An excited babble rippled through the room. Grat Duvall and Bob Pratt talked excitedly. Masterson and Río, quieter men, and more deadly than Duvall and Pratt, were talking in subdued tones to each other. Lanie watched them. Each one was visibly excited, and she knew with a sense of exaltation that her idea had been good! *It's going to work,* she thought triumphantly. *They're going for the bait!*

Suddenly Angela's rich voice commanded the attention of the room. "And how do we know all this is true?" Her dark eyes were a feline glow in the lantern light, reflecting its yellow flame. Coolly she stared at Lobo and Lanie. "These two come out of nowhere and have this big scheme," she said disdainfully, "and I don't believe a word of it!"

Perrago gave Angela a thoughtful glance. She was a smart woman, he knew. "You may be right." He turned back to Lobo. "You've never done anything like this before, Lobo. You may have done a little holdup work, but you've always been a lone wolf."

"And what have I got to show for it?" Lobo shrugged. "A horse, a gun, and a blanket." Every eye in the room locked on him, and he felt the tension. This was the moment in which they would stand or fall. His voice grew rock-hard as he said to Vic, "I'm not proposing to join you, Perrago." Looking around scornfully he went on, "I don't want to live in a shack out in the desert somewhere, running from Parker's marshals! Not me! I'm gonna do one job, make a pile, and buy a ranch somewhere. Somewhere out of this forsaken territory!"

There was a loaded silence in the room. Lobo banged his cup down on the table and told the group curtly, "But I can see you're more interested in listening to Angela than anything I've got to say." He rolled to his feet and said, "C'mon, honey, let's get a little sleep. Tomorrow we're gonna pull outta here and find us a bunch with some backbone."

Lanie got up and went down the hall, followed by Lobo. As soon as they stepped inside the room, he shut the door and leaned back against it. His forehead was gleaming with perspiration. It was hot in the room—hot in the whole house. Grinning at her crookedly he said, "I never would make an actor! What do you think?"

"I think they believed you. All except for the woman." She watched his face as she mentioned Angela, but Lobo's expression didn't change. Lanie thought about the woman's strange attitude. "She hates you, Lobo! You—you two were pretty close once, weren't you?"

"How do you know that?"

"A woman doesn't have that kind of animosity unless she's loved a man," Lanie shrugged.

Lobo ran his hand through his hair and wiped his forehead lightly. "We were friends at one time," he said briefly.

From that one sentence, Lanie could tell that what she had suspected was true. *Lobo and Angela Montoya had been lovers,* she thought. *That's why she hates him. He must have walked off and left her, or done something awful.* Bluntly she said, "So, you were lovers."

Strangely enough, her words embarrassed him, but he lifted his chin a little and gazed at her unflinchingly. "Why do you care, Lanie?"

"I don't care," she retorted crossly. Then, even as she said it, Lanie realized that she did care. She cared very much! Resolutely she thrust the thought away from her. "But if she was in love with you once, you may have to use her to get us out of here."

"No."

The refusal was so flat that Lanie knew instantly there was no use in pursuing it. She was embarrassed by the scene and agitated by her own show of jealousy when faced with Lobo and Angela's relationship. Confusing and conflicting thoughts crowded her mind. She said lamely, "Well, Betsy's here and she's all right. So we have a chance."

"Yeah, we've got a chance," he replied. "And I don't want to mess this up. It's gonna be tough. They're going to be watching us like hawks, no matter what we do." He pushed himself away from the door, walked to the window, and looked outside for a few moments. Then he turned back to Lanie and continued. "They've already put a man out front. We've got to be careful, 'cause they could sneak up here. Mateo's watching this window. Someone will be watchin' it all night. They're not about to let us leave here unexpectedly."

Lanie's shoulders drooped. The hard ride and the immense

strain of the past few hours were beginning to affect her. Lobo glanced at the single bed. "You take the bed. I'll take the floor."

It was early, but they were both tired. "I'll blow out the light, and you can get undressed," he said.

"I'll just sleep in my clothes," she said hastily.

He did not reply. Finding a blanket in the gear they had brought in, he made a bed beneath the window, took off his boots, and started to lie down. Instead, he walked over to the single chair in the room, carried it to the door, and shoved it underneath the doorknob. Shrugging, he told Lanie, "Somebody might come bustin' in here, and they'd expect us to be in the same bed."

Lanie didn't reply as Lobo lay down. For days now she and Lobo had slept within five feet of each other beside campfires. But somehow being in a bedroom with him was totally different. She was apprehensive, almost afraid. She lay down on the bed stiffly, unmoving and tense, until she heard his even breathing, and then she relaxed.

Sleep didn't come at once, though. Lanie lay quiet, thinking of the strangeness of it all. Her other life—her life of teas and parties and balls and fancy dresses—seemed a million miles away. With a mental start Lanie realized that she could not easily go back to such a life. It would seem so—so tame after all she had gone through!

Suddenly she thought of her father. *Why, this is what Dad has always talked about! He's never liked it in the city!* She thought about the land she was in, how sprawling and open it was, how it made her feel so small, yet very important. *This is what Dad loves—wide open spaces. I wish we could go back to Montana, see some of those places he and Mother talk about.*

She began to worry a little about the next day. *What will we do? How will we get away? What will—*

"I'm glad Betsy's all right." Lobo's voice was quiet but it startled her.

"Yes. I was afraid. But I had a chance to talk with her a little." Lanie sighed. "She's going to have a hard time, even when we get her away from here. She's ashamed of what she's done. It's going to be very difficult for her."

"Never easy to get over your bad deeds."

His words intrigued her. "You're speaking from experience, I take it."

Lobo didn't answer her for a few moments, but finally he said, "Well, we're not on this earth here for very long, and sometimes I think it's all meaningless. But once in a while, I meet someone who's found more meaning and purpose than I ever have. Like Lorenzo." His voice grew gentle as he spoke of the marshal. "I've thought a lot about him. I knew him for a long time, and he was a good man, one whose life *meant* something."

"He died well, didn't he." Lanie's voice, too, was filled with tenderness as she thought of Lorenzo Dawkins—so hard yet so gentle and faithful to the end. "I admired him very much."

Lobo didn't answer. He considered Lorenzo, and how he'd gone out to meet death with ease and in such peace.

Sleep started to steal over him as he began thinking about how extremely careful they would have to be tomorrow. *Wouldn't put it past Vic to put a bullet in me, just out of pure suspicion. Or just plain meanness.*

And then he thought of Angela Montoya and the days they had had together. Wildly sweet memories they were to him, and yet there had been no giving in it—just total selfishness. They had used each other to feel loved but had never given of their inner selves. He then drifted off into a fitful sleep.

★　★　★　★

When Lanie awoke the next morning she looked around anxiously before remembering where she was. She glanced uneasily at the floor and saw that Lobo was gone, the blankets folded up. She got to her feet and pulled on her boots, then washed up at the basin and tried to fix her hair.

I would give anything I own to bathe and wash my hair! she thought, petulantly yanking her hair as she tried to arrange it. Then the gravity of her situation crowded her mind. She stopped fidgeting with her hair and straightened up. *Who cares what I look like? The important thing is to get Betsy away from here.*

When she walked out of the bedroom, the smell of frying bacon drifted toward her. Coming into the kitchen she looked around for Lobo, but he wasn't there, nor was Betsy. Only Buckley Ogg and Vic Perrago were in the room.

"Sit down," Vic ordered. "Your boyfriend's gone for a walk with Angela." His tone was bitter and he walked to the window to stare outside.

Ogg ignored him and said in a friendly tone, "Sit down there, Miss Johnson." He busied himself getting up to pour some coffee. "Don't worry about Vic. He's just a little irritable." His round face broke into a grin. "I guess you may not have heard, but Lobo and Angela was pretty close at one time. Looks like they might be startin' up again, and Vic's a little bit touchy about that. Aren't you, Vic?"

Perrago turned a venomous look on Ogg and walked out the door. "I'm going to go get 'em," he muttered. "We gotta talk."

Lanie heard him on the porch, calling out loudly, and then he entered the room again. He walked to the table, his legs wide apart, his arms crossed, his eyes narrow. "You sure about this, Buck?"

Ogg looked sleek and self-satisfied, almost like a Buddha, as he nodded to Perrago. "We'll look into it, Vic. Won't cost anything to listen."

The two must not have been far away, because Angela entered almost at once, followed by Lobo. Furtively scanning Angela's face, Lanie saw that the anger and animosity of the day before was gone. *Well! He said he wasn't going to use her—but it looks like that's exactly what he's doing.*

Perrago waited until the pair was seated, then said brusquely, "All right. Give us the layout on this, Lobo."

"Sure, Vic! It's simple!" Lobo said enthusiastically. "I got a man working for me—he's the go-between. Between me and Ralph Johnson, Irene's father. As soon as her father finds out she's all right, he'll send us the information about shipping." He continued to explain the plan as he, Lanie, and Woman Killer had worked it out and ended by saying, "What will happen is this—as soon as we find out that the goods are on the train, we go do the job."

"What about her?" Perrago demanded, nodding at Lanie.

"We're gonna need every man we can get on this job, so I've got a special spot all picked out for her. We shut her up in there"—he nodded toward the bedroom—"and your woman, too, I guess. We can't take 'em out to hold up a train, and we can't spare anyone to watch 'em."

Perrago considered the scheme, gnawing on his lower lip. "All right. And what about your man? How are you gonna contact him?"

Lobo leaned back in his chair nonchalantly. "Well, Vic," he drawled, "reckon if I told you everything I know, you might not need me anymore. So I'm not telling where my meeting place is with my man, and I'm not telling you who he is. What I *will* tell you—when I get the lowdown—is which train to hit. And I know the place to hit it."

Ogg broke in suddenly, "They're bound to be carrying plenty of guards with a big shipment."

"Nope. That's one thing I found out from Johnson. They don't send out a whole lot more guards when they ship out the real stuff. They figure it'd be sorta like posting a sign: 'Gold and Silver on This Here Train.' " Amused laughter rumbled in the room and Lobo continued. "Sometimes they don't send out even one more guard than usual. And that," he smiled beatifically at Lanie, "is what's gonna happen this time."

No one said anything; Vic Perrago grunted noncommitally. Lobo's chair dropped down with a crash and he leaned forward, his eye glittering. "Come on, Vic! Look at it! No guards, lots of money, one train—" With a loud clap, Lobo smashed his fist into the table. "Hit it! We're gone, and that's the last you'll see of me—any of you."

A thick silence fell over the room, and Lobo knew they were greedily weighing the possibility. His eyes surveyed the faces— Ogg, Perrago, Montoya.

"What do you think, Buck?" Vic demanded. He put great faith in the fat man's keen insight and would make no move without his agreement.

Ogg eyed Lobo as he said pleasantly, "I put no trust in any man. But I think Lobo's hungry enough to pull it off." Then his voice changed slightly and his heavy lips twisted with cruelty. "We're gonna watch you, Lobo. You're gonna be in the crosshairs at all times. One thing goes wrong, and you get a bullet in the brain. You got that?"

"Sure, Buck, I know that," Lobo said carelessly. "But don't *you* forget—I want to be rich worse than any of the rest of you." His tone couldn't have been more mild, but every person there recognized the seriousness in his words.

Approval flitted across Buckley's face and he said, "All right, Vic. Let's do it!"

"It's on," Perrago agreed. He looked around the room and added, "One more thing. I'll get some cash out of this Winslow girl. It'll take some doing, but I'm gonna get word to her old man to lay his hands on some cash and get it to me or I'll send her head in a sack."

"Gonna be hard, doin' two things at once, won't it?" Ogg said blandly.

But Vic was adamant. "No. I'll send a telegram to her old man and tell him to have the cash in Fort Smith and we'll hand the girl over."

"What's her name? Betsy what?" Lobo asked innocently.

"Winslow."

"There was a man named Winslow in town," Lobo observed helpfully. "Fella in a wheelchair. Talk was, he'd come out from Chicago, lookin' for his girl."

"That's him!" Perrago said, grinning broadly. "Good! Now I won't have to go hunting him down. I'll send Grat into town to contact him. Make him have the money ready just before the robbery, and we'll bring him the girl. Two birds with one stone."

Ogg shook his head. "Too complicated." But as Vic's face grew mutinous, Ogg saw that Perrago had made up his mind, and decided to cut his losses. "All right, all right," he said placatingly, holding up one fat hand. "I guess it can happen. You can sure use the money."

Then Ogg turned to Angela. "You been awful quiet, Angela. How about it? You for it?"

Lanie watched Angela, observing that the woman was dressed to the tee. Her entire demeanor was softer, more pliable, less threatening than the previous evening. Obviously something had happened between her and Lobo to cause these changes. As Lanie thought about it, anger stirred within her.

"It's all right with me," Angela answered, her eyes on Lobo. "I think it'll work."

Betsy came through the front door, carrying a bucket of water. Her eyes downcast, she walked into the kitchen and set the bucket on a cabinet. Perrago said expansively, "Looks like you're going home soon, honey! That is, if your old man comes up with enough hard cash." Scraping his chair back from the table, he walked to her and turned her around. Cupping her face with both hands, he leaned down and kissed her. "Think he'll pay enough for you to make a trip to town?"

Held powerless in his strong hands, Betsy did not move, nor did she answer. As always, this irritated Vic Perrago. Brutally shoving her away, he hissed, "I'll be glad to get rid of you! You're as cold as a dead fish!"

He turned back to the others and said shortly, "Lobo, the message. When's it coming?"

"I've got a spot staked out," Lobo answered. "I'll have to ride out and check it every day."

"You're not going alone," Perrago snapped.

"I'll go with him," Angela said.

Her even tone angered Perrago. He had tried his best with this woman, and at one time thought he possessed her. But now he seethed at her preference for Lobo Smith and said viciously, "I don't think I trust you, either."

"Shut up, Vic," Angela shot back. "You do your job, and I'll do mine. That's the way it'll be."

Lanie was amazed at Perrago's reaction; she had steeled herself for an explosion. But Vic merely stared at Angela, his handsome face turning slightly pale. She had some sort of control over him; perhaps it was the fearlessness in her eyes, and he finally nodded. "All right. Then that's the way it'll be."

"Might as well ride out today," Lobo said diffidently. "I don't think it'll be there, but I don't want to risk missing it." He nodded to Angela. "Whenever you're ready, Angela, we'll take us a little ride."

"All right, Lobo."

They left within a few minutes and Lanie stood at a window, watching them. Betsy came up close beside her, saying loudly, "If you need any clothes washed, Miss Johnson, I'll be glad to help you."

Still staring at the departing pair, Lanie answered distractedly, "What?—Oh yes, thank you."

A few minutes later they were outside, washing clothes in a number ten washtub. They were far enough out of earshot of the men, but had to be careful lest their actions betray them. Betsy said, without looking at her, "I'm afraid, Lanie. What if Lobo goes away and doesn't come back?"

"He'll be back," Lanie answered briefly,

Betsy looked sharply at her, turning only slightly. Then scrubbed harder. "What—who is he? What kind of a man is Lobo? The others talk about him and Angela being sweethearts once."

The words cut Lanie much deeper than she cared to admit to herself or anyone else. She shrugged her shoulders and said nothing, her eyes on the clothes in the huge tub.

But Betsy didn't give in. "Well, he does look awfully hard— that Lobo. I suppose he's just another hired killer, like everybody else around here."

"A man should learn to fight! Or put skirts about his knees!" Lanie rasped, trying to hold her anger in check. Savagely she scrubbed a shirt, her face grim.

Betsy had never seen her sister so passionately defend a man, and she stammered, "I'm—I'm sorry, Lanie! I didn't mean it! I didn't mean anything wrong! I'm just—I'm just—so scared!"

Lanie closed her eyes, her hands growing slack. Slowly, she expelled the anger she felt and forced herself to calm down. Then she opened her eyes and looked into Betsy's dismayed face. "Don't worry about Lobo, sweetie. He is a hard man, and in this particular situation, I think that's a good thing. And he *will* get us out of this. He will!"

She stared at the two riders disappearing into the distant shimmer of heat far on the horizon. "I don't know what he'll do after that—but I know he'll never quit until he does what he sets out to do."

The two women continued washing clothes, speaking quietly, both of them thinking thoughts that they didn't care to share. Betsy was thinking of trying to pick up the pieces of her life, when she saw herself as stained and soiled. And Lanie was thinking of the long ride that Angela and Lobo would take—and what that ride would be like.

CHAPTER NINETEEN

A COSTLY LOYALTY

★ ★ ★ ★

As soon as Zach Winslow looked up, he knew he was going to have trouble with Wesley Stone. Zach was sitting outside on the front porch of his hotel, the late afternoon sun going down and the air becoming cooler. He had taken to sitting out here each day, letting the air cool not only the heat of his body but also the rising temperature of his spirit.

"What's the matter, Wes?" he asked, looking up as the tall, lanky young man stalked down the boardwalk and loomed over him.

"I'll tell you what's wrong, Mr. Winslow!" Wesley said, his voice harsh and imperious. "I've stood all I can, sitting around here waiting for something to happen!" He had recovered quickly after reaching Fort Smith, and now the only sign of his wound was a hesitation and awkwardness as he moved his arm. But his face revealed the strain he had been under. "I've got to do something! I can't just sit around while Betsy and Lanie are out there!"

"Sit down, take a load off your feet." Zach Winslow knew how to handle men; and he waved toward the chair beside him. He waited until Stone sat down before he continued. "I know how you feel, Wes," he said easily. "This bum leg of mine's got me tied down like it was an anchor! If it wasn't for that, I guess

I'd be riding off in a cloud of dust, going out to find Perrago's bunch." Zach's eyes looked off into the distance to the west; out there, past the Arkansas River valley, were his two daughters, struggling for their very lives. "Guess I'd get myself killed first thing if I did. But I'd go anyway."

"Yes, you would, and that's what I'm going to do," Wesley stated vehemently.

His eyes twinkling, Zach innocently asked, "What? Get yourself killed first thing?"

"No! Go anyway!" Wesley was not amused in the least. "I'm going out there and find them, that's what I'm going to do! I heard Woman Killer giving directions to the new hideout to Lobo—I'm certain I can find it."

"And s'pose you did find 'em," Zach countered. "Are you going to gun down Perrago? Why, you can't even use a gun right now."

Frustration crossed Wesley Stone's homely features and he clenched his jaw, the muscles taut. "I know that. But I can go talk to them! Maybe Perrago's the kind of man you can talk to with money. I don't have any, but you'd pay to get Betsy back! I've heard you say so!"

Of course Zach had thought of this possibility, and several other options, only to find himself caught in a mire of conflicting desires. One was to hire a bunch of tough men to go out, surround Perrago's band and shoot it out with them; the other was simply to go offer Vic Perrago money. He sighed deeply, the lines of fatigue and weariness on his own face beginning to show. "I know, Wes. And I really think that's what it's going to come to. That scheme of Lanie's—" Zach's face was troubled, and he bit his lip nervously. "It's just too tricky. I never did like complicated situations. You lawyers like 'em—put as many complications as you can up before somebody. But I always like to go straight through. That was the way it was in the war," he said. "The fancy generals marched around, trying this and that and the other till we didn't know which way we were facing. But men like Grant—they'd see a flag and drive us forward! No turning, no backing off, no lying down! Just go take it! That's what I always liked about Grant. Heard someone say one time that he looked like a man that had lowered his head and was about to run it through a solid oak door!" He smiled faintly, saying, "I guess I'm kinda like that, Wes."

Stone had listened quietly to Zach and now thought over what the older man had said. Finally he admitted, "You're right about lawyers. We do like complicated things. But I agree with you on this: that stunt of Lanie's is dangerous." He turned to Zach and asked earnestly, "If I go out there and talk to Perrago, how much would you be willing to pay?"

"Everything I've got," Zach declared, "but that wouldn't suit him. He'd want more. So what we'd have to do is ask his price and make a counter offer, and sooner or later he'd get reasonable." The more he thought of it the more he liked it. "You know, Wes, I wouldn't be opposed if you'd go out there and talk to Perrago."

"I could find him, I think. I'm not much of a plainsman, but the directions sounded simple enough. I believe I could get to it," Wesley said speculatively.

Zach Winslow thought it over carefully for a while. Finally he said reluctantly, "No, Wes, I guess not. If you had just a little more experience, I'd say to give it a try. I wish now I'd just told Lobo to go out and deal with Perrago. But I wasn't thinking clearly, I was so mad!" Stiffly Zach shifted in the wheelchair, grunting a little. "Anyway, if we tried it now, we might mess up whatever Lobo's got going. So we better just dig in and wait."

Wesley leaned back in the chair and said meekly, "All right, Mr. Winslow."

Zach was surprised that the young man had given up so easily. He was a stubborn man, a trait Zach secretly admired, and which he thought would give him more of a problem with the young lawyer. But he merely said, "Thanks, son. I know how hard it is for you. That's a costly loyalty you have, willing to risk your life for my girls. But this time it just wouldn't work."

The next morning, however, when Tom pushed Zach into the dining hall for breakfast, Zach was handed a note by the manager of the hotel. "Mr. Stone asked me to give you this, Mr. Winslow," he said.

Zach opened the note and stared at it.

"What does it say, Dad?" Tom asked curiously.

Looking up into the boy's clear eyes he answered calmly,

"Stone has gone out to find your sister. He's going to negotiate her return." But inside, Zach was furiously berating himself. *I should have known it! By the horns of the devil himself, I should have known this was what he was going to do!* he thought with rising fury at his own blindness. *When Wes gave up like that, I knew that wasn't like him at all! Now what am I going to do? Four of them out there, dancing to Vic Perrago's music. Blast this leg!*

"What's the matter, Dad?" Tom asked. He had always been sensitive to his father's moods and knew that despite Zach's calm words, there was a seething anger inside his father.

Zach took a deep breath. He had learned long ago that if you can't whip a situation, you may just have to sit and wait. And now that was all he could do. "It's—nothing, Tom. We just have to sit and wait. It's hard, but we'll just have to grit our teeth and do it."

★ ★ ★ ★

"How much farther is it, Lobo?" Angela asked. The two were riding along and the sun was halfway down the sky. "It'll be dark by the time we get back, even if we started back right now."

"You were never afraid of the dark, Angela," he teased. "Or anything else, that I ever found out."

They had ridden steadily, stopping only at noon for an hour's rest from the hot sun. They had eaten a lunch that Angela had had foresight to bring, and then they had forged on without lingering. All afternoon the two had kept their horses at a steady pace. Lobo said nothing to her about their destination; he knew he had to deceive Angela, and he knew also that she was a hard woman to deceive.

To conceal his motives he kept up a light conversation for most of the afternoon, but she had finally asked about their destination. He pointed and said, "About four or five miles down that trail and we're there."

She looked in the direction of his gesture and saw a low line of hills, broken by a high outcropping of stone. It was a huge trunk of molten, rough stone, at least as big as a house, and it made a natural landmark among the smoothly rolling hills. "I've been by here before," she told Lobo. "Everybody sees that stone and remembers it."

"Yeah, that's why I chose it, so my man could find it," Lobo said lightly. He had worked all of this out with Woman Killer.

"That big rock will be our checkpoint," Lobo had told Woman Killer. "There's a place at the base of it, a sort of a crevice, that I found one time out there wandering around. You can't see it. You can walk right by it, but it's carved out of the rock and covered by a scrub growth. I put a glass jar in there, and that's how we'll pass messages. When I want you to do something, I'll put a note in there."

It was Woman Killer's job to watch this secret place. They rode up to the rock, seeing no one, but Lobo knew that somewhere out there the Indian was watching carefully, and that as soon as they left, the message would be immediately taken to Zach Winslow.

Pulling up to the rock, he dismounted, saying, "This is it."

Angela swung off her horse and they tied the reins to a sapling, and he led her around the base of the rock to the eastern side. He looked at her and said, "I wouldn't have let anyone else come but you, Angela. I don't trust Vic Perrago any farther than I could throw him."

Her eyes were very dark as she met his gaze. "He doesn't trust you either, Lobo. You know that."

"I know Vic," Lobo nodded. "He never trusted anybody in his life."

Lobo suddenly turned and bent down. "Here it is," he told her. With his back to Angela, he slipped his hand in the tiny cave, scratching around in the crevice to get the jar.

Now he turned to her, holding the jar, and said casually, "Well, we got something here." He pulled out the piece of paper and studied it carefully, even though he knew Woman Killer had printed it last night.

Angela was watching him closely, and he handed her the message. She read it quickly: *Your man says that the train you want will be leaving within three days. He won't say which train it is until you send a letter from his daughter, proving she's still alive.*

Angela looked up and handed the note back. "So we have to go back and get a letter from the girl."

"That's right. Means another long ride tomorrow. Maybe you won't have to make it, though."

"I don't mind, Lobo," she said.

Lobo studied her for a moment, wondering what was on her mind. He had never understood Angela Montoya, and she was still a puzzle to him. He admired her strength and clean beauty, but as for her inner qualities, he had never gotten past the barriers she had erected—in that sense she was still a stranger.

Pushing it out of his mind, he pulled a stub of a pencil and a small piece of paper out of his shirt pocket. Bending down, he laid the paper on a rock, scribbled something, stuck it back into the jar, and started to place it in the crevice.

"Let me see what you've written," Angela said lightly.

He looked up at her quickly with humor in his eye. "Don't trust me?"

"I don't trust any man," she answered evenly. "You should know that."

He slowly unscrewed the jar cap, saying, "I thought you did, once." He handed her the paper. "At least I thought you had some kind of feeling for me."

Angela took the paper, her dark eyes fixed on his face. "You were the one who rode away, Lobo." She looked down at the note, which said merely: *Be here tomorrow for the letter.* It was unsigned.

Wordlessly she handed it back to him, and he put it back in the jar, capped it, and replaced it in the small hiding place.

Straightening up he said, "Well, long ride home."

"Let's walk for a minute. I get stiff from so much riding," which wasn't the truth; she just wanted to talk to Lobo.

There was no landscape to admire, nothing but the rolling country, broken in places by far-off low-lying hills. The sky was clear. The sun glared down on them like a malevolent eye, bathing them in a heat so intense it was almost like a physical blow.

They walked around the rock and meandered out to a group of nearby cottonwoods that marked a creek bed. But when they got there the creek was dry. The unmistakable rattle of a snake startled Angela and she turned quickly, brushing against Lobo.

"Big one," Lobo said, nodding at the huge diamondback that lay coiled in the middle of the dry, cracked creek bed. They stood still; the snake finally was convinced that he was not being attacked. Languidly he uncoiled and went slithering soundlessly off into the brush.

They stood close together and Angela looked up into Lobo's face. "I'll be glad when the sun goes down. It'll be cooler then."

Abruptly he asked, "How are you, Angela?"

In the old times she had gotten accustomed to his coded questions, and she had learned how to read them. *He's really asking me,* she thought, *why I'm wasting my time out here with this worthless bunch of outlaws. I wish I had an answer to give him.*

She pushed her hat off so it hung down her back by the leather thong around her neck. Her hair had been carelessly stuffed up into the hat, and now it fell down around her shoulders like a black cascade. Lobo stared at the silky veil. *He always liked my hair,* she thought. She said with a streak of whimsy, "So you still like my hair. Sometimes I think that's all you did like about me."

Lobo was taken aback by her shrewdness, and embarrassed by her frank honesty. He looked at the ground and muttered, "Well, sure, Angela. I mean, yes, I always liked your hair. But I liked other things about you, too."

"I remember," she said with emphasis.

The simplicity of her words brought heat to his face, for they brought back memories of intimacy that Lobo had never forgotten.

She saw his discomfort and was amused by it momentarily. Then she sobered and asked, "Why did you leave, Lobo?"

"I don't know," Lobo shrugged. "Never had a good answer to that question. Wasn't your fault, though," he added quickly. "I'm just fiddle-footed. Still don't know what to do with myself."

"So," Angela said matter-of-factly, "I guess that is my answer to your question: How am I?" She reached up and pushed her hair away from her face with an impatient gesture. To Lobo, Angela seemed restless, angry, hopeless, and defiant—all at the same time. "I don't know what I'm doing out here. Every day I think I'll leave. But the next day I'm still here." She turned to stare out across the glaring plains. "Six months ago I went off to Little Rock. Stayed for two weeks."

Lobo waited for her to finish, but she did not. She turned and he could not help admiring the smooth lines of her rounded body, revealed clearly by the thin white shirt that she wore. "Why'd you come back?" he prodded her.

"I don't know," she shrugged. "I was bored."

She turned back toward the horses and Lobo followed. Lobo couldn't see the strange light that came into her eyes and the enigmatic smile on her lips. Without warning she turned. They were close together and without preamble she reached up, put her arms around him, and drew his head down to meet hers. Startled, Lobo met her lips and without thinking clasped her tightly in his arms. She fell against him, holding him fiercely. Immediately Lobo felt the stirrings of old memories of the times he'd had with this woman, the softness of her lips, the firmness of her body against his. Angela had always been able to awaken his desires in this way, to bring out the hunger in him.

He clasped even closer. Abruptly she pulled back, both hands against his chest, and looked at him defiantly. "I wanted you to remember what you threw away," she said coldly. Then without another word she turned and went straight to the horses. Swinging up in the saddle, she prompted the mare and was a hundred yards away by the time Lobo got mounted and turned his horse around.

He was half angry at the woman—but at the same time amused at her game. *She did that on purpose,* he thought, *just to unnerve me! Nothing that woman ever does is accidental. She wanted to stir me up. I'll have to watch her.*

As he touched his spurs to his mount, he was oblivious to everything but their encounter and found that he could not dismiss the memories that had flowed over him when she pressed against him with her lips—the hungers and stirrings she had awakened within him.

★　★　★　★

"Seems late to have lights on," Lobo commented. They had pulled up on the rise overlooking the cabin. It was after one a.m., and the windows were bright yellowed squares as the amber light shed itself on the ground outside. "Isn't everyone usually in bed by this time?"

"C'mon, let's go see," Angela said, and spurred her horse forward.

When they were within two hundred yards of the house a voice called out, "Who's there?"

"Angela! What's going on, Bob?"

Pratt strode out of the darkness, his rifle in hand. "Caught a fella sneaking up around here," he said. "We think he was with that bunch that cut down on us a while back when Honey got killed."

A dread chill struck Lobo, and when they walked inside the cabin his fears were confirmed. Wesley Stone! Stone looked a mess—his face was bleeding and twisted with pain, blood streaming from one eyebrow, his hands tied behind his back. But he gave no sign that he recognized Lobo.

"Look what we caught, Angela!" Vic said, sounding like a child giving her a gift. He reached out and grabbed Wesley's hair, jerking his head backward. "He's a pretty stubborn one. Tougher'n he looks, I'll give him that."

A slight involuntary groan escaped Stone's lips as Perrago gave his victim's head another bone-cracking jerk. "Won't talk a bit," Vic said angrily, "except for some phoney story."

"What's the story?" Angela demanded.

Ogg spoke up. "I'm not so sure it's a lie. He claims he works for Betsy's father."

"He does work for my father," Betsy said. "I've told you that. Leave him alone!"

"He may work for Winslow, all right," Perrago said, "but that don't mean nothin'. He could've led a whole bunch out here." He appeared worried as he looked at Mateo Río. "Mateo, you go out and watch with Bob. Need two pair of sharp eyes out there."

Río nodded. "That might not be a bad idea, Vic. We could get boxed in here real easy." He sauntered out the door.

Angela stared dispassionately at Wesley's battered face. "Tell me your story," she commanded coolly.

Stone blinked his eyes and licked his cracked and dry lips. "I work for Zachary Winslow," he croaked. His tongue moved across his lips again as he tried to speak.

Angela walked over, poured some water into a cup, and put it to Wesley's lips. "Untie him, Lobo," she ordered. Lobo quickly stepped forward and removed the knotted ropes holding Wesley to the chair.

A quick flush spread over Vic Perrago's cheeks. "I'll give the orders around here, Angela—"

"You're a *fool*, Vic!" Angela snapped back. "The chance to make that money on her"—she nodded disdainfully at Betsy—"that you've been yelling about just walks in through the front door. And now you act like a stupid kid! What are you scared of, shadows or something?"

Her stinging derision turned his angry flush to a pasty gray, his hazel eyes to smoldering hatred. "That's enough, Angela," he snarled. "I know you're tough, but I'm not putting up with that smart mouth of yours anymore."

His malevolent gaze shifted to Lobo. "And you're not taking over this bunch, either! Got that, Lobo?"

"Never intended to," Lobo shrugged. He knew enough to keep quiet and let Angela handle it.

Stone rose unsteadily to his feet, rubbed his wrists, and downed the water left in the cup. "Here's the way it is," Wesley said to Angela. "Mr. Winslow is in Fort Smith. He's willing to pay to get his daughter back. I am here to make the arrangements, and that's all there is to it."

"We've got too much at stake to be trying to do two things at once," Angela said meaningfully to Vic, her hands on her hips.

Perrago's eyes shifted to Lobo, then back to her. "What'd you find out?"

"The deal's on," she said. "We have to take a letter from the woman." She glanced at Lanie, who was backed up against a wall. She had remained completely silent since Stone had been brought in. At the sight of him, her heart had sunk. Now everything was even more complicated.

Perrago furrowed his brow and came to a decision. "All right. Let's kill two birds with one stone. You'll take that letter in from the woman tomorrow. But we're not going to let this joker go back—you can write a letter, too, tenderfoot," he nodded to Stone. "You're going to let Winslow know how much he's got to come up with for his daughter, and where he needs to put it. And we'll just hang on to you for a little extra—uh, surety, we'll say."

This is getting out of hand, Lobo thought apprehensively but didn't say anything. Then another thought eased his nerves: *The more Vic has to keep up with, the better chance we have of getting away with it.*

Later that night, when Lobo and Lanie were in their room alone, Lobo told her about the message and the instructions. She listened anxiously and asked, "Now what do you think?"

Lobo knew she was worried about the complications Wesley's presence had brought. He said reassuringly, "I think we can pull it off. We've just gotta work it so that the ransom helps to keep things moving. Keep Perrago thinkin' about that, and he won't have his mind so much on me and on this train robbery. That way, we'll have a good chance to trip him up."

They both sat silently for a while; then Lanie said abruptly, "Did you have a good ride with Angela?" Once the words escaped her lips, she was embarrassed she'd asked.

"Why—yeah, I guess," he said, caught off guard. "Pretty long ride."

Lanie's body tensed, her face grew stiff and cold. "Bet you didn't mind," she muttered, then stalked across the room to stare out the window. "I suppose you're taking her back tomorrow."

"I guess they'll send her with me." He was puzzled, wary of the underlying messages Lanie left unspoken, but he didn't understand why she was upset. Lanie glanced sharply at him over her shoulder but said nothing else.

They turned out the lights and Lanie finally lay on the bed, Lobo on his pallet on the floor. He wondered about her attitude, why she had turned on him so suddenly, but his questions remained unanswered as sleep overtook him.

CHAPTER TWENTY

A NEW KIND OF FEELING

★ ★ ★ ★

Two days had passed since Perrago had captured Stone, but the atmosphere inside the cabin still remained charged. There was an ominous silence, almost a breathless quality in the air; but it was as deceptive as the peaceful weather before a tornado that could be broken at any moment by the screaming violence of a twister.

The strain made Betsy feel uneasy, so she took some clothes down to the creek that ran close to the house, and was scrubbing them energetically on a washboard perched inside her washtub when Stone approached her. Both of them were acutely aware that Jack Masterson sat on the front porch, his rifle across his knees, his dark eyes never wavering from them.

Betsy picked up a bar of lye soap, grabbed a shirt, and began to rub it briskly across the washboard with the soap, lathering it up with frolicky soap bubbles. As she worked she said quietly, "I'm sorry you came, Wes."

He looked at her with surprise. The deep cut over his right eyebrow was crusted over now, but was still swollen and discolored, an unpleasant mixture of yellow and purple. It appeared he would have an angry red scar there; it should have been sewn up, but there was no one there with the skill or the materials to do it.

"I had to come," he said finally, picking up a stick where he had sat down under the cottonwood trees. "I just couldn't sit around Fort Smith, waiting for something to happen."

"I know you're worried about Lanie," she said evenly.

Stone eyed her carefully as she spoke. Betsy was wearing a simple brown dress that billowed slightly in the hot breeze. Her gaze was averted as she carefully scrubbed, and Wes thought of the times he had spent with this young girl. "I really don't think it was Lanie I was so worried about," he said simply. She stopped scrubbing and looked up in surprise, and he shrugged. Twirling the stick in his hand he said, "She has Lobo with her, and I think he's well able to take care of anyone. It was you I was thinking about." Still Betsy didn't move, she merely stood there with the same look of surprise. He grinned. "I guess you're kind of like my kid sister, Betsy. We've spent a lot of time together."

Those times seemed far and distant now, back when she was—different. "Yes, we did have fun times," she said softly, and sighed. Then she smiled up at him and began her business-like scrubbing again. "I was always glad when Lanie wouldn't go with you, 'cause I knew then that I'd have you to myself."

"You are a designing female!" Wesley declared, grinning at her.

Betsy bit her lip and ducked her head to hide her face. It seemed to Wesley that she scrubbed with unnecessary violence. It was early in the morning and the desert was already beginning to simmer. Stone realized he had said something that bothered her, but thinking over his words, he could not understand what it was. He studied her, wondering what she was thinking. Wesley had been surprised—even amazed—at the depth of his emotions when Perrago had taken her, and still he could not quite define his feelings toward Betsy.

He picked up a stone and threw it in the creek. He was restless, but there was nothing to do but wait. Lanie stayed in the house under the watchful eye of one of the men. Lobo and Angela had ridden out quite early that morning. Last night Lobo had made enough casual comments in his presence so that Stone understood exactly what they were doing. To cheer Betsy up he said idly, "We'll be out of here soon and you'll be home again."

"I'm not going home."

Stone's head jerked sharply as he turned to look at Betsy's face. "What do you mean, you're not going home?"

The hot, dry wind blew harder, and Betsy's hair lifted around her face. She reached up and impatiently shoved a lock back. Looking very young and vulnerable, she turned to Wesley and murmured, "I can never go home." Her soft lips trembled.

Wesley knew Betsy well, and he understood that she was afraid—and ashamed. Ordinarily Stone was good with words, concise and articulate. But he had no idea how to speak comfort to this young woman he was so fond of. Carefully he said, "Of course you're going home, Betsy! Where else would you go? Your parents are worried sick about you."

Betsy did not answer for a time. Then she looked at him and tears shimmered in her eyes. "You know why I can't go back, Wesley," she said sadly. "You've always known what I was thinking."

"Because of Perrago?"

"Yes." The single word was hard as granite, and Wesley saw that, in Betsy's mind, she was condemned and guilty. He longed to console her. *I'll have to be very gentle*, he thought as he watched her. "Betsy, I know it seems bad right now," he said softly, "but I promise that time will help. You don't see that now, I know, but it always does." Betsy ducked her head again and stood motionless.

Wesley knew the whole story; how Perrago had deceived her and then pretended to marry her. Stone spoke firmly. "Your heart was right, Betsy. Your actions were impetuous and careless—but the outcome of it wasn't your fault. God's not going to hold you accountable for Vic Perrago's sin."

"I hold myself accountable," she said, almost inaudibly. "I'm—ruined, Wesley, and you know it. No man will ever want me now!"

"Why—why—that's crazy, Betsy!" He jumped to his feet and took a step closer to her. Her humiliation and shame ran much deeper than he had thought. "No man is going to hold this against you, Betsy!"

Betsy did not answer; slowly she began scrubbing the clothes again. Stone moved closer and put his hand on her shoulder and she turned her eyes up to meet his gaze. "No one who knows you, Betsy," he said passionately, "would ever think that you're anything but a sweet girl! Impulsive and rash sometimes—but good!"

Betsy blinked back tears. She murmured, "Thank you, Wes. That's like you!"

He knew he had not convinced her, and he sighed deeply. *There's time*, he told himself firmly. *Just need to get her out of this place, and she'll be all right. We'll get her back home. I'm not going to let her brood on all this.* Lightly Wesley squeezed her shoulder and returned to sit back down under the tree.

He stayed with her until she finished the washing and they returned to the cabin. When they passed close to Masterson he drawled, "I was kinda hopin' you'd make a break for it, Mr. Lawyer. Lookin' forward to blowin' the top of your head off." His voice was light and mocking, which made his words even more chilling, his face wreathed in unbridled cruelty. There was no doubt in Wesley's mind that the outlaw would do exactly as he said. Neither he nor Betsy answered. Betsy went into the house, and Wesley sat down on the porch by the open door of the cabin, staring out across the hills.

Wesley had no opportunity to speak to Betsy alone again, and he was afraid to even look at Lanie. He wasn't supposed to know her, of course, or be at all concerned with what she was doing there. These outlaws were crafty and watchful; and Wesley knew that an unguarded word or even a look might tip them off.

Perrago and Grat Duvall had ridden off earlier in the day. At noon Wesley, still sitting on the porch, saw them ride in. Their horses were lathered, and both men were covered with the gray dust of the trail. Looking up, Perrago said brusquely, "Here, you. Take these horses and unsaddle 'em. Rub 'em down and give 'em a little water—not too much—and grain."

"All right." Wesley took the reins of the two weary horses and led them into the barn. He stripped the saddles off warily; he didn't know much about horses and was slightly afraid of these two. They seemed like half-wild, rowdy mustangs to him. But he managed to carry out Perrago's instructions without too much fumbling. Turning the two animals loose into the corral, he went back to the cabin.

As Wesley arrived he saw Vic Perrago looming over Betsy, cursing her in a slow, steady tone. Clutching her arm in a cruel grip, he started dragging her through the kitchen toward the hall—and the bedrooms. Betsy was furiously fighting him. Vic's hand shot out and he struck Betsy across the cheek, sounding a loud crack in the room. Betsy stumbled and fell headlong against a cabinet.

Without thinking, Wesley threw himself at Vic Perrago and caught him high on the cheekbone with a wild blow. Perrago staggered back; then instantly grabbed his gun. Buckley Ogg yelled, "Don't kill him, Vic!"

Murderous anger flashed in Perrago's eyes. For one moment, as Wesley stared into the black hole of the gun, he was certain that he was a dead man. Suddenly Perrago shoved the gun back into his holster and in a liquid movement brought his hand back up to land a stunning blow to Stone's face. Vic's rocklike fist caught Wesley square on the mouth. Instant pain darkened Wesley's mind and he reeled backward, half conscious, doubled over, and fell. As he hit the floor, a boot landed dead center over his kidney, sending a searing bolt of pain through him unlike anything Wesley had ever known. He tried to rise, desperately trying to shield himself from the rain of blows, but again and again Perrago's blows and kicks threw him to the floor.

"That's enough, Vic!" Ogg yelled, stepping between them. "We've got to use him, and he ain't gonna be worth a dime if you don't stop it."

Perrago's handsome features had twisted into those of an almost unrecognizable monster of rage, so consumed with fury and frenzy that he had lost all sense of reason. No man crossed Vic Perrago, and being struck by a rawboned, tenderfoot lawyer had unveiled all the black malice that lay beneath the well-groomed surface. His face was pale and sweaty, his lips drawn back in a wolfish grimace.

His voice came in rasps as he finally drew in a deep, shuddering breath, his eyes focused on Stone, a motionless form at his feet. "Don't open your mouth, you hear me! Not ever again, or I'll kill you!" He turned on his heel and stalked out of the house.

"You women, help me clean him up," Ogg muttered as he

bent over Wesley. Masterson had come in to watch with vicious amusement, and Grat Duvall also stood close by, showing no emotion whatsoever. Mateo Río watched with ill-disguised enjoyment. But none of them offered to help Buckley as he struggled to get the battered man over to a bunk under the window of the main room.

Carefully Ogg laid him down and said, "Betsy, do the best you can for him, and you, too, Irene. Hope he ain't got no ribs busted." Quickly Lanie and Betsy began ministering to the still figure.

Though Wesley had taken a terrible beating, he was still conscious, so Betsy gently touched his ribs, asking, "Does that hurt? This?" They were relieved to find that most of the damage had been done to the flesh, that no bones seemed to be broken. Wesley had some contusions and was going to have some nasty bruises; already his face was swollen.

In a low voice, Lanie said to Betsy, "Go get some hot water. Let's get these cuts washed out before they close up."

All the next day, Stone lay there weakly, his entire body racked with pain. Of course, there was nothing but whiskey to give him to ease the pain. Finally all the men except Buckley Ogg left. While Wesley slept Betsy sat beside him. When his eyes opened she leaned over and brushed his hair back from his eyes. "Be still," she whispered. "Don't move." Her hand felt soft and cool on his forehead. "Why did you do this, Wes?" she asked with great distress. "Vic might have killed you!"

"I—I couldn't stand it when he hit you, Betsy," he said through thick, swollen lips. "I've never wanted to use a gun before, but I would've killed him if I'd had one!"

Betsy was touched by his kind words. Somehow it made her proud that, despite what she had become, this man had been willing to risk injury, or even death, for her. She rested her hand on his feverish forehead, then leaned over and kissed his cheek softly. "Thank you, Wes," she whispered, "but you must never do it again."

He looked up at her, a stubborn glint in his swollen slitted eyes and through thick lips said, "I'll do it again—if he hits you again."

★ ★ ★ ★

Vic Perrago was pacing impatiently when Lobo and Angela rode in, just after eight that evening. Before they were even dismounted he snapped, "Well? What have you got?"

"Looks good," Lobo said. He handed Perrago the paper that Woman Killer had left in the bottle.

Perrago took it, held it up to the light that streamed out of the cabin window, and squinted. " 'Shipment on three-thirty headed south out of Seligman,' " he read aloud, " 'No guards.' " He lowered the message and glared at Lobo. "I don't know that route."

"I do," Lobo said cheerfully.

Perrago rasped, "Well, come on in. We gotta plan this."

They walked inside and their eyes fell on Wesley sitting in a chair, his face puffy, his eyes dark with pain. Lobo said nothing, but threw a furtive glance at Betsy. She shook her head, almost imperceptibly.

"You women get outta here," Perrago snarled. He had been like a bad-tempered dog all day after the incident with Wesley, grunting and snarling at everyone. He sat down at the table, glancing balefully at Wesley and added, "And take this lawyer with you."

When they were gone, Vic tossed the note to Ogg, who read it and looked up at Lobo. "This all?"

Lobo shrugged. "What else do you want? We know when and where to get the money—the three-thirty just outside of Eureka Springs."

"That's just a little feeder line," Ogg frowned. "We never bothered with it. Never operated anywhere around that territory before."

Lobo pushed his hat back and leaned over, putting his forearms on the table. "I know the territory. There's a spot on that line that looks like they mighta built it just for holding up trains."

"Show me." Ogg's words were noncommittal, and he handed Lobo a piece of paper and a pencil from a pocket inside his massive vest.

Lobo sketched quickly, explaining, "After the line comes through Seligman, it has to come down and make connections with the AV Railroad. Then it'll turn east. Don't know why they got so much shipment this time, but Johnson's being straight.

He knows his daughter won't live long if it ain't right."

"So where do we hit it?" Perrago demanded. "We gotta go check out the spot." He despised being in the hands of another man—especially an unknown quantity like Lobo.

"No time for that," Ogg complained. "If we hit it, we're just gonna have time to get there."

"What'll we do with these two women? And the lawyer?" Mateo Río demanded. "We can't leave 'em here! Soon's we're out of sight, they'll be kickin' up dust back to Fort Smith. Reckon we'd have a welcome home party waitin' for us when we get back."

Lobo shook his head. "We take 'em with us." He drew a quick map, saying, "Here's the Frisco, where it comes out of Seligman. Here's Fort Smith, where it turns to take the AV to the east. Right here, at the foothills of the Bostons, the line has to go between two steep hills. And it goes between 'em after the tracks make a sharp turn." He looked up and grinned. "That means the train's gotta slow down to no more than ten miles an hour to make that turn—or it'll jump the track. And it means they can't see a thing in front of 'em 'til they're right between those hills."

Immediately Perrago saw the layout in his mind. "So when it slows down and goes between these two hills, we hit it?"

"That's it," Lobo said with satisfaction. "Never been a holdup in that part of the world. They're not gonna be lookin' for anything. Note says there won't be any guards—it'll be like taking candy from a baby!"

"Well, that don't answer my question," Río said darkly, "about those three."

"I been thinking on that," Lobo nodded with a thoughtful air. He put a small cross at the spot that he had indicated for the robbery. "Now—less than two miles away from where we hit the train, there's an empty house. Been empty a long time. Kind of funny that no one's squatted there—'course, there's nothing there. Somebody tried to start a ranch, but there ain't a drop of water close around. Anyway, it's just a one-room outfit. But the thing is, it's built outta stone, with big timbers on the roof." He looked around, and everyone seemed to be listening avidly. "So, what we do," he continued, gesturing to Perrago, "we take the two women and the lawyer and lock 'em up cozy in the house while we hold up the train. And Vic, if you wanna get the money for that Betsy, you oughta have somebody bring the ransom money someplace close around there."

Perrago stared thoughtfully at the map, then looked back up at Lobo questioningly. "That way," Lobo went on, "nobody has to come nosin' around the hideout here to get the money to you. So you turn loose the girl and the lawyer, and I turn loose the Johnson girl. You'll have the money from Winslow, we'll all have the money from the train, and we don't have to worry about those three anymore. We're finished—" Lobo leaned back in his chair and grinned again, "and we're rich."

Ogg at once began to drill Lobo with questions, who fielded them easily. He had known they would pick him to pieces, and he had known that it would be Buckley Ogg who would be the toughest to please. He and Lanie had spent long hours trying to anticipate every contingency, every factor, every possible result; they had studied the maps and asked each other every question they could think of. Occasionally Lobo was careful to say, "I don't know. Didn't think about that." It would give Ogg some room to manipulate, and soon no one interrupted Buckley Ogg as he grilled Lobo.

Finally Ogg took a deep breath, leaned back in his chair, and buckled his hands over his massive paunch. "Reckon it's all right, Vic," he nodded. "If we do it right, it's gonna go."

Grat Duvall spoke up for the first time. "I don't like it," he muttered in an ugly tone. "If we let 'em go, they're gonna squeal on us."

Lobo laughed out loud. "Squeal on you?" he said with derision. "Be a little late, won't it? It's all over with, and they're free! What, do you think they might run and tell Judge Parker that you're a bad boy? Why, Grat, the judge would be more than happy to hang you right now for that man you shot up in the Osage reserve!"

"He was just an Indian," Grat said sulkily.

"No, he wasn't," Lobo said, still grinning. Angela Montoya knew how deadly his grin was. "He was a half-breed, and he was under white man's law." Lobo continued, "You know that, Grat, and you know you don't have anything to lose anyway." He shot a look around the room and added meaningfully, "But the rest of us do—"

To his satisfaction, the others glanced furtively around, avoiding Grat Duvall's eyes. Though the others might have killed, so far no one except Duvall was actually tagged. Lobo continued. "If we kill those three people, it'll be murder, pure and simple. Parker will send Heck Thomas and twenty marshals after us. And I'm tellin' you right now, I ain't got no intention of decoratin' Maledon's scaffold."

Ogg nodded sagely, "I agree with you, Lobo. Let's keep this as easy and simple as we can. Vic, you get the money from Winslow, we get the goods from the train, and turn 'em all loose."

Perrago sat like a statue, and for one moment Lobo was afraid he was going to argue. If he did, it was all off. Finally Perrago shrugged. "If there's enough money in it, I don't care about 'em. Let 'em go."

Lobo said with satisfaction, "That's smart, Vic. We'll make a fortune outta this, and get any woman we want. Right?"

Vic Perrago turned a cold gaze on him. For long moments he didn't answer, and the chilling silence touched everyone in the room. "I don't trust you, Smith," he said, the words dropping like stones in the quiet room. "Never did. Everywhere we go, I'm going right with you. When we hold up the train, I'll be right beside you. The first thing that goes wrong, I'll put a bullet right in your head."

"If anything goes wrong, I'll know it about one second before you do, Vic," Lobo said calmly. "I'm that much smarter than you are."

Ogg snickered quietly and Angela Montoya smiled faintly. The inference of who might get shot first was wasted on the rest of the room; the men's faces were blank, as was Perrago's for a moment. Then his face grew ugly and he opened his mouth to speak, but Lobo interrupted in the same quiet voice.

"Make up your mind, Vic. I'm in because, in case you've forgotten, this is my job. And I'm not gonna dawdle around and wait for you to blow my brains out. So," Lobo sighed delicately, "I'm gonna give you the same warning you gave me. You even look sideways at me, and you won't live to spend a dime of that million dollars."

"Hey, wait a minute," Ogg said soothingly. "Let's don't be

a-carryin' on like this. Vic, what's wrong with you? This is the biggest chance we've ever had!" Ogg's voice was mild, but his face shone with perspiration, his tiny eyes gleaming with excitement. "But if all you're payin' attention to is how quick you can shoot Lobo, you ain't gonna be worth a dime! And what good is it gonna do to put a bullet in Vic, Lobo? That what's gonna put any money in your pocket? No. So you two settle down."

Vic Perrago listened to Ogg, a surly look on his face. Taking a deep breath he said, "All right. Forget it, Lobo."

"Sure."

Pratt, Río, Masterson, and Duvall proceeded to get drunk, bragging about what they were going to do with their money. Ogg, Perrago, Lobo, and Angela continued to sit at the table, talking quietly about the job.

Back in the room where the three captives were, Lanie said, "If he hurts you, Betsy, Father will have the bones hot from his body," using the same Welsh expression her mother had spoken.

Betsy looked at Wesley, and he knew what she was thinking. Neither of them said anything, but Lanie noticed that Betsy was staying close beside Stone as though she needed his nearness as reassurance. *Right you, girl,* Lanie thought, *there would be a man for you!* Then her heart went heavy as she thought of the dangers that lay ahead—and the room was silent.

CHAPTER TWENTY-ONE

A WOMAN CAN CHANGE

★ ★ ★ ★

"Everything's moving quickly," Lobo murmured. "When things break, they'll go fast, so we need to be straight about what to do."

He was standing by the corral, Lanie close beside him, watching the horses as they moved aimlessly around inside the stout posts and crosspieces. He had wanted to talk to her alone. "I expect we'll be pullin' out in the morning."

Lanie looked at him, and once again a ghost of apprehension swept her face. Now that the time was actually upon them—they were standing on the very edge of violence—her voice echoed her uncertainty as she asked, "How much chance do we have to get away, Lobo?"

"Better chance than some I've had."

The stark realism and harshness of his reply did not encourage her. She picked out a splinter of wood from the corral rail, toyed with it for a moment, then tossed it down. Turning to face him, she drew his glance, saying quietly, "It's something we had to do. If it doesn't work—if someone—" She drew a deep breath and began again. "If I get hurt, you mustn't blame yourself."

The sweeping feminine curve of her cheek drew his eye. He studied her carefully, not speaking his thoughts, but finally stated flatly, "How could a man help that? If something happened to you—"

He stopped, and Lanie waited, but Lobo stared across the corral and said no more. She turned and began to walk slowly around the corral. Lobo followed her, grabbed her arm, and gave her a shake. "You do as I say!" he yelled. She looked up at him, startled. He said, "Masterson's watching us over there. He thinks we're having an argument. Gotta make it look real." Lobo's back was to the gunman, and he smiled down at Lanie. "Be hard to have an argument with a girl as pretty as you."

His comment startled her. Lobo was different from most men that way; Lanie had learned to accept compliments from men as a matter of course. From him it seemed out of place, but in his eye, she saw sincerity. Now she frowned and shook his hand off—for Masterson's benefit—and said, "You just don't know me. I'm impossible to live with! Ask anyone. My father, for one."

"You've got him wrapped around your little finger, Lanie," Lobo grinned. "I saw that even in the time I was with you both."

Lanie reached up and covered her mouth as if she were coughing. "I guess you're right. I learned when I was a little girl how to handle Dad. If I wanted something, I'd go sit in his lap, and stroke his hair, or rub his shoulders. Sometimes he'd say no." A fond smile touched her wide lips. "So I wouldn't argue, I'd just go away. But the next day I'd be back, trying something different."

"Bet you usually ended up getting it, too."

"Yes, I did. Dad said he'd look up, and there I'd be, with whatever it was I was pestering him for. And he was never quite sure how I wiggled it out of him."

The hot breeze caused the tops of the cottonwoods to tremble. Far off in the desert a trail of dust was rising faintly. Lobo studied it and murmured, "Probably an Indian headed for Fort Smith." Then he turned back to Lanie. "I've wondered what it was like to have a family. Fella that has that—why, he has everything."

There was a hint of sadness in his voice, but his face remained undisturbed. Lobo had learned, she knew very well, to cover his emotions. But during their brief time together she had been able to read some of what went on inside Lobo's mind. Her brow wrinkled and she asked, "Lobo, do you think you'll ever marry?"

The question caught him off guard. Lifting his eyebrows he glanced at her. "You sure seem to have my marital status on your mind a lot." Then he shook his head briefly. "Doubt it."

His reply was laconic, but Lanie wasn't satisfied. She had always been able to manipulate people; this man, however, was beyond her reach. Drawn to him in a way she could not explain, she started to question him further. But even as she began to speak she looked up to see Angela Montoya coming out of the house, dressed for riding. "There comes Angela," she said, studying Lobo's face as he watched the dark, beautiful girl approach. "You might marry *her*," Lanie said flatly.

"Marry Angela?" he echoed in amazement. "I don't think so," he said, shaking his head forcefully. "Angela will never marry anybody. She wants her own way all the time—and no wife can have that."

"She *is* beautiful," Lanie remarked, but by now Angela had reached them and she could say no more.

"Lobo, let's take a little ride. I want to talk to you about tomorrow," she commanded, pulling on leather riding gloves.

"It's on then?" he asked.

Surprise touched Angela's face. "Of course! You didn't think we'd back out, did you?"

Lobo shrugged. "Vic's not too hot on the whole thing. You have a talk with him?"

Angela glanced at Lanie before answering. "Let's go saddle up," she said brusquely and headed for the barn.

When she was out of hearing distance, Lobo murmured to Lanie, his voice summer-soft, "I better go with her. She's the key to this whole thing. Angela can handle Perrago in a way not even Ogg can."

"I guess she can handle most men."

There was a clipped edge to Lanie's voice, which surprised Lobo. "You're not—" Then he caught himself and walked away.

Lanie stalked back to the cabin, as though angry, for Masterson was watching her with narrowed eyes. "Looks like them two are gettin' real thick again, don't it?" He grinned wickedly. "Lobo better watch his back. Vic's a little touchy about somebody stealin' his woman."

"That's all any of you men want—women and money!" Lanie said curtly and went inside. As soon as she closed the door she looked out the window to watch the pair lead their horses out of the barn, mount up, and ride out toward the east.

Angela was wearing an outfit Lobo had not seen: a black riding skirt with a white silk blouse, and a low-crowned, wide-brimmed riding hat, tied on by a leather lanyard. As always she looked fresh; fatigue never seemed to overcome her as it did other women. Lobo admired her endless supply of energy. She would have been the object of admiration of many men, he knew, with her full-bodied beauty and classic features.

"Good-looking woman you brought, Lobo," Angela commented with studied casualness.

"Yeah," he readily agreed, "but she's a pretty cold number."

"No, she's not cold," Angela pronounced firmly. They had been riding along for the best part of an hour and had reached one of the few stands of timber of any size. It was a small forest of cottonwoods, with a few stunted pines, and they had found a small creek and had stopped to water the horses. Angela slipped from her horse and stood quietly, looking at the small stream as it trickled over the rocks.

Lobo dismounted and stood beside her. There seemed to be no way to crack this woman's shell; if there was, Lobo had never found it. Suddenly he said, "I never know what's going on inside you, Angela. It was always hard for me to guess. Why don't you let a man know what you're thinking?"

She turned to him, her eyes questioning. "I don't think most men really want to know what's going on inside a woman," she said abruptly. "Most men are interested only in what's on the outside." She looked back up at him with the same peculiar expression. "I thought at one time you were different."

Lobo was watching her carefully; she was very beautiful. "We *were* pretty close, once," he said quietly. "I've never forgotten those days."

Her eyes were fixed almost hungrily on his face. "Lobo," she said, desperation in her voice, "you know what I am, and what I have been. But there's some part of me, deep inside, that is good." Her mouth twisted in a harsh, bitter smile. "That sounds funny, coming from me; but I know it's true."

Without thinking, Lobo reached out to touch her cheek, letting his fingers run down its smoothness. "I've always known that, Angela," he said, his voice gravelly. "You're a lot like me, I guess. We've lived like the devil, but deep inside we've always been looking for something better. Never found it," he shrugged, "but I saw little bits of it in you. And it's still there." Impulsively Lobo wanted to do something for her. He had ridden away from her before because of inadequacies he saw in himself—not in Angela. He would've married her in a moment if he had loved her. But the time had come when he knew he could never help her break out of the circle of crime they had fallen in to.

She reached out, caught his hand, and pressed it to her cheek. Her voice, when it came, was a raw whisper. "Could we forget? Isn't there some way we can go back, start over, and be new and clean again? Wipe out the past?"

"I don't know," Lobo said, wishing he could reassure her. He smelled lavender, the scent she always wore. He was very much aware of her beauty; it drew him like a magnet. Thoughtfully he went on. "That's the way people of God are. Always clean," he said. "Friend of mine used those words: 'always clean before God.' Get all refreshed every morning, just like the dew on the grass. Go to God, all forgiven, and your wrongs all taken care of." Lobo was thinking of Lorenzo Dawkins.

Angela had once had a dream that someday she'd find a man—and for that man she'd fill all his needs and desires, and he would fill the empty place in her heart. She hated to see that dream slip away. Placing her hand on his chest, she asked, "Could we go back and start over again, Lobo?" There was a breathless quality in her voice and suddenly Lobo knew that she was—for that moment—a helpless child.

He wanted to agree, but the knowledge that he was betraying her burned in him like a hot iron. He had always been a man of single ideas, and now he was caught between two terrible forces. He thought of Lanie and Betsy and Stone, their lives held by a thin thread; part of the price of saving them was deceiving Angela. But as he looked at her, the old days reached for him and the smoothness of her cheeks and the desire in her eyes caught at him as well, its seductive tentacles pulling him back—back—

Suddenly the choice was taken from him. She came into his

arms, her lips lifted and, hating himself, he kissed her. She clung to him, taking his kiss as some sort of sign, and when she pulled back, her eyes sparkled with happiness. "We'll find what we had once. After this is all over, you and I, we'll go away, maybe St. Louis. Do you remember St. Louis?"

Lobo murmured, "Yes, I do." In his heart, he knew he'd never be able to forgive himself for what he was about to do to this woman.

They mounted up and she talked cheerfully on the way back, like a young girl again. When they dismounted and met Perrago on the porch, he glared at her, saying merely, "You two had a good ride, I see." He had not missed the flush in Angela's cheeks, the happiness in her eyes. He grunted, "Come on in, get this thing straight. We're pulling out before dawn."

Angela laughed, holding on to Lobo's arm. "Don't worry, Vic, we'll be rich, and that's what you've always wanted."

When they entered the room, Lobo glanced at Lanie on the far side of the room. She had seen the change in Angela Montoya, but Lobo made no sign to her at all.

She still loves him, and he must love her. The thought closed about Lanie's heart with a desolate barrenness she could almost touch. She moved over to the window, staring out but seeing nothing, shutting her mind to everything that went on inside the room.

★　★　★　★

Marshal Heck Thomas rarely had any trouble with anyone except outlaws. His personality was so forceful that the mere statement of what he intended to do was sufficient to stop those set on wrongdoing. But now the calm demeanor of Marshal Thomas was ruffled and anger flashed in his steady black eyes. He stared across the desk at the man who sat with his leg propped up on a chair and said bluntly, "Why don't you leave the law work to us, Mr. Winslow? We've done a pretty good job of it in the past, I reckon."

Zach Winslow put his blue eyes on Heck Thomas and answered blandly, "I'm sure you have, Marshal. Everyone speaks well of you." A sly look came to his eyes. "I had you checked out when I found out you were assigned to getting my daughter back."

"You did, did you?"

Zach ignored Thomas's sarcastic question. Nodding cheerfully, he went on. "Yes, sir, I did—and you're *exactly* the man for the job." He ran his hands through his hair. "But this is my daughter, not yours, and I'm going along to be sure things go right," he said firmly.

Heck Thomas sat back in his chair and wondered why he was listening to Winslow. He was not usually given to taking advice on his profession from laymen. He was the best of Judge Parker's marshals, and his scientific methods of detection had sent many a man to the rope. However, there was something about Zach Winslow that gave him a patience he didn't ordinarily have. Leaning forward, he cocked his head to one side and drummed his fingers on the desk. "Why is it that amateurs always think they can do the job better than the professionals?"

"I don't know, but I'll agree that you're right about that. In this case, I think you'll just have to agree to let me go with you."

Zach considered telling Thomas about his stint as one of the original vigilantes at Alder Gulch when he'd been sent against violent men. He didn't know that Thomas already had this information. Now Zach said, "Look, let's compromise, Marshal. I'll stay out of your way as much as possible—but I've got to go." He lowered his head, his voice grew soft. "I'm worried sick about my girls—and now Wesley Stone is involved. You and I both know they can make all the plans they want, but just like in a war, when the first shot's fired, all bets are off."

Thomas stared at Winslow and made up his mind. "All right. I don't know what good you'll be with your leg like it is, but you can go."

"I appreciate that, Marshal. Now, can you tell me how you plan to handle it?"

Thomas nodded. "I'll have six men on that train. They'll get on separately and nobody will be able to tell they're guards. They'll be scattered throughout the train. I suspect Perrago will have somebody watching the train, so we'll have to have them get on singly. Six men—plus you and me makes eight. We know where they'll jump the train, so we won't be taken by surprise.

I'll be with the engineer, and another will be in the caboose. We'll let 'em stop the train, and when they do, we'll let 'em make their play. They'll probably gather at the express car—the mail car, that is. They'll try to get the guard inside to open it, or try to blast the door off. As soon as they bunch up in front of the car, we'll swarm out and let 'em have it. It's a good thing that Indian friend of yours brought us news about their plans to rob the train."

Winslow considered the plan, then nodded. "Yeah. Woman Killer has been invaluable in this whole thing. I don't think a white man could do nearly the things he has. Ought to work, I hope. I won't be able to get out and help much, except through the window—but I'll do what I can."

"You just stay out of it." He leaned back, and said thoughtfully, "We've been after Perrago a long time. Be doing the court a favor if we killed them all."

They continued discussing the plan for another ten minutes, then Winslow called, "Tom—come and get me!"

Tom entered from the hall and stood beside his father. His eyes were lit with admiration at the sight of Heck Thomas.

Thomas smiled, saying, "Come back in a couple of years, young fellow. We can use good men like you!"

After the Winslows departed, Thomas called, "Jake, we're gonna need some good men. Going to nail that curly wolf Perrago—or I'll take off my star!"

CHAPTER TWENTY-TWO

WAITING

★ ★ ★ ★

"All right, Stone—"

Perrago had suddenly appeared on the porch next to Wesley. The pale edge of the sunlight made a thin line in the east, and the men were already out, saddling their horses. He turned to look at Perrago, who had his hat pulled over his eyes, and asked, "What is it?"

"You're going into Fort Smith," Perrago answered, "to get the money for the girl."

"I thought you were going to use somebody else for that."

"Never mind what you thought! Bob's saddling your horse. You ride into Fort Smith, get the money from Winslow. You bring it out, and you get the girl."

Stone was taken off guard by the outlaw's offer. He stared at Perrago, though he knew he had no say in the matter. "All right. Where do I bring the money?"

Perrago pulled a sheet of paper from his pocket and handed it to Stone. "Here's the map. Not hard to find—it's the only house around. The only thing is I'll have a look-out there. If anybody but you shows up, we won't wait to ask questions," he said harshly. "I'll kill that girl. You know I'll do it, don't you?"

Stone stared at him and nodded. "I know," he said tightly. He'd never hated anyone as he did Perrago, and it disturbed him to let his emotions go that way. "What time do we meet?"

They talked about the details for delivering the ransom money; then Pratt came up with a saddled horse. "Get going," Perrago said. "I'll see you one more time. You have the money— you get the girl. You don't show—or you try any tricks, all bets are off!"

"Let me talk to Betsy," Stone asked.

"Do it then—and quick."

Wesley quickly walked into the house and found Betsy cooking. "Betsy," he said, "I have to go. He's sending me to get the money."

Betsy's eyes filled with alarm. "Be careful," she warned. "I don't trust him. Even if you bring the money, he might just take it and kill you."

They were alone in the room for once. "We only have a second," Stone said. "I want to tell you something."

"Yes?"

Wesley Stone, the man of words, suddenly had none. Without warning, he reached out, pulled her close and kissed her. "I want you to know," he whispered, "I love you. I don't know how it came about, Betsy, but that's the way it is."

Held in his arms, Betsy felt a warm sense of security such as she'd seldom known. It came to her in such a flash that she was nearly speechless. "Why, I love you, too!" she whispered. "I guess I have for a long time, Wes!"

Steps sounded on the porch, and he released her. Stepping back he said loudly, "Don't worry, Betsy, I'll be there with the money, and you'll be home again in no time."

"Goodbye, Wes," she said as he left.

Lobo came in and headed straight past Betsy toward the bedroom where Lanie was. "Perrago's changed his mind," he said quickly. "He's sending Wes to get the money from your father. Come on, we've got to go."

Lanie stared at him, then whispered, "Will it be all right? Will Vic let her go?"

"I don't think he'll have the chance. It'll be over by the time Wes shows up with the money."

They walked out of the bedroom with blankets and personal items in their arms, passing Angela on the way. Giving Lanie a shove, Lobo said roughly, "Get on your horse and don't give me any trouble."

After Lanie left, he said, "Angela, did Vic tell you about sending Stone in to get the money?"

"Yes, a good idea. Frees another man for the job," she said. As she came over to him, she said harshly, "I wish it were over—I want to leave here and never *see* this place again!"

"Sure. But we have to get this over first." Taking her arm, he led her outside, filled with bitterness at the deception he was forced to use. They mounted up and the band rode out toward the north.

★ ★ ★ ★

Late the next afternoon they reached the house where the women were to be kept. It had been a hard ride and they were all weary. They'd brought extra horses, each man having two mounts. Perrago said, "Bob, you and Jack take care of the horses. Be sure they're rested. We'll have to push 'em hard after the job."

He had stepped down from his horse in front of the low stone house. Reaching into his saddlebag, he pulled out a package and walked over to the door. It was a sturdy oak door that opened easily. He peered inside cautiously, then turned to say, "All right, nobody here."

The rest dismounted and Lanie went over to Betsy. Lobo walked up behind them. "All right, you two get inside."

At the farthest end of the one-room cabin stood a large fireplace, a battered old table, and a few chairs. At the other end of the room was a bed and a small table with a lamp on it. "We can nail the windows down so the women can't get out," Perrago said. Tossing the sack in his hand to Río, he said, "Mateo, put this lock on the front door. We'll lock them in while we're doing the job."

Mateo Río was looking around. "They must have expected Indian attacks," he remarked. "It's almost like a jail."

"That's right. They can't get out of here," Lobo said. "That's why I thought of this place. We can lock 'em in, come back after the job's over, and then turn 'em loose."

"This one doesn't go until Stone gets here with the money," Perrago said, looking at Betsy. "Now let's go take a look at the place where we hit the train. Lobo, you come and show us."

"All right."

Lobo and Perrago went outside, mounted, and rode off toward the west. Inside, Ogg glanced at the two women. "Might as well make yourselves comfortable. Maybe fix up something to eat."

Lanie and Betsy, anxious to have something to do, brought in the blankets and made pallets, then Lanie said, "We've got to have some firewood to cook with."

"I'll take care of that," Pratt said. "I saw an old ax around back." He left and was soon back with enough firewood to build a fire. Lanie and Betsy fixed a meal from some of the supplies they'd brought. After the men had eaten, they went outside, leaving the three women alone. Angela hadn't assisted in making the meal, but took a portion anyway. Finally she said, "I guess you two will be glad after tomorrow is over."

"Yes, I will," Betsy said. The woman had been decent to her.

Angela looked at Lanie. "I guess you will, too, won't you, Irene?"

Lanie nodded, looking up from where she was washing dishes. "Yes, it's been awful. I want to get back to my family."

"You two don't belong out here," Angela shrugged.

Her observation surprised Lanie, and she asked suddenly, "Have you always lived in the West?"

Angela smiled. "You don't want to hear my life story. It's not very pleasant."

She walked outside, past the men who were guarding the place.

"She's a strange one, isn't she, Lanie?" Betsy said, who had joined her.

"Very beautiful," Lanie replied shortly. They walked a little farther, out of earshot of the men.

"She and Lobo are in love—at least *she* is," Betsy said. "She doesn't look at him like she looks at the other men." Betsy spoke indifferently, but when she looked up and saw the effect of her words on her sister's face, she asked, "What's the matter? What did I say?"

"Nothing—nothing at all. I'm just tired."

Betsy knew her sister well. "You're not *interested* in Lobo, are you, Lanie?"

"Of course not!"

The answer was blurted out so suddenly that Betsy knew she had touched a sensitive nerve in her sister—that she'd hurt her somehow. "Why—Lanie! He's no man for you! He's nothing but an outlaw!"

"You don't understand him!" Lanie retorted sharply, trying to keep her voice low. "He hasn't had any chance at all. Why, he could be anything he wanted to!" Then she broke off, her face flushed. "Sorry, Betsy. I didn't mean to snap at you."

"He and Angela were lovers," Betsy said cautiously. It troubled her to see her sister drawn to such a man as Smith. Her own experience with Perrago had made her afraid, and she didn't want Lanie to have to go through anything like that. "Lanie—you're too wise to fall in love with a man like Lobo," she said.

Lanie looked at her sister, a strained expression in her eyes. "It is dull you are, girl! When did women ever do anything wise where men are concerned?"

Betsy stared at Lanie for a moment. When she saw the tears in her sister's eyes, she put her arms around her and said, "Lanie—" Then stopped. What could she say? The two women simply stood, engulfed in their sadness.

★   ★   ★   ★

"Right there, Vic. That's where the train has to make the turn." The two men had reached the canyon where the raid would take place, and Lobo pointed up at the rocks, then at the track. "We could pile logs on the rails—but that'd stop it fast. Be easier to put a gun on the engineer."

"How fast does the train move through this cut?" Perrago asked.

Lobo shrugged, saying, "Slow enough so that a man on a horse could hide in one of those thickets, then come alongside and pull himself on."

"Do you want the job?"

Lobo said, "You're the boss. Why don't you try it?"

Suddenly animosity flamed in Perrago's face. "I never liked

you, Lobo," he said tersely. "You're brash."

Lobo stared at him. "I know that. A few times I thought we'd have it out."

"You think you could take me?" Perrago demanded.

"Don't be a fool, Vic!" Lobo snapped. "I don't know about that—and neither do you. We've both smelled powder—but no matter who wins—we both lose. We need every man we've got to do this job. Then you won't have to look at me anymore. I'll be out of your sight forever. I'm pulling out of this place."

"That's good," Perrago said, but the urge to fight was still in him. He said, "You tried to make a fool out of me with Angela. She's after you now—but I want you to know, if I wanted her, I'd fight you for her." Then he shrugged, saying, "There's plenty of women in the world."

"What about the train? You or me?"

Perrago checked the site again and said, "You do it. I don't like you—but you're nervy enough for it." He stared at the terrain, then at Lobo. "You think you can do it?"

Lobo had studied their plan for a long time. "Sure. If I put my horse in those bushes, nobody can see me. As soon as the engine passes, I'll pull out and come to the cars. Be easy to climb on. If the engineer or the firemen give me any trouble, I'll shoot 'em in the legs and stop the train myself."

"You want any help?"

"I don't need anybody else. The problems start after we get the train stopped."

"We'll get in with this if there's any resistance." Vic pulled a bundle of dynamite sticks from his saddlebag. "Let's get back to the house and go over this thing. Some of my boys are pretty thick-headed. I want this thing done without a hitch!"

All afternoon Perrago had Ogg drill the plan into the men. Ogg insisted on treating the gang as if they were children, going over each aspect of their jobs and quizzing them on the details. Ogg was meticulous and careful. Lobo only hoped Zach Winslow and the marshals would come through as Lanie had promised they would, otherwise Ogg was certain to make the heist successful.

Darkness came, and they ate a meal, after which Perrago said, "Everybody get to bed." He walked over to Betsy. "Last chance to give me a big kiss—how about it?"

Betsy stared up at him, saying quietly, "Don't touch me!"

Perrago reached for her, hesitated, then laughed harshly. "You're no woman," he scoffed as he turned from her. "All right, men, let these women have the cabin," he said.

"I got to talk to Irene, Vic, " Lobo said.

Perrago stared at him a moment. "Make it quick!" he barked. "I want everybody fresh in the morning. "

When Vic and the others left, Lobo walked over to Lanie. "I know I've given you a rough deal, Irene," he said. "But you'll be back with your dad tomorrow."

He walked outside and Angela followed him. As he found his blanket, she asked, "Will it be all right, Lobo?"

"Should be." Darkness had brought a coolness over the land, so the men busied themselves getting settled around a small fire that Pratt had made. Lobo turned to her. "Angela, you stay out of it tomorrow. Stay clear of that train."

She looked at him in surprise, and a smile softened her lips. "I wasn't going to—but it's good to know you care." She glanced at the men and saw that Perrago was watching them. "Watch out for Vic. He'd kill you in a minute."

"I know that."

The men began to settle into their blankets, and finally she said, "I'd better get inside. In case I don't have a chance to tell you tomorrow, Lobo—" She hesitated and said softly, "I feel like a young girl again." Wonder shone in her eyes, and she whispered, "It's like turning the pages back in a book—back to the time I had hoped and dreamed that everything would turn out right." In the moonlight he could see that her face was sober and radiant. "I haven't felt like that in a long time." She reached out tentatively and took his hand in hers.

His heart sank at her trust—and the betrayal he must carry out. *I hurt her once—and now I'm about to do it again!*

Leaning forward she put her arms around him, then drew away, saying, "After this—we'll be all right!" With that she turned and walked back into the house and shut the door.

Lobo rolled up in his blankets and looked up at the skies. *What kind of a man am I to be doin' this to her? I loved her once—and she still loves me, I guess. Yet here I am lying to her! What'll happen to her when this is all over—and she sees what I've done to her?*

CHAPTER TWENTY-THREE

THE HOLDUP

★ ★ ★ ★

All morning the band moved nervously around, their eyes searching the foothills for any sign of movement. "I wish we could get at it," Pratt said to Jack Masterson. "This waitin' around makes me nervous!"

Masterson raised his eyes to the younger man. "It don't do to be nervous on a job like this, Pratt. All we need is one man to do the wrong thing and we're all in trouble."

His words stirred the chesty young man full of pride. Pratt retorted, "Don't worry about me, Jack. I'll be there when the fun starts—and when it's over, too!" Masterson snorted at him, turned around, and rode off to look into the short hills over to the east.

Lanie and Betsy stayed close together, watching as the men moved about. Lanie looked for a chance to speak to Lobo, but none came. Finally at noon, Ogg said, "Let's get on with this, Vic. We need time to get the men set."

"All right—everybody get mounted." Vic turned to Angela, saying, "I decided that we need you to stay here to guard the women. I'd hate to lose 'em if something went wrong. Besides, I don't trust that Stone guy—he could set 'em free while we're gone, without ever collecting any ransom money—he knows where we are. If you have to use that .38 on these two, don't kill 'em. Just shoot 'em in the legs."

Surprised, Angela asked, "You sure you don't need me, Vic? Might get pretty nasty out there."

"I'm certain," he replied. Then he glanced to where Lobo was tightening his cinch. "Made up your mind, have you, Angela?"

"That's none of your business, Vic."

Perrago shook his head. "It's too late for you two. Whatever you had, it's gone. You'll come back to me." He smiled, making a handsome picture as he stood before her, his hazel eyes glowing with confidence. "I never let a woman get away from me. After this job, I'll show you a thing or two."

Angela shook her head. "No, it's all over between us. Find yourself another woman. There's plenty willing to go with you."

Perrago shrugged his shoulders, but said no more. He turned and walked to his horse. Swinging into the saddle he called out, "We'll be back after the job's over."

"All right, Vic." Angela watched as the band rode out, then she turned to Betsy. "I hope your man gets here with the money soon. Vic doesn't like to be shortchanged."

"Why don't you let us go now?" Betsy said.

"Let you go? No—not without the money. And don't try to run for it. I'd hate to shoot you—but I'd do it."

"I know you would," Lanie said calmly. "Is there any gentleness in you? What kind of a woman are you?"

Angela considered the question for a moment, a thought forming in her mind. Then her lips hardened. "I'll show as much softness as I've had shown to me," she said as she walked away.

Betsy and Lanie watched as Angela mounted her horse. "She won't go far," Betsy nodded. She looked off into the distance and murmured, "I hope Dad's on the train with some marshals. I wish it were all over!"

Lanie put her arm around the younger girl, watching the dust rising in the distance. "Don't worry, Bets, it'll be over soon."

★　★　★　★

Perrago led the band at a hard pace and an hour later pulled up at the bend in the low foothills. He set the men out, spacing them carefully where they could be concealed. To each one he gave specific instructions. "Lobo hops the train, makes the engineer stop. It won't be going fast, so it'll stop about there—by those trees. As soon as it does, we come out and hit the train. Anybody sticks their head out the windows—let 'em have it. Then we hit the express car."

All had been planned to the last instant, and every man knew his job. Pratt had been given the job of guarding the train, and Perrago asked, "Can I count on you, Bob?"

"Sure! I'll handle it, Vic!"

"Good man!" Perrago knew how to make a man feel important. It was his way of drawing younger members into the group. But he also knew how to use them up—Pratt would have to take much of the fire.

When he got to Lobo, he asked tightly, "All set?"

"All set here."

"Never thought you and I'd be working together again, Lobo," Perrago said, and shrugged. "Doesn't matter. What matters is getting the loot—and getting away with it."

"That's it, Vic," he agreed, sizing the man up carefully. "You always were a smart one."

Perrago studied the smaller man. *He thinks he's got me buffaloed—but he'll find out different soon enough!*

"I'll go on down the line," Perrago told him. "Some of the boys are a little jumpy. Remember, you have to hold the crew in the engine. Tie 'em up, then come and give us a hand."

"I'm with you, Vic."

Perrago smiled. "We do this right and we're in clover, Lobo!" He pulled his horse around and rode down the tracks at a fast trot.

Lobo dismounted, loosed the saddle so his horse could breathe easier, and then moved the animal back into the shade, from time to time, giving him a drink from his canteen.

An hour later, he saw the black turn his head and pitch his ears toward the east. Quickly Lobo cinched his saddle and mounted the animal. He moved the horse to the edge of the woods. He had second thoughts about what he was going to do. *Should have told the marshals not to shoot me—but I didn't know I'd be piling on this train,* he thought. He heard the faint reverberations of a distant whistle. *Better not try the engine,* he decided. *I'll go up a car and get on top. Some of these engineers are pretty tough old cobs!*

He sat there, his stomach in a knot. His horse began to shift nervously. Lobo leaned over and patted him on the shoulder. "Good boy—just like a race—we've done that before, haven't we? This time, though, you've got to catch a whole train." He talked to the horse steadily as the sound of the train grew louder. Then he heard the drivers as the engine came around the bend, and could tell that the engineer was slowing down. "Won't be long now." He caught the first glimpse of smoke; then the black engine appeared coming down the narrow-gauge line. He held the reins lightly, waiting, and the sound swelled and the train was upon them. He got a glimpse of the engineer leaning out of the black cab, and as soon as it passed, Lobo was out on the narrow band beside the track. "Get 'em, boy!"

The black hit a driving run in five jumps, and Lobo saw the steel ladder at the end of the car. He leaned over in rhythm with the stride of the black—but had to lean farther than his lone eye had estimated. His left hand caught, but his right scraped down the steel wall. The force of the moving train swung his body downward so that he hung by one hand, the ties flashing beneath him. Then like a pendulum he swung back and managed to grasp the rung of the ladder with both hands.

Quickly he pulled himself up the ladder, seeing that the horse was clear. He scrambled up, and when he got to the top, crawled the length of the car. He could see the engineer and the fireman over the coal tender, but their backs were to him. He jumped down, almost falling as he scrambled over the coals, and then as his feet hit the steel deck of the engine, he felt the hard barrel of a gun rammed into his side.

He turned, keeping his hands very still.

"Well, Lobo, we meet again!" Lobo stared into the cold eyes of Marshal Heck Thomas, but the lawman suddenly grinned, shouting over the noise of the engine, "Mr. Winslow said you'd like to be joining us. You ready?"

"Stop the train—they're waiting!"

The engineer, at Thomas's nod, slammed on the brake. "What's the play, Heck?" Lobo demanded.

"I got men planted in every car," Thomas said. "Soon as the

gang hits the express car, we move out and get 'em in a crossfire. What do you want to do?"

"Soon as the train stops, I'll drop out on the other side of the door. I'll run down to the express car. That's where Perrago will be. I'll try to nail him, Heck. If I miss, you take care of him." The train had ground to a stop, and quickly he said, "There's a house about five miles northeast by a big cut—old stone house—anybody can tell you where it is. "The Winslow girls are there. Case I get hit, you find 'em, Heck!"

"Okay, Lobo," Heck said, then warned, "Watch yourself, that Perrago's the wolf!"

Pulling out his gun, Lobo leaped to the ground and ran as fast as he could toward the rear of the train. The baggage car was behind the last passenger car, and already Lobo heard shots and glass breaking. *Vic's shootin' the windows to keep the vigilantes out of it*, he thought.

He turned between the last passenger car and the express car, scrambling over the couplings, then jumped to the ground. He peered out cautiously. He saw that the raid was unfolding, with Duvall, Ogg, and Masterson lined up. Río and Pratt were farther off, peppering the train windows with rifle fire. Lobo almost got a shot at Perrago, but Río swept down and came between them.

"Open up—or we'll blast you to purgatory!" Perrago shouted.

A voice inside yelled out, "Blast away!"

"We'll have to blow it, boys! Keep firing! Anyone sticks their head up, let 'em have it!" Lobo saw Perrago jump off his horse and hand the reins to Río, then run toward the express car, holding the dynamite.

Can't let him blow the car! Lobo laid a shot toward Perrago's racing form. Perrago looked toward the end of the car, yelled, "There's someone over there. Get him, boys!" Instantly a fusillade of shots rang out, driving Lobo back. At the same time, he looked at the front of the train and saw men piling out of the cars, holding their guns ready—*marshals*, he thought. Then Heck came scurrying down beside the train, calling out, "Around the end—Bill, you and Shorty and Ed! We got to flank 'em!" Three men scurried by Lobo, disappearing around the end of the caboose. Looking in the other direction, he saw Heck and two others disappear between two cars. *They'll fan out and get 'em in a crossfire*, Lobo thought. But he saw at once that Bob Pratt and Ogg were laying down a withering fire in that direction—and at the other end, Masterson, Duvall, and Río were holding off the marshals behind the caboose.

Carefully, Lobo stepped out from behind the car, knowing he had to break up the fire so that the marshals could move out into the clear. He called out, "Give it up, Vic! We've got you pinned!"

His voice caught the gangsters off guard. Perrago wheeled around and stared at him—and his face contorted with rage. "He sold us out—get him!"

Instantly, Mateo Río aimed his rifle and got off three shots—one of them knocked the hat from Lobo's head, the other two close enough for Lobo to feel the wind. Masterson joined in, and Lobo was forced back between the cars.

"Go get him!" Perrago was yelling. "Knock him down!"

Knowing that he couldn't beat both Río and Masterson, Lobo made a dive, cleared the coupling, and ran toward the engine, thinking they'd expect him to go the other way. But a thought came to him, and getting to the end of the car, he climbed the ladder and threw himself on top of the car. He could see Ogg and Pratt clearly, both concealed behind a low ridge. They were keeping Heck Thomas's men pinned down with a vicious fire.

Moving to the edge, he peered to his right and saw that Vic had fastened the dynamite to the door of the express car. Below him Mateo and Masterson were keeping the lawmen locked in behind the caboose. Lobo hated to do it, and found that he couldn't shoot them cold. "Río!" he shouted. "Up here!" He waited until Río looked up, and the Mexican lifted his gun quicker than Lobo thought he could and fired. It split the air next to Lobo's cheek, and Lobo's shot rang out almost simultaneously. It struck Río in the chest, driving him back in the saddle. Río glared at Lobo, hatred in his eyes, and he tried to lift his gun for another shot, but it was too heavy for him. His eyes went blank and he fell to one side. As he struck the ground, the horse panicked and galloped off, the dead outlaw bounding along the ground, his foot still in the stirrup.

Masterson got off another shot, striking Lobo. It burned

along Lobo's side. He fired and missed, and then had to duck as shots came from Ogg and Pratt. Lying flat, they couldn't hit him, but neither could he get up to return their fire.

Masterson shouted, "How much longer, Vic? We can't stand much more of this!"

Grat Duvall replied above the gunfire, "Hold 'em, Jack—we've almost got it—!"

Lobo rolled over and felt the blood drip from the wound in his side. Coming down the ladder, he looked down the track to see that the situation was unchanged—Heck Thomas moved back and came toward him. "They got us pinned down, Lobo! What about if we pull the train away?"

"No good," Lobo said. "They'll get away—and the women are lost."

"Any ideas?"

"I'm gonna go down and get behind the express car, Heck."

"If you come out there, Masterson and Duvall will catch you cold!"

"No other way," Lobo reasoned. "Listen—when I come out, they'll all be looking to get me. You step out and pepper them while they're busy."

"You'll never make it, Lobo," Heck cried out, but Lobo was already running for the express car. "Crazy fool!" Thomas said angrily, but was filled with admiration for the man. He informed his men of the plan, "Soon as we hear the shots, we step out and let 'em have it." Then he reloaded his revolver.

Lobo stopped at the baggage car, then went to the three marshals at the end and told them the plan. "We'll be ready, Lobo, but you're in a bad spot!" one of them said.

Lobo went to the express car, ducked under it, stopping only to reload. As he crawled under the train, he could see the legs of the horses ridden by the band, and knew that he'd be facing their guns as soon as he stepped out. Suddenly he thought about the dynamite. *That's all I need, to get blown up*, he thought wryly.

There was no time for thought—in fact, when in a fight, Lobo actually *thought* very little. It was all instinct and reaction for him. Suddenly he exploded into action, rolling out into the clear, looking for a target. Instantly, before he could get off a shot, he heard

Grat Duvall scream, "Look out! There he is!" and the outlaw began to open fire on Lobo.

Lobo rolled as the slugs from Duvall's revolver made dust geysers beside him. One of the slugs ripped his moccasin, tearing off the sole, and at the same time, he stopped rolling long enough to see Perrago strike a match. Lobo threw one shot, which grazed Perrago, who let out a cry and dropped the match. He was not hurt bad, however, for he whirled and, seeing Lobo on the ground, let out a shrill cry and pulled his gun, throwing his fire at the traitor.

Lobo never stopped moving. He knew that one of the marshals would get Vic sooner or later. He kept his fire directed at Vic and was glad to hear other shots ringing out. *Heck's into it,* he thought.

Gunfire shook the air, but it was no longer concentrated on him. Duvall and Masterson had turned their guns on the marshals, moving at them from both ends. Needing a respite from the intense fighting, Lobo rolled to his feet, in a crouch, and before he knew it Masterson had turned to face him, evidently driven back by Thomas's fire.

The lean gunman's face was twisted with hate as he aimed his gun at Lobo. Lobo swung his gun up, pulled the trigger— and it clicked on an empty shell!

Masterson laughed, shouting, "So long, Lobo! Live in the pit!" He leveled his pistol and Lobo stared into the black muzzle. He knew he was a dead man!

Suddenly an isolated shot rang out, and Lobo saw Masterson jerk to one side. He reached up as if to slap a mosquito, but a slug had torn through his neck, and as he opened his mouth, a gush of scarlet blood spattered his lips. His eyes turned opaque, and he fell to the ground, his legs kicking as he clutched at his throat.

Lobo looked to his left and saw Zach Winslow standing there, his leg in a cast, hanging on with one hand to the side of the passenger car, a smoking gun in his right hand. Lobo yelled, "Thanks, Zach!" then turned and saw Duvall pulling away and shouting, "Come on, Vic, we've got to get out of here!"

But when Perrago saw him riding away, he uttered an insane cry of rage and fired at Duvall. The bullet struck Duvall, knocking him from the saddle. He was not fatally hit, for he got up and tried to run, only to throw up his hands as the marshals called on him to surrender.

Perrago turned to face Lobo, raised his gun, and Lobo dived under the car and tried to load his gun. Shouts and more gunfire filled the air, and when he crawled out, Lobo saw that the marshals had driven off Ogg, who was fleeing after Perrago. Pratt, in excess loyalty to Perrago, tried to cover their retreat. The marshals zeroed in on him, and Pratt was struck by half a dozen slugs. He was dead before he hit the ground.

Lobo groaned as he saw Perrago disappear into the trees.

"Lobo—!"

Lobo saw Winslow calling him. "I'm glad you were here, Winslow," he said. "He'd have got me for sure."

"He got away, didn't he—Perrago?"

"I'll get him. You pray—and I'll go!" Lobo saw Masterson's horse fifty feet away and ran to him, speaking softly. The animal lifted his head, but didn't try to run. Gently Lobo got the reins and swung into the saddle.

He knew that he could never catch Perrago on Masterson's horse, but he had no time to hunt for his black. Touching the animal with his heels, he left at a dead run, calling out, "Heck, come after me—I may not get him!"

Vic would be at the house before he could hope to get there, he thought as he drove the horse at a hard run. He kept the horse going, glad for the animal's stamina. His thoughts were on Perrago; he knew the man was like a mad dog. When these wild moods came on him, there was nothing Vic Perrago wouldn't do! And now, he had nothing to lose!

When he had been riding for less than five minutes, Lobo saw Ogg ahead. Ogg turned his horse around and drew a rifle from the saddle. Ogg was shooting from a still position with a rifle, while all Lobo had was his Colt. Lobo got off a shot that came so close that Ogg flinched, sending his shot high into the air. But then Ogg pulled down, and in a desperate maneuver, Lobo pulled the horse to one side, shouting, "Give up, Ogg!"

Ogg ignored Lobo's pleas and kept throwing a hard fire at him. Lobo felt his horse falter and knew it had been struck by one of the bullets. One of Lobo's bullets must have stung Ogg's horse, for the animal pitched wildly. Ogg was thrown to the ground but managed to hang on to his rifle.

When Lobo was about thirty yards away, he fired at Ogg, the bullet catching him low in the stomach, driving him backward. He dropped the rifle, clutching his stomach.

Lobo leaped from his horse to the ground, his gun ready. The fat man lay groaning in agony as the crimson flood issued from his body. Lobo grabbed the dying man's rifle, saying, "I'd help you, but I've got to go help the women."

Ogg glared at him out of hate-filled eyes and said nothing. Lobo ran toward the bay the fat man had been riding, mounted, and rode off, shouting, "I'll come back when I take care of Vic—!" But Ogg didn't even glance at him.

Lobo was glad his bullet had only creased the animal, though as he put the bay at a hard run, he discovered the horse was no faster than Masterson's. But there was no other choice. *I'll never get there in time*, he thought desperately as he drove toward the house.

The long ride seemed to take forever, but finally he pulled up over the ridge and looked down. He saw no sign of Perrago's horse. *Maybe he took off.* He checked the loads in his gun, holstered it, then rode down the ridge. When he was within thirty yards, he saw nothing, and called out, "Hello—Angela!"

The door opened and he was relieved to see her come out. She walked to the edge of the porch and stepped down. He moved his horse toward her. By the time he had slipped down from the saddle, she had reached him. He said, "Perrago's on the way—"

"Too late, Lobo—!"

Lobo whirled and started to draw his gun but saw that Perrago held a rifle in his hands aimed right at him. "I knew you'd come here, Lobo," he said, his lips drawn in a cruel tight smile.

"Vic," Angela said. "The marshals will be here soon. You have to get away."

"They'll never catch me—not on my horse. And I wouldn't leave without saying goodbye to our friend Lobo, would I?" His lips drew back in a grin and his eyes glittered like ice. "I'd walk through fire to get to you, Lobo! You think you could leave after the way you set us up and killed my boys?"

Lobo stood there, his hands beside his gun, but he knew that no man was fast enough to draw a .44 before Vic could pull a trigger. He said nothing, then a movement drew his eye. Lanie had come out of the house and was standing on the edge of the porch. It drew Vic's attention, and Lobo moved his hand closer to his gun, thinking his chance had come, but then Perrago's eyes shot back to him. "You women stay where you won't get hurt. And you might as well say goodbye to this one."

"Vic, let him go," Angela pleaded. "I've got plenty of money. I—I'll go with you. We can do anything we want to."

Surprise washed across Perrago's face and he lowered the rifle a few inches. "You mean that, Angela?"

Angela's face was pale, but she nodded. "You ever know me to lie, Vic? Let him go and you and I can get out of here—just the two of us, like you've wanted."

She stepped forward so that she was standing beside Lobo, her face drained. "Don't do it, Angela," Lobo said softly. "You're better than he is."

This sent Perrago over the edge, cursing and shouting. "You think that, do you? We'll see what kind of a man this makes you!" He threw the rifle up, but before Lobo had time to draw his gun, he felt Angela fall against him, crying, "Look out, Lobo—!"

He heard the sound of the rifle and knew the slug had struck her in the back, driving them both to the ground. Finally, he cleared his own gun from its leather holster, lifted it and pulled the trigger.

The slug took Perrago in the shoulder and the rifle dropped, but Perrago pulled his pistol with his left hand. "I'll get both of you!" he yelled, and lifted the gun.

But as he raised the .44, Lobo fired again, and this time the slug struck Perrago in the heart. His eyes suddenly bulged out, he grunted—and fell to the ground. His fingers clawed at the dirt—then relaxed.

As soon as Perrago fell, Lobo dropped his gun and took Angela in his arms. Carefully he lowered her and felt the wetness on her back stain his fingers.

"Angela—Angela!" he whispered urgently. Her eyes opened

and she looked at him blankly for a moment. The pain twisted her lips, and then she gasped for breath.

"Angela—you shouldn't have done it!" Lobo spoke thickly. "You shouldn't have taken that bullet for me!"

She tried to speak, and he lowered his head to catch her words. "We—won't be going—to St. Louis—!"

He held her tightly, grief written on his face. Reaching up she touched his cheek, whispering, "I've always—loved you—!" And then her hand fell back and her body went limp.

Lobo stared at her, holding her tightly. He had not wept since he was a small boy, but now the tears flowed freely and his shoulders shook.

On the porch, Lanie and Betsy were stunned by the scene. It had happened so quickly! One thing, however, was clear to Lanie. *Angela died for him! She really did love him!* She began to tremble.

Sensing Lanie's reaction, Betsy asked, "What are we going to do?"

"Nothing," Lanie said. "There's nothing more to do now."

She turned and walked back into the house and fell in a heap on the bunk, her head pressed into the rough blanket. Betsy came inside and looked at her in bewilderment. Like a slow sunset, Betsy began to realize that her sister was in love. She loved Lobo. Trying to comfort her, she held Lanie, whispering soothing words into her ears, but there was no comfort to give. Quietly she rocked the heartbroken girl, holding her tightly.

Outside in the dust, Lobo knelt, the still body of Angela Montoya in his arms. The world seemed to have stopped, and his face was filled with despair and anger and grief.

CHAPTER TWENTY-FOUR

A NEW NAME

★ ★ ★ ★

Fort Smith had seldom seen such a spectacle as when Marshal Heck Thomas brought in the remnants of Vic Perrago's gang. True enough, "remnants" was all that could be said of the gang. Grat Duvall and Buckley Ogg were the only survivors. Amazingly, one of the marshals found Ogg and managed to stop the bleeding from his stomach. The bodies of the rest were put on display in the glass window of the funeral parlor. The undertaker did a magnificent job of making everyone look natural. Victor Perrago was as handsome in death as he had been in life. The others looked more villainous—like the characters they were.

Young Tom Winslow was drawn to the mortuary as if it were a magnet, driving his father to distraction.

When Wesley and Betsy came to Zach Winslow's hotel room, they heard her father's voice before they entered the door.

" . . . and if I have to tell you one more time to stay away from that funeral home, it'll be too bad for you. I've put up with a lot, but it's just not decent, staring at those poor fellows as if they were some sort of side show."

Tom had the grace to duck his head and mumble, "I'm sorry, Dad, I won't go back there anymore." He looked up quickly as Betsy and Wesley entered, relieved at the interruption. "Wes, you promised to take me for a ride this afternoon!" Tom said.

Wesley laughed and put his hand on the boy's shoulder. "How come you never forget a promise that gets you something, but you always forget anything that means work?" Then he added, "All right, go to the stable and pick yourself a horse. I'll be right down."

"Great! I'm gonna pick out that black horse I like so much!"

When the boy had gone through the door, Zach grinned. "Gone crazy over horses! I was the same at his age, though."

He looked at Wes and Betsy, thinking it had been only two days since they'd all been together again. He had feared that Betsy was deeply troubled, for she refused to come to him. He'd had to send Tom to get her. She'd been so broken with grief that it was all Zach could do to soothe her and convince her the past was over, that it was time to look ahead.

Now he realized it hadn't been his words but the steady support of Wesley Stone that had done the job. He saw how close they stood to each other, how their eyes always seemed to meet. *They're going to be all right*, he thought with relief. *Couldn't have worked out better if I'd planned it all! Wesley will be a fine son-in-law. Always wanted to have a preacher in the family—which is what he'll be after he gets through fooling with this law business! Bron will be so happy.*

Aloud he said, "Wish I could go with you on that ride. This leg of mine took a banging when I jumped off that train."

"Mother will have you for that!" Betsy nodded.

"Not if you don't tell her!"

"Everyone knows about it, Zach," Wesley said. "They're making you out to be quite a hero. Way I hear it, if you hadn't drilled Masterson, he would have killed Lobo."

Zach disliked the conversation. "Well, that's over. Where's Lanie? Haven't seen her all day."

"In her room," Betsy said. "She hasn't said ten words since we got back."

Zach studied her carefully. They'd talked about this before, and now he said, "Go tell her to come here. I need to see her. If she won't come, Wesley, haul her down here."

Wesley and Betsy left, promising to come back in time for lunch, and Zach went to stare out the window. He tried his leg, grunted, but knew he was better. He thought of all that had happened, and when the door opened and closed, he turned to face Lanie. "Hello, daughter," he greeted her.

"Hello, Dad." Lanie came over and looked out the window with him. "You seem pretty tired."

"That was a pretty rough thing—that train robbery. And the rest of it, as well."

"Yes, it was. I don't think I'll ever forget it."

"You'll forget the worst parts." He reached out, patted her shoulder, and she turned to face him. "When bad things come, we think they'll last forever. But then they go from us somehow. Time washes over them, and if we think of them at all, it's with some small regret."

"I guess you're right, Dad."

Her reply was weak, so he asked, "What's wrong, Lanie? You've acted strangely ever since you got back to town. What happened out there to make you like this?"

"Oh, nothing."

He shook his head. "You're too old to start lying to me. I know you better than that." He hesitated, then said, "I have a feeling it has something to do with Lobo Smith."

Lanie blinked with surprise and turned away from him. She didn't answer, just continued staring out the window, not really seeing the wagon that drove by or the people walking on the wooden sidewalk below. "I . . . don't know what you mean," she whispered.

After a few moments of silence, he took her face in his hands, his eyes filled with love. "Lanie," he said, "you're a poor liar. You always were. Can't you tell me about it? Do you care for this man?"

"I don't know!" she cried. "I'm so mixed up, Dad!" Her eyes were full of misery and she shook her head. "He's not the kind of man I ever thought I'd love. I feel—oh, sorry—for him. He could do so much—but he needs a chance. You don't know how hard a life he's had!"

"I know a little bit about him," Zach said evenly. "I know he's brave and honest." He hesitated, then added, "Those are the things I'd like to have in a son-in-law. What's the matter? You don't really love him—is that it?"

"I don't know—but it wouldn't matter if I did. He doesn't love me."

"He tell you that, did he?"

"No, of course not! But I know it's true." Lanie began to walk around the room, wringing her hands. "I thought he did once—that he cared for me. We were alone, and I got to know him. He's—not like I thought he was when I first met him. I thought he was just a cold, hard man with no feelings, but—" She lifted her eyes to her father and seemed to be pleading. "Dad, in some ways he's as vulnerable as a child! I didn't know any man could be like that!" Then she said again, "He doesn't love me! He loves the woman that was killed trying to save him!"

Zach listened to her, thinking, *I know she loves him. She's afraid he doesn't love her—but there's only one way to find out.*

He waited until Lanie had finished. "Well," he sighed heavily, "we've prayed about this a lot, haven't we?" It was true; Zach had prayed with all his children. Sometimes it seemed to go over their heads, and sometimes they seemed to think he was crazy, but he had drawn each one of them aside, telling them, "One thing I care about—and that's what happens to you. So I'll pray that God will open the right doors for you to go through!"

Lanie had listened less than the others. She had been the most self-confident and secure of them all. But her self-assurance had been broken by the recent events, and Zach saw a vulnerability and a gentleness in her that had been lacking before. Now he said softly, "We'll be leaving for home pretty soon—but we need to get this settled first."

"Settled?" She turned to stare at him. "What do you mean, settled?"

"I mean, you can't walk away and leave this thing. Why, I've known men—and women, too—who walked away from a situation like this. Years later you could hear it echoing in them. Before we leave Fort Smith, you're going to know whether that man loves you or not! One way or another, you've got to find out!"

Lanie laughed. "Dad, you're so—*simple*. I can't think of another word for what you are! What am I going to do, just walk up and demand, 'Well, Lobo Smith—do you love me?' "

"No, you don't want to do that. Let *me* take care of it."

"Are you becoming a marriage broker? Dad, I don't think this is a very good idea—" She stopped, tears smarting her eyes, and without another word walked away, slamming the door behind her.

"Well, she thinks I'm a fool—and she may be right." Zach thought hard for a moment, then he picked up his crutches and headed out of the room.

★ ★ ★ ★

Angela Montoya's funeral left Lobo Smith numb, almost as if he were moving through a foggy dream. He'd been so stunned by her death, so shaken that he could remember little about the trip back to Fort Smith, or the days afterward. He'd stood at the grave and vaguely heard a preacher read some words. He saw a few people, including Woman Killer, who nodded at him somberly. Lanie, too, had been there, standing across the grave, watching him with some sort of emotion he couldn't read.

After the body was lowered, he'd walked away quickly so that he wouldn't hear the dirt clods falling on the casket. He'd gone to a saloon, ordered a drink, and had stood there downing one after another until he almost passed out, when he felt a touch on his arm. "Come on, Lobo," Heck Thomas had said. "You ain't doing yourself no good here." Lobo had stared at him, muttering, "Get away from me, Heck, or I'll knock your head off!"

"Now, that ain't no way to talk," Thomas had said. He'd reached over and pulled Lobo's gun from the holster. Lobo struck at him, trying vainly to find a target, falling against him instead. The lawman had taken him to a building and shoved him into a cot.

"You lay down there and sleep it off, son," he said quietly. "I don't blame you a bit. That was some lady. I'd do the same thing my ownself!"

When Lobo left, he had retrieved his gun from Heck but continued to drink for several days. Somewhere along the line, however, he remembered a tall form standing beside him. "Have a drink," Lobo offered.

Wesley leaned against the bar, waving the bartender away. "I need to talk to you, Lobo."

"Talk away!"

"Not here—!"

"This is as good a place as any—better than some I could name. If you're too holy to stand here in a bar, then get out!"

Stone had merely nodded. "All right, this will do. I want to talk to you about Angela."

"Shut up, Wes! I don't wanna hear it!" Lobo began to curse, and Wesley waited until he was finished. Finally, Lobo had stalked away and sunk into a chair near the door. Stone had followed him. Sitting down he said, "I don't want to say much. But get this. That was a woman who loved you. I don't know how you felt about her, but I know one thing. The only way Angela's death will have any meaning, Lobo, is if you *give* it meaning."

Lobo had stared at Wesley, trying to focus. He felt numb all over, but the words struck him hard. "What—did you say?" he asked.

"I said, Angela's death means nothing if you become a drunk and an outlaw. Only if you become a man with something to give will what she did for you give meaning." He went on speaking, easily, slowly, so that the man with the black eye patch could understand. He was a good speaker, Wesley Stone, and he never made a better speech than he did in that saloon. He managed to give dignity and honor to Angela Montoya—and made her death something full of pride and love. He finally said, "I don't know how she stood with God. We never really know about other people—but I do know how she stood with you. She gave her life for you, and I hate to see anybody give their life for a drunk and a hardcase." He waited, expecting to see Lobo slash out in anger, but Lobo sat silently. Wesley finally said, "Nobody can make you do what you don't want to do. I could see that she had something good inside her, Lobo. She missed her chances down the way, but let me tell you this—if you don't live a better life than you're living right now, Angela died for nothing!"

He got up, saying, "You'll have to decide. Do you remember Lorenzo?"

Lobo's head bobbed. "Yes," he said. "I remember him."

"Then you remember how he died—how he went out trusting in God. You think he was a hypocrite?"

"No, he wasn't that!" Lobo put his head in his hands. "Get

out of here, Wes—leave me alone!"

Stone left then, saying, "I'll be around if you want to talk."

That had been Lobo's last drink. He'd slept all night and never touched a drop. He'd struggled with Wesley's words. He felt lost—without hope.

Finally he'd risen before daybreak and ridden out of Fort Smith, driven by the storm inside his spirit. Aimlessly he wandered across the broken countryside, thinking, *How am I going to live like that lawyer wants me to?*

Finally he drew his horse to a stop, dismounted, tied his mount to a sapling, and walked along a bluff that fell away sharply to the floor of a small valley. He continued on along the edge, head down, struggling with the misery that had gripped him since Angela's death. He felt strange, as if he'd been wounded and hadn't known what he was doing. His perception of the whole thing *had* been blown out of proportion, as Wesley had indicated. Angela's love, sacrifice, and death had left him open and helpless. He'd come to the end of something in his life, something he'd experienced before, but there'd always been a new trail—a new challenge to go for. Now there was nothing.

Half an hour later he looked up as the red rays of the rising sun burned along the crests of the distant hills. There was a stillness over the land, like a holy silence, and he longed to stay there in the quietness.

And then it came to him so clearly that he spoke aloud. "Why—peace isn't in a valley! When a man's right with God, he can have peace in the middle of a war!" Immediately he thought of Lorenzo dying with such quiet dignity, and he seemed to hear the old man speaking: *Lobo, it's Jesus who gives peace—and there ain't no other way to git it!*

Lobo had little experience with formal religion, but he'd seen a man die a horrible death—but with a smile, as if he were going to bed for the night. And he realized as he stood there watching the light grow stronger that he'd have to choose. He thought of his past, and the little good it held—and the future, which held less.

Without much hope, he took off his hat and bowed his head. The silence was deafening and his voice sounded hoarse when he said, "Lord—I don't know about you. Lorenzo said that Jesus is the only hope a man's got." He struggled with the doubts that rose to torment him, then desperately cried out, "Oh, God— I've done every wrong thing a man can find to do—but I'm askin' you to forgive all of it—make me different—and I'm believing in Jesus right now!"

His words floated over the edge of the bluff. He stood there for a few moments, then slowly sank to his knees. Tears rose in his eyes, but he ignored them. Bowing his head, he began to pray silently, remaining in that position for quite a while. His horse grew restive and nickered at him, jerking his head with impatience.

Finally Lobo got to his feet. He wiped his eyes, put his hat on, and walked stiffly back to his horse. Patting the animal on the neck, he swung into the saddle, then looked back to the place where he'd found God.

"Well, Lord, you know what I am," he murmured. "I'm believing you're going to help me—because I sure can't help myself!" Then he turned the horse toward town and let out a loud whoop as he slapped his heels against the startled animal's flank, driving him into a dead run.

★ ★ ★ ★

Lobo dismounted, his mind filled with what had just happened to him. A voice broke into his thoughts and he whirled around.

"Come along, Lobo," Heck Thomas said.

"Come along where?"

"To the jail. You're under arrest."

"Under arrest! What for?"

"Something about whiskey. Don't you remember? You were in jail for it."

Lobo stared at Heck Thomas. "You mean Parker is gonna put me in jail for *that* after what I did for him?"

"You know the judge," Heck shrugged. "He says to arrest you, so gimme your gun."

Handing over the gun, he said angrily, "All right, here it is."

"You know the way, I guess."

As they entered, Lobo headed for the stairs, but Heck said, "Not down there. Fellow wants to see you first." He led Lobo down the hall to one of the offices and knocked on the door.

"Come in," a voice called.

As they stepped in, Heck said, "Mr. Winslow, I'll be right out here when you get through."

Lobo fixed his eyes on Zach, who was seated in a chair, his crutches leaning against the wall. "Hello, Lobo," he said. "Sit down. We got some talking to do."

Lobo shrugged and sat down. "What do we have to talk about?"

The office was small and hot. It had an open door that led to another office, and one window, which was open, letting a slight breeze come in. "Hot, isn't it? Gonna be hotter down in that jail."

Lobo said nothing.

"Well, I might as well get right down to it," Winslow said. "To tell the truth, you're not going to jail." He saw Lobo's eyes open with surprise, then added, "Judge Parker and me, we had a little talk. He's proud as punch over getting Perrago and his bunch out of commission. He'd make you mayor if he could— and you could sure stay on as one of his marshals if you like."

Lobo shook his head. "No—I don't think so. I've had enough of that sort of thing."

"That so? I'm glad to hear it." Zach leaned back in his chair. "I went through something like this in Alder Gulch. Had to use my gun—and got sick of it! It does something to a man when he has to turn to the gun. Stay with it too long and it makes a man sour and bitter. What are you going to do?"

"I don't know. I'll find something." He almost told him that he'd just found something rich and new, but felt awkward and uncertain speaking about it.

Winslow asked abruptly, "Do you love my daughter?"

Lobo's eyes shot open. "Lanie?" he asked, surprised. The past days of closeness they'd shared flashed through his mind. "I don't think I need to tell you about things like that."

"You think I'm not interested in my own daughter?"

"What difference does it make how I feel about her?" He hesitated and shook his head, despair in his eyes. "She'd never have anything to do with me."

"Know that for sure, do you? You ask her? You told her you loved her?"

"No, I didn't tell her. She'd laugh if I did—you oughta know that, Winslow!"

"I don't know anything of the sort! What I do know is—she's in love with you."

"Why—that's *crazy*!" Lobo exclaimed. "What kind of a father are you? You know I'm not a fit man for her!"

"We talked about that. I told her you're honest and have a lot to offer. The stuff that don't matter like education and money— why, you can pick those things up along the line. What I'm interested in is—do you love her? If you don't—why, just say so and the conversation is over!"

"I don't know," Lobo said, confused. "I never met anybody like her. Any man would be proud to have her as a wife." Then he ducked his head. "But—it's too late."

Zach got to his feet, picked up his crutches, swung across the room, and put his hand out. Surprised, Lobo took it. "Son," Zach continued, "you saved both my daughters. I could spend a lifetime and not get across what that means to me. I'm telling you now one thing I *can* do. I'm leaving Chicago, buying a ranch in Montana. Never did get my heart out of that country. I need a man there—a young man. Somebody who can fight anybody who stands in the way—to make a place for me and my family. I'd like you to be that man. It's yours if you want it."

Lobo sat there numbly as Winslow left the room, his mind whirling. Out the window he could see a small peach tree with a mockingbird preening its feathers, then breaking into a song. At the same moment, a movement in the room caught his eye. He glanced toward the door that led to the other office—Lanie!

He jumped to his feet, faced her, feeling awkward in her presence. Her face was pale, but she was smiling. Without a word she came to him. He took her hands, searching her eyes.

"I was afraid you loved her—Angela," Lanie whispered. "Maybe you did." She waited, then asked, "Did you?"

Lobo shook his head. "Not like that—but, she died for me. Nobody can do that for somebody unless they love them, can they, Lanie?"

"No. She did love you. You can be proud of that all your life.

She was a brave woman—and she died for what she loved. Not many people can do that." Then she asked, her voice light but strong, "Lobo, I have to know: Did you *love* her?"

"Once we had something," he said. "It wasn't much, and after it was over, there was nothing left." He shook his head. "And I lied to her, deceived her! Lanie, I'll never get over that!"

"Yes, you will," she said. "We always get over things—at least the pain of it. Betsy will get over what happened to her. Time will change things. It can even change hearts."

He looked at her, a peculiar expression on his face. "You heard all your dad said?"

"Yes."

"It was a lot of nonsense!"

"Was it?"

" 'Course it was! You're a fine lady, educated. I'm nothing but a gunman."

"You're what you are—gallant and brave. If it weren't for you, both Betsy and I might be dead." There was pride in her eyes as she spoke. "I want to ask one thing—and I'll ask only once—"

"What is it?" he asked.

She hesitated, then whispered, "Do you love me?"

His eyes shone as he remembered her pride and arrogance when they first met. Now it was gone! She was broken, and stood before him with all the sweetness and loveliness that a woman could have.

He knew how difficult it must have been for her to come to him like this—and he admired her strength and determination as much as he admired her beauty and goodness.

Suddenly Lobo Smith knew what lay within his grasp. Putting his arms around her, he drew her in. He held her close, pressing his cheek against hers. "I love you," he said. "I always will—but I can't ask you to marry me. I don't have anything to bring to you."

She drew back, and he saw tears in her eyes. "It is slow you are! A little kindness I'll have from you!"

"Maybe—I'll work for your dad."

"He's a smart man, my dad! He said you'd never marry me—not for a while."

He took in her fineness, the honest look of her, and without meaning to, told her of his experience on the bluff. "I—I've got a long way to go—to learn how to serve God like Lorenzo did. But I know Jesus is real!"

"Oh, Lobo!" Lanie cried out, "I'm so happy for you!"

"Someday," he said, "I'll come courting you, Lanie. When I really find myself. You wait!" Then he kissed her—savoring the wild sweetness of her.

Quickly she drew back, her face bright with hope. "One thing I'll know right now—no argument, is it?"

"What's that?"

"What *is* your first name?" she demanded. "I can't go on calling you 'Lobo,' can I?"

He looked at her, then glanced around as if he were about to reveal a dreadful secret. "All right, you asked for it." He hesitated, then shrugged his shoulders. "Faye," he said defiantly.

"Faye? Your name is *Faye*?"

"Well—it's Lafayette, actually—but that's *worse*! Everybody shortened it to Faye. I got tired of whipping men who laughed at me for having a girl's name." He made a sour face and said, "Awful, isn't it?"

"Faye—" Lanie tapped her full lower lip with her finger, then smiled and put her hands on his shoulders. "I like it!" She drew him close, saying firmly, "When I get very angry with you, I'll call you Lafayette Smith!"

And then she slipped her arms around his neck and whispered, "But sometimes I'll say, 'I love you, Faye!' "

He smiled happily. "You know—it doesn't sound so bad the way you say it!"

"You'll have a lifetime to get used to it," she assured him. Then she asked pertly, "Well—are you going to kiss me—or not?"

Their lips met in powerful completeness as the mockingbird, perched on the peach tree limb, sang a musical carol to heaven.

———

Watch for Book 16 in the HOUSE OF WINSLOW series, to be released in the Fall of 1994.